A PRAYER FOR MY SON

A NOVEL

by

HUGH WALPOLE

ORIGINALLY PUBLISHED 1936

FOR

COLONEL W. A. T. FERRIS

TO WHOM

TWENTY-EIGHT YEARS AGO

MY FIRST NOVEL

WAS DEDICATED--

THIS STORY

IS OFFERED

IN GRATITUDE

FOR A SPLENDID

FRIENDSHIP

My homeward course led up a long ascent,

Where the road's watery surface, to the top

Of that sharp rising, glittered to the moon

And bore the semblance of another stream

Stealing with silent lapse to join the brook

That murmured in the vale. All else was still:

No living thing appeared in earth or air,

And, save the flowing water's peaceful voice,

Sound there was none--but lo! an uncouth shape . . .

WORDSWORTH, The Prelude.

No characters or incidents in this book have been in any way suggested by characters or incidents outside this book

Contents

PART I - THE QUIET ENTRY

CHAPTER I - SNOW-SHINE FOR ARRIVAL

This moment of anticipation was the worst of her life--never before had she been so utterly alone.

Her loneliness now was emphasized by the strange dead-white glow that seemed to bathe her room. She had just switched off the electric light, and the curtains were not drawn upon the long gaunt windows. Although it was after five on that winter afternoon, the light of the snow still illuminated the scene. Beyond the windows a broad field ran slowly up to a thin bare hedge; above the hedge, the fell, thick in snow, mounted to a grey sky, which lay like one shadow upon another against the lower flanks of Blencathra.

Rose had learnt the name of this mountain from the first instant of her arrival at the Keswick station. She had not known whether she would be met or not, and she had asked a porter whether he knew of Scarfe Hall. He knew of it well enough. It lay near the Sanatorium right under Saddleback. And then, because she was obviously a stranger, and he unlike many of his countrymen was loquacious, he explained to her that Saddleback was the common name for Blencathra. 'What a pity,' she murmured. 'Blencathra is much finer.' But he was not interested in that. He found the motorcar from the Hall and soon she was moving downhill from the station, turning sharply to the left by the river, and so to her destination.

She had had tea alone with Janet Fawcus in the drawing-room downstairs; such a strange, old-fashioned, overcrowded room, with photographs in silver frames and a large oil painting over the marble fireplace of Humphrey's father. So odd, Rose thought, to have so large a painting of yourself so prominently displayed. She had seen before, of course, photographs of Humphrey's father and had always liked the kindliness, the good-humour in his round chubby face, the beautiful purity of his white hair, his broad manly shoulders, but this oil paint-ing, made obviously a number of years ago, gave him a kind of dignified splendour. She had always thought him like Mr. Pickwick, but now he was a Mr. Pickwick raised to a degree of authority that yet had not robbed him of his geniality.

So she and Janet Fawcus had shared an embarrassed tea. It was no surprise to her to discover in Janet the perfect spinster--that is, a woman of middle age whose certainty that virginity is a triumph is mingled with an everlasting disappointment. Janet was dressed in the hard and serviceable tweeds of the English dweller in the country. She talked to Rose with all the kindliness of a hostess and the patronage of a successful headmistress. Rose saw at once that Janet had always hated her and that meeting her had not weakened that emotion.

However, she had expected this, counted on it, in fact, and she sat now in this old curiosity shop of a drawing-room, the heavy, dark, an-cient curtains drawn against the snow, brightly and falsely amiable about Geneva and the League of Nations and the selfishness of France, and what a pity it was that despotism was beginning to rule the world. It was explained to her that young John was out with his tutor skating on some pond towards St. John's in the Vale and that Colonel Fawcus himself was at a meeting in Keswick about pylons, and that was why Janet must do the honours alone. 'But, of course,' Janet said, 'you will see John when he comes in. He is so excited about your coming.' In that last sentence Rose knew there was something sinister; that im-maculate tweed-clad virgin would not give an inch. 'But then,' Rose thought, 'I have no intention of asking her. I have not come here to fight. There is no battle in the air. John's grandfather has invited me out of kindness and generosity. There was nothing in the signed agreement, which compelled him to do this. It has been simply warm-hearted kindness on his part. I am not here to fight. I am not here to get my son back. I am not here to win his affection away from anyone

2

else. He is not mine. I surrendered him deliberately, fully knowing what I was about. I am not here for any contest of any kind with this unagreeable, tiresome, self-satisfied prig of an Englishwoman.' But as she smiled and said that, yes, she would have another cup of tea, and how good it was after a long cold journey--she was forced to repeat to herself: 'I am not a mother. I surrendered John not only because it would be for his good, and because he would be given so many things I could never give him, but also because I was not meant to be a mother. There were other things that I could do better. I am not mater- nal. I am a modern woman of my time. I do not wish to be hampered with a child. I have things I want to do for my generation and civiliza- tion and, although it is true that I am now thirty years of age and have done as yet very little for anybody, there is still plenty of time. I have surrendered John, and no amount of disliking his aunt from the bottom of my heart must make me want to take John away from her.' She thought further: 'She is looking at my clothes. She is envious of them and that makes her dislike me the more. I am very pleased. My clothes are certainly not remarkable and at least they do not look like a sheet of mail armour.'

'I expect,' Janet said, with her considerate, indulgent smile, 'you would like to come to your room now?'

To her room Rose was taken. What a strange, old, confused place it was! It must be, she realized with a thrill of excitement, the actual room of which Humphrey had often told her. The room where he had slept as a boy. Also it must be very little changed from those long-ago days, for there hanging near a window and opposite the four-poster bed was the oil painting of Abraham offering up Isaac for sacrifice. All the details that Humphrey had given her--the dark, angry hill painted a sinister red, the white body of the boy, the Patriarch with knife raised, and a black cloud breaking into spears of lightning, through which God's voice spoke. Humphrey had told her how, as a child, he had lain in bed and seen the mounting field beyond the window, the sky above it, the serried edge of Blencathra, almost walk into the room and min- gle with the old oil painting, so that he used to fancy that Abraham and his knife were waiting there on Blencathra for himself as the appointed victim.

This, then, was the very room that Humphrey had had. All the fur- niture in it was old and black. There were dark-green hangings with a red pattern on the four-poster, and the only concessions to modern life in the room were the electric light, an electric fire in the old stone fireplace and a small collection of recent books in gay colours near the bed. Then Rose made her first really serious mistake. 'Why,' she said, 'this must be the very room that Humphrey had.' Her impetuosity that she thought by now she had learnt to control had once again betrayed her. She felt Janet's whole body stiffen, and she knew with her quickness of apprehension that Janet had loved her brother with an intense passion. Why, Rose wondered, had she been put in Humphrey's room? They could not have forgotten. Perhaps it was the only spare room in the house. No, she knew that the place was of a rambling, undisciplined size. There must be many spare rooms. Janet had not answered. She had gone to the door and switched on the light. They had been for a moment standing together in the dusky white-stained twilight. Janet said, 'As soon as John comes I will bring him up to see you,' and went.

As soon as she was alone Rose switched off the light again and stood without moving, looking on to the fields that grew with every moment darker, seeming to smell that sharp, friendly, aromatic scent of freshly fallen snow. At last she went to the door and switched on the light again, then stood in front of the long old looking glass bordered with dim gold that hung between the bed and the door. She looked at herself with a new interest. She was a woman devoid almost entirely of personal vanity. She liked to be clean, to be healthy, to be equipped for whatever she might have to do. Since Humphrey's death she had thought very little about men except as, indirectly, companions. She had had no sexual life at all. She had been living, she fancied, in a world entirely of ideas, and now, looking into the mirror, she suddenly wondered for the first time whether the ideas had been worthwhile. In this old room, with the intense stillness of the snowy world beyond it, things altered their values. She saw herself one of an eager group of men and women at a table in a Geneva café, or in somebody's room, or in the bureau where she worked, sharp, opinionative voices saying, 'But then, of course, Barthou means something quite different,' or 'But, I ask you, Simon and Mussolini, how could they ever understand one another?' or again, 'Americans go only skin-deep: that is why the world is in the mess it is.' Yes, these voices, so sure, so clever, so brittle, echoed with a kind of ludicrous inefficiency, which came down in front of that old mirror. Five minutes' talk with Janet Fawcus seemed to have changed, in spite of herself, the whole world. She did not want

4

it to change. She was paying this visit because she was sure that she was impregnable, but now, was she sure? What unexpected influences were beginning to work upon her?

She looked back at herself in the mirror--slim, slight, dark-haired, much too youthful-looking for her thirty years, she impatiently reflected. She wished to impress them all with her stability, her firm security. She was on a visit to her little son whom she had definitely surrendered, coming from outside, remaining outside, a safe modern woman who was at work for the world's good, rather than for personal maternity. 'How detestably priggish that is,' she thought. 'But perhaps the whole of Geneva is priggish? What have I done coming here? I did not expect to feel so defenceless.'

It was then, standing in the middle of the room, that she knew her moment of wild, terrified anticipation. What would John be like? How would he greet her? How had he been taught to think of her? It was ten years since she had surrendered him, and she saw again that last dreadful minute in the cold room of the London hotel when she had delivered him up to the nurse and to the family man of affairs, and, seeing that minute again, she thought to herself: 'It was not because I did not want him that I gave him up, but because I knew that it would be so much better for him; and it shall be. I must have no personal relationship with him. I must let them keep him from me as much as they wish.'

It was at that moment that she heard, even through the closed door, the sharp, clear call of a boy. The door opened, and John, his aunt just behind him, stood there looking at her.

There were two things she at once realized when she saw him; one was that he was strangely like the baby she had surrendered, the other that he had an astonishing and most moving resemblance to his father. It was the second of these two things that instantly warned her, like an inner voice: 'Take care, take care. You must not be affected by this'--for indeed it was most desperately moving.

John, now twelve years of age, was small and slight and very fair in colouring. His hair, which was rather stiff (a little tuft of it stood up sharply on the back of his head), was pale honey-colour. His face was sharp and thin. His most remarkable feature, which you saw at once as you had done in his father before him, was the eyes, grey-blue in colour, strong, fearless, masculine, full of character. His nose and mouth were thin and pointed. The shape of his upper lip might have been, as his father's had been inclined to be, cynical and sarcastic. But John's mouth had suddenly a rather babyish softness, which was probably transitory but, at the moment, very appealing. His slim child's body was as straight as a dart. He was dressed in a light blue pullover and short grey flannel trousers, but you felt the nervous activity of his body beneath his clothes. He stood urgently on his feet as though he were about to start a race, but this may have been because he was feeling the excitement and strangeness of this meeting. His pale hair, his sharp-boned, delicate colouring, the athletic urgency of his poise gave him at once an air of life and spirit that scarcely seemed to belong to that old, dark room, nor had it anything to do with the spare, thin figure of the woman who stood beside him, her hand lightly touching his arm. But he was like the baby Rose had left and like the man she had lost, and it was no sentimental weakness for her to feel a catch in her throat, or to see the room suddenly sway behind a misty cloud of uncertainty.

'Here's John,' Janet said.

'Hullo,' John said, and then he held out his hand. 'How are you?'

She felt and shared his own sense of intolerable shyness. He did not in all probability realize all the implications of this meeting, but he knew enough of them to feel a deep awkwardness and possibly strong, urgent resentment.

She went forward and took his hand. 'How are you, John?' she said. She bent down and kissed his forehead.

He received her kiss as though he had known that this ghastly thing must occur. She realized that that had been one of the moments he had been dreading and that now everything would be a little easier. She realized, too, that to the virgin mind of Janet Fawcus all this was of a dreadful indecency--the unmarried mother greeting her bastard child-- and suddenly she thought: 'How inconceivably stupid of me! Janet must have fought her father's decision to invite me here with all the force she possessed. I had never realized how abandoned she must have thought me.' She felt it exasperating that Janet should be present at her first meeting with her own son. She longed to have the courage

6

to say, 'Leave us for a moment, won't you?' but she could not and the woman did not move. Something had to be done, the pause had already lasted too long.

'You have been skating, John, haven't you?'

His eyes were eating into her face. He was studying her with an absorbed attention, having forgotten completely all the rules of conduct, that you must not stare at strangers, and so on. His eyes never wavered from her face as he answered:

'Yes. The pond's been frozen for a week. I'm getting quite good.'

'John, dear,' Janet said softly, but he gave a little impatient wriggle of his shoulders.

'Oh! I'm not swanking, but Mr. Brighouse said so and he can skate like anything.'

'I live in Switzerland most of the time,' said Rose, 'so I get plenty of skating, or could have if I wanted it.'

'Why, don't you want it?' he asked, his eyes wider than ever, staring at her.

'Yes, but you know what it is,' she said, smiling, 'when you have so much of anything all round you, you don't value it in the same way.'

'No, I suppose you don't,' he said. 'It's like being an assistant in a sweet-shop. They get as bored as anything with chocolates and cakes.' He drew a quick little breath. 'I don't think I'd ever be bored with marzipan,' he said.

Janet pressed her hand in a little on his shoulder. 'Come, John,' she said.

And it was at that moment that Rose knew her first instant of sharp, intense rebellion. What right had this woman to tell her son to go at this moment? This was her moment. If the woman had had any kind of decency she would have left them alone together. Then Rose remembered. She smiled, looked him full in the eyes, nodded and lightly said:

'Good night, John. See you to-morrow.'

7

He said, his eyes still on her face: 'Yes. I hope the frost holds, don't you?' Then turned and went out with his aunt.

The room was very quiet. There was a gentle tap on the door. Rose said, 'Come in,' and a small, rather pinched-faced little maid stood in the doorway. She asked whether she might pull the curtains. Then, standing near the window, she asked whether everything was all right, please, miss?

'I didn't know,' she said, 'whether that would be the dress you'd be wanting to wear.'

Rose looked and saw--what she had not noticed before--that her evening frock was laid out on the bed, and that it was the smart one of grey and silver. She smiled. 'Oh, thank you. How nice everything is! But I think that I'll have the black one to-night.'

'Oh yes, miss. I didn't know.' And she moved very quickly to the drawer, brought out the black taffeta dress and put the other one away, then drew the heavy thick mulberry-coloured curtains across the windows and moved to the door. Again she said: 'Will that be everything, miss? Dinner's at quarter to eight.'

'Yes, thank you,' Rose said. 'What is your name?'

'Sally, miss.' The girl gave her a sharp, inquisitive look.

'I suppose,' Rose thought, 'they already know all about everything.' But there was more in the look than mere personal curiosity. It said not only 'I wonder whether all they say about you is true,' but also 'I wonder how much you know about us.'

There was something pleasant about the girl's face, something una-greeable too. But Rose felt, without having any real reason for her instinct, that this young girl was important in the house. While she dressed she had to struggle against the cold. The electric fire gave out heat, but the room seemed to contain cold as a well contains ancient water. The walls gave off cold so concretely that she could almost see it, and the cold from the world outside seemed to press in from the windows. 'I suppose,' she thought, 'it is the central heating I have been

8

used to in Geneva that makes me feel this. I have never been so cold in my life before. It is as though there were something personal about it.'

When, however, she went down to the drawing-room, there was a great fire leaping wildly in the old dark fireplace, and all the many many things in the room leaped and sparkled with it. The room seemed filled with a kind of aimless chatter. Two clocks were ticking away. Two canaries in a gilt cage near the window were twittering. There was the noise of the fire. And behind all these things a kind of undertone, as though people out of sight were whispering together.

'The fact is,' Rose reflected, 'this house is so old that you feel the past in it more than the present.' She stood, one shoe up on the fender, her skirts a little raised, warming her ankles, looking into the fire.

The door opened and a young man came in. He was slim and dark, with a bright intelligent face--that was all she noticed about him. He seemed to her a perfectly ordinary boy with that odd gesture of surprise that belongs to so many of his generation as though he were discovering that things were very different from what he had been told they would be. She noticed all this--his dark good looks, his friendliness and his rather surprised eagerness as he shook hands with her and said:

'My name is Michael Brighouse. I'm John's tutor. I know who you are.'

And she showed that at once they were friends when she said to him: 'And I know who you are. You are the first person John mentioned to me.'

'He is a jolly good kid,' Michael Brighouse said. 'I'd have known anywhere you were his mother,' he added, staring at her, she knew, with admiration and liking.

'He is very young for his age,' she thought, 'but we are going to be friends, and that is a good thing. I shall need a friend here.'

The door opened again and Colonel Fawcus came in. Her impression of him at once was of height and breadth rather than the stout Pickwick rotundity that she had expected. He must have been well over six feet in height, his shoulders seemed tremendous, and only his

9

round, bespectacled red face and snow-white hair carried on the Pick-wick illusion. But she was bathed at once in the full tide of his kindly congeniality.

He came forward with both hands outstretched and caught hers, and, all his face smiling even to his large, rather protruding ears, he said: 'Welcome, my dear Rose, welcome. How kind of you to come.'

She noticed that in some trick of light his round glasses caught the glare so that she could not see his eyes. What she did see were his mouth, his nose, his cheeks, his high red forehead and, above all, his ears. All these were smiling in a kind of ecstasy of welcome, but it was at that moment as though a blind man were greeting her.

'You know Brighouse?' he said, putting his hand on the boy's shoulder. 'I expect he has introduced himself.'

'Yes,' she answered, 'and I had heard of him from John before that.'

'Ah! you have seen John,' Colonel Fawcus said quickly.

'Yes. He came to my room for a moment.'

'And what did you think of him? It must have been extraordinary after so long.'

She realized that he intended to deny and hide nothing. He was welcoming her with all the facts on the table. She had not expected to find him so large, so strong, so breezy. She had known that he was kind.

Then Janet came in wearing a black dress that fitted her badly and emphasized her bony neck and her thin arms. She did not use any kind of make-up. Her nose was a little red, pinched with the cold, and there were faint streaks of purple veins on her sallow cheeks. But the great thing about her was that however plain she might be she did not care.

'She is full of pride,' Rose thought, 'of self-satisfaction. She knows just what she wants and always gets it. She is by far the strongest person in this room.'

The echoes of the gong rolled in the distance.

10

'Dinner, dinner,' Colonel Fawcus cried, as though he were announcing a wonderful new event that was about to change the world's history. 'Come, my dear Rose, you must, I am sure, be ravenous,' and the two clocks, the canaries and the undertone of whispering chatter repeated 'ravenous.'

Seated at the old mahogany table, the impression that Colonel Fawcus made was overwhelming. Sitting, he looked more massive than ever, more massive, more benevolent, more completely head of the family, more entirely commander of all he surveyed; and he surveyed, she noticed, a very great deal. His eyes were everywhere. While he talked--and he talked voluminously, words pouring from his lips--his eyes darted like fish in a pool up and down the room. You could feel that the maid, Sally, was immensely conscious of his supervision. Rose was interested to notice that here at the table Janet Fawcus counted for nothing. It was the big, hearty, benevolent man who dominated everyone. He talked to Rose exclusively, once and again saying genially:

'Well, Michael, what do you think of it?' or 'I am sure Michael would tell you the same,' or 'Michael knows what I feel about it.'

He spoke to her as though he were almost bursting with happiness at her arrival. She could not but wonder. She was of a generation brought up to regard simple kindness as extremely suspect. Let anyone be accused of the worst crimes in the human calendar and she would offer them the friendly protection of Freudian analysis. Just as the works of John Galsworthy, Sir James Barrie, Mr. Milne and other kindly creatures were to her pernicious, so if she were told that anyone was kind or good she assumed instantly that they must also be false and hypocritical. And yet here she was surrendering at once to kindness, goodness, benevolent hospitality, eager friendship, because that was what he was. It was long since anyone had shown her so plainly that he meant well by her. People did not show you that in Geneva unless they wanted something either sexual or financial.

'I do hope you will enjoy your time with us, Rose. Of course there will be John, who will be a host in himself, and we have neighbours who should interest you--the Parkins, for instance, eh, Michael?'

'Oh! the Parkins certainly,' said Michael, laughing.

'Who are the Parkins?' Rose asked.

'The Verdurins,' Michael said, smiling at her.

'The Verdurins?' she repeated.

'Yes, Proust.'

'Oh! Proust,' she said, laughing. 'I'm afraid I haven't read him for ages. In smart circles in Geneva he is more old-fashioned than Anatole France, and that is more old-fashioned than'--she laughed and looked about her--'I can't think of anything more old-fashioned,' she said.

'Well,' Michael said, 'when you have met the Parkins once or twice you have read certain parts of Chez Swann again.'

Rose fancied that Colonel Fawcus did not altogether enjoy this little literary interruption; although he had not moved, he yet seemed restless. He looked at them benevolently as a kind guardian watches children hunting for sea-shells on the shore. Then he said to her that he did not get half the time he would have liked to keep up with modern literature.

He was, of course, although she did not know it, an author himself. He told her very modestly of the two little books that he had published, one on Ancient Monuments in the Cockermouth district and the second on Old Cumberland Churches. He had been for many years, he remarked, president of the Cumberland-Westmorland Antiquarian Society. He had been forced to give it up because of the accumulation of business. If he ever had time again he planned a work on Anglo-Saxon life in Cumberland, which would, he hoped, be of some general interest. He had accumulated much material, but alas! try as he would, each day seemed busier than the last.

'And my age,' he cried to her joyfully. 'How old do you think I am?'

Although she knew that he was more, she suggested, 'Sixty.'

'Sixty,' he cried. 'Sixty-eight--sixty-nine in a month or two.' He was so plainly delighted with his health and vigour that she was delighted too.

He was more of a scholar than she had imagined. She had not known that he had all this antiquarian knowledge. Why had Humphrey never told her? She could now faintly remember Humphrey once saying something like, 'Oh! Dad's all right if you flatter him on his hobbies.' This, perhaps, was one of them. She saw that he took a child's delight in his own little affairs; so many men did and that was why so many women felt maternal. She looked up at him. Their eyes met. They both smiled. She felt for a moment as though she were his mother.

During the meal, which was plain and good--a rich thick soup, fried sole, roast beef and apple tart--Janet Fawcus spoke very little.

Once she said to Michael Brighouse: 'How did John behave to-day?'

'Very well,' said Michael. 'He is getting on with his skating like anything.'

'You mustn't flatter him too much.'

'On the contrary,' said Michael, 'I'm sometimes afraid I don't encourage him enough. He is very easily discouraged, you know.'

She said nothing to that, but there was an implication in the grave authority with, which she considered the food on her plate, that she did not wish instructions from Michael about John, that she knew quite enough without his telling. Later in the meal she said:

'Father, Mr. Cautley rang up.'

'Oh! did he?' said Colonel Fawcus, suddenly changed from gay to grave. 'What did he want?'

'Oh! the usual thing,' said Janet. 'He wanted to come and have a talk with you about the pylons.'

'Oh! did he?' said Colonel Fawcus. 'Well, he can wait. He can take his stuffy self-importance somewhere else. You'd imagine that I'd nothing to do but fuss about little men who do not know their proper place. Cautley, indeed! I should have thought I'd snubbed that man enough to last him a lifetime.'

'How like Geneva!' Rose thought. 'How like everywhere in the world! How like every portrayal of daily life in every novel! Always there is somebody in the way of somebody else. Always everywhere there is someone who just prevents life from being perfect.' Her sympathies were all alive for poor Colonel Fawcus. She could just figure to herself the kind of self-important, interfering little man who would drive a great, generous, impulsive creature like Humphrey's father to frenzies of irritation. There were so many of them in Geneva.

After dinner she had a little conversation with Michael Brighouse. This contained one or two odd things, which she was to remember afterwards. Janet disappeared about some household business. Colonel Fawcus said:

'Will you excuse me for half an hour? I have a little business to finish and then I am at your service.'

So Michael and Rose were left alone in the lively, whispering drawing-room, and sat by the side of the fire and had a little talk.

She looked at him and decided that she not only liked him, but trusted him too.

'Tell me about John,' she said.

'No,' he answered quickly, 'not yet. I've thought it all out before you came. I want you to see him for two or three days yourself first and make your own conclusions. I don't want to say anything about him until you see for yourself.'

She nodded her head. 'That's right. I think that's wise.'

'I only want to say one thing,' he went on promptly. 'There is so much more going on here than you know, and if at any time later you want a friend, I offer myself.'

'It's very nice of you,' she said, and also rapidly, 'You may detest me. We may fight over John. You cannot promise friendship so quickly as that.'

'Oh yes, I can,' he answered eagerly, 'in this case, at least. However much I might dislike you, I would be with you in this affair for John's sake.'

'You speak,' she said, 'as though there were going to be an inevitable taking of sides.'

'There will be much more than that,' he answered.

'You want to frighten me.'

'No,' he said, 'of course not. I hope you will have a lovely time. I know it will be an interesting one.'

She looked at him. Her eyes dwelt on his face. 'I am sure I can trust you,' she said. 'That is one thing I know about people at once. Tell me yourself. Do you like it here?'

She was aware that they were both speaking urgently, almost furtively, as though they knew there would be an interruption, almost as though they were sure that someone was listening. She looked about the room.

'This is a funny place. You can almost believe there are people in the room you cannot see. But tell me. I want to know. Do you like it here?'

'Like it?' He laughed. 'That's a mild word. There's more than liking or disliking here, as you will soon find. But I am glad to be here for two reasons: one John, the other the country.'

'The country?' She gave a little shiver. 'Isn't it terribly cold and bleak and rough? Doesn't it rain all the time? But perhaps you are North-country by birth. That would make a difference.'

'No,' he said. 'As a matter of fact, I'm not. I was born in Dorset, near Corfe Castle. I have never been north before I came here, and it isn't the North that I thought I loved so much, but this immediate piece of country.'

'Why?' she asked. 'Of course I know the lakes are beautiful, but aren't they desolate in the winter, and tripper-haunted in the summer, and isn't the Wordsworth-Coleridge inheritance dreadfully dreary?'

'That has nothing to do with it,' he said. 'I can't explain to you now. Besides, you may not feel it, and if you don't, nothing that I say will be of the slightest use. If you do, you won't need me to explain it to you.

15

It's lovely. It's perfect. Every inch of ground is exciting. For instance, there is snow everywhere to-night; well, it never lies for long except on the mountain-tops and in a day or two, perhaps to-morrow, the fields will slowly reveal themselves again, and then every detail of them will be important. You will go, for instance, beyond the pond where we were skating to-day, to the road that leads up to St. John's in the Vale, and every tree and every field, every hedgerow, will have some shape, or some colour, or some effect under the changing sky that will make it exciting. I had a friend at Oxford who was great at Anglo-Saxon. He would have some piece of manuscript that he would study, a square of parchment, and every letter and every scrap of colour would mean beauty and history and human interest. So I feel about every inch of country here.'

'I suppose,' Rose said, 'that whenever anyone loves the country they feel that?'

'Perhaps so,' he answered. 'I don't know. I have never felt it about anywhere before. Listen, here's a little poem.

"Close-fitting house of velvet, foxglove bell,

My heart within your walls might live at ease

And never heed Time's knell;

And you, like rose, upturned by infinite seas,

To bleach here on the foam-remembering fell,

Could teach my spirit by obscure degrees

Of gossamer tension between heaven and hell;

But heart and spirit are roving, hiveless bees."'

'How beautiful!' she said. 'Who's that by?'

'A friend of mine copied it out and sent it to me from Oxford. He said it was by somebody called Bowes-Lyon, a new poet. But it has

16

exactly the quality that this place has for me. "Close-fitting house of velvet"--that is what this is, as you will find, and "foam-remembering fell"--that is what the country is.' And he added, his voice almost sinking to a whisper: 'There is a battle here. Our own battle, of which the poet of course knows nothing, scarcely anybody knows.'

'Battle? What battle?' she asked.

But before he could answer her there was the strong, friendly voice at the door:

'Finished sooner than I expected. Now, Rose, let us have a cosy talk.'

CHAPTER II - HEART AND SOUL OF A YOUNG MAN

Michael Brighouse was twenty-three years of age. He was two years old and a little bit on August 4th, 1914, six years of age and a little more on November 11th, 1918: the War, therefore, meant nothing to him at all and this inexperience was shared by all his contemporaries. He was not moved in the slightest by Armistice Day, or by any appeal to remember war veterans, or by Mr. Lloyd George's aspersions on Earl Haig's war conduct, or by the few remaining sentimental poets who still wailed about the unhappy time that they had had in the trenches. The War meant nothing to him also because he had all his life lived in a state of war. From the time when he had been at all conscious of any happening outside the excitement of his own rectory garden, there had been war going on somewhere, or if not actually war, at least conflict.

He had seen the kings fall and the despots rise; he had seen the American boom and the American slump; he had seen the quiet absorption of Manchukuo by the Japanese; he had seen the rise of Hitler, the flight of the Jews, the murder of Dollfuss, and only a week or two ago the plebiscite in the Saar. His generation, therefore, did not despair of the world as had the generation before them. Poets of Michael's day, Auden, Stephen Spender, Day Lewis, were the only figures at this moment in the world of art who were at all representing him. But there were thousands upon thousands of young men like Michael, who out of an extraordinary welter of machinery, speed, half-baked science, complete sexual frankness, poverty, cynicism and unemployment were achieving a new calm, not of indifference, but of a kind of philosophical humorous fortitude. The world was indeed a ludicrous mess, but it was a new world, as new as the early Elizabethan one had been. It offered, no doubt, every kind of parallel to that other splendid epoch--the speed, the machinery and the unemployment were all necessary parts of it. What a time to be alive in!

On the other hand, he had no illusions; above all, no sentimentality, no unbalanced idealism: 'Keep calm whatever may be offered you, be it death, supreme beauty, or a job at three pounds a week.' Michael was like his generation in all these things. He was like his generation, too, in that underneath the superficial colouring of his period he was like every other young man who had ever been--idealistic, sentimental, patriotic, sometimes very childish.

His father was rector of a small Dorset parish, and lived in perfect contentment there in a charming old rectory, with a high-walled garden, and a view from the upper windows over rolling down to the sea. Michael's father and mother were very philosophical people, that is, practically nothing disturbed them. Michael was their only son and they loved him, but they were quite happy when he was away, and always believed that all was for the best in God's world, even though Michael's mother had severe rheumatism in one leg and his father a heart that might kill him at any moment.

Michael went to school at Uppingham, had a history scholarship at Cambridge, got a double first and must, therefore, be considered a brilliant young man. He was not, however, really brilliant, but had a ready capacity for putting things on paper and a good memory. He knew very well that he was not brilliant. He knew that he might be a don--he didn't wish to be that. He thought that he would make a good journalist, but he didn't wish to be that either. He did not know until he had come to Cumberland what it was he wanted to be.

He knew his character pretty well. There was something weak in the middle of it, a soft, oozing spot somewhere. He was consistently to his own chagrin coming upon this mossy, boggy centre. It was not that he was sentimental so much as that he gave way before he knew it to unreasonable emotions, desires, impulses. He did not realize that no young man is a nice young man if he is hard right through. What exasperated him was that his consistent weakness was the result of no logic. He was quite ready to excuse weakness on definite philosophic grounds, but he hated to be ashamed of himself without a reason. The friends that he had made at Cambridge--Horlock, Redmayne, Burnam--were all perfectly aware of why they were weak when they wanted to be weak and what the results of their weakness would be. 'You see,' Redmayne would say, 'my doing that the other night proves what Jung says in his book'; or Horlock would simply cry, 'One must get one's fun where one can. It's poor fun. Isn't it astonishing that for thousands of years people have made such a fuss about love when this is all it comes to?' But Michael, alas! was far more unreasonable than his friends. One day when he was walking from Wastwater over to Eskdale he faced it quite frankly.

'I'm soft. I get bowled over by anything, but perhaps I am right. Perhaps there is more in this business than Horlock or Redmayne imagines.'

What he meant by 'this business' was the look-back from the spur of the fell to Wastwater, which lay black as jet in the Screes. The silence everywhere was so beautiful and comforting that it offered a true reassurance against these black waters. A sheep-trod running in front of him was also comforting. When he slept in Eskdale that night he determined to write to Horlock about it.

'You see, Horlock,' he meant to say, 'everything that we talked about at Cambridge is nonsense.' But of course in the morning he thought better of it. Every day in Cumberland put Horlock more out of touch. He began to grow a new spiritual skin.

He had always supposed that the tutoring of a small boy was as unpleasant a job as could ever be imagined. He did not care about small boys. He disliked the idea of teaching them anything. The word tutor was an offence. Some old schoolmaster friend wrote to his father to ask whether he knew of a likely young man who would give six months in a very lovely part of England to looking after a nice small boy. The point was that the pay was excellent and the work easy; the young man would have leisure to study for his own purposes. The point in Michael's case was that, lying in bed, he saw the white road, which ran like the spine of a fish into a cluster of stars scattered about a moonlit sky. In this sky, and on either side of the road, rolled smaller hills, whitened with moonlit powder. This surprising scene had for him

21

miraculous power. 'That,' he thought, 'is because I am nearly asleep,' but in the morning the power remained, and to his own astonishment he said to his father at breakfast:

'I think I'll go to these people--Fawcus, or whatever they are called.'

'It's time,' his father said gently,' that you should make up your mind what you are going to do.'

'I know quite well what I am going to do,' Michael said. 'I am going into the City to sell ivory collar-studs and make a lot of money. Then I am going to devote the money to--' He stopped.

'To what?' asked his mother. 'I hope you are enjoying the kedgeree because Cook made a great fuss when I said we were going to have it.'

'To what, I don't know,' Michael went on. 'The trouble is all the things you really care about seem to do better when you don't help them than when you do.'

'Why collar-studs?' asked his father.

'Because I know the man who has asked me to go in with him. He has inherited his father's business--it isn't only collar-studs of course.'

So in this indeterminate manner he went up to Cumberland. Before he went the schoolmaster friend of his father wrote to him:

'Old Fawcus is all right,' he said, 'if you remember the things that he has done in the past. He has been M.P. for the Penrith Division of Cumberland, but years ago. He served in the Boer War, which is why he is a colonel; but he isn't as real a colonel as he would like people to think he is. He has written monographs about monuments--bad ones. He is very easy to manage if you think him important. The boy is his grandson, illegitimate, but being brought up as heir to a great deal more than a non-existent estate. Fawcus has a spinster daughter. The house is ancient, and dark and cold, but the country is lovely, and the rain is not so bad as it sounds. I consider the pay more than adequate for what you will do, because the little boy is not tiresome and old Fawcus easily placated. There are, however, ghosts in the house--a certain madness--and I advise you, if anyone starts throwing spells, to watch out.'

This friend of his father was called Mr. Harris, and Michael thought he sounded so nice in his letter that he wanted to meet him in London, but Mr. Harris did not wish to be met. He was quite frank:

'I am sure you are a very nice young man,' he wrote. 'I had a great affection once for your father, but I care now only for chess, Bach and Handel. I live in Eastbourne and hate coming to London. Good-bye. Let me know how you get on in Cumberland.'

When later on Michael asked Colonel Fawcus about Mr. Harris, Fawcus said:

'Poor old Harris, as mad as a hatter! Went into King's Chapel once without his trousers.'

Be that as it might, Michael found everything that Mr. Harris had said very strangely true. The house was dark and ancient and cold; Miss Fawcus was a spinster all right; the Colonel liked flattery; the little boy was a nice little boy. These were the things that he discovered at first. It was only when he had been there some little while that the business of witchcraft and spells began to be apparent. It lay, of course, partly in the country. Michael read certain books about Cumberland and Westmorland. A man called Collingwood, he decided, was the only one who knew anything about the matter. Popular novels, with a great deal of highly coloured scenery, revolted him. The guidebooks were for the most part concerned only with the tracks, stiles, stone walls, and seeing as many named places as possible from one particular point. Only two men since Wordsworth and Coleridge had written any poetry about the Lake District worthy of the name; nothing that anyone had written except Wordsworth and Collingwood, nothing that anybody said accounted for the curious spell that the country laid upon him. He could not put it into words, except that its main appeal at first was to his personal vanity. The little stone walls, the fell, the fields and the streams whispered to him, 'Nobody has ever understood us before you. We cannot tell you how relieved we are that you have come.' While they did this he knew that they were mocking. He determined at first that he would not allow himself to be cheap about the colour simply because popular novelists were so easily cheap about it, but he could not deny that one mulberry-tinted cloud resting its chin upon the white powdered line of Saddleback (the rest of the sky grey with impending snow) held an intangible delicacy beyond anything he had ever seen. He stared at it from the windows of the Hall waiting for it to go, because clouds are so lovely the shade must be impermanent. But the dark mulberry only lightened as he watched it to a sharper purple.

Snow began very faintly to fall across the shadow of the fell, and the dark trees of the Hall garden. But even this did not diminish the mulberry cloud. Shadows of pale gold, a final suggestion of a sun that had not appeared all day, broke into the grey expanse of sky, and then, steadily supporting the cloud, this was the only fragment of light and colour in all the world. As the falling snow thickened, the garden grew ever darker, and over the fell a whiteness gleamed. At last, when all was dark, he fancied that he could still see the mulberry cloud. He was never quite to lose sight of it again. Now coloured clouds and falling snow are not the property of the North of England alone, but he discovered that in this country, because the hills are so near and the stretches of water so personal, many things happen that seem personally significant. He decided that the whole country was bad for one's egotism.

He was forced, however, very abruptly to think of people rather than places. He had never before lived intimately with a family not in any way of his own kind. He had been brought up, as are most young men, to congratulate himself on circumstances and surroundings that were in fact exactly right for him. Now he was an intruder, almost, he felt at times, a spy upon the lives of people who were as alien to him as West African natives. He had been brought there for a purpose, which was, he very quickly perceived, not at all the education and development of one small boy. The boy himself he found easy. In the first place he had from the very beginning a kind of tenderness towards him because of his illegitimacy. He would not have pitied himself had he been illegitimate, but he had not been in the house two days before Miss Fawcus very sternly, very briefly, and as though she were reciting to him one of the more indecent passages of the Old Testament, gave him the bare bones of the facts.

'My brother,' she said, 'my only brother, was one of the finest men I have ever known. He was everything in the world to me. He had one weakness--women--only because of his kindness of heart, not because he had a horrid nature. He was married--well, some people said unhappily, I believe not. I think that Gertrude and he might have had a most successful marriage had not others interfered. However, that's as may be.

'Gertrude was in some ways an odd woman. She needed under-standing. I frankly disliked her very much. In any case, after he had been married some five years a dreadful thing occurred. He lost his head, ran away with a girl of eighteen. Gertrude very rightly refused to divorce him. He had a child in Switzerland. John is that child.' She paused.

Michael perceived that she was labouring under stress of terrible emotion. There were tears in her eyes. She could scarcely speak. With a tremendous effort, which he could not but admire, she recaptured her self-command.

'My brother was killed climbing the Alps. It became evident later that the girl who had ruined his life had no means, and my father, very nobly as I thought, made her an offer that if she would surrender her boy entirely, never see him again, or have any kind of claim on him, the child should be brought up with every advantage of my father's special care. Not to my surprise, the woman consented, so little had she of any real feeling. But quite calmly she gave up her baby. John was brought here when he was two years old--ten years ago. She kept her part of the bargain. We had no word from her of any kind.

'I think, Mr. Brighouse, you ought to know these facts if you are going to be John's constant companion. You will find him a good little boy, I think--at times strangely like his father, he seems to me. It would be better, I think, to make no allusion whatever to his mother.'

It was not long, however, before Michael realized that Miss Fawcus meant little in the house in comparison with her father. After his first week Michael knew that there was no one in the place, from Miss Fawcus herself down to the small spotty boy who helped under com-pulsion in the garden, not aware of the Colonel during every minute of the day and even more aware of him when his bodily presence was felt rather than seen. There was something curious in this, Michael thought, because the Colonel's robust geniality was anything rather than frightening--a kinder and more agreeable man surely did not exist anywhere. He was generous and open, more than fatherly with Mi-chael from the very first moment. He had a way of putting his hand on

Michael's shoulder, of gripping his arm, that was extremely pleasant, so cordial, so spontaneous. As a rule, Michael fastidiously disliked any kind of physical contact with his friends and acquaintances. He inherited this possibly from his father, who had never kissed him although they were such excellent friends. The Colonel pressed his hand into Michael's shoulder, drew him a little towards him, looked him laughingly in the face, and then said with such spontaneous, cordial honesty:

'We're in luck, Brighouse. You're just the man I've been wanting.'

And Michael replied: 'I'm the lucky one, sir.'

He found himself after a while eagerly sharing in the Colonel's past triumphs: the present ones were, he was bound to admit, very small and he wondered that a man of the Colonel's character and broad-minded good-nature should value so seriously the little encounters in Keswick, trifling compliments paid him in a letter, foolish little nothings that the wife of Mr. Broster, the clergyman, or old Mrs. Page-Hunter had paid him. 'But that,' he thought, 'is what happens when you live for a long time in the country; little things become so important and the old boy's getting on. It is natural for him to wish to live in the past. The fact that he is a bit of an egotist is nothing against him: we are all egotists together and as we grow old we are afraid of being left alone.'

After a month or two, it might be said that Michael almost loved the Colonel. He was excited at his approach. He had never before thought very much of the physical appearance of any man, but the Colonel's cleanliness and physique and freshness of colour, a faint aroma of an extraordinarily healthy soap, a very fine virile tobacco, a tang of open-air health that the Colonel carried with him, gave Michael an intimate satisfaction, and when the Colonel drew him a little towards him and he could see those clear bright-blue eyes and the rough cleanly strength of the stiff white hair, and measure the broadness of the chest and appreciate the fine set-back of the shoulders, then Michael felt a warmth of almost filial affection.

One morning going to his bath, the door being open, he went in and found the Colonel singing in a funny high treble that was almost falsetto and rubbing himself fiercely with an enormous towel.

'Come in, my boy, come in,' the Colonel cried. 'Room for us both.'

And it was then that Michael was compelled to admire the splendid physical strength of that body, its freshness and symmetry and energetic happiness.

'Wouldn't think I was nearly seventy, would you, my boy?' said the Colonel, punching his chest. 'Like to see me touch my toes? How's this for an old man's exercise?' And obviously extremely proud of his strength he bent and twisted and turned, his beautiful white hair standing up on end, the muscles of his shoulders and thighs rippling under the fair skin.

'My word!' said Michael. 'I wish I could be like that when I am nearly seventy. How have you managed it, sir?'

'Luck,' said the Colonel, his whole face smiling like that of a happy child. 'Luck and obeying a few sensible rules, watching the teeth and the colon, exercises every day. Here, let me see you do an exercise or two.'

Michael was ashamed of his thin, meagre body. The Colonel felt his muscles, slapped him on the back, and then looking at him with real fatherly affection said:

'I can tell you, my boy, it's a happy thing that you've come here. It makes a difference to all of us.'

'Do I indeed?' said Michael, blushing with pleasure. 'I want to do my best; you are all so very good to me.'

One individual with whom intimate relations were not at once established was little John. He was from the beginning polite and obedient, but at first he kept absolutely aloof.

'How much does he know of his history?' wondered Michael. 'Does he suffer because of it? Is he aware of his own loneliness and isolation?'--because lonely it seemed the boy was. It was clear that he admired his grandfather intensely and that he obeyed in every instance his aunt. But it was not so clear that he loved either of them. His affections were elsewhere. First and above all other, the Parkin boy, who was three years older than himself. After that the mongrel kitchen dog named Romp by the cook and more vulgarly Rump by everybody else. Rump was of the engaging kind of mongrel as common in life as in fiction. He was a sort of terrier, but with a round, amiable, friendly face that belonged more to the sheep-dog kind. He was a dog who had been brought up from the beginning in the worst kind of social snobbery. He was gay and merry in the kitchen quarters, but if ever he ventured higher he became painfully subservient, crawling across the floor, wagging his tail, looking up into Miss Fawcus' face with a beseeching manner--and well he might, for if she found him in any part of the house other than the servants' rooms he was swished and shooed and driven away. He would run for his very life. This creature John loved. The third item in his affections was the gardener, old Lewcomb, an absolutely silent, saturnine man, who so far as anyone could see hated mankind. Nevertheless John worshipped him. He would sit by him for hours in the very depressed garden under the fell, would ask him endless questions, which Lewcomb did not answer. He had an irresistible fascination for John, who thought him infinite, wise and omniscient.

Into this select company of three Michael was not admitted. On the other hand, John after a while did more than tolerate him. He liked being with him. He liked being taught by him. He was obedient and very seldom sulky, but he did not surrender himself, and after four months Michael knew the boy very little better than he had at first.

Then came Miss Fawcus' extraordinary announcement.

Miss Clennell, John's abominable mother, had been asked by the Colonel to pay a visit. Miss Fawcus' horror was almost pathetic in its ineffectiveness.

'My father has invited the woman to stay here. His reasons I cannot imagine. I have argued with him, protested, done all that I could. You are a young man, Mr. Brighouse, but you will understand the scandals to which this visit must inevitably give rise in a small community like this. My father, as you know, has been a Member of Parliament for this district and has lived here for many years. Even small day-by-day occurrences give rise to much comment. The appearance here of Miss Clennell will be the talk of the place. But in addition to that, I consider it an insult that she should be brought into this house. What her influence on the boy may be I shudder to think.'

28

Miss Fawcus' announcement left him in a state of curious excitement and he realized very quickly that it was not the anticipation of Miss Clennell's arrival that excited him so much as his sharpened consciousness of some kind of mysterious conflict that was going on in the house. Where did the conflict lie? Was it between Miss Fawcus and her father? Was it between the Colonel and some person or persons whom he, Michael, had not yet realized? Was it between the servants in the house and their superiors? Was John the centre of it? Was it simply the house itself and the country that surrounded it?

Why was it that he, who until this visit had never been afraid of anything, was conscious so often of little moments of apprehension? Yet he was happy here. He was happy partly because of the very excitement that the place produced in him. Was his love of this country making him more sharply perceptive than the facts warranted? In any case, putting these vague sensations aside, what an extraordinary thing for the Colonel to do--Miss Fawcus was right there--to ask his son's mistress to the house where her child was, when he had made the sharpest condition that she should never see the child again. He had imagined that in spite of his vigour and full body the Colonel was a strict moralist, in fact he told Michael on more than one occasion that he disliked this modern broad-mindedness and that if he had his way young people should be taught to obey the old rules again; especially he emphasized his opinion that women to-day were surrendering almost everything that made them valuable and attractive.

'I may be old-fashioned,' he said, 'most men are at sixty-eight, but the world will find out one day that I am right.'

But Michael was by this time more than suspicious that there was a great deal in the Colonel that he had not yet perceived. One family of friends, the Parkins, confirmed him in this.

Mrs. Parkin was a little, thin, very tidy woman, with short well-cared-for grey hair and a rather pinched white face. She was immensely energetic and vivacious. Her husband, who had made money in buttons or something of the kind and had now retired from business, was a thin, tall man, completely under the domination of his wife. Mrs. Parkin lived for her circle of friends. This circle was by far the most important thing in her life and meant much more to her than either her husband or her child. Every member of the circle had to be distinguished for something or other. It was not so very easy in a little neighbourhood like this to find a number of distinguished people, but Mrs. Parkin had achieved marvels.

There was, for instance, Mr. Latter who played the piano: Mrs. Lincoln who had sung solos in oratorio. Then there were Mr. Morphew, his wife and daughter, who all wrote. They were naturalists, and in one of the Northern papers once a week there were delightful things by Mr. Morphew about what the blackbird was doing, why owls made the noises they did at night, and so on. Amy Morphew knew all about dogs, and quite often little articles would appear hither and thither about the skins of dogs and the right biscuits to give them. But Mrs. Parkin had failed, alas! to capture the greatest prize of all, Mr. Bauman, who lived on the other side of the Lake, a quite famous novelist. He was in appearance a stout cheery-faced man who could be seen walking furiously on the fell or along the road, swinging a stick, and as he went he would often sing aloud. He seemed so cheerful a person that he should have been easy for Mrs. Parkin to capture, but he refused absolutely. He was, in fact, extremely rude to her, and if you wanted to please Mrs. Parkin, even if it were very easy, all you had to do was to abuse Mr. Bauman.

Mrs. Parkin was extremely tenacious of her friends. Once you were a member of the circle it cost you your very social life to forsake it. It might be that all her geese were swans, but there was something very charming about her enthusiasm. To listen to her you would think that Mr. Latter played the piano like Cortot, that the Morphews were naturalists like Monsieur Fabre, and that Mrs. Lincoln was the recognized equal of Clara Butt. Unfortunately this enthusiasm instantly died did you refuse one of Mrs. Parkin's invitations, or, still worse, pretend you were ill and then be discovered at some other person's house.

Mrs. Parkin was a lady of immense character and determination.

'We may live in the depths of the country,' she would say, 'but we can find our culture wherever we are.'

Now the one person of whom Mrs. Parkin was afraid was the Colonel. It was difficult to see why, for the Colonel was always charming to her, laughed and joked with her, complimented her, went to her parties. But if he did not, if he said to her quite sharply: 'Nonsense, Emmeline, I have no time to waste on that foolishness,' Emmeline Parkin would smile and say: 'The dear Colonel, he is sometimes out of sorts. I understand him so very well.'

Michael had, of course, been drawn into the Parkins' circle. He found it indeed one of the trials of his young life, for he had not the mature courage to refuse an invitation. Once he had said he must go back home and work, and instead of that had visited some extremely sophisticated friends of his, the Lascelles, whom Mrs. Parkin detested even as she detested Mr. Bauman and for the same reason that they would have nothing at all to do with her. Mrs. Parkin discovered his falseness as she always discovered everything, and he found that, within a week, the most dreadful suspicions about him were being circulated in Keswick and the district: that no girl was safe from his amorous advances, that he had been sent down from College in disgrace, that his father was ashamed of him, and that he was the worst possible young man to be tutor to a small boy. He did not know that Mrs. Parkin had said any of these things, but in sheer cowardice he went and made his peace with her and his character seemed suddenly to recover its pristine innocence. May and Kate Lascelles chaffed him brilliantly for his cowardice. He frankly admitted it. He wanted to live at peace with all the world. It was the Parkins whom he had specially in mind when he heard of the visit of John's mother. What excitement there would be, what chatter, what gossip!

At the first sight of Rose Clennell in that warm, old, crowded, whispering drawing-room, he forgot all about gossip, all about local curiosity and chatter, all about the Colonel, all about Miss Fawcus, even all about John. He fell at once, completely, entirely, for the first time in his young life, in love. He did not know why. He had never had any experience of this before, so that he could offer to himself no comparisons. It was as though his heart and soul were bared to himself for the first time. He was, from that instant of experience, no longer a rather aimless, rather clever, rather characterless young man. He was sublimated there on that drawing-room floor into a knight-errant, a worshipping servant, a humble friend. It was not that his breath was taken away by her beauty; he knew at once that she was not in the general sense a beautiful woman. It was not that he could discern any special ability of character or wisdom. There was no divine air, no heavenly music. He kept his head. He did not stare at her in any kind

31

of breathless fashion. He had no wish at all to catch her in his arms and embrace her. He scarcely even wished to be near her. He only felt within himself such a surrender of his personality to another, such a fire of a desire for service, for unselfish action, that it was really a dedication of all that he was and ever had been.

After his first little talk before the Colonel interrupted them he decided for himself that she was very young for her age--exactly the opposite impression from that which Rose thought she gave him. Her talk about Geneva and the League, foreign politics in general, seemed to him to be very simple and inexperienced. He decided that what she wanted to be was very different from what she was. In his room alone afterwards, as he was undressing, his principal thought was: 'She needs protecting: she needs looking after. I shall be able to help her.' And he lay awake for hours, feeling as though his invisible room were lit with every kind of beauty.

This sudden and so unexpected experience coincided with the revelation that the country had been to him. The two things came together. In the confused and busy hours that follow a sudden falling in love one cannot remember anything of the beloved in actual fact--very often scarcely the name. One can see nothing of the features. One hears the voice as a very distant echo of something much more beautiful. One is sunk, lapped round by a fire as bright and fierce as ever lapped protectingly about Brunnhilde. There are two fires: one, the flames of glory that come from one's own ecstasy; the other, a mysterious, smoky flame that veils the loved one. Both fires die down, and when, afterwards, there is only the cold hillside and all iridescence has faded from the sky, then the first real meeting takes place.

Michael may have conjured up for himself these immature rhapsodies, but at least he knew for a certainty that his life would never be the same again and that the country and Rose Clennell had come to him together.

As he lay in bed, staring into the darkness, he saw as though from a great distance line upon line of little hills, mouse-grey, and then, as though he himself ran towards them, the background expanded into long, rough expanses of fell. He climbed the rocky, twisting path and now he was on the top, the wind whistling about his feet. He could move now all day over turf that sprang with the running touch of his step, and he turned the corner, as he had done only a week before, starting from Cat Bells, and saw the valley of Newlands lying with its farms, stone walls, and marvellous, shapeless symmetry, stained with colour between the hills, an intense green, and then grey, like smoke, where threads of mist drifted in between the hollows.

He passed from vision to vision, from recapture to recapture of little places that he knew, of journeys that he had taken, and whether he stood on Esk Hause and looked down the rolling slopes to Eskdale, or climbed the hill above Hawkshead and saw Coniston in a blue mist, or watched small blue waves curl about the reeds on Rydal, or from the downs above Uldale stared at the Scottish border and the silver line of the Firth, it was always the same--Rose Clennell was the country and the country was Rose, and he himself was happier than he had ever been in his life before.

CHAPTER III - BIRTHDAY PARTY

On the second day after Rose's arrival Mrs. Parkin appeared at the Hall.

It was at once evident that she had come for one purpose and one purpose only--to look at Rose. She was a little bird-like woman whose eyes instantly spoke her mind. Over her tongue she had some command, over her eyes none at all. Were she bored with you her eyes showed it. Were she expecting the entrance into the room of someone more important or interesting than yourself her eyes showed it, for, while her tongue addressed you, her eyes were fixed over your shoulder at the door.

In this present instance her eyes devoured Rose. Her gaze absorbed everything. She stripped Rose of every shred of clothing, then dressed her slowly again, considering every article before she neatly readjusted it. While her eyes were thus occupied her tongue chattered. She scattered about her absent-minded friendliness. You would think to listen to her that her only desire was that Rose should be happy now that she had arrived, for the first time in her life, in 'the dear, delightful, soaking Lake District.' She could not help but speak of the Lakes as though she had invented and owned them, but in this she was only one of many, for everyone who lives in the Lake District does the same. She apologized for the rainfall rather as a lady letting her house apologizes for the hot-water system: 'We must make you happy, dear Miss Clennell. We will show you our Lakes and you shall tell us about the League of Nations. That is Mrs. Broster's hobby--the League, I mean, she is so very good about it and so enthusiastic. She gives us almost too many pamphlets!

'You must come soon to see us. We live most simply but we have our little Circle. Music--do you care for music? There is Mr. Latter--he plays the piano quite delightfully. And Mrs. Lincoln sings--she has one of the most powerful contraltos I've ever heard. But you must come and try us out. Now Friday--next Friday. That is Roger's birth-day--our only boy. He is a great friend of John's although he is three years older. They are the greatest friends. John thinks the world of him. Now come you must. I'll take no refusal. John is coming, of course, and Michael Brighouse and perhaps the Colonel if he hasn't a stupid meeting. Of course you'll come. It will be a good opportunity to meet my friends. Maybe we shall have a little music--we older ones-- while the children have their games.'

Rose promised. Mrs. Parkin vanished into her little Austin, eager, smiling, her eyes fixed on her next horizon.

During the following two days and nights the heavens opened and the rain descended. The rain never ceased for a single instant. It thun-dered down upon the house, personally, savagely, as though it wished to beat it to the ground. The house was so dark that, in the passages, Rose moved with her hand in front of her face as though she expected a bat or some other obscene animal to fly at her eyes.

Beyond the windows the whole world surrendered to the rain, hills, trees, stone walls, and always there was a roar of water beating with a kind of drumming rhythm in the air. The people in the house were en-tirely unconcerned with the rain and went about their duties placidly. Rose noticed that automatically they raised their voices to a higher pitch. She looked out of window and saw the white, almost phospho-rescent stream on the fell-side leaping through the air. The old gardener, a sack over his shoulders, moved quietly along, water drip-ping from his cap.

On the second afternoon she was moving cautiously down the up-per landing to her bedroom when she encountered John. He was dragging Rump by the collar. Rump with a look of blind and obsequi-ous obstinacy was resisting at every step.

'He hates to come upstairs,' John explained. 'He thinks Aunt Janet will be after him.'

'Ought you to bring him upstairs,' Rose asked, 'if Aunt Janet doesn't like it?'

'Oh, she doesn't mind. She only thinks she minds. Unless he's very dirty of course. But he's awfully afraid of her.'

'He seems afraid of me too,' Rose said. She knelt down and began to stroke him. He submitted but the whites of his eyes were turned towards the stairs. He was ready to run at a moment's notice. On her knees she was very close to John. He did not move away. He considered her gravely.

'You're my mother, aren't you?' he said.

'Yes, I am.'

'And father's dead?'

'Yes.'

He drew a short trembling breath. 'You haven't bothered about me much all this time,' he said.

The rain was thundering down but they could hear one another very easily.

She looked at him steadily.

'Why haven't you?'

'I'll tell you,' she answered. 'Because I knew your grandfather could give you so much that I couldn't. He could send you to a fine school and I couldn't. When you were a baby I had very little money.'

'You might have come to see us sometimes,' he said.

'Would you have liked me to?' she asked.

That question closed him up entirely.

'Oh! it's very decent here,' he said casually. 'Come on, Rump! There's nothing to be frightened of.' And he marched off down the passage.

Safe in her room she tried to read a book. But was she safe? She got up and began to walk about, the rain, as it seemed, marching with her. She saw herself in the long mirror and despised the small insignificant figure that she saw there. She was not far from tears. She had not cried for ten years and she would not cry now, but John, in those few short sentences, had brought back John's father to her almost beyond endurance.

'Humphrey!' she murmured. 'Humphrey!' He had said to her once: 'Rose, darling, you're not at all what you think you are! You want to be hard and wise and sophisticated, but really you're soft and not very wise and simple. You've got to love someone--otherwise you're lost.' Well, he had been wrong. For all these years she had been wise and sophisticated. She had hated sentimental people, sentimental ideas, sentimental books and plays, weak, flaccid philosophies. But she had been lonely. It came on her now in a flash that she had been unhappy and had known it but had never admitted it. Her obstinacy had carried her through, but carried her to what? To nothing at all. Nothing had been so real to her as that sentence of John's a moment ago--'You might have come to see us sometimes.'

Biting her lip, she fought her weakness. This was the sentimentality that she had always despised. She imagined what she would have thought and said if some woman had come to her and said: 'So I gave up my child because I thought it was right, and then ten years later when I saw him again I wept and wanted him back.'

She must go. That was clear. She must leave this house and never return. She would throw herself into her work and perfect that self-training that would make her one of those wise controlled modern women to whom a cause was more than any person and a stern ideal more beautiful than any relationship.

But Humphrey! John, with the tuft of fair hair, the shy honesty, the physical independence, had brought Humphrey back so that he was with her in the room, his room where he had slept and dreamed--and from that very window he had looked out and seen the climbing fell.

His arms were round her, his cheek against hers, and his voice saying: 'It won't be easy, darling. It won't be easy unless you love me enough . . .' She brushed her eyes with her hand, blew her nose and went down to find Colonel Fawcus.

She knocked on his study door and went in. He was there, seated at a large official-looking table, and in front of him a big book. Before him was a bottle of paste, in his hand a pair of scissors. He was very busy, his cheerful countenance grave, his eyes bent sternly on his task.

'Who is it?' he said quite fiercely, not looking up. 'I thought I said--'

Then when he saw who it was he beamed.

'Well, my dear--'

She stood some way from the desk, her hands at her side.

'I'm disturbing you, I know--'

'Not at all. I'm delighted to see you, my dear.'

'I had to come. I couldn't wait. I had to tell you that I must go away--at once. I must leave to-morrow.'

He stood up. He smiled at her like a benevolent father. He stretched out his hand.

'Why, dear Rose, whatever is the matter? Go away? What nonsense! Come and sit down and tell me all about it.'

'No. I won't sit down, thank you.'

He came towards her. His large fresh healthy body closed in some of her horizon.

'Colonel Fawcus,' she said, 'why did you ask me to come here?'

'Why do you think I did?'

'I don't know. I've no idea.'

'Mightn't it have been--curiosity?'

'Curiosity? If that was it you would have asked me before.'

'Perhaps not. Perhaps for a long while I felt rather bitterly. And then, maybe, after all these years, I felt that I had done wrong.'

'But you knew what asking me here would mean--the gossip, the difficult position for John--'

'Why, has anyone been rude or unkind to you?'

'No--everyone has been very kind. That isn't why I'm going.'

'What then?'

Her voice faltered. 'I hadn't realized, I hadn't known--what I would feel when I saw John again.'

He waited, looking at her with the greatest kindness and even tenderness.

She cried out almost desperately: 'Oh, I can't tell you! I can't explain! And why should I? We are under no obligation to one another. We made a bargain and we've kept to it. I've seen John. I realize that he is in splendid hands, and so, having seen him, I can go away with a quiet mind.'

'Have you had,' he asked her, 'a quiet mind all these years? You have never enquired about him, never written--'

'I didn't dare,' she said very quietly. 'I see now that he was never out of my mind. I pretended to myself. I was always thinking of him--'

'And won't you now, if you go away--?'

'Perhaps I shall. But that will be better than staying here, loving him--' She broke off. Her voice was trembling.

'Must you?' he said to her very gently and with such kindliness that suddenly her very soul revolted against the softness and sentimentality of her state. There was something uneasy, unreal, about their conversation, about her own feelings, even about his looks, and beneath all the unreality, some two layers down, there was a hidden reality of most important significance. The very fact that their conversation was unreal meant that something was developing, something that was using this unreality for its own purpose.

She shook her head as though she had come to some sudden re-solve.

'I don't think we're saying what we really think. I know you're be-ing very kind, trying not to hurt me. All that has happened to me is that I saw John half an hour ago and that he was so like Humphrey that I began to be soft and sentimental. I hate to be sentimental, and that's why I am going.'

She had expected that at the mention of Humphrey's name some emotion would have been expressed by him--in the eyes, in the corners of the mouth, in those eyes that were so kind and generous and yet, as she was beginning to realize, eyes upon eyes, so that in all probability there lurked quite another pair behind those bright ones.

He answered her very quietly. 'My dear Rose, I don't like sentimen-tality either. Of course you must go if you wish to. We all like you here--'

'Not Janet,' she broke in angrily.

'Oh, Janet! Is she the cause of the trouble? Janet doesn't matter. But if you like I will speak to her.'

'Over my dead body,' Rose cried out. 'I admire Janet for not liking me. I'd have hated myself if I had been her. She's perfectly polite to me and it's not Janet that's the trouble.'

'Who then?'

'Myself. I didn't realize before I came how alive Humphrey would be in this house.'

'And that's why I want you to stay a little longer,' he said. 'You asked me just now why I invited you. Perhaps you are the only person in the world beside myself who knew really what Humphrey was. Per-haps I have been looking for that someone who knew him.'

'Janet did,' she cried.

'Janet loved him, but never knew him. And that's why Janet is jeal-ous of you.'

'No,' Rose thought, 'that is not the reason and he knows it's not the reason. And it is not because of Humphrey that he asked me here.'

But she felt herself submitting. It was extraordinary the influence that he had. When you were with him in a room you wanted to do as he wished. He was almost double-sized, that is, he seemed to be on every side of you and you did not resent him because his kindness and his intelligence were so attractive. Yes, he was extremely intelligent and she had never realized it before. Why, with his charm and intelligence, then, hadn't he become something much more than he was? Why had he not gone much further? Was he, knowing in himself how intelligent he was, deeply disappointed, and did he perhaps hope that she would understand and give him some kind of compensation? She had moved, without knowing it, nearer him, and at that instant he put his hand on her arm--a strong, fine hand with an almost iron pressure. She did not dislike his touch.

'Stay,' he said. 'We all need you--myself, Janet, John. Don't think about any gossip there may be. That will very soon die down. I don't think you should run away from this before you have tested it a little. You are not a coward.'

She made no answer.

He went back to the table and sat down. He took up the paste-pot and looked over it at her, smiling, so exactly like a boy who was sticking stamps into an album.

'Well,' she said shyly, 'I seem to have no will of my own.'

'Is that a bad thing?' he asked her.

'Certainly it's a bad thing,' she answered almost fiercely. 'I hate weak women.'

'You're not weak,' he said, 'only kind to a rather lonely old man.' He threw up his head, laughing. 'See how senile I am. I am arranging old press-cuttings of one or two feeble speeches I have made. Look.'

She came forward and glanced over his shoulder, and saw something that had just been pasted into the book headed: 'Lt.-Col. Fawcus opens Rose Show at Carstairs.' She thought: 'What an extraordinary

42

thing for him to take pleasure in! As though it mattered to anyone, his opening a rose show.'

They looked at one another and in his gaze she saw something pathetic and almost arrogant, as though he said to her: 'You think it foolish of me to do this? One day you shall know.'

She felt a sudden curious nervousness and left the room.

On the Friday was the Parkins' party and at first all that Rose could think of was young John's excitement about this event. He had bought his present entirely with his own money. What he had bought was a small red writing-case, and this was because young Parkin had once said to John: 'Oh, what a ripping writing-case!' John's had been all blue leather and he was very proud of it. He would have liked to offer it to young Parkin, but it had been given him by his grandfather. He had seen that young Parkin wanted it and there had been rather uncomfortable moments. Young Parkin had so clearly expected John to offer it and John had thought: 'I can't give him this case, because Grandfather gave it me, but I will get him one for his next birthday.'

Rose realized on this morning how very highly strung John was. She was almost frightened by the intensity of his feeling.

'Why do you like him so much?' she asked him.

'Oh! I don't know,' John said. 'He's awfully decent. I'm three years younger, you know, but he lets me do things with him and he never minds my not knowing as much as he does.'

'I should think not,' said Rose indignantly. 'I'm sure you know a lot of things he doesn't know.'

'He's most frightfully clever,' said John. 'He's good at exams and games too. He's good at practically everything, except swimming.' He dropped his voice and into his eyes there came a look of awe. 'It's pretty rotten for him,' John said, 'but he's frightened of the water. He is, really. His nurse, or someone, held his head under once. He gets blue all over the legs and arms before he is in the water at all, and he had an uncle who threw him in out of a boat. It's dreadful, because at school he has to dive and everything so that the other boys won't know. It's a terrible secret. Nobody knows but me.'

'Well,' said Rose, who hated young Parkin already in prospect, 'I'm glad there is something he can't do.'

'That's the only thing,' said John. 'He's teaching me to box.'

'Do you like that?' Rose asked, looking at his slender body and very sensitive face.

'I don't terribly,' said John, 'but I shall, he says, if I keep on at it. It isn't much fun at first, you know, because you're hit all the time. He just hits me where he likes and the other day I came back with my nose all swollen and Aunt Janet was very angry, but Grandfather said it was all right--it would make a man of me. Only you see,' he went on more confidentially, 'I've got to get thicker in the chest and I don't know how to. I do exercises and everything, but perhaps I am young yet: they say two or three years make an awful difference.'

He packed up his red leather writing-case himself with the utmost care and wrote on the outside in his large, boyish handwriting: 'For Roger William Parkin from his sinsere friend, John Fawcus.'

Rose noticed that he had spelt 'sincere' with an 's' instead of a 'c,' but she said nothing. She only wondered whether Roger Parkin would point out this mistake to her John. If he did she thought that she would probably kill him.

'Do you think he can see through the tissue paper what it is?' John asked. 'I don't want him to know until he has taken all the paper off.'

So Rose lied. 'He won't have the least idea what it is,' she said.

They walked to the party, for the Parkins' house was not very far away--Michael, Rose and John.

After that great tempest how dry the land was! But in the sky the soft watery spaces seemed to hold a bloom like flowers after rain. The Helvellyn range, where it approached the sky, also was faintly iris-coloured and thus the slopes ran almost into spring-warmed country. The brown of fell and tree had a feathery promise, the sun was hot, the snow all gone save for thin white shadows on the tops.

As they reached the bend of the climbing hill and saw St. John's in the Vale below them it was all that Rose could do to keep back a cry, for the little narrow valley was bursting with life. Every tree seemed to be swelling with importance, the purple-veined tranquil smoke from the farm chimney moved upward with an exultant promise, sheep and cows raised their heads to gaze as though they expected some skyward manifestation. The light was so clear that detail, the green glitter of a leaf, the bubbling pause of the stream before a black stone, the dark lustre of a heap of manure, these things shone like sharp jewelled fragments. And the hills were so close. The rough fell was personally concerned in the civilized world of farm and garden; every hill had its double service of intercourse with man and the upward movement to the freedom of air and space. The sky was marbled with white feathers of cloud that formed changing patterns on the blue.

All was light and all was movement. Freedom and anticipation of some universal holiday were everywhere; the sky was water-dimpled, blue, trembling, the hillside damascened, the life of the valley tumultuous with colour, sharp green, ice-grey in the stream, amber brown of the tree-branches.

'And that's the Parkins' house,' said Michael.

Rose looked down to a white rambling house that was charming with its dovecote, its old rose-garden wall and a green lawn on which she could see figures moving like little dolls. Sometimes in March there comes surprisingly one of those warm days, almost a day of early summer. This moment's pause before the move downwards seemed to her for some reason to be one of infinite importance. She was waiting, suspended in this world of white and blue sky, stirring breeze. For the last time perhaps she could make her choice. She could go back. She could run away. Once involved, once she risked that downward step, she was irrevocably caught. She looked about her, back to the rough and rolling fell, up to the soft, almost iridescent sky, then down to the detail of farms and animals and puppet human beings. She looked at John, who had already started down the side path. Then, with a little toss of the head, she followed him.

Michael, beside her, said: 'Don't be afraid of the people down there, of their gossip, I mean; or of their looking at you too sharply. It means nothing. It will only be a nine days' wonder.'

She smiled. 'You're a noticing kind of young man. You thought I hesitated. Well, I did, and I'll tell you honestly I didn't know all I would be in for. If I had I expect I would have never come.'

'Oh yes, you would,' he said confidently, 'and it's a good thing you have. It's probably saved John.'

'Saved him from what?' she asked, looking at the small figure ahead of them absorbed in its own thoughts and interests.

'Oh, I don't know,' Michael answered lightly. 'A boy ought to have a mother, oughtn't he?'

'I'm afraid he doesn't like me very much,' she said doubtfully.

'Oh, he will,' said Michael. 'The story's only just beginning.'

And then they were at the Parkins' and Mrs. Parkin was there looking over Rose's shoulder at the garden gate, her eyes wandering about like little magnets, hoping to attract as many steel filings as possible.

'Well, Miss Clennell, this is good of you! And the Colonel couldn't come? Too tiresome of him. But he's such a busy man. What we would all do without him--'

She broke off and her eye picked up her son, a nice-looking boy, with black hair, dark eyes and a strong self-confident nose and chin.

'Roger, here's your friend, John. Miss Clennell, this is my boy-- Roger.'

The boy had excellent manners. He seemed quite a grown little man already and he was perfectly at ease with everybody. But Rose's attention was absorbed by her son. John was in a quiver of emotion and sensitive feeling. He was clutching his parcel and at the moment the boy joined them John pushed it into Roger's hand. His face was crimson and he muttered something that nobody heard. Roger took the parcel rather like a monarch receiving tribute from one of his subjects.

'Oh, I say, John, that's awfully decent of you. How ripping!'

And he was about to investigate it when a boy came running across the lawn, calling out: 'Roger, they say we are going to have races and there will be prizes,' and he turned, holding his parcel, joined his friend, and with a rather hurried 'Wait a minute. I'll be back' to John, ran across the lawn carrying the unopened parcel in his hand.

Rose's whole soul seemed to be caught by her son. She did not appear to be looking at him, but was, it seemed, listening to some of Mrs. Parkin's chatter. She did not, in fact, hear a single word. Only about her head a bee-swarm of voices. She was caught up by her son as though she were a part of him and he of her, physically as well as spiritually. His disappointment was so naked to her that her only longing was to protect him. No one, perhaps, saw it but herself, although she fancied that Michael was aware of it. John was making a courageous effort to cover it and stood looking at Mrs. Parkin and shifting from one small leg to the other. But his lips were trembling; there were tears in his eyes, and the defiant way in which he had thrown back his head as though he were challenging all the world to try and hurt him was simply his father over and over again. Roger had not even looked at the parcel. He had scarcely thanked the giver of it. And Rose at that moment felt for Mrs. Parkin's offspring a hatred stronger than anything that even the Führer himself had ever been able to arouse in her.

She was soon compelled to think of herself, for Mrs. Parkin was bringing up to her one or two friends.

'Miss Clennell, you must know Mr. Latter. What the Parkin family would do without Mr. Latter, it simply doesn't know. You're part of us, Reggie, aren't you? Bone of our bone, we might almost say.'

And this, Rose thought, was especially applicable to Mr. Latter, who was very tall, very thin, and resembled a telegraph-pole in that he was constantly humming little indistinct tunes to himself just as the wires hum above your head as you walk in the country.

'Reggie plays the piano, Miss Clennell, better than any amateur I have ever heard in my life. And to call you an amateur, Reggie, is a terrible insult. It simply is, Miss Clennell, that he plays for the love of playing and refuses to take a penny for his beautiful art, don't you, Reggie? This is Miss Clennell, Reggie, a friend of Colonel Fawcus, and she is passionately fond of music, and the one thing in the world she wants is to hear you play.'

Rose knew at once that this long thin man with the high cheek-bones and a hungry look in his eye, as though he never had enough to eat, had heard all about her and probably knew much more of her private history than she knew herself. He did not look unkind or patronizing, but terribly unhappy, as though the one thing in the world he wanted was to escape, and she fancied that she detected a look almost of hatred that flashed from his despairing eyes to the little bird-like figure of Mrs. Parkin. However, she had not very much time to consider him because other ladies and gentlemen were speedily brought up to her and she detected in them all that same glance of inquisitive recognition. They, having heard everything about her but seeing her for the first time, were busily adding experience to surmise. She felt a panic rising within her and it was roused in her especially by the Morphew family, who curiously resembled rabbits, Miss Morphew in particular, having had her front teeth sadly neglected in early youth. In fact, as so often happens with people, physical appearances fitted in very exactly with occupation and interests. The Morphews were the famous naturalists, Mrs. Parkin explained, and there was nothing about cuckoos and moles and ferrets that they did not know. But Rose perceived that she herself was the animal whose habits they were just then intently studying. They stared at her as though they were stripping the very clothes off her back. She could detect Mrs. Morphew busily writing in her brain: 'This little animal is unusual in several particulars. Its plumage is bright, but its appearance altogether deceptive, for as the dusk falls it flits from tree to tree uttering a shrill sharp note--' and so on and so on.

Miss Morphew was especially excited. She was a plain girl, very badly dressed, self-conscious in all her movements, but her eyes were soft and pleading as though she were saying: 'Oh, Miss Clennell, I do so want to get away from Papa and Mama. I don't care about natural history a bit. I would like to be bold and daring as you have been, and I do hope you will tell me how I can manage it.'

But now the whole scene was becoming exceedingly animated. Mrs. Parkin was here, there and everywhere. She was stirring everyone up to show their very best paces, rather as a trainer with performing lions goes round from lion to lion trying to rouse them from their sleepy indifference. Rouse them she did. There were a number of children who passed with surprising quickness from the instructed politeness as proper little visitors to the excited horse-play of small animals released from their cages.

Rose heard Mrs. Parkin's cheerful impersonal voice saying:

'And now that the children are happy, shall we go indoors and have some music?'

'How terribly difficult it is,' she thought, 'to be a really good hostess! Just when you have learnt the technique sufficiently you are ruined, because you are at last a professional and that is the one thing a hostess must not be.' Mrs. Parkin was so thoroughly professional that Rose felt as though she were one of the Albert Hall choir being driven on to the platform to rehearse Elijah. What she wanted to do was to see that John was all right. As she moved to the door of the house she saw him waiting with several other anxious-looking children, while Roger Parkin and another boy picked sides for a game. She knew so well the embarrassment of that waiting. Would you be chosen? Or would you be left to that terrible lonely position when, in a kind of tortured agony, you heard someone say: 'Well, I suppose I have got to have Rose.' She knew just what John was feeling; how desperately he would be wanting to be on Roger's side. She was on the point of saying: 'Oh! I must just stay in the garden another few minutes. It's quite warm even though it is March!' but she hadn't the courage, and meekly she followed her hostess in.

She found herself in an overcrowded drawing-room--a room containing a vast piano, many signed photographs, and an extraordinary, high, thin, white Chinese pagoda under glass--with a nervous little woman, with a voice like the rustle of dry autumn leaves, sitting beside her. This little lady told Rose frankly that she did not like music at all, but that she adored Mrs. Parkin.

'I can't help thinking that it's a pity on a nice afternoon, with the sun shining, we should all sit in here listening to Beethoven. I never know which is Beethoven, and which is Bach and which is Brahms, and I am so dreadfully afraid of giving myself away.'

'Why,' asked Rose, 'do you come if you dislike music so much?'

'Well, of course, I love Emmeline and I do think she should be supported for the way in which she is trying to bring culture into Keswick.'

'Does Keswick really want culture?' Rose asked.

'No, I don't suppose it does,' said the little lady, 'any more than any other place. You either have culture, or you haven't, don't you think? And if you haven't got it, you really don't want somebody else to give it to you. You don't want it and you ought to have it. That's the way I look at it.'

'Oh! I don't agree at all,' Rose said. 'If you don't want it, don't have it. If you really hate music you will never like it however often Mrs. Parkin has concerts.'

'Well,' said the little lady, 'Emmeline promises me that I shall like it one day. She says that it all seems difficult at first, but that suddenly one morning you find that you love it.' Then she dropped her voice. 'Of course I don't think they play very well, Mr. Latter, I mean, and the Bunnings. And then I really do dislike Mrs. Lincoln's singing. I know that she's got a splendid voice, but she ought to be heard in the Rocky Mountains or in the African desert--somewhere where there is plenty of space. I have wondered sometimes whether the windows would not be broken in this little room: they shake like anything when she sings. Hush! they are going to begin.'

They did. Mr. Latter had sat at the piano with the melancholy anger of a prisoner picking hemp. He looked round the room with a complete loathing for everybody. Then he bent towards the piano and his face became more gentle, happier. He seemed suddenly to be wearing the right clothes and his figure looked no longer stiff and awkward. He played very well--Chopin and Delius and Holst. He was a real musician and a sudden peace came into the room as the beautiful notes softly stole about it, and very faintly, beyond the windows, came the cries and laughter of the children.

But Mrs. Parkin was restless, so as soon as one of her trained performers had begun his exercises she was eagerly thinking what the next item in the entertainment would be. She did not want the performance in the least, only that the performers should perform, and so when the last note of the gentle Holst chorale had died away, Mrs.

Lincoln was being whispered to. She was indeed only too ready to sing. She rushed at the piano like a trained seal opening its mouth for sardines. Mr. Bunning was to play her accompaniment--a little man who had a resemblance to the Hatter in Alice. This was perhaps because of his large mouth, his almost imbecile, friendly smile at everyone in the room. Mrs Lincoln sang 'O Rest in the Lord' at such a pace and with such violent determination that Mr. Bunning was left far behind. It was just as she finished and said in her jolly, deep, policeman's voice: 'And what will you all have next?' that Rose saw the door open and a very surprising person enter.

The newcomer was a small, stout, untidy clergyman. He had a round, red face and his trousers were still bound with clips. He had plainly just come off a bicycle. His face was pleasant and agreeable, but, as Rose at once noticed, a little unsteady. He held his soft black hat in his hand and he smiled at everybody, but rather, Rose noticed, as though he were not sure of his welcome. It was at once clear that there was a reason for this, for Mrs. Parkin had just said to Mrs. Lincoln: 'What's that lovely thing, Hilda dear, about the moon and running water you sing so beautifully?' when she was aware of her new visitor. She gave him a look of sharp and even angry disapproval.

'How are you all?' said the little clergyman. 'I wasn't asked, but I knew it was Roger's birthday and I've brought him a present. Go on with your music now and don't mind me.'

There was an empty chair on the other side of Rose and into this he dumped with a violent movement as though he had been dropped out of something. He seemed, Rose thought, a trifle unsteady on his legs. He regarded everyone most merrily in spite of Mrs. Parkin's discontent and went on, sotto voce, to Rose:

'Dear Mrs. Parkin doesn't like my coming. She's long given up asking me, but I come all the same, because I think it's good for her. Do you ever do things to people because you think it's good for them?'

'No,' said Rose. She was feeling uncomfortable because Mrs. Lincoln was just beginning to sing and their whispered conversation was plainly disconcerting her. 'I'm not ever sure of what is good for people.'

51

The little clergyman nodded his head. 'I always know exactly,' he said. 'It's one of my gifts.'

Mrs. Lincoln began to sing.

There was a great deal of music. The Bunnings played duets and Mr. Latter the Moonlight Sonata. It became exceedingly difficult to stop Mrs. Lincoln, who almost before she had finished her song cried out: 'And what will you have next, all of you?' When at last tea arrived and she could sing no longer, she stood in the middle of the room, large and hearty and jolly, eating whatever came her way.

She cried out: 'I like to sing. It does me good. No, I assure you, it's no trouble at all. I sing as naturally as I breathe. Have done ever since I was a baby. So if you nice, dear, kind things enjoy listening and I enjoy singing, that's all right, isn't it?'

'It would be all right,' the little clergyman remarked to Rose, 'if dear Mrs. Lincoln was not so sure it was all right. I like a little diffidence in public performers, don't you?'

'I don't know that I do,' said Rose. 'A really diffident public performer is pretty terrible--you know, a lecturer with a whole bundle of apologies, or a singer who isn't sure where the next bar is coming from.'

She did not quite know what she was saying, for she was longing to get away to rescue John, to be secure from all the curious eyes that inspected her. Only a few weeks ago she was sure she was completely indifferent to public opinion, and now a few country people in this little country room embarrassed her and made her angry. Some of them were moving out into the garden. She went too, the little clergyman at her side.

'My name is Rackstraw,' he said, 'and you are Miss Clennell, I know. I heard all about you half an hour after your arrival at the Hall. There's not a man, woman or child in Keswick, or its surroundings, who doesn't know that you are John's mother. That doesn't worry you, does it?'

'I don't know,' she answered. What right had this little man to fasten himself upon her and speak to her so intimately? As she stood on the lawn and looked at the quiet sun-burned hills under a sky that was now all a milky blue, without a cloud upon it, she prayed that she might not make a scene. The sun was setting and it would soon be very cold. Everyone would be going home. She thought that she could hold on for the few minutes that remained. But what she wanted to do was to turn and cry out to all of them: 'What has it to do with you whether I am John's mother, or not?'

The little man went on:

'Mrs. Parkin is very vexed at my coming to-day. There is nothing that she could possibly dislike more. That's because I sometimes drink too much and always talk too much and always say what I mean.'

He drank too much?

Yes. His words came a little thickly and his eyes had that faint look of anxiety as of a dog who sometimes behaves badly in public and is so anxious not to shame his master.

Mr. Rackstraw went on: 'I'm a clergyman, but I have no church. I believe in God, but no one listens to me because they all think my habits disgraceful. You might call me,' he continued cheerfully, 'the real scandal of the neighbourhood.' Then his voice became almost pleading. 'I'm not really very scandalous, but I was drunk once publicly in my church, and now if I have a cold or a slight indigestion, or talk in a voice so that the words are indistinct, everyone thinks I have been drinking again.'

'Why do you tell me all this?' Rose asked.

'Because,' he answered, 'I liked you the moment I saw you. People will tell you all this about me and more, but I'd rather you had it first-hand.' Then he added: 'If you stay here and are in any kind of trouble, remember that I'm not so foolish as I look.'

'Yes, I will,' Rose said. And they shook hands.

Afterwards, walking home, she thought that that was a very rude thing to have said.

The party was over. She, Michael and John walked up the dusky road, seeing the hills now like shadows against a white sky, in which stars were beginning to sparkle.

'Have you enjoyed it?' Michael asked. 'Was it very tiresome?'

Rose shook her head.

'I don't know. Enjoyment certainly isn't the word. The only thing I know is, I am going to stay and see it through.'

Her heart beating, she took John's hand in hers. He let it lie there for a little while and then very gently withdrew it. They walked in silence over the brow of the hill.

CHAPTER IV - LIFE AND DEATH OF JANET FAWCUS

Janet Fawcus was born on September 23rd, 1895. The first thing she consciously saw and remembered was a bright green curtain blowing in an open window and a tempest of rain driving into the room. She lay in her cot and screamed. Her father stood in the doorway, a giant he seemed to her; he was bare to the waist and his face was covered with soap, for he was shaving. From the middle of the white lather came a nose and two large bright eyes. On his chest there was hair, and round his neck a gold chain, and hanging to the chain a gold locket, which swung a little and gleamed. He bent down, picked her up and pressed her against his hairy chest. She would have screamed the louder, but she did not, because his eyes told her that if she did something quite terrible would happen. With one hand he closed the window. On her cheek she felt the white drops. He carried her into the bath-room, sat her on a chair. He took off all his clothes, stepped into the bath and stood there, shaving. She heard the storm beating against the window. When he had finished shaving he lay down in the bath and she saw only the top of his head and then suddenly two large white knees. When he stood up again he was pink all over.

Every detail of this she remembered; the noise of the rain, the smell of the steam, of soap, of human skin. She must have been about three years of age.

When she was nine she had a governess, Miss Spanner. When she was ten her mother died. She remembered her mother as a slight woman with very pretty hair and a nervous way of saying: 'I don't know, I'm sure.' She connected her mother also with the Keswick church, St. John's. They drove there in a pony trap. When her mother prayed a look came into her face of passionate intensity. Her lips would move in prayer as though she were asking for something with the greatest urgency.

The day of her mother's funeral there was snow on the ground, and the black figures moving through the garden were like long thin holes in the snow.

Miss Spanner, her governess, was a small plump woman who laughed a great deal. Janet came into a room unexpectedly one day and saw her sitting on her father's knee. Miss Spanner on the whole was kind to her and taught her French, History and Geography very well. But when Janet was about fourteen Miss Spanner told her all about sex in a very unpleasant way.

After that Janet loathed her. All this time there was Humphrey, her brother, whom Janet adored. Humphrey went away to school at Giggleswick but in the holidays he was generally at home. Everyone loved him except his father. Janet could not understand why her father was always so sharp and unkind to Humphrey when he was so charming and friendly to everyone else. Charming, that is, if you did what he told you. Janet soon discovered that he must be absolutely obeyed and she obeyed him. Humphrey also obeyed him but he could not do right. Sometimes his father whipped him and after a whipping he was for a little while kind to him--but only for a little while. However, Humphrey seemed to care very little about it; he was always cheerful and happy and good-natured with everyone. As Janet grew up this love of Humphrey became the great passion of her life. When he was away she thought of him, dreamt of him, and wrote him letters into which she poured all her thoughts. He never wrote to her in reply, but then boys do not write to their sisters.

When she was nineteen years of age she fell in love with Miss Hetty Francis, the sister of a doctor in the neighbourhood. Hetty Francis was over thirty and not beautiful, for she was masculine in appearance, wore stiff white collars and a coat and waistcoat like a man. For a while Miss Francis was very kind to Janet, and Janet knew some months of frenzied happiness and agitation. Then, quite suddenly, and for no apparent reason, Miss Francis was bored with Janet and told her so. Janet nearly died. Indeed she thought a great deal about suicide.

Miss Francis left the neighbourhood, and Janet was now austere, reserved, cynical. Only her brother was still adored by her. The rest of mankind was vile.

She had learnt by now to manage the house extremely well. 'What an efficient woman Miss Fawcus is!' people said. She was very severe with the maids, who disliked and admired her. She took some pride in the excellence of her management but more pride in her general scorn of mankind. Nothing pleased her better than to discover the little vanities, meannesses, selfishnesses of her neighbours, and there were plenty, of course, to discover. Yet, all the while, how she was longing to be loved! But not sexual love. When she thought of sex--and she was compelled to think of it very often because books, newspapers and animals are for ever reminding one--she saw her father rising, all pink from his bath, and Miss Spanner saying 'And then, after he has taken you on his knee, he . . .' and Hetty Francis, on their first meeting, kissing her as no one had ever kissed her before, and Hetty Francis saying only a month or two later: 'The truth is, dear, you're rather a bore. I like to be honest with everyone and it's just as well you should know that you made me feel an awful fool the other night. . . .'

So she hated sex and all those who exalted it, wrote or sung or pictured it. A maid, Mary Bess, was discovered to be with child and was dismissed with ignominy. Mary Bess, tossing her head, cried defiantly: 'I'd rather be me than you, miss, any day. Anyways I knows what a man's made of.' Her father agreed that Mary Bess had always been a wanton.

As time went on she realized that she would one day be a bitter old maid, and oh! that was not at all what she wanted to be. She wasted her heart on Humphrey who was now always in London and seldom wrote to her. She made once and again timid advances, now to a child, now to a new-comer, now to someone who spoke a friendly word to her at a party. But she did not know how to do these things gracefully. Her figure was austere in its uniform tweeds, her face stiff and unbending. A pretty girl came once to stay at the Parkins' and one evening at a musical party, walking in the garden (a lovely June night), this girl poured out her heart to Janet, how she loved a clerk in a bank and her parents would never allow it and she had no money and neither had he and so on and so on. . . . Janet listened and gave advice. Her eyes were tender, her voice soft. The girl cried, 'How good you are to me! No one has ever been so good!' and threw her arms around her and kissed her. Janet lay awake all that night thinking that a new life had begun for her. She would help the child and be her guide, friend, mother to the two young people. . . . Next day the girl was gone. Janet wrote but there was no answer.

Meanwhile there was her father. Her relations with him were very odd, for they were twofold and the one half did not belong to the other.

First she admired him, aided and abetted him, was his intimate. Secondly she feared him and was a stranger to him. She often, when she was near to him enough to smell the rough cloth of his country clothes, the faint aroma of soap, of tobacco, saw him rising all pink from his bath. Then she hated him. She knew that he had a constant energetic sexual life. For many years he went away at intervals, to London, to Manchester, to anywhere you like. Letters were forwarded always to the Savile Club, London. She knew why he went away and she imagined to herself what his mistresses might be--plump, jolly, greedy women. She saw him sitting with such a woman on his knee, just as she had seen him in her childhood with Miss Spanner. But she fancied that he also enjoyed sexual pleasures nearer home. Had he not been so jolly and cheerful a man and so popular there would, she thought, have been more said. There had been maids in the house who came to her quite suddenly familiar and impertinent, but when she dismissed them her father made no protest.

He never opposed her in any of her domestic plans, and here they were strong allies and even friends.

He treated her in all these things like a man, a good fellow. He kept her up to the mark as an officer a soldier in his regiment, and she responded to this, listening in silence to his anger when something had been wrong. In matters of affairs he was always just, but in relation to himself, his past history, his inner feelings, he was frequently unjust. That is, he moved then in a world that had laws and rules only for himself. Anyone outside that world must be often bewildered and confused. When he was angry it was often, it seemed, for no reason at all, or if there were a reason it was something so trivial as to be incredible.

Janet knew that his strange and arrogant tempers (cruel, fierce, savage) were aroused by some inner discomfort or need. She tried to satisfy these, but moved in the dark world of his impulses so uncertainly that she grew cautious.

Finally the situation was this: that in the management of the material life of the house they worked together in complete understanding-- in everything else they were strangers.

Janet lived with some vitality until Humphrey's marriage. Five weeks after that event she died. Humphrey married a Miss Gertrude Penner. Miss Penner was the only daughter of a Birmingham manufacturer and was wealthy. When, after a honeymoon in Italy, Humphrey brought her for his father's inspection, it was Humphrey who was inspected rather than Gertrude. Gertrude presented her husband as though he had never been seen by any of them before, saying: 'This is a very handsome thing that I have bought. It looks well, speaks well, my money will keep it smart and efficient. Please congratulate me.'

Gertrude, who was handsome--she reminded you of a magnificent mare, trained to the minute--was complete mistress of all situations. Within a week of her arrival she was ordering meals and altering the furniture. To say that Janet hated her is to say nothing--it was much more than hatred. And she loved Humphrey with a deeper, more yearning, more maternal passion than ever before.

She saw the great danger that she was in. For a fortnight she controlled herself admirably, then one afternoon she told Gertrude all that she thought of her. Humphrey was present.

He was physically obsessed by his wife, so completely absorbed by her body that he spoke like a thin, small voice, whispering from behind Gertrude's fine cold eyes.

So he told Janet that he would never forgive her, that she had grown cantankerous, peevish, that everyone detested her, that he was ashamed to possess such a sister. Janet picked up the novel that she had been reading, gave him a glance, almost shy, of bitter reproach and died. No one knew at dinner that night that she was dead, for her ghost talked very brightly about garden parties, Mrs. Parkin and the summer weather. Her ghost also apologized to Gertrude.

The years passed. Humphrey, rid of his physical obsession, grew up and realized that Gertrude was too equine for intimacy. He fell truly in love for the first time in his life with Rose Clennell, gave her a son and died. Gertrude married a fine horse who made much money in the stock-market, and was very happy indeed.

Janet's ghost lived on in the dark house and managed the accounts and the servants quite as efficiently as Janet herself had done.

It is the property of ghosts that they may return to human life again if they can only connect. The link, however, must be there. One link there was and that was the country in which Janet lived. That hung about her, with its streams, its clouds and mountain-tops, urging that life should return. The connection may one day be made. At present, no.

It was not so much that she loved this country as that she was part of it. She was able therefore to abuse it, and this she did, but when she left it on a visit to cousins in Durham or for a brief stay in London, she hungered for it as many a ghost hungers for its home. Above every-thing she resented all those who praised it. She would never forgive Wordsworth for his comments on daffodils, or Dorothy because she saw the last leaf on the tree, or Coleridge because he borrowed from Dorothy. As to the modern ecstatics there was murder in her heart when she saw the red car of Mr. Bauman, the popular novelist who had a house in Newlands and was often photographed in his Lakeland garden, tempting his dog with cake.

When someone said 'How beautiful are the Lakes!' the ghost almost connected with life again, so bitter and intense was the resentment. But never quite. Only the room grew chill, the window-curtains blew a little in an unexpected breeze and, out of space, a sharp spinsterish voice said: 'Oh, do you think so? It rains constantly, you know. We, who live here always, find the country monotonous often enough.' And at those words of betrayal there was mocking laughter in heaven.

Then John, Humphrey's boy, came to live with them for ever and ever. At the first sight of the baby, very white, very still, the connec-tion was almost made; Janet Fawcus almost lived again. Even now the child had so strong a look of his father. But there was a nurse, very efficient, very sure of herself. The child disliked Janet's cold hands and bellowed. The connection was not made.

John grew and Michael Brighouse came.

In a thick orange-backed book, locked with a key, Janet scattered in a spidery hand the white paper with a broken, ghostly monologue. She wrote at night in her ugly bedroom, wearing her hideous dressing-gown of brown and white squares. 'Dust all over the dining-room mantelpiece. Spoke to Millie about it, but dust means nothing to her. She revels in it. Dust. Dust. Dust. Could write it a thousand times over, I hate it so. Visiting Miss Babbitt. Water below Friar's Crag translucent green with a grey flurry like worm-castings on surface.

'Miss Babbitt said "I won't go to St. John's again unless they promise me 'Abide with me'."'

30642

10321

24340

  36 1/2

65339 1/2 + . . . 103

       104

     207

'The more I bother about these figures for father the less he cares. Yet he gives me sheets of them just now. Says it's something to do with the town water-supply. . . .

'. . . yes, and *Anthony Adverse*. I read and read the thing. Why? I don't know; it bores me. . . .

'John very naughty last night. I had to look after him. . . . Michael went to the pictures. John said that he had fleas. Insisted so I undressed him. No sign of anything. I put him to bed then and kissed him. He didn't like it. . . .

'I like the house when everyone is out of it. The garden was moonlit and sheep were crying on the fell. In the afternoon I had motored over to Grasmere to see Mrs. Bricknall. She's sillier than most. Saw some swifts, glossy and dark, chins white. Spring weather-- blustering with sunny rain against very dark fell. . . .

'Seemed to be out of my body altogether last night. Old frustrated maids go mad, they say. Saw myself in mirror reflected six times, the last a shadow, only the two white buttons of my sleeves showing. I don't care.

'Father furious temper to-night. When angry his lips are grey, he doubles his right fist and the knuckles are bone white. All because Mr. Grayson passed him in Keswick without speaking. But he's been rude to Mr. G. at meetings for years. What does he expect?

'Quite cheerful at times though. But he laughs too loud after a temper. As though he were throwing something out of himself. He liked the new savoury with herring-roe and bacon. . . .

'Rose Clennell arrived this afternoon. Young-looking. Her being here an insult. . . .'

CHAPTER V - GLORY OF THIS WORLD

That moment when, after leaving the Parkins', Rose told Michael that she was going to see this through was, as she saw long afterwards, one of the major crises of her life. She knew, directly after she had spoken, that John was more to her than anything in this world or the next.

'More than anything in this world or the next,' she repeated to God that night in a dream. God was clothed in a long woollen dressing-gown and was standing at the foot of her bed. He had a face like an ivory hatchet, with horns on his head like Michael Angelo's Moses, and on the second finger of his right hand he wore a purple signet-ring.

'I'm glad you've realized that at last,' God said.

'I can't think how I've been so stupid all these years,' Rose observed.

'Well, now see if you can rescue him,' God said, and at once Rose realized that on the other side of the dark-panelled wall John was in deadly peril.

Although she could not see him she knew that he was standing, his small hands clenched, his mouth trembling, his eyes dim with fright.

'John! John!' she cried. 'I'm coming!' But she could not move. It was as though she were tied with invisible cords to her bed.

'You've got to do more than that,' God said, and only his dressing-gown remained, hanging in midair with the cords quivering.

On the road above Manesty, some days later, with Michael and John, she had a wild notion that she would take John by the hand, find a car, drive to Carlisle, catch a train and never return. The temptation was as real and as sudden as though it were sensual. She stood there, looking at the Lake, her heart thumping.

The glory of the day made the absurd impulse more positive. On a day like this anything was possible. The March winds had died away. Only birds broke the depths of silence. Recently trees had been cut down here and the logs lay piled on the turf. The Lake was held in a half-circle by larch and fir. On the farther bank, above sloping fields, Blencathra rose to a sharp serried edge against a sky that was all shining light--tremulous with light.

A thin scattering of snow on the jagged ridge was opalescent.

But the colour of the Lake was the wonder. Violets pressed down and pressed again but alive in spite of that pressing. You could almost scent them from where you stood, while the naked brown of the tree-branches was translucent, light quivering through brittle stem upon stem. Then a breeze, the voice of the sunlight, stirred the flower-depths of the Lake to a surface ruffle of silver, but a movement so slender, so sparkling that Rose held her breath lest she should disturb it. Quick lines of darker steel ran like whips toward the border of sun-lit golden bank on the other side, then scattered into a fan-shape of stars. The breeze died back into the sun again and all the violet-field lay still. The colour of the water now, as though encouraged by silence, grew deeper and deeper, spreading in pools of purple on the blue expanse. The cliff of the hill towards Lodore threw out spears of ebony, along its flank, in the shelter of its rocky hollows.

John had turned up the hill towards the Cat Bells path. Rose said to Michael: 'I had the maddest impulse then--to run off with John to Carlisle and then London and never come back.'

'I'm afraid you'd have to give him up. You resigned all your rights. He belongs to his grandfather.'

'There was a case the other day,' Rose said. 'Some woman gave her little girl to another woman to look after when the child was a baby. Then years later she wanted her child back and the judge said she must have her.'

'Yes, but you signed papers, didn't you?'

'The judge said a child ought never to be kept from its mother unless the mother was cruel or abandoned or--'

She paused. She pressed up the fell after her son. Then she looked back.

'This is beginning to be more than I can manage,' she said.

She came back a step or two to Michael and put her hand on his shoulder. 'You must tell me,' she said. 'I've no one else to ask but you. In fact you're my only friend here. Janet hates me, the Colonel I don't understand. John himself won't yield an inch. I must seem to you a most awful fool. I seem so to myself. To have given up my baby like that, never to have tried to see him all those years . . .' She caught her breath. He thought that she was near to tears. 'I was so sure of myself. I thought I was so wise. I thought all our talk, in Geneva, I mean, all the things we bothered about, so important. I was forcing myself to be something I wasn't. Do you understand that, Michael? And how could I have been so blind? Conceited, self-satisfied . . . And now I don't know what I am. I don't know what to do next. I seem to have no common sense. And the Colonel. What has he invited me here for? What's his plan? What's he going to do? Michael, you've got to help me, to advise me. Tell me how I'm to win John, how I'm to make him fond of me. How am I to get him back? Because I must have him. I must! He's mine! He belongs to me and to no one else in the world!'

Michael was bewildered. She had seemed to him, ever since the day of her arrival, so self-controlled, so certain of what she was doing. He had wondered often whether she cared for John at all and, because he had fallen in love with her, he had excused that lack in her by defences that, he knew now, had never been sufficient. The one thing that he had wanted was that she should love John, but now that he saw how passionate that love was, ironically he wanted her to love him as well--and he had known her for only a week or two!

She felt his shoulder tremble under her hand and, looking at him, saw that his face had flushed and his lip was quivering.

'What is it?' she said.

'Nothing,' he answered. 'Only I've wanted to be sure that you loved John. It seemed so unnatural somehow--' He broke off. 'You see, I admire you more than anyone I've ever known.'

'Admire me? Me? But that's absurd, Michael. Look at me! I'm the most miserable failure in the world--and the world's full of them. I'm grown-up, a woman, I'm John's mother, and I haven't a spark of character, a scrap of wisdom. If I had I'd go to Colonel Fawcus to-night and tell him he can do what he likes. John's mine. We're leaving by the first train in the morning and he's got to make the best of it.' She looked away, out to the Lake. 'I believe I'm afraid of that man. I thought I was afraid of no one but I'm discovering that everything I thought about myself was wrong. I'm not clever, not strong, not wise. I've no character. I'm rotten to the core. All the same I needn't wallow in it. I'll do something about it and you'll help me.'

'Of course I'll help you,' Michael said. 'I'd do anything in the world for you. Anything. Murder Fawcus if you like.'

'It isn't so simple as that,' she said slowly. 'We've got to think of something better. And he's kind, he's friendly. When I'm with him I like him. When I'm away from him I'm afraid of him. I don't like the house either. It's dark under that fell--and then there's Janet. How she does hate me, that woman!'

'She's unhappy,' Michael said. 'And she worshipped her brother.'

'Yes. I understand that,' Rose said. 'It's natural for her to hate me. I don't blame her. But I hate to be hated. I want to be liked. I want everyone round me to say: "Ah, that Miss Clennell. She's a dear." But even the servants don't like me. Or is that Cumbrian reserve? But the funny thing is that in Geneva I never cared whether anyone liked me or no. And they did. They said: "Rose Clennell's delightful. She's clever and good company and doesn't care a damn about anything." But now . . . When I kiss John good-night his cheek shrinks. I feel it.'

'He doesn't like being kissed,' Michael said.

66

John ran back down the little steep winding path and joined them.

'Was that a heron,' he asked Michael, 'going into the wood just now? I do hope it was.'

'I didn't see it,' Michael said.

'When are we going to eat?' John asked.

'When we get to the top.'

'I'm awfully hungry.'

He didn't look at Rose. They walked on in single file up the path.

At the top (and the top of Cat Bells is so gentle, the turf so resilient) they saw, recumbent in the sun, a strange sight. It was the little clergyman, Mr. Rackstraw.

He lay on his side, reading, and one grey trouser-leg was rucked up to the knee, showing his bare leg. His round childlike face was dug deeply into his book. One arm was raised aimlessly in the air, flourishing a twig. You would not think a clergyman could lie on the top of a hill in the middle of March (it was March 13th to be exact) in Cumberland, but, in fact, the sun was so hot that even as they looked at him he felt his leg was burning and pulled down his trouser. As he did so he turned round and saw them all. 'Hullo!' he said, and waved the twig at them as though he had known them all his life.

'Do you want us not to notice you?' asked Michael, 'because if so we can walk on as though we had not seen you.'

'Oh no, not at all,' Mr. Rackstraw said, getting up as far as his knees. 'For they are very nice,' he thought. 'Three most agreeable young things and how young they are and how young I am, for I am reading Homer with the greatest enjoyment and feeling quite extraordinarily hungry and I could kiss that nice girl with the greatest of pleasure although I wouldn't dream of doing so.'

He looked so very comic on his knees, for his body was short and fat and his posterior very prominent.

67

But Rose was glad to see that he was looking in the best of health to-day, very different from the bemused caller on Mrs. Parkin. He had evidently been drinking nothing but God's air. His eyes were especially bright, she noticed, like dogs' eyes, that is, lambent and soft. Not eyes to be trusted perhaps. But his nose, which was short and strong, and his mouth, which was humorous and kind, these are to be trusted! And the mouth is the thing. The mouth will tell you everything, which is why Victorian men wore beards.

She saw that he was not very tidy; there was a small tear in his shirt to the left of his tie, and a hole in the heel of one sock.

'If you'll keep quite still, a moment, all of you,' he said, 'I'll read you something.' And still kneeling, he began to read, the sun shining on his face, and the breeze blowing through his hair:

'Odysseus the while lingered before the gate of Alcinous' renowned dwelling. He stood there, not crossing its copper threshold, because of the host of thoughts thronging his heart. Indeed the brilliance within the high-ceiled rooms of noble Alcinous was like the sheen of sun or moon; the inner walls were copper-plated in sections from the entering in to the furthest recesses of the house; and the cornice, which ran round them was glazed in blue. Gates of gold closed the great house. The door-posts, which stood up from the brazen threshold were of silver, and silver, too, was the lintel overhead: while the handle of the door was gold. Each side the porch stood figures of dogs ingeniously contrived by Hephaestus the craftsman out of gold and silver, to be ageless, undying watch-dogs for this house of great-hearted Alcinous.

'Here and there along the walls were thrones, spaced from the inmost part to the outer door; the feasters in the great hall after dark were lighted by the flaring torches, which golden figures of youths, standing on well-made pedestals, held in their hands.

'From outside the court, by its entry, extends a great garden of four acres, fenced each way. In it flourish tall trees; pears or pomegranates, stone fruits gaudy with their ripening load, also sweet figs and heavy-bearing olives. The fruit of these trees never blights or fails to set, winter and summer, through all the years. A west wind blows upon them perpetually, maturing one crop and making another. Pear grows old upon pear and apple upon apple, with bunch after bunch of grapes and fig after fig. Here, too, a fertile vineyard has been planted for the king. A part of this lies open to the sun, whose rays bake its grapes to raisins, while men gather ripe grapes from the next part and in a third part tread out the perfected vintage in wine-presses. On one side are baby grapes whose petals yet fall; on another the clusters empurple towards full growth.

'Beyond the last row of trees, well-laid garden plots have been arranged, blooming all the year with flowers. And there are two springs, one led throughout the orchard-ground, whilst the other dives beneath the sill of the great court to gush out beside the stately house: from it the citizens draw their water.

'Such were the noble gifts the gods had lavished upon the palace of Alcinous.'

He got up from his knees, which must by now have been very stiff. He was holding the orange-coloured book in his hand lovingly. He had read in a clear ringing voice as though he wanted all the valley to hear.

'There!' he cried. 'That's the way Alcinous lived!'

Rose noticed that nothing that Mr. Rackstraw did seemed at all strange to John. He clearly knew him well. All he said now was: 'Mr. Brighouse, I want to go on walking. Can we?'

Rose said quietly: 'You and John go on for a bit, Michael. I'll stay with Mr. Rackstraw. Come back in half an hour and we'll have lunch here.'

Michael gave her one sharp look of kindness, understanding, sympathy (it irritated her: she thought, 'I don't want his sympathy. If John behaves as though I'm not there I can deal with it'), and followed John, who was already running up the slope.

Rose sat down.

'You see how my son feels about me,' she said.

He had undone a packet of sandwiches and was looking at it with longing.

'Have I got to wait half an hour before I eat? Must I?'

'No, of course not.'

'Will you eat with me? I've sandwiches enough for a village.'

'No. I'll wait till they come back,' Rose said. 'Oh, damn!' She clenched her hands on her lap. 'John behaves as though I don't exist. . . . Help me! I want him to love me. How can I make him?'

Rackstraw finished his sandwich, drank half a bottle of ginger ale, then said: 'You can't make anyone love you. You've neglected your job for years. What do you expect?'

'I'm not asking for comfort,' she replied angrily. 'I don't expect anything. I thought you'd give me good advice.'

'Why should you think so?' said Rackstraw. 'On one side are baby grapes whose petals yet fall. That's fine. The orchards, the pears, the pomegranates and the palace, shining with copper, silver and gold. The day as fair as this one and Nausicaa with her maidens. Why should I bother with you and your child?'

She got up. 'I'll catch the others up,' she said.

He looked up at her. He was now lying on his back and eating an apple. 'Don't be silly,' he said. 'You're very young for your age, aren't you?' He sat up. 'You must realize--although how can you, for you don't know me at all?--that it's my passion to give advice, that I've been thrown out of place after place for giving it. So that now when I'm asked for it I'm cautious.'

He patted the ground with his hand. 'Now sit down and be friends. The sun's so warm and it will soon be gone. Tell me what the trouble is.'

She sat down, looking very unhappy. He put his hand on hers.

'I like you very much,' he said. 'I would suggest that we pledge our friendship if it were not that I'm not a very good friend for you. At least that's what people would say. As a matter of fact I'm an excellent friend--none better.'

She let her hand rest in his.

'Of course we'll be friends,' she said. 'I liked you the moment I saw you at Mrs. Parkin's.'

'That's good,' he said, greatly pleased. 'But I must warn you that to be a friend of mine won't make your job here any easier. I must also warn you that Colonel Fawcus abominates me.'

'Why?' Rose asked.

'For every possible reason. Fawcus is a very strange man. He plays a part and it's very important for him that the scene should be set properly. I'm as irritating to him as Osric must have been to Fortinbras.'

'What do you mean--"he plays a part"?'

He shook his head. 'I'm not going to tell you all I think about Colonel Fawcus. I shall leave you to your own discoveries.'

'Tell me this at least,' Rose said. 'Why am I afraid of him when he is so charming and kind and apparently likes me?'

'Oh, you're afraid of him, are you?' He shook his head. 'You mustn't be afraid of anyone. Never, never, never! And I'm surprised. I shouldn't have thought you like that.'

'I've never been afraid of anyone before so far as I know,' Rose said, 'but now, in that house, he seems to take my strength away. I do what he says.'

'Do you?' He reflected. 'Later on you won't. Then he'll fight you. He won't be charming any longer.'

'Why?' asked Rose. 'What does he want? Why did he ask me to come? Why, when I wanted to leave the other day, did he press me to stay?'

'You wanted to leave, did you?' Rackstraw said, looking at her curiously.

'Why do you look at me like that? What is there behind all this?'

'I don't know,' Rackstraw said. 'Fawcus is a tremendous egotist. He sees himself as a kind of Napoleon, and he's been spoilt all his life. He was of some importance in the place once, and so long as that was so he was satisfied. He isn't any longer and it irks him. You know when Napoleon invaded Russia he halted at Smolensk. That was before Borodino. He ought to have waited there because Jerome had failed in his job of separating the Russian armies. He should have postponed his invasion over the winter. But he couldn't stop. His egotism drove him on to his destruction. Fawcus is being driven on. Many things that were harmless in him when he had some power are evil in him now that he hasn't. I expect he wants to keep you and the boy, for ever perhaps. He invited you in the first place, I expect, partly from curiosity, partly because it amused him to show you how completely he owned your boy. When you came he found you very charming. It is a new interest for him to have power over you as well as the boy. It has begun, you see. You admitted it yourself. You can't go because you find that you love your child. He has of course seen that. He is a man of very active passions, which he has never learnt to control. Had he been a great financier or a successful Cabinet Minister or Archbishop of Canterbury he would have been a good man. As it is--'

Rose said at last: 'Thank you. That's cleared up a number of things. I must get away with John as soon as ever I can.'

He went on: 'I'm glad you came. It's now or never with John. That's a very charming boy, but he's very sensitive and feels everything passionately. It has been bad enough for him already to be shut away in that house as he has been. You've no time to waste.'

Rose nodded.

'I know. I felt that from the first moment. I'll do my best.'

'And don't count on my appearing your friend too openly. As I've told you already, it won't help you. I am your friend, but remember always that I'm a reprobate old clergyman. People laugh and say, "There goes old Rackstraw, drunk again." Generally I'm not, sometimes I am. Not badly drunk, you know, but enough to slur my words and sometimes stumble a bit--'

'Oh, why?' Rose broke in. 'Why do you? Now, both of us sitting here like this, you seem so strong, so--'

'Ah--why? That's a long story. Nobody but God knows all about it and, although I don't suppose for a moment that He excuses me, He is very wise, very tolerant. I had a living up to three years ago, over Shap way, and I was prouder of my little church--it was a thousand years old, part of it--and of the people in my parish than any clergyman ever was. They trusted me, too, and believed in me. But others--from outside mostly--complained, so I gave it up before they turned me out.

'My dear'--he took her hand again--'there's nothing so terrible as the blood. Things from outside you can fight, but when it's in your blood, when your own blood betrays you, you're lost. I'm lost--but being lost,' he went on more cheerfully, 'I make the best of it. There are days like this, you know, and the company of the Lord Jesus Christ Who turned water into wine. And there's always the chance that it may never happen again. Here with you, this afternoon, it seems impossible, but there will be an evening and the door of "The Jolly Huntsman" will be open and there'll be light and a fire and good talk and a glass of ale. One glass and another and another--'

'Perhaps I can help you,' Rose said.

'You do help me. You've promised to be my friend and I shall think of that. . . . But one day I'll be free of this body and have work entrusted to me where there'll be no hindrance and I'll be happy again as I was in Little Boding. Bring that day near, O Lord, bring that day near, for I am still Thy faithful servant.'

They were silent and it was after a long while that Rackstraw said: 'Don't let's ever speak of this again. I only wanted you to understand why one of these days I may pass you without a greeting. And don't pity me, I'm my own failure. It's no one's fault but mine. Remember--I don't pity myself. Pity's the poorest of all human weaknesses. And if there comes a day when you're ashamed of me, when you don't want to see me any more, don't be distressed. I'll understand only too well.'

They saw Michael and John coming down the hill.

Luncheon was eaten and there was desultory conversation. Rackstraw was now very silent. He might even be considered sulky. He answered in monosyllables, and suddenly, getting up, nodded to them, said good-bye and was off towards Robinson.

'I do hope he's not hurt,' Rose said.

'Hurt?' Michael answered. 'No. Why should he be? But he's unhappy.' He said no more because John was there.

When they started down, the sun was about to fall behind the line of hills. A little way down they looked back and were almost blinded by the intense light that lay over Newlands. One slope was a sheet of sun-mist without shape and vivid. It seemed to swing in the air as they watched. The air about them was odorous. There was perfect calm in the lee of the fell--not a breath stirred and, although they were on the bare hillside, the motionless sunlit haze seemed to draw up the scents of the valley so that they felt the resinous sap of the trees, the liquid delicacy of the new grasses and the deep richness of the soil itself. The ranges across the valley were burning with a red glow while the sky behind them grew ever whiter as though with the intensity of its own light. Derwentwater was silver-shielded, the islands reflected in dark metallic circles.

Michael was walking ahead, and Rose, encouraged by her talk with Rackstraw, but painfully alarmed as though she were attempting some desperate assay, challenged her son.

'John, don't let's catch up Mr. Brighouse for a minute. I want to say something to you.'

He gave her an apprehensive look. He was flushed and tumbled with his exercise and the sun and air. He reminded her of a ruffled bird who suddenly wonders whether danger is near.

'John, I'm your mother and I love you very much. It can't seem that I can love you when I've been away for so long, but it's true all the same. I want you to tell me--quite honestly. You wish I'd go away again, don't you?'

Her heart ached for the distress that she was giving him. She knew that something he had been dreading had at last happened to him.

He murmured something that she didn't catch.

'Don't mind if it sounds rude,' she said. 'I want to know.'

He said:

'It's funny--having a mother suddenly. Most boys have them always.'

'Yes, I know. It's all been my fault. But here we are. This is how it is. We can't alter it. And I think we ought to understand one another.'

He seemed to appreciate that she was talking to him as one grown-up person to another.

'Are you going to be with me always?' he asked.

'I want to be,' she answered.

'Because Grandfather said you'd only come for a week or two.'

'Yes. That's what I meant to do. But now that I've seen you I don't want to leave you.'

He considered that.

'I expect,' he said in a small strangled voice, 'we'll get used to it after a bit.'

'What,' she said, 'do you find it hard to get used to?'

'I'm not good at making friends,' he said. He spoke for a moment like an elderly man. 'You see, I haven't been to school like other boys. Roger's the only friend I've got.'

'Will you try and be friends with me?' she asked.

'Yes, I'll try,' he said.

They came down into deep shadow and the world about them was suddenly chill.

Before they joined Michael, John gave her a quick shy smile.

CHAPTER VI - JOHN LISTENING

John had been, from the very first, a listening child. His earliest memory had been of Black Maria snoring. He did not know at that time, of course, what she was called, but he did know that she was black. She was a large voluminous woman with hair so dark that it shone in the candlelight, and she had on her upper lip a faint black moustache. He was asleep in his cot and would wake with a start. On the little brown table there glimmered the night-light, and in the jumping flame of the fire Black Maria moved up and down while from her person there issued earthquaking snores. The sound was friendly and comfortable because it meant that someone was there. He could not then be attacked by the creeping enemies from floor, wall, ceiling, that so often, when he was alone, invaded him. His early impulse had been to cry aloud whenever he was in danger, but he discovered that to cry brought dangers more actual than the unseen ones. Hands were raised, his body was shaken, and worst of all, the big shape with the deep deep voice appeared towering above him to threaten--what? He never knew, but he held his breath and let his tears dry on his cheeks while he stared and stared and listened and listened.

He became then very quickly a docile child. Three figures in these years filled his world. The first was Black Maria, who was all softness and yet was not truly soft. She washed him (and oh, how he hated that!), fed him and took him out in the perambulator. The words that he learnt before any others were: 'Oh, my poor stummick!' He did not know their meaning, but they were always followed by a great heave of the bosom against which his head so often reluctantly leant. He learnt that beneath that bosom there was a hard bony structure (for Black Maria wore stays), which it was well to avoid. He studied during many hours that great expanse of sallow countenance, learning every detail of the thick strong nose, the black wiry eyebrows, the little mound on the left cheek with black hairs upon it, and the two chins that shook sometimes so that you expected them to tumble off and roll on the carpet.

Black Maria was not unkind but she was not friendly either. Years later he was to learn that the smell so intimately connected with her was of beer and a cheap soap, a faded and musty odour of turpentine.

When she washed him she breathed so stertorously that he was bathed in this odour rather than in soap and water. When she turned him over on her knee she breathed on to his bare back like a fiery furnace. She slapped his buttocks with her rough, gnarled hand. 'Drat my hair,' she said, for she had a great deal of it and it tumbled into her eyes.

When he was older she told him stories of her astonishing life, and most of this was obscure to him. But there was a man called Harry who 'fought in his cups,' and a grand piano, a cat without a tail, and a little girl, Lucy, who was an angel from Paradise.

No, Black Maria was not unkind, but she was not kind either.

The other two figures of this early world were his Aunt Janet and his grandfather. His aunt, in those first years, he greatly disliked because whenever she touched him she hurt him. She kissed him and his cheeks were sore for hours after. She took him on her knee, which, through her dress, cut his tender flesh like a knife. He realized, too, as very young children, cats, dogs and parrots immediately realize, that she had not the least idea of the way to handle him. She was nervous and ill at ease and angry with herself for being so.

When he was grown a little older she was for ever checking him. 'Where are you going, John?' 'Don't do that, John.' 'Auntie told you not to touch, John.' But she had not the courage of her decisions. Told not to touch, he would wait and then, after a while, do what he was forbidden. But she had not the courage to repeat her order. She tried very earnestly to be affectionate, and when he was five or so she bestowed on him some bursts of emotional feeling.

'Come here, John, and Aunt Janet will tell you a story.' He did come, but instead of the story he was caught up, pressed and hugged, his face covered with kisses. He disliked this intensely and soon she realized his dislike and pushed him away. She talked to him a great deal about his father. Then there came a day (he was seven years old) when at a children's party he realized very vividly that other boys and girls had mothers.

'Where's my mother?' he asked Aunt Janet.

'She's dead,' his aunt said.

At the age of ten he learnt from Roger Parkin that his mother was not dead but lived in Switzerland.

'Mother told me all about her,' Roger said.

'Why isn't she here with me then?' John asked.

'Because your mother didn't marry your father,' Roger said. 'You're what's called a bastard.'

He then explained all about babies to John, who until that moment had never considered the matter. He told John how boys behaved at school and why three boys had been expelled from his house a year ago. Something very deep down in John absorbed this knowledge and was disgusted by it. Had he not admired and loved Roger so deeply he would henceforth have avoided him. But Roger was always right.

He felt, however, that his mother had done him a great wrong. He said to his aunt:

'Why did you tell me that my mother is dead? She isn't. She lives in Switzerland.'

'She is dead as far as you are concerned,' Aunt Janet said. 'She gave up all rights to you when you were a baby.'

'Why?' asked John.

'She did not want to be bothered about you.'

He bore his mother a deep grudge, but he thought of her very often. What was she like? Why had she wanted not to be bothered with him?

Other mothers cared for their children. He was what was called a bastard and it was apparently a disgraceful thing to be.

The third person in his life was his grandfather, and here very deep and dangerous elements were involved, for he admired his grandfather and longed that his grandfather should love him. Also he was afraid of his grandfather as he was of no one else in the world. The admiration he had always known; the fear had been created in him by a scene that occurred in his ninth year.

When he was a very little boy it was made clear to him by everyone that his grandfather was monarch of all this world. Whatever his grandfather did or said was right. That great man was very kind to him. He would catch him up and swing him towards the ceiling, he would ride him on his shoulder, he would give him sweets and toys out of his pockets. But John knew from the very earliest days that he must do exactly what his grandfather told him; he must be very quiet when his grandfather was near by; he must answer when he was spoken to and be quick about it too.

Sometimes, when he was a little older, he would be taken in the car to Keswick and he would sit very still and upright beside the great man. How proud he was as the people in Keswick touched their hats, as he heard reverential voices say: 'Yes, Colonel.' 'Why, certainly, Colonel. It shall be done at once.' And sometimes, on the return journey, he would feel weary and his grandfather would put his arm around him and hold him close, and he would lean his head against the hairy, heather-smelling stuff of the warm coat and would fall asleep very happily.

His grandfather seemed to him simply the grandest, biggest, most wonderful man in the world. He did not quite love him because there was always a distance between them, but until his eighth birthday he looked up to him as a king, almost as God Himself.

His life long he will never forget any detail of that afternoon. It had been a day of misted rain. John broke Aunt Janet's blue glass bowl. There are times for all of us when the Devil is very active and uses the liver, the bowels, the weather or the second post for his evil purposes. On this day he crept in from the wet-spidered garden, warmed himself in front of the fire and whispered in Janet Fawcus' ear. His whisper was so impertinent that to relieve herself of his company she said, 'Now, John, don't do that!'

The Devil then crossed to John and whispered in his ear so that John, greatly to his own surprise, answered: 'I shall if I like.' No one was more astonished than Janet, for John was seldom rude and was almost always obedient.

As usual she was frightened at her own responsibility, but she said very warmly:

'You naughty rude boy! Go to your room!'

The Devil answered 'Shan't!' and no one was more surprised than John who, in his bewildered astonishment, moved his arm and knocked on to the floor Janet's blue bowl. It lay there piteously in pieces, and the Devil, having done sufficient in this stupid dull house, went out into the wet garden again.

So then John found himself in his grandfather's room, for, thought Janet, my beautiful blue bowl is broken, my lower gums ache again, which is monstrously unfair, for there are no longer any teeth there, and the child is too much for me. I will go and lie down.

In his grandfather's room John felt a sudden terror. Although sensitive and nervous, he was not a coward. He had also, quietly within himself, a sense of humour which, on many occasions, had saved desperate situations. But now, in a moment of comprehension, he realized that he was in serious danger. As always at any crisis he began to listen.

First he heard the thin rain weeping against the window. Sometimes rain was triumphant, sometimes querulous, sometimes angry. To-day it was simply laying its long grey fingers on the window-pane and drearily weeping. In the fireplace there was the spit and stutter of fading coals. Amongst the books on the shelves there was a busy murmur of anticipation. Something is going to happen! Something is going to happen! We are glad that we are here to see! He realized that his grandfather was speaking to him. Then he looked up into his face. What he saw there frightened him so badly that his heart jumped into his throat. For his grandfather seemed to him to have swollen to twice his usual size so that he blocked out the windows and the dark garden.

81

Staring out of this great body were two cold eyes. These eyes looked at John as though they would catch him up and drag him in, away, under the eyebrows into some dreadful confused darkness.

'Well, what have you to say for yourself? Can't you speak?' The voice did not seem to be his grandfather's voice: it was rich, deep, slow--it had in it the purring accent of a cat that is being stroked by an understanding hand.

John said that he was very sorry and that he hadn't intended to knock over the blue bowl. He heard the books remark that that was not enough. Oh, not nearly enough! He must think of something better than that. . . .

His grandfather's hand lifted and touched his shoulder.

'Sorry is not enough. What has happened to you lately, John? You're not the good boy you used to be. I'm afraid you must be taught a lesson.' His grandfather went to the corner of the room and returned with a small riding-whip. He told John to take down his trousers. John had never been beaten before and he felt now a fear much greater than belonged to the beating.

He did not then know what it was he felt, but later, looking back and facing it, he knew that he had been conscious of a dreadful shame as though a thousand eyes were watching him lose the privacy of his body.

He would have run naked into Keswick (if it were warm enough and nobody objected). But now he stood, his trousers about his ankles and the low-lying malicious coals of the fire hissing contempt.

He shuffled to the table and bent over it as he was ordered. He set his teeth and made no sound or movement at the first two blows. At the third he cried out, at the fifth he was sobbing in agony of spirit while with one hand he guarded his eyes and with the other fumblingly tried to draw up his trousers.

His grandfather, who was now kind, assisted him. Then he drew him to him, held him close and comforted him.

'No more shall be said of this,' his grandfather said. 'Be a good boy. We all love you. We all love you very much indeed.'

After this he listened more intently than before because there were enemies about. He was not at all an unhappy boy, but now he was reserved, cautious, very careful, and his fear of his grandfather never left him. The admiration, the desire to be loved by him was as constant as ever, but he was afraid, not because he had been whipped but because of the eyes that had looked at him before the whipping. Nevertheless he was on the whole a very happy boy. Michael Brighouse came, and before Michael there had begun his friendship with Roger Parkin.

It was at a children's party in Keswick that John first saw Roger. He worshipped at the first instant of beholding. Roger was one of those boys determined to command, and as in this world nine out of ten persons are not sure what they want, a strong determination generally has its way. Roger had all the qualities of the preordained boss: he was healthy, happy, conceited, possessive, unaware of his limitations, clear-headed, supremely self-confident. He always knew what he wanted and was regardless of the feelings of others.

All through his life he would have what he wanted. He would not have that love and devotion that is given only to the humble of heart, but he would never be aware that he had missed anything. He was a very good-looking boy, dark and flashing, strong of body and finely active.

When it came to a game in which sides were chosen, Roger, who was one of the captains, chose, to the general surprise, young John.

'Here, you! I'll have you! What's your name?'

'John Fawcus.'

'All right. Can you run?'

'Yes,' said John, who felt, in this triumphant moment, that he could do anything. He was in fact quick and adroit, and after the victory Roger said:

'That was grand. What do you say your name is?'

'John Fawcus.'

83

'Colonel Fawcus' grandson? That's fine! We've come to live near you.'

The love of one boy for another is considered a dangerous subject for everyone, but it is in fact very often the purest, most selfless, most heroic emotion that many men will ever know. John had never had anyone or anything to love until now, so he gave himself, body and soul, to this worship. Roger was away at school for a large part of the year, so that John did not see him very often. The flame burnt the more brightly. Also John said nothing to anybody.

Roger was not a bad boy nor a heartless. He thought young Fawcus a very decent kid, a bit soft though. He thought that he was being generous in his efforts to harden him, and he made John run, fight, and perform many feats of endurance. There were, for a year or two, no other boys in the neighbourhood of especial interest, so John went often to the Parkins'. Roger liked to talk a great deal about himself, and as with all masters of men he was sure that no detail of his life could be uninteresting. So John listened and worshipped.

'I wish I could go to your school,' John said one day with a sigh.

'Oh, well, you wouldn't see much of me if you did,' Roger answered. 'I shall be having a fag soon though. Perhaps you'd be my fag.'

'Oh, I should love that!' John said, and indeed he thought that he would.

John's love was the greatest of all kinds of love--that of the imagination. He made Roger into a glorious creature and round this figure built a beautiful world of service. He asked for nothing but to serve. In this world he went to Roger's school; he was his fag. There was nothing that he did not do for him. And Roger was indeed glorious. He was captain of cricket, football, hockey, everything. He did not notice John very often, but John was always there, and sometimes Roger said: 'That's fine, John. Thank you.' John knew nothing about school except from the things that Roger told him and from the books that he read-- Tom Brown, The Cock House at Fellsgarth, The Hill--but it was clear to him that in any and every circumstance he would be there, ready for every sacrifice. While Roger was away he tried to do the things that Roger would wish him to do--he ran, he threw balls, he did exercises. But he had no one with whom to play and it was difficult alone.

'Shall I be going to school soon?' he asked his grandfather.

'Of course. Of course.'

He did not dare to ask whether he would be going to Roger's school.

It was now that his grandfather began to take a closer interest in him, and in some ways it was a strange interest.

'What you need,' said his grandfather, 'is discipline. We will have some lessons.'

What happened was that he went to his grandfather's room, the door was shut and the discipline began.

'Look at me,' said the Colonel, but in a very kindly way. He was in fact smiling. John looked and saw this broad, stout, fresh body, as strong as a tree, as confident as an eagle, as clean as a lemon. In the pocket of his russet-coloured jacket there would be a silk handkerchief, brown with white spots. He took off his coat and his waistcoat. John was instructed to do the same.

'Now bend. Touch your toes. . . . No, without bending your knees. See. Look at me,' and the Colonel bent, his shoulders seeming ever broader and broader, and touched the toes of his shining brown shoes.

'Do it twelve times.'

John did it twelve times and the Colonel did it twelve times.

'You're out of breath. That's absurd. Look at me.'

John looked.

'Come here. Put your hand here and feel my heart.' John did so. 'Now do you see? It's absolutely steady.' As a matter of fact it was not, but John did not say so.

He had to do stranger things than this.

'Go into the corner and stand with your face to the wall. No. I'm not punishing you. I'm just seeing how obedient you are.'

It was queer indeed standing with your face to the wall because after a very short time you were sure that many unusual things were happening behind your back. John did not know what the Colonel was doing.

'Now,' said the Colonel in his rich, deep, happy voice. 'Don't you turn round, whatever happens.'

There was absolute silence in the room except for the ticking of the clock and, very often, the noise of the wind down the chimney. Where was the Colonel? Was he just behind you? Had he crept up on stockinged feet? (He did this once.) Would his hand suddenly descend on your shoulder? Had he left the room and if he had would John remain standing there for ever and ever? Was there someone else in the room (for such ideas do occur to you when you have been staring at a dark-green wallpaper for, so it seems, an eternity) and what was this other person like? Was he not a little man with a bald brown head like a geography globe and long brown fingers? Once John turned round before leave had been given, and the Colonel was angry.

'Come here,' he said. 'Kneel down. Lay your head on my knee.' John did so. Something cold touched the back of his neck. It was only the ivory paper-knife with the silver head, but it had been very terrifying.

'Do you want to obey me, John?'

'Yes, Grandfather.'

'Do you see how people look up to me and respect me and do what I tell them?'

'Yes, Grandfather.'

'Do you love me?'

'Yes, Grandfather.'

'Very well, then.'

This room of the Colonel's became a very special place to John with an atmosphere all its own.

It had high tall windows, and beyond these the garden and the fell ran as though they were a continuation of the room, as though, in fact, there was no glass. What happened in the garden belonged to the room, and John had often noticed that very peculiar things happened in the garden when he was with his grandfather. From these windows the trees seemed to be twice as alive as from any others, and a dog, a strange dog, would run along the garden path and leap the stone wall on to the fell. A fat black cat would crouch on the flower-bed watching a bird. Sudden winds would rise and the branches would shake like mad, a mist would come down the fell, enveloping the garden, and through the mist a faint sun would glimmer like a turnip-lantern and everything would appear double.

It was only, of course, that the windows were large and so high that the sky became part of the room as well as the garden and the fell.

Inside the room there were certain objects that affected John very strongly. One was a bust in some pale material. The Colonel said it was a bust of Julius Caesar. It had naked shoulders and blind eyes and a long, sneering nose. Then there was the rug in front of the fire with a tiger's head. Not only was this head very easy to trip over but the teeth snarled and grinned both at the same time. In general the room con-tained very little furniture, but it had the atmosphere of being very full of something. What it was full of, so far as John was concerned, was the Colonel.

On the whole, however, up to this time things had gone well with John. He loved the country in which he was, although as yet it seemed to him chiefly a place to play in, but because he had been here most of his life he had absorbed the fells, the streams, the Lake, like food that nourished his soul and body. Nobody was unkind, he had Roger to worship, and soon he was sure he would be going to school.

Then Michael Brighouse came. John liked Michael well enough but formed no intimacy with him. He worked at his lessons and found His-tory, Geography, English, easy. But he was quite hopeless at anything to do with Mathematics and Science. These were also the subjects at which Michael was not very clever.

Then two more things happened. One was the arrival in the district of a boy. Bill Finch was his name and he was the son of a retired colonel who bought a house near Friar's Crag. Bill Finch was the same age as Roger, he was dark, stocky, very strong. Roger took to him at once and John hated him. He despised and mocked at John.

The other thing was that one day Michael said to him:

'John, I have some news for you. Your mother is coming to stay with us.'

'My mother!'

'Yes.'

'But Aunt Janet said she was never to see me again.'

'All the same she's coming.'

John drew a deep breath.

'Will she be here long?'

'A week or two, I expect.'

His delicate sensitive face was flushed and his body trembling.

'I don't want to see her. Roger says she made me a bastard.'

The moment when, on Cat Bells, he smiled at his mother marked the end of the prelude to the events that followed.

END OF PART I

PART II - THROUGH A GLASS DARKLY

CHAPTER VII - THE PARTY RETURNED

'The North! The North! I am taken prisoner by the North! This room is like a refrigerator,' Rose thought, trying to brush her hair in front of the glass, but her hands were so cold that the brushes trembled in them. 'And yet this is the beginning of April, and in March we had those warm opalescent days of gold mist and the Lake filled with violets and the trees odorous. Now there is snow on Skiddaw again and the daffodils are blowing in the wind.'

When, a little later, pressing her cold feet about the hot-water bottle, she tumbled into an uneasy sleep, it was the North who appeared to her, naked and flourishing a club, with long blue-shadowed icicles on his chin. She surrendered without an instant's resistance, for behind him there was a landscape that seemed to her of the very noblest and most heroic. Hills, like mounds covering the historic dead, tossed about the expanse of country, and at the edge of it a grey ugly sea sulked over muddy flats.

But the plain was pierced with flashes of sun that tore thick clouds like a sword; scattered about the plain were turreted strongholds, little keeps of grey stone at whose feet ran brown horseback-coloured turbulent streams. About the keeps there was constant battle, torches flaring, men in armour mounting and falling while the peasants prayed to the Virgin Mary in little strong churches whose bells clanged in the wind.

The heavy grey clouds drove above the moor, and the wind tugged at tree-clumps, isolated and sturdy, while the men from the Border drove the cattle towards Scotland and the village flamed against the sky. . . .

This is the North and it has no weakness. This is the North and it has no confined closeness. 'This is the North,' thought Rose, suddenly waking and hearing the rain beat against the glass. 'I shall never be able to live in the South again. . . .' She turned on the electric light. 'This house is always worst at night. I wish I had someone sleeping with me for nothing but reassurance and consolation, so that I do not always think that there's someone out there in the rain tapping at the window.'

She could not sleep. The cold crept about the room, not entering the bed with her but breathing little chill wisps of discomfort now on her forehead, now on the tip of her nose, now on the hand that she stretched towards Mr. Sackville-West's Sun in Capricorn on the little rickety table with a broken leg.

'That's Janet's fault and mine because I forget to tell her. No, she is a perfect housekeeper and I like her. The appalling thing is that I like her and she detests me. She has a lot of Humphrey about her. She is the part of Humphrey that was frustrated.'

What was frustrated in him? His wife had not given him what he wanted, nor, she was beginning to perceive just before he died, was she herself all that he wanted. No woman is all that any man wants, and wise is the wife or mistress who perceives it. Well, then--where does the lack lie? 'Perhaps,' she thought in the misty confusion that heralds the return of sleep, 'I can learn from Janet. I can make up to her for all that Humphrey missed.

'Yet he loved me. He loved me with every day more dearly. So he would put his arm about me and touch my breast . . . and into his arms she fell, her last act, before that happy surrender, to switch off the light. . . .

So, on the afternoon of the next day, she said:

'Janet, I want us to be friends.' And then before the other could speak she went on: 'No, no. Wait a moment. Don't go. Soon you shall tell me all the horrid things you can think of. No, don't switch on the light. The firelight's enough. Listen--this is important--for you as well as myself.

'Perhaps we can't be friends. I know you're thinking that that's the most impossible thing that could ever happen. But I want you to remember this. We have something in common. We shall always have. We both loved Humphrey. I think it's been silly, all these weeks in the same house and neither of us saying a word. I understand exactly what you must feel. In your place I'd feel the same, but it's wasted emotion. It is indeed. Humphrey's gone, but if he were here he'd want us to be friends. You know he would. Don't you remember how he hated rows, how he did everything always to avoid them? I don't want to be sentimental. I'm not really a sentimental person at all, but I can't help liking you, admiring you. It would probably be easier for me if I didn't. But there it is. On my side there's nothing to be done about it. Whatever you do, that can't change.'

Janet, who had risen as though she were leaving the room, turned back.

'I don't care what you feel. It's a disgrace that you should be here. The sooner you go, the better for everyone.'

'Why is it a disgrace?' Rose asked. 'It's true that Humphrey and I weren't married, but we would have been if we could. If we had been, if Humphrey had lived and we had come here to stay, you and I would have been friends--I know we would. Is it simply because we weren't married?'

'We would never have been friends. Never, never!' Janet said quickly, drawing her breath as though she had been running. 'Now let me tell you something. You invited me to be truthful, so I will be. You are the type of modern woman I despise--greedy, selfish, vain. You have come here into a house that you should be ashamed to enter. You gave up your baby without a care just because you couldn't be bothered with it. You say you loved Humphrey--you never thought that it was his child when you surrendered it. And now when you see that John has grown into a charming little boy you want to have him back

91

again, although in all these years you have never thought of him but have led your own selfish self-satisfied life.'

She paused. She had never been so rude to anyone before. But the woman had asked for it.

'Yes,' Rose said quietly, 'I can see how it must seem to you just like that, but it isn't so really. When Humphrey died I hadn't a penny. I didn't know whether I'd get a job and I'll tell you frankly that I was frightened for John. It isn't true that I didn't love him, but I was very young and to give John up seemed to make him safe for ever. It isn't true that I didn't think of him. I was always thinking of him, but I wanted to keep my part of the bargain. I knew that if I once saw him again it would make it terribly hard. And it has--it's made it impossible. I can't leave John now. I don't know what his grandfather will do, but somehow I must see him, must keep in touch with him.' She stopped. She was afraid of what she might say.

'You've left it too late,' Janet said grimly. 'You've been away from him too long. He's grown used to having no mother.'

'But that can't prevent what I feel!' Rose cried. 'If I love him I love him whatever he may do or say. And it's the same with you. If I like you I like you. You can't help my liking you!

'Oh, you won't like me long,' Janet said. 'I'll see to that!' and she left the room.

This was to be an unusual afternoon for Rose. A minute after Janet's departure Michael looked in.

'Oh, I beg your pardon. I thought John might be here.'

'No. He isn't. Can I do anything?'

It was a relief to her just then that here at least was someone who liked her. He was only a boy. Her feeling for him was all maternal. In fact she felt for him rather as he felt for herself, always a good ground for friendship.

'Come in a minute. Are you so busy?'

'No, I'm not . . . .' He came forward, hesitating, smiling. 'It's only that I wondered where John was.' He stood looking at her.

'Sit down,' Rose said, 'and let's be comfortable.'

He sat down. 'Have you heard?' he asked. 'Has the Colonel told you? He's going to give a party.'

'A party? Oh dear! . . .'

'Yes. A children's party. He's never done such a thing before--since I've been here anyway.'

'Why is he?' Rose asked.

'I don't know. Who can tell why the Colonel does anything? All he says is that it's for John to return some of the kindness.'

'Have people been so kind?'

'The Colonel never seemed to think so. It's your doing, I expect.'

'Mine? Oh, I hope not! I've nothing to do with the Colonel's mind.'

'Of course you have. And mine. And John's. And Miss Fawcus'.'

'Yours?' Rose asked, smiling.

He leant forward, looking at her intently.

'I'm in love with you. I've told you already. I've never been in love with anyone before and now I really don't know what to do about it. Look here! I have to know! Do you care for me at all?--a little bit? Are there perhaps the signs of the beginning of something? Just the begin-ning?'

She thought that she would treat this lightly although she was deeply moved.

'This is a remarkable afternoon,' she said. 'First someone comes in and tells me that she hates me; then someone comes and tells me that he loves me. What is it about this place? And there was never anyone more ordinary. All those years in Geneva--'

'No--please,' he said.

'Michael, dear.' She looked at him with a tenderness that in the circumstances he found maddening. 'I'm not in love with anyone--I've never been in love except once, and that was Humphrey. Besides, here, just now, I can think of only one thing and that is John. Anyway, Michael, I'd never be the woman for you! I'm too old, too unsatisfactory in every way. I think that at this particular moment I'm feeling my inferiority more than is normal. Janet Fawcus has just been very straightforward about my character and my abilities generally. But in any case it's true. You've got to marry someone better than me, Michael--much, much better.'

'One doesn't marry people because they're perfect,' Michael said.

'No. Certainly not for that reason, although for almost every other. Listen. I'm proud that you care for me and I can't tell you what a help it is to me just now and in this very odd place. I'm a bit frightened, I'll tell you frankly, and now I know that I've got a friend who'll be there whatever happens.'

'I'll do anything--anything!' Michael breathed. But he went on: 'What am I to do about loving you? How am I to stop it, stop feeling like this, I mean, so that my heart beats like a hammer every time I see you and I lie awake thinking and I want to touch you, be near you--?'

'Think of John,' she said quickly, 'as I'm doing. Let's concentrate on that together, both of us. And then, when this is over, you'll find that you don't think of me romantically any more, but only that we're splendid friends, and John and I will come to your wedding. . . . No, really, I mean it. If I did love you--which I don't and never will--I wouldn't be able, here and now, to think about it. You've got to help me to do two things--to win John over and then to get him away--'

'To get him away? To steal him, do you mean? You'd only have to give him up again.'

'Perhaps I wouldn't have to. Anyway it's not come to that yet. Perhaps it won't ever. The Colonel perhaps will understand. We'll come to some arrangement. . . .'

She suddenly discovered that they were whispering together. There was only the light of the fire in the room, which, as on the afternoon of her arrival, seemed to be stirring with little sounds, tinklings, rustlings, the movement of curtains, the whisper of leaves or of rain.

'What I mean,' Rose said, 'is--'

The door opened and Colonel Fawcus came in.

'Hullo, you two!' he said cheerfully. 'Sitting in the dark? I'll leave it like that. It's damned cosy.'

He plunged into the old rose-coloured arm-chair near the fire. He stretched out his strong legs and leaned back, yawning, his hands clasped behind his head.

'What are you two talking about?' he asked. 'Secrets?'

'Oh no,' Michael said. 'I was telling Rose about the party.'

'Ah, the party. Don't you think it's a good idea, Rose?'

'It's very kind of you to take the trouble to have the house upset.'

'Trouble be blowed! It's yourself and Janet will have the trouble. It's time we returned some of their kindness to John. Mrs. Parkin, for instance, has been enormously kind--enormously kind. Although she's done it partly out of courtesy to me, of course.'

'Yes, I know. John will be very proud.'

'There are a dozen children or more we can ask. If it's fine they can play in the garden.'

Then Rose was conscious of something. She was aware that Colonel Fawcus wished Michael to leave the room and was furious with him because he did not go.

She was not sure how it was that she was so certain of this, except that perhaps the fire, which had leapt into a new energy, was illuminating his face and it stood out so strongly that it seemed to be close to hers. She could see his little veins that would one day be purple and the kindly wrinkles at the corners of the eyes. Yes, he was kindly enough but at that moment was directing an energy of force against Michael that filled the room as though with the sinister rumble of drums.

But the boy was entirely unaware of it and after five minutes of this it seemed to her that the Colonel would soon attempt a physical assault. For the first time she realized fully the power, physical and psychical, that he possessed.

He made a movement. She almost cried out in fear. But he only said, very quietly: 'You'd better go and see what John's doing, Michael.'

'Yes, sir,' Michael said, and went out.

'I hope you're happy here now,' said the Colonel. 'You worried me by what you said the other day. You mustn't think of going--unless you're bored.'

'Oh, bored!' said Rose, laughing. 'No, that's the last thing I am.'

'That's right,' he said comfortably, as though everything were settled. 'You don't understand me yet--but you will--you certainly will.'

'No, I don't quite,' Rose said.

'What don't you understand?' he asked, stretching his powerful thighs, spreading himself in the chair.

'For one thing, as I've told you many times already, I don't know why you asked me here: now when I am here, why you want to keep me.'

'Ah,' he said, smiling. 'I'm rather an unusual man. You don't mind my talking about myself for a moment, do you?'

'No. Of course not,' said Rose.

'I'm a man of tremendous energy and I've never had the chance to do all I might. Of course I've been an influence in the place--a greater influence than you've any idea of. I might say without exaggeration that almost everything here is what it is because of my influence. Do you think that very arrogant? Well, perhaps I am arrogant. I wouldn't say this to most people, of course, but with you I can be frank, so I'll tell you that my power is tremendous and it reaches maybe a great deal further than locally. Did you see my letter in The Times the other day about War and Peace? No. I won't bother you with it now, but it had its effect, undoubtedly it had its effect. Men seem important on the surface--Cabinet Ministers, writers, industrialists--but often it's the men behind the men in power who affect the country's destinies. And even in so remote a place as this, one's working. A word here, a word there. But it isn't enough. You may be surprised one day at the turn events will take.'

'Does he really think,' she considered, looking at him, 'that he has power? Is he cheating himself? And power over whom?'

While he had been speaking he had gradually sat upright, then forward in his chair until at last he was leaning towards her, his big body thrust at her, his eyes willing hers as though, in another moment, he would say: 'Come here, Rose. Do what I tell you.'

The room seemed now very close and hot. She even wondered fantastically whether his gaze was not hypnotizing her, and she looked down and then away at the fire.

'Do you want power so much?' she asked.

'Yes,' he said. 'I want it. I must have it, and I've got it.' The tone of his voice had changed: it was heavy with a kind of sergeant-major thud in it. 'Right wheel! Right wheel!'

'You see,' he went on, 'to take a small example, how I've influenced you--even in this short time. You came for only a day or two. But now--who knows how long you'll remain?'

'If I do stay,' she wanted to cry, 'it's not because of you but because of John,' but she was aware how dangerous that would be. The sense of danger to John and herself was quite new to her. She had never been afraid of anyone in her life before.

He got up. 'I must go on with my work.' He stood over her. He put his hand on her shoulder. 'I'm so glad that we are friends,' he said.

When John heard about the party he was greatly excited.

97

In his own private world of imagination he often saw himself as an opulent and exultant host. He was owner of a wonderful house with high white pillars, a bell-tower and a marble staircase and a gigantic dovecote. In front of this mansion stretched lawns with lakes, rivers and a grove of trees. Behind the house was a great garden and on the cherry-coloured walls nectarines and peaches ripened. There were peacocks and dogs and horses: he stood on the steps while the lawns shimmered in the sun, welcoming his guests, the principal of them being Roger.

'By Jove!' Roger would say, 'I didn't know you had a place like this!'

'It's all yours, Roger,' John would answer, 'to do what you like with. You can live here and ride and hunt and play tennis and football and eat as much as you like.'

He and Roger together then entertained the guests, and the lawns were scattered with the most gracious and beautiful figures. In the evening there was a magnificent supper and footmen with splendid calves carried in superb dishes. The long tables in the great hall were illuminated with branching silver candlesticks, and at last, when everyone had eaten enough, Roger rose and proposed John's health.

'Our host!' he cried. 'My best friend, the man whose kindness and loyalty I can never repay!' Everyone drank his health. Then the orchestra played, there was dancing, and, beyond the windows, the moon rose and bathed the world in her silver light.

Now, with Rump at his side, John considered reality. It was a pity that Rump was not more of a social dog, was indeed at his very worst in any fine society. Rump alone with John, as he now was, appeared perfectly happy and content, sitting on his hinder part surveying the world with an imbecile look of satisfaction on his face, one ear down and one ear up, unapprehensive and sedate. But let anyone in authority appear and he became at once sycophantic, obsequious, low-born and ill-bred. That was why John both loved and despised him, for his sympathies were immediately aroused for anyone who was frightened. Himself he knew what those terrors were and longed for the time when no one could give his heart that twist of alarm, when he would no longer start at an angry voice nor watch with apprehension an opening door.

This made him think of his grandfather. Why was his grandfather giving this party? He had never given one before. Was it because of his mother? And at that thought he stirred uneasily, pulling Rump closer to him, moving restlessly his eyes.

He wished that his mother would go away. Nothing had been the same since she had come. It was not that he disliked her but rather that she was a strange mysterious figure to him. Ever since she had spoken to him on Cat Bells he had wondered what he ought to do about her. She wanted him to love her but he did not, he could not. He loved no one but Roger. Women in any case were not to be loved, because they had nothing about them to make them lovable. Black Maria, Aunt Janet, Mrs. Parkin--who would wish to be with them if he need not? They did nothing well, were always in the way, were always forbidding and objecting and complaining.

Yet there was something about his mother that he could not quite dismiss. No one had ever before asked for his affection and, because his nature was generous, he always wanted to give if he were asked. He liked her face, her voice, yet he wished to disappear when he saw her coming. Everything had been settled before her arrival. There were his grandfather, Aunt Janet, Mr. Brighouse, and soon he would be going to school. But now everything was unsettled. There was a stranger in the house and with her an atmosphere of drama as though something unusual might at any moment occur. Then his aunt said that his mother had been wicked. She did not look as though she had been, but then his aunt must know. On the other hand his grandfather and Mr. Brighouse liked her.

He sighed. What was going to happen? Was he going to school? And this new boy Finch, who was Roger's friend, what about him? John hated him, and the thought of this hatred made him as uncomfortable and miserable as though the room had become suddenly darkened and filled with grey cloud. Meanwhile there was the party. He was immediately happy again. There would be games and a splendid tea although there would not be peacocks and no one would drink his health. His heart warmed towards his grandfather who was so good to him, although only last evening he had made him march up and down twenty times in the study, stopping at the word of command and saluting as though his grandfather were general of an army. He sighed again. Would they never send him to school? He asked Rump, but Rump had no answer.

On the day of the party it poured with rain. The landscape wrapped itself in its shabby cloak like a charwoman going home, then came close to the house and peered in at the windows. Everything must be indoors. Clear the drawing-room for games. There can be hide-and-seek around the house. Tea in the dining-room.

The house, although apparently spacious, was not so in reality. Old age occupied so much of it. As it does in many places, old age, if given permission, is easily vain and spreads itself complacently. So it was here; prowling black furniture, four-posters, and the large oak chest with the arms of Sir Herbert Malmesbury . . . a good house, though, for hide-and-seek.

There would, it was thought, be eleven children besides John--one Parkin, two Meadows, three Thompson-Wests, two Bullens, one Marberry and two Lazenbys. The Colonel was greatly pleased that Lady Thompson-West permitted her treasures to drink his tea and eat his cake (the plainer sort, for the Thompson-Wests were always on diet). Lady Thompson-West was a widow and took from April to October a large gloomy tree-ridden house under Skiddaw. Her children were brought up with so much care that there was no disease possible for children that they did not catch. The children of Dr. Meadows were boisterous and noisy, the two Bullens were phlegmatic and greedy, the Marberry boy short-sighted and mathematical, the Lazenbys jolly and stupid.

Mrs. Parkin, Roger as her guard, arrived easily first. Out of the rain she emerged, bright-eyed, eager, and looking around for the Thompson-West children because for so long she had been striving to add their mother to her circle.

'Well, now, isn't this nice? Isn't this splendid? Fancy you giving a party, Colonel! You did surprise me! And yet why not? Why not indeed? Lady Thompson-West here yet? No? Rain may be too much for her children? Oh, I hope not! I hope not indeed! I remember she was at the Trials at Threlkeld with her little girl in much worse weather than this. Well, perhaps not worse than this, because it is pouring, is it not? Oh no, too kind! I shall be perfectly happy here--I like to move about, you know. Who else is coming? The Bullens? Why, that's marvellous of you, Colonel, because we are quite agreed about Mrs. Bullen, aren't we? Yes, I know. We'll keep it to ourselves. Ah, Miss Clennell! How charming you're looking! Don't mind an old woman. I must say what I think. About the seventeenth. I sent you a note. Only a little music and perhaps a discussion. Would you mind a discussion? Something about the Greeks and Romans, we thought. Which has meant the most to world civilization? Ah, there are the Lazenbys, poor things. How very wet they look! Yes, Mrs. Lazenby's father was a bookmaker, I believe, and did extremely well. . . . No, no, how wicked of you! I meant nothing of the kind!'

Rose had neither looked nor said anything at all, but it was one of Mrs. Parkin's traits to father some of her more malicious criticisms on an innocent audience and proclaim loudly, thereafter, the false parentage. Rose had been scarcely aware of Mrs. Parkin's pleasant chatter, for all her attention was absorbed by John's attitude to young Roger.

She had seen her son, of whose every thought and movement she seemed now to be part, transformed by Roger's entrance. The great moment of the party had occurred for him when, as yet, it was scarcely begun.

'Hullo, John!' she heard Roger say. What a good-looking boy and how supremely confident! What a child, a baby almost, John seemed beside him with the tuft of hair sticking up on the back of his head, his gentle unformed colouring--and how beautifully he does it, this difficult business of being host, how Humphrey's blood comes out in him and how unordinary he is with his nervous sensitiveness, his perception of so much that is going on around him without his knowing that he perceives it!

'Hullo, Roger!'

There was a pause.

'We're the first, aren't we?'

'Yes.'

'Hope you don't mind. I told mother we'd be early.'

'Oh no, I'm jolly glad!'

The Colonel was there with his white hair, his rosy cheeks, his beaming friendliness, and even as he beamed on the Parkins so did his portrait on the wall beam down upon him. The room seemed to be filled with beaming Colonels.

'How do you do, sir? Very jolly of you to ask me!' Roger was quite grown-up in his neatness, his aplomb, his self-confidence.

'Not at all! Not at all! Of course I must ask John's best friend. Glad to have you, my boy. How's school?'

'All right, I think, sir.'

'That's good! That's good!'

John was standing there, staring at his friend. Rose thought: 'When he is older he will learn not to do that. He will discover by bitter experience that the last thing that the beloved wishes is to be stared at in public. It is certainly the last thing that Roger wishes.'

For he was moving restlessly and his mother's blood in him was demanding that he should, in some way, take up a commanding position, figure in a situation that would show off his brilliant accomplishments. He was already moving away from John.

Others were arriving, the Lazenbys stout and jolly, the Bullens wondering when the tea was to be, the Meadows at once demanding games. And here at last was Lady Thompson-West with her treasures. She was a massive lady with a very large bosom, a lot of white hair, and weak piercing eyes, for once she had been handsome and would not imperil her beauty with glasses. She had a wearied languid voice and her attitude to life was that the world contained only some dozen people, all of them Thompson-West or Bastingham (she had been a Miss Bastingham of Coventry).

'A wet afternoon. I wondered whether I should bring the children, but in the car they could not, I think, come to much harm. I've brought their governess, Miss Hastings, with me. I hope you don't mind. Yes, Miss Hastings--not too near the fire. Very heating after the drive . . .

102

Ah, how-do-you-do, Mrs. Parkin? . . . Alice, Alice, come here, dear. Stay with Miss Hastings. Thank you, Mrs. Parkin, but I'm afraid I never go out in the evening. Afternoon? That's too kind. I fear that I may be in London. Lucy Bastingham's girl is being married. They want me for the wedding, but whether I can leave the children . . . Harold, stay by Miss Hastings, dear. No, not for the moment, darling. It's such a very heating game. You can play later on.'

For they had decided to start with Musical Chairs, a well-known breaker of ice. Rose would play the piano.

From her seat there she could view the whole room, watch the elders gathered uneasily together (for will the children behave, and if they do not can one succeed in blaming others?). Janet Fawcus is doing her best to unbend and is so uncomfortable that it is distressing. For against every woman present she has a grudge, and yet, Rose thought, were they suddenly to applaud her, if, for instance, Lady Thompson-West were to stand on a sofa now and cry: 'Three cheers for Janet Fawcus!' how exceedingly delighted she would be, how she would blush and bloom, how her heart would expand, what generosities she would commit!

The chairs were arranged, the music began, with solemn caution the children moved forward. Roger Parkin and Harry Meadows were the vital spirits--Roger was stepping out, his eyes shining, and already he had given little Ruth Bullen a push so that she nearly fell. 'He shall not win!' Rose thought vindictively and, just as he turned the corner at the end, at the moment when no chair was at hand, she stopped the music. Roger darted for a place, but the Marberry boy, short-sighted though he was, was there before him. Roger, the great splendid Roger, was 'out' first time, and oh! didn't he mind it! He threw up his head, he smiled, she heard him say to his mother 'A lot of kids--I wanted to give them a chance,' but Rose saw too John's distress, how his eyes followed his friend. In the next round John was out. He didn't want to win if Roger were not there.

Roger had drawn near to the piano and was standing, a look of haughty indifference on his face. John came up to him.

'I'm awfully sorry, Roger.'

'It's a kids' game. I only played because--'

'Yes, I know.'

'When's tea?'

'Oh, soon, I expect.' John looked at him. Rose knew that he wanted to ask him to come and see his things, to go with him alone about the house, but he did not dare lest Roger should refuse.

The game became exciting: only Harry Meadows, the Marberry boy and big fat Lettice Lazenby remained. They moved like little tigers round the two chairs. Rose stopped, and fat Lettice, jolting Harry Meadows in the stomach with her stout arm, sat down.

Meadows cried 'Oh, I say!' then like an injured but still noble Roman moved away. Lettice won.

She sat on the one remaining chair in a trance of satisfaction while everyone clapped.

'That's just like Lettice,' Mrs. Lazenby cried triumphantly to the world. 'You never saw such a child for winning things. Last year at St. Bees she beat all the other children in the races on the sands. She just makes up her mind. . . .'

The room was now very hot and the rain beat frantically on the windows. Children's parties are dangerous. The child's world is all its own--no mature person can tell what happens in it. All the passions rage and only a lucky providence can sometimes keep them in check.

Rose, standing near Mrs. Parkin, noticed how extremely excited the Colonel was. His eyes shone, his rosy cheeks flamed. And from him, she thought, the children themselves caught an added zest, a wilder freedom.

Tea was announced and in they trooped.

'One should see the Taj Mahal,' Mrs. Meadows said to Mrs. Parkin, of whom she was greatly afraid.

'Yes, I suppose one should. No. Let your little girl sit beside my boy, Lady Thompson-West. He'll look after her! Oh, no trouble at all. There, dear--Roger will see you have everything you want.'

'Of course,' Mrs. Meadows went on, 'some people have been disappointed, but not if you see it by moonlight--no one can be disappointed then.'

She would like to be invited to Mrs. Parkin's parties. She could not understand it. Often, lying in one of the twin beds, she had discussed it with her husband.

'We're not clever enough,' he said, turning on his side and longing for sleep. 'That's what it is--and Ma Parkin can go to hell for all I care.'

Nevertheless Mrs. Meadows thought: 'I could have been clever. But bearing children and bringing them up when you haven't enough money, and although Crosby (her husband) works his fingers to the bone, so often it's for nothing and we never have a real holiday.' She looked at the Thompson-West little girl and hated her. Her own children were rough, untidy, bad-mannered. There was something they terribly lacked. And she could have been clever had she only time. . . .

The children sat at table while the parents stood about. But the tea was not a success. Why? No one could tell. Everything was there, a large cake with pink and white icing, small cakes, scones, jam, rum butter, honey. But things were not right. Quite suddenly the little Bullen girl began to cry. No one knew the reason. It may have been the lightning, which flashed once quite visibly through the lighted room. Thunder muttered like a grumpy old man in the garden. The Lazenby children cared nothing for the thunder, for they were intent upon eating. You would think, to look at them, that they had never seen food before. Mrs. Lazenby did not mind. Red-faced and jolly, she encouraged her offspring.

'Would you mind passing the plum cake? So good of you. There, Lettice--mother will cut you a piece. Don't grab, darling.'

'Yes,' she said, smiling on Rose. 'It does one good to see them enjoying themselves. I know they say Lettice is too fat, but I'm too fat myself and has it ever done me any harm? None in the least. I know it's all the fashion now to have no shape, but you'll never persuade me that men like it. They have to put up with it, that's all.'

She had not known, before she turned, that it was Rose to whom she was speaking. She was a little uncomfortable. Although she wanted everyone to be happy, she must, in spite of herself, grudge something to a woman who had had a lover and not had to pay for it. Here Rose was, sin and all, as though she had done nothing reprehensible! All the fun of marriage without the ties! Perhaps that was why the Colonel had invited them. (He had never asked them inside the house before.) That they should be kind to the girl. Well, she was a pretty thing and that was a nice little boy. Who was she to judge others? There had been a time or two when she might herself . . .

'Let Mother spread it, Lettice. Honey's messy if you aren't careful.'

Hide-and-seek followed. The Colonel insisted but Rose knew at once that it would be a great mistake. The children were in too disorderly a state for it to be safe. But it was only when she went, the little Bullen girl's hand in hers, to hide in one of the rooms, that she knew what a mistake it was. Her mind was set upon John. Where was he? With whom was he? Was Roger kind to him? And so, absent-minded, she found herself with the little Bullen in one of the spare rooms--a large cold room with a black bed, black chairs, and a picture of Saint Sebastian's martyrdom over the fireplace. The little Bullen girl looked at the arrows with frightened interest. Did it hurt? Oh, it must have, because once she stuck a pin in her leg just to see. . . .

'Yes, dear, I know. Come. Shall we hide here behind the bed? They'll never find us here.'

So there they were pressed between the bed and the window. The little girl's hand in Rose's was like a warm squashed tomato. From this window you could see the hills, the Helvellyn range, the low running shoulders of the slope soot-black now under the thunderstorm. The sheets of rain above St. John's in the Vale were coming down fan-shape or like the corded strands of an inverted basket. The cloud was so black that it was metallic. But behind it the Helvellyn slopes were already clearing, and a faint shimmer, light seen through gauze, began to spread, and Rose knew that Grasmere would soon be lying, a platter of gold, in the sun.

She thought of Grasmere and of how in a very clever novel about India that she had been re-reading the author had used Grasmere as a symbol of England's smugness, smallness, security as against the passion, vastness, timelessness, danger of India. Well, India was dangerous. But so could this be! Oh, so could this be.

'Do you think they'll find us here?' the Bullen child whispered. 'I don't like this room, do you?'

No, it was a beastly room as though murder had been done in it. Unkind words at least had surely been spoken. They listened. The house was quite silent. The little Bullen girl was trembling. Hide-and-seek had been all wrong. But the Colonel had wished it, and Rose saw in a flash of clarity how fierce and almost insane his egotism was-- when he had wished Michael to leave the room, or now when a children's game had made his voice ring, his eyes flash . . . What was happening? Cries rang out.

'Somebody's been found,' Rose said.

'Oh, let's see! Let's see!' the child cried as though they had been in darkness. A moment later they were in the passage, and here indeed was a scene.

Roger stood facing John. The passage was so dark that there were voices only here, no faces.

'What are you following me around for all the time? I didn't ask you to come up here, did I?'

'No. But--' John's voice said.

'All right. Now you know. I'm sick to death of you. You can't play a game decently and I can't stand your hanging round looking like a sick cow--'

'Yes,' said John's voice.

Roger must have turned because as though they had been flung by a humorous immortal out of space he collided with Rose. Shameful! Shameful! Attribute its origins where you will. She slapped his face. Mrs. Parkin, coming with the Colonel to collect scattered children, heard it. She also heard:

'You conceited little swine! I've been wanting to do that for weeks. Leave John alone. As though--he--cared' (breathlessly now) 'for anything you say. You can--'

'Roger!' Mrs. Parkin cried.

'She hit me, mother! I hadn't done a thing--' and he began to snuffle, his pride (although it had been dark) desperately hurt. Also Rose's hand had not been soft. And there was a ring on it, although not a wedding one.

'What's up?' the Colonel demanded. (Rose fancied that there was joy in his heart. But why? Had he wanted this to occur?)

She addressed herself to apologies.

'I am very sorry, Mrs. Parkin. I lost my temper.'

'And why?' asked Mrs. Parkin, her voice like reluctant silver striking the church offertory-plate.

'He was rude to John--'

'Come, Roger.'

They were seen for a moment as the new sun, thunder-burnished, struck the passage-window, mother and son. Rose had made an enemy for ever. John was nowhere to be seen.

Only the little Bullen girl, her eyes round with wonder, was collecting amazing news for her mother.

CHAPTER VIII - THRESHOLD OF DANGER--OR ISN'T IT?

Rose, on waking the following morning, was instantly conscious that dramatic events awaited her. She stared about, sat up, saw the sun pour like a soundless primrose river from window to floor, then realized how things were. The party had ended; everyone had gone away. She had seen John only for a moment flit past her down the passage as she went to her room. She had cried after him quietly 'John!' but if he had heard he had given no sign.

At dinner she had expected to be scolded, but as seemed to her now the rule in this house, the opposite occurred.

'I beg your pardon,' she had said quite suddenly. 'I'm afraid you'll never forgive me for being so rude to one of your guests in your house.'

But the Colonel, as fresh and lusty as a prize bull at a show, had cried: 'My dear Rose, not at all. Not at all. She'll never forgive you, of course.'

Janet looked up.

'Has anything happened?' she asked.

'Yes,' said Rose. 'I slapped the face of Mrs. Parkin's boy.'

'Oh!' Janet breathed--and for the first time since Rose's entry into the house, Janet looked at her amiably. Even she smiled. 'You slapped Roger's face?'

'He was rude to John. I'm afraid I lost my temper.'

'You did?' Janet returned to her fish. 'He's wanted a slap a long time.'

So the boy had been rude to Janet: at one time or another he had offended that maiden lady.

'I've never slapped anyone before,' Rose said.

'Never too late to begin,' the Colonel remarked cheerily.

'I'm afraid Mrs. Parkin will never come here again.'

'Oh yes, she will. Don't you fear. Whenever I ask her. But I'm afraid you'll not be going to her house again.'

Michael burst out laughing.

'Did you really, Rose? When and why?'

There was something rather shameful to her in this triumphant discussion of her misbehaviour. It was not a thing of which she was in the least proud.

'While they were playing hide-and-seek. Upstairs. He was brutal to John.'

'Yes, he's a bit of a cad, young Parkin,' Michael remarked. 'He wasn't always. It's a pity.'

'You'll be a marked figure now,' the Colonel said. 'It's almost as though you'd slapped Mrs. Parkin herself.'

She felt as though in some way he were implying that this incident had given him a new hold over her. Why was he so greatly delighted and why did she feel that he had arranged it? Because he had not. She was a free and independent creature.

But John was the only important thing. That morning she sought him out and found him.

She had left the dining-room after breakfast and saw him crossing the garden. He opened the little wooden gate that led on to the fell, hesitated, then passed through it. It was a soft and warm morning, the daffodils were golden against the hedge, and the fell shone with a faint green shadow promising summer. She ran across the garden and caught him as he began very slowly, his whole body dejected, to climb.

When he turned and saw her he started as though he were trapped. Then, without a word, he began to climb again.

'John,' she said. 'I can't help it. We've got to talk. It can't go on like this.'

'Like what?' he asked in a muffled voice, his face averted.

'Walk more slowly. It's no use. You can't escape me.'

He slackened his pace. She saw that he had been crying.

'You're ashamed of me, I suppose,' she said as nonchalantly as she could. 'Of what I did to Roger.'

He produced a very dirty handkerchief out of his pocket and blew his nose.

'It doesn't matter,' he said.

'That's nonsense. It matters terribly. I'm not sorry that I slapped Roger's face and I never will be, but I want to tell you why you mustn't be sorry about it--about Roger, I mean.

'I know,' she went on, 'you must hate my talking about something very private like your friendship with Roger. But I have to do it be-cause I'm older than you are and know more than you do about friendship. Forget all about my being your mother just now. That has nothing to do with it.' He was walking more slowly and she knew that he was listening. 'Friendship's like this,' she said. 'There must be two people who care. It's hopeless otherwise. I know there are some people who think it's fine to go on caring for someone who doesn't want them,

111

unselfish, self-sacrificing, and all that. Well, I think it's rotten and self-indulgent. It's cruel to the other person, too, because it bores them stiff and often forces them to pretend to feelings that they haven't got. Roger never cared for you and never would. He's selfish and conceited and cares for no one but himself.'

'That isn't true,' John burst out. 'He did care for me before you came and spoilt it.'

'Did he? Be honest with yourself. I haven't been here for long, but at that party that day at his mother's when you gave him the present I saw at once how it was.'

John blew his nose again. Then he said, his voice trembling as though tears were not far away:

'He's the only friend I had. I'd have done anything--'

'Yes, you would. And he'd have taken it until somebody else came along--'

'It's been my fault,' John went on. 'Because I couldn't play games like he wanted me to. I tried and tried, but I've never been to school and there's nobody here to play with.' He gave her then the most hostile look she'd yet had from him.

'You're a woman and you wouldn't understand.'

'What's being a woman got to do with it?'

'I hate women. I want to go to school. Why can't I go to school? Grandfather said I should.'

'You shall go to school,' she cried. 'That I swear. I'm your mother and I'll see to it.'

He looked at her curiously. 'But you gave me up to Grandfather,' he said. 'You can't do anything if he doesn't like it and no one else can either.'

'You see,' she said. They were on the brow now and the haze was on their faces. They stopped and looked across the valley to Helvellyn.

'You must forget I'm your mother. I'm just your friend. There's not such a terrible difference in our ages. If we both live I'll be fifty-eight one day and you'll be forty. We'll seem almost the same age.'

That seemed to strike him. He stood looking at the small clouds that furled and unfurled before the sun. His body was warmed and strengthened. She felt as though the sun were binding them together.

She took his hand.

'I'm no age,' she said, 'and I never felt as young and inexperienced in my life as I do now. I'm quite as lonely as you are. If it comes to that I don't suppose I have a real friend in the world at this moment.'

'Mr. Brighouse likes you,' John said. 'I know he does because I've seen him looking at you.'

She realized that this time he hadn't taken his hand away. Her heart was beating furiously and she longed to put her arm around him and draw him close to her, but she knew that any sentiment at this moment would be fatal.

'Oh, Mr. Brighouse!' she said. 'He's kind and attentive, but it's you I want to be my friend. Do you think you could be?'

'I don't know,' he said.

There was a little pause.

'Let's go down now, shall we?' she said. 'They'll be wondering where we are.'

All the way down she told him cheerfully about adventures she'd had, how she'd been lost in Palermo once, and the old blind man in Geneva who'd tried to rob her, and the mad dog who bit a policeman in Athens, and the great Nazi demonstration in Munich.

He said never a word: only as they entered the garden he cried, 'There's Rump!' and ran off.

Michael from his bedroom window had seen her cross the garden. He had seen the crocuses like sparks of white and blue fire star the grass, and the young beginning daffodils tugging a little at their roots against the breeze, the fell with the sun smoothing it, and a cloud as once, steaming towards Greece, looking back, he had seen Etna a white cumulus in mid-air, blue above and below it. Through this beauty Rose hurried to her son, and as Michael watched her he climbed a step in maturity because for the first time he wanted to take a woman in his arms and feel her heart beat against his. Until this instant of the daffodils tugging at their roots he had wanted to kiss Rose and he knelt at her feet. Now suddenly in his mind he got up, stood beside her, took her, kissed her eyes and, his hand on her breast, murmured 'I love you.'

He saw her join John, knew that he had eaten too much breakfast because he could not resist sausages, and wondered what, in all the long dreary future, he would find to do. 'Because I shall love only her all my life long, never anyone else. Am I then to be a celibate, a hermit? Shall I, through abstinence, become a sexless withered thing? Will she perhaps one day repent when, after many years, she learns how fickle men are and only I am faithful? And will,' he honestly asked himself, 'pleasure remain when we are both old, possibly toothless and certainly rheumatic?'

And he remembered an awful story that a friend had told him about a man who had loved faithfully for years, and the lady had married another, and then after so, so long the husband had died, the faithful lover was at last rewarded.

But alas, the lady snored. One snoring night had undone the devotion of twenty years. It had not, of course, been true love, a romantic sentimentality . . .

Rose might snore an she wished . . . but at the thought of being in so close a communion with her his heart constricted, his temples pressed in upon the skull, his nose was cold at the tip.

He sat on his bed and saw her stand naked before him, but it was only at her face that he looked, her face, eyes, nose, mouth, so young, so kindly, so courageous, in colour, delicate form, dark of the eyes, rose of the lips like a--like a--and then it was terrible, for he could think only of the most dreadful images, a candle-lit turnip, an inverted basin, a Stilton cheese . . . not that Rose's face resembled any of these things, but that was what fate did in its malicious perversity. Oh, the horrible, horrible images that pass through the minds of the Saints of God! Then his eyes passed downwards and he considered the small breasts, the navel, the flanks, the thighs, the feet. She has had a child. Once there was a man who enjoyed all this, to whom she surrendered everything. . . .

Oh, the horrible, horrible images that pass through the minds of the Saints of God! Everything is holy and for the true lover nothing is common. And yet, true lover, take not too many risks!

'Always shave in private,' a friend had told Michael. 'The secret of a happy marriage is never to see your wife dressing.'

But Michael made his vows, standing in front of the glass, drawn up stiffly as though someone were playing the National Anthem: 'I swear that I will love and serve her, faithfully, without expecting any reward, so long as she may need me!'

And indeed he was to keep his vow before all were ended.

And on that same morning John unburdened his mind. Geography just then was the thing, and Michael had made the astonishing statement that some enterprising men were thinking of draining the Mediterranean and flooding the Sahara with it, when John unexpectedly remarked:

'Do you think it's no use being friends with someone if he doesn't want you?'

'Anything's of use,' Michael said sententiously, 'if it makes you feel fine.'

'That's not what mother says,' John remarked. 'But I don't know how much mother knows. What do you think, Mr. Brighouse?'

'What do I think about what?'

'About mother.'

'How do you mean--what do I think?'

'Well--it's rather extraordinary, isn't it? We've been here for years and years and she never writes a word or bothers. Then she comes for a day or two and stays weeks and upsets everybody--and she says she wants to be my friend!' he ended breathlessly.

'Do you think you ought to tell me what she says?' asked Michael. 'Wasn't it in confidence?'

'Oh, I came to you because I know you like her awfully. I've seen you looking at her.'

'Yes,' said Michael. 'She's the finest, grandest person I've ever known.'

John considered this very seriously.

'Is that because she smacked Roger's face?'

'Oh no--I don't consider that very important.' He looked at John and, with a kind of new perception that had come to him in some strange way, on this very morning, realized what the boy was going through, how resolutely determined he was that no one should know that his whole world had crumbled about him, how many stiff and new problems he was facing, how lonely he must feel with Roger gone for ever. Michael forgot everything in this new perception of John's courage. He realized another thing--that he and Rose and John were all young and inexperienced together in a dangerous and very ancient world.

'How have I not seen this before?' he thought. 'We are linked together whether we wish it or no, whether she wishes it or no,' he thought, his heart triumphantly accelerating.

John was talking.

'Now--after yesterday--I must go to school, mustn't I, Mr. Brighouse?'

Michael knew what he meant. 'Now that Roger has said those things to me and everyone heard, I must go to school and do fine things just to show him!'

116

'Roger didn't mean what mother thought he meant. You see, Roger doesn't understand. He thinks you'd be able to swim and play rugby and everything just the same whether you're at school or you aren't. And then, of course, he thinks I'm awfully slow. I'd be the same in his place. And if she hadn't got angry with him it would have been all right.'

'She loves you very much,' Michael said slowly. 'You're lucky.'

'It's very lately, then, that she has,' John said. 'She's only been here a week or two.'

'Shall I explain that to you, John? It's very important that you should understand it.'

John said nothing. He looked down at his geography book, then up and out of the window.

'All right,' he said. 'But Roger says I'm a bastard.'

'He did, did he?' Michael said furiously, and jumping up, he began to walk about the room. 'Now, listen to this, John. I've never talked to you about it before because it wasn't my business anyway and I wasn't sure whether you were old enough. But now I know you are old enough and it is my business. Listen!'

He sat on the edge of the table close to the boy.

'Your mother and father loved one another devotedly. They couldn't marry because your father was married already, but they would have done if he'd been free. I expect you know how children are born. It is the result of two people who care for one another coming together. The man gives the woman the seed of his body for her to keep and cherish. She does keep it for him months inside her body, and all those nine months it grows, then when it is big enough it pushes its way out of her body and begins its own life in the world. But the important thing is that some children are the result of true love, some are not, and to me this matters more than whether the father or mother were properly married or no, although marriage does matter too. I'm not very old myself yet, but I've seen enough of life to know that a happy marriage between two people who love one another is the happiest lot on this earth, but loving someone else is very complicated.

117

For one thing both people must be worthy of it. One isn't enough. Now your father and mother were both worthy of it, and although they weren't officially married you are the result of their love, and all your life you must be proud of it. There is nothing to be ashamed of. Always be proud of your mother and father.'

John said: 'Why didn't she want me when I was a baby?'

'She did want you. Only she was very young and she'd had such a short time with your father. When he died it must have killed something in her. She probably felt she didn't mind what happened. She felt, too, that life could be terrible, could suddenly step in and kill the thing you loved best in the world without warning, for no reason. The one thing she wanted was for you to be safe. You were only a baby; she had no money and no prospects. She knew that if you went to your grandfather your future was secure.

'I expect she thought of you all the time after you were gone, but she'd made a bargain. She felt she ought to keep to it. It wasn't until she came here and saw you that she realized that she'd always loved you and always would love you. And since she's stayed here she's got to love you more and more.'

'I see,' John said. 'So she'll always be where I am?'

'No. Not with you always. Not when you go to school, and later on you'll grow up and go off on your own. But she'll be there to help you if you want her, to stick to you if things go wrong, never to change whatever you do or say.'

'I think,' John said, 'that I'd rather be alone.'

'Why?' Michael asked.

'I don't want to be friends with anyone any more. If you're not friends there's nobody can say that you hang around too much or that you're a nuisance.'

'She'll never think you a nuisance,' Michael said.

'She might. And then there's Grandfather. Perhaps if I like her he'll tell me I'm not to see her any more.'

'It's certainly high time,' Michael thought, 'that he got away from this house.' He asked a question that he had often wished to ask.

'Are you afraid of your grandfather, John?'

'Yes.'

'Why?'

'He's so funny. If you don't do what he says he's very angry. That's one reason I want to go to school.'

'He's angry, is he?' Michael asked.

'Yes. In a funny way. He smiles at the same time.'

'That's enough,' thought Michael. 'I'm discovering too much.'

'Come on,' he said. 'Let's do some geography.'

Twice on that strange afternoon, one of the queerest and most sinister that Rose had ever known, she was to think of Mr. Rackstraw.

The rather silly chattering clock in the drawing-room had just struck three when for no very actual reason she went out of the front gate and stood looking across the fields towards the Druid Circle. That misnamed but superbly situated group of stones she of course could not see--and yet at this moment in the faint April sun that threw shadows of the most delicate apricot over hedgerows and sloping field she thought she could see them. We are told that nothing visible is really seen, nothing tangible is to be touched, nothing occurs but in the past and in the future. We see then what to the human eye is invisible, and so for Rose the stones were there, cows were grazing and the altarstone had suffered sacrifices of orange-peel and silver chocolate-paper. There was nothing unusual about that, for tourists offer the gods the things that are of no value to themselves, but what was interesting was that Mr. Rackstraw in a shirt and trousers was doing obeisance before the altar, bowing his head and turning his body north, south, east and west. She saw his grey coat and waistcoat folded on the grass. The cows cropped undisturbed and a line of birds, imitating aeroplane formation, swung with steady purpose across the blue.

119

She gave her body a shake. This was absurd. And of course it was, for the stones were not there, a dog barked and the hill rose calmly where the stones had been.

She returned into the house, and with that simple crossing the threshold her whole life on this cinder of a planet was changed.

The door of the Colonel's room opened and John came out, sobbing, his arm across his face. He stood for a moment thus, then he ran upstairs as though the fallen chief of the angels were at his heels. Satan, not the Devil. She remembered afterwards that she was aware of this distinction as though she knew at once that this was no ordinary occasion either for her son or herself. Her first impulse was to hurry after him, her second was to go, without knocking, into the Colonel's room. This she did, but as soon as she was inside some friendly power warned her. Say nothing. Do nothing. Discover what this is. If ever you have learnt control, use it now.

The Colonel was seated at his table, licking with his rosy tongue a stamp that he might stick it on an envelope.

He did so. Then he smiled at her.

'Why, Rose, my dear!' he said.

She smiled back at him. She stood by the door, her hand upon it.

'Come for a walk,' she said. 'It's such a lovely afternoon.'

He looked at the things on his table, then got up.

'Why, certainly,' he said. 'What a good idea!'

She went up to her room for her hat. It needed all the control she could find, within herself and beyond herself, not to knock on John's door. 'I must find out first,' she said to herself. 'I must discover everything.'

When she came down the Colonel was ready. They went out.

'Where shall we go?' he asked.

'Oh, anywhere.'

They turned down into the Penrith road towards Keswick, then off to the left towards the Vale.

At first they were silent. Then he said: 'Have you been here long enough to notice that nothing in this country is what it seems to be?'

'How do you mean?'

'What I mean is that everything turns over on its back as you look at it. It's a trick of light perhaps. You see a field, a running brook, a clump of trees. You glance away for a moment. When you look back the trees have shifted, the stream has another formation, the field is flat instead of sloping. That is why so few can paint this country. It's like an artist who told me once that in New York he went out to etch a building that was to be pulled down. He worked all morning, went for his lunch, and when he came back everything was gone. There was only a hole where the building had been.'

He stopped her, his hand on her arm. She discovered that she liked his touch although at this moment she was hating him.

'Turn round. Look to the left for a moment.'

She did so. They stood in silence staring out towards Shap.

'Now turn back. . . . Don't you see? The wood seems to have come a little closer.'

Yes, it certainly seemed so.

'But we must walk on. The sun will be down behind the hill soon and then it will be cold.'

On the brow of the hill she asked: 'Tell me. What do you intend to do about John? Is he to go to school soon?'

He said: 'You're his mother. What do you think?'

'Yes, I'm his mother. But you have all the rights.'

'Well,' he said, 'John's been living with us all this time. I've come to some conclusions about him. All the same--I repeat, you're his mother.'

'What conclusions have you come to?'

'About John?'

'Yes.'

'He's a charming, shy, sensitive boy. Discipline is good for him. He has a sweet, loving nature--'

'Yes. Don't you think he should go to school?'

'Why?'

The Colonel stopped, turned until he was directly in her path, and looked at her. She noticed that behind them the whole valley was filling with a thin purple light that lay almost like a transparency above a world of gathering smoke into which it was beginning to penetrate. The hill-tops were a glory, blazing with powdered bronze, and through the shadowed valley streams were running, singing, breaking the rhythm, singing again.

She had the impression that the valley was supporting the Colonel, forming a wall, as though behind him, through its streams, it whispered: 'Yes. This is so. No movement without the Colonel's permission.'

'Why?' he said.

She answered as lightly as she could: 'Oh, because it's not good for a boy to be so much by himself. Roger's too old for him; besides I've smacked his face. There's no one else here of his own age whom he likes. Certainly he should go to school.'

He stood there, not moving, and to her excited fancy he seemed to grow in size.

'I'm not sure that I agree. He's not ready for school.'

She laughed. 'He wants to go terribly.'

'Yes. But he has to learn that he can't have everything he wants. That's what I'm trying to teach him.'

'Oh,' she said, 'but he's not at all a greedy or selfish boy. He's almost too sensitive to other people's wishes.'

The Colonel smiled.

'You love him very much, don't you? I suppose that I ought to say--"Well, dear Rose, take him. I give him back to you." I'm not sure that I can though. For one thing I'm not quite certain that you're ready to look after him yet. You're very young. Very young. Although you're his mother you might be his elder sister. Then he's been with Janet and myself for ten years. We've grown very fond of him. It's not easy to give him up.' He looked round him. 'Shall we start back? The light is failing. There's a cold breeze.'

She looked at the valley and saw that it was like a vat in which purple clouds were bubbling. He kept his hand on her arm.

'No, my idea, Rose, is this. Now I'm going to make you jump. Don't answer at once. Stop and think it over. My suggestion is that we should both look after John. In fact I want you to stay with us always.'

She thought that she had heard the words, then she was sure that she had not.

'I don't--' she began.

'Oh yes, you do,' he said, most genially. His grasp now was tight on her arm and she fancied even that his fingers gently caressed it.

'You know just what I mean. I want you to make the Hall your home. We'll be John's joint guardians. I'm old enough to be your father, my dear, but I'm going to say something quite revolting--which is that I should ask you to marry me if it were not within the prohibited degrees.

'Instead I invite you to make my home yours until I die--and then after that if you wish.'

Her tongue was dry; her knees trembled a little so that she paused to feel the breeze on her cheek and to see a stream shining in the fading sheen, leaping quartz, running into quicksilver gestures, then dead dusk. White again.

She was able to say very quietly:

'There would be a good deal of scandal, wouldn't there?'

'Do you mind that? Does it matter in the least what they think? Isn't John more important?'

She looked him in the eyes and seemed by them to be drawn closer.

'And there's my work. You forget that is very important to me, that I couldn't leave it.'

'Not as important as John, is it?'

'Perhaps not.' They were at the brow of the hill again. 'Do you mean that I can only be with John on condition that I remain here?'

'Yes. I mean exactly that. I wish you to stay.'

'Why?'

'You have become very precious to me, my dear Rose--just as John has. I am an old man--probably only a few years to live.' (She could see him in the dusk, shoulders back, chest spread, head up, as though he were challenging the world.) 'I am, as you have probably noticed, a very unusual man. I should have been in a very different position. I would have enjoyed great power. I might, had things been a little different, have changed the world's whole history. As it is--I must do what I can. I have for some time had the notion that I would make John carry on what I should have begun. John can be, if he obeys me, one of the world's great men, and in years to come he will tell the world that it is to me that he owes his greatness. You shall do your part in moulding him. Together we can do wonderful things for him. . . . Now you perhaps can understand why I can't let him go--even to school.'

'You promised him that,' she said.

'Yes, but when he understands that it is not my wish he will agree.'

'You want him to have no will of his own?'

'I want him to have my will, my thoughts, my power--'

'But he isn't, so far as I can see, that kind of boy. He isn't unusual in any way. He's only rather gentle, shy, very sensitive.'

The Colonel spread his arms. 'My dear Rose, I can do anything--anything. With you to help me.' Then he repeated more softly: 'With you to help me.'

He put out his hand and touched her cheek. She had a dreadful revulsion--but she did not move away.

As they turned into the Penrith road she sent out a prayer for help.

He passed into the house in front of her, humming to himself, gaily swinging his stick. An idea suddenly came to her. She waited in the dusk, then turned and, very softly, went back to the road. It shone whitely against the grey country that now was very silent and cautious like an old man with his finger to his lip.

Rackstraw's cottage was up a little lane just above the village of Threlkeld--no distance. She ran up the road, walked slowly through the first part of the village, turned to the left, and there was the cottage.

She knocked on the door. He came himself. At the sight of his funny face with its crows'-feet, the mouth a little humorously twisted, she knew an extraordinary relief as though all her troubles were over.

'May I come in a moment?'

'Miss Clennell! Why, of course!'

She followed him into a sitting-room, a shabby comfortable place with a hole in the carpet, bookcases with worn and tattered books, one print over the fireplace, a coloured reproduction of Constable's 'Hay Wain,' a long rack with many old and much-used pipes, and on the table a vase with daffodils, a pot of tea, a Stilton cheese, a tin of sardines, a loaf of bread and a pat of butter, a large pot of apple- and-blackberry jam. A fire was burning and there was a piebald cat asleep in front of it. All these insignificant things seemed, as she stood there, to have a warm and welcoming life. That other house was against her: this was for her.

'Sit down. Have some tea.'

'No, thank you. I'm so sorry I've interrupted you. Go on, won't you?'

'Yes, I will.' He sat down and began to spread a very thick chunk of bread with butter and jam.

'I have my chief meal of the day now. Then I have the whole evening free.'

'Yes.' She found it difficult to begin. 'I came on an impulse. I'm in bad trouble.'

'Why,' he thought, 'she doesn't look a day more than eighteen.' Her cheeks were flushed with running, a strand of hair had blown over her forehead.

'What is it?'

'It's simply that John and I have got to escape from here as soon as we can.'

He nodded, his mouth full of bread and jam.

'It all happened this afternoon, although I suppose it really started from the moment I arrived. With every day two things have been happening--I have been loving John more and understanding the Colonel less. I can't help it. I love John so much that I am changed, entirely altered. Nothing that seemed to me important matters to me any more. Soon after I came I saw that something was wrong. He was so shy, so nervous, not what a boy ought to be. Of course I meant nothing to him. That was natural. But he seemed to care for nothing except that Parkin boy. We've talked about this before.'

'Yes, I know. Go on,' Rackstraw said.

'I mustn't stay. They'll be missing me. But this is what happened this afternoon. While I was in the passage John came out of the Colonel's room crying bitterly. He ran past me. When I saw that, I was frantic. I don't know what the Colonel is, what he does, but John has got to be taken away--and at once. I tried to do what I thought was wise. I asked the Colonel to go out for a walk. He was only too pleased. As we walked he told me that if it were possible he would ask me to marry him. As it wasn't he wanted me to stay there, at the Hall, always. . . . He said,' she began to stammer in her agitation, 'that he was training John to be a great man and to take his place as his, the Colonel's, representative, so that all the world should see through John what a great man he, the Colonel, was. I was to stay and help in this.' She paused. Then she threw out her hands towards him. 'Mr. Rackstraw, tell me--is he mad?'

The old man smiled.

'Don't be frightened, my dear. I knew this was coming. We'll manage it. No, he's not mad, but he's got an egotism, an egomaniac energy that is starved. I told you the other day on the fell--he doesn't count for anything here any more. He doesn't count for anything anywhere. So he fixed on John. His idea isn't mad, but if it grows into an obsession it may lead to what people call madness--that lonely, empty place filled with voices and culs-de-sac. You came. He'd asked you, as I've said before, to show you his power over John. But when he saw you, his desire for power extended to you. He sees you perhaps as part of John, part of Humphrey whom he loved, who ran away to escape his father's egotism, part of himself even. Can you understand that? Understand that, pity him, forgive him and take John away as soon as you can.'

She looked at him with real fear in her eyes.

'I don't want to go back. . . . I don't want to go back. I wouldn't if it weren't for John. And I've no rights. If I did get John away I wouldn't be able to keep him.'

'You might,' Rackstraw said. 'The Colonel might be afraid of any kind of publicity.'

'But I can't get away--not with John. We are both watched every minute of the day. There's himself and Janet and the servants. I'm not even sure that John would go. I mean almost nothing to him.'

'We'll think of a plan. We'll have a plot. I'm a wonder at plots.' He came over to her and put his arm round her. She rested her head against his shoulder for a moment. Then she got up.

'It's nice here. Cosy, comfortable. Everything's friendly.'

He sighed.

'I'm glad you like it. It isn't always so. Now I'm in on this. By to-morrow I'll have thought of something. Go back, give no sign of any-thing but peace of mind. He's suspicious, he's clever, he's always the last thing you'd expect.'

She kissed him.

'You're a darling. I feel safer, more secure.'

She ran through the darkness.

CHAPTER IX - CONQUEST OF JANET-- THE HOUSE HAS A COLD--MR. RACKSTRAW IS NOT WELL--ROSE LIGHTS A CANDLE

Someone else besides Rose had seen John come out of the Colonel's room. Sally the maid had seen him and she smiled. Janet saw him and she did not smile. Janet had been scolding the cook and, refreshed as one who has taken a vigorous piece of exercise, she stood on the top step of the stairs that led down to the kitchen. She saw her father's door open. John came out, Rose standing in the passage. She saw Rose's face, she saw her enter the Colonel's room.

Then very slowly she went up to her own room. This was an austere, bare, uncomfortable place. She sat down in the little wicker chair in which she had been sitting for a part of every day ever since she was ten, and looking in front of her at the timetable of household events pinned on the wall, sought for personal honesty. The thing on which above all others she prided herself was her honesty about herself. 'I am a plain old maid. I am unattractive to absolutely everybody. I have no purpose in life except to do my duty. I might just as well be dead. But I am honest. I do do my duty. I stand no nonsense either from myself or anyone else. All the same I might just as well be dead.'

The time-table said:

Called 7.30

Breakfast 8.30

Visit to Cook . . 9.30

'I might just as well be dead.'

She knew, however, that today she was not dead. This might be possibly because she was not feeling well. She had not been well for several days. It was one of those indeterminate malaises than which there is nothing more irritating, when there is a universal weakness and lack of energy and, at the same time, a continuous sequence of mild aches and pains--first the right temple, then the left, now an eye-ball, soon a nostril, a knee, a great toe, the larynx, an ear and, so that it may not be forgotten, the impertinent officiousness of the upper gums. Janet was accustomed to aches and pains, but, contrary to the common opinion, she did not love them the better for that. She had written last evening in her Journal:

'My body is nothing but a piece of impudence. I wash it, clothe it, and pay it constant and tiresome attention. I have never outraged it. It owes me gratitude. It shows me none. I refuse to grant it obsequious attention. I refuse to consider it a miracle of ingenious construction. It is one of the clumsiest, stupidest things, confused with unnecessary intricacies. Whoever thought it all out was a tiresome, meddlesome fool.'

She had felt better after that, but nevertheless slept badly and suffered in the morning from a violent neuralgia that jumped from place to place like an energetic but inefficient performer on the piano.

It was not now, however, of her neuralgia that she was thinking. It was of John's crying and Rose's face. It was of her own responsibility in this matter. Why had John left her father's room in tears? This was not for the first time. No one, she reflected, left her father's room quite as she or he entered it. She had seen Sally the maid leave it with a smile. Also some of Sally's predecessors.

She thought of Rose. She did not hate her quite so badly after she had smacked Roger Parkin's face. To be entirely honest, she had not hated the woman so badly ever since she had told her that she liked her and would like her whatever might occur. Nobody had ever spontaneously told Janet that she liked her, and although here there was undoubtedly some further purpose, Rose's face--her eyes, her mouth--had been even more convincing than her voice.

Rose's face. It had expressed, at that moment of John's passing her, a distress, a fear, an unhappiness that Janet, however hard she might try, could not forget. There was something maternal that Janet would have given all that she possessed to experience; not that she possessed very much--a time-table, a fur coat and a diamond brooch that her poor mother had left her.

Janet did not sleep very well that night. She suffered from an old familiar dream in which she chased an omnibus down a crowded street, was mocked with jeers, dropped parcels, caught the balustrade of the omnibus, was dragged along the pavement, then fell through a dark hole down, down, into a bottomless pit.

When she woke for the fifth time it was seven-thirty. Sally brought her tea, impertinently as usual. Janet sat up in her rather worn bed-jacket, sipped her tea and realized that she had a headache, a sore throat, and pains in her legs.

She was, however, not easily beaten, and dressed as though she were ten different pieces of ten different women, all severed in the wrong places.

She discovered that it was the worst kind of day for anyone suffering from chill. There was no rain, but a cold April wind swept across the garden and up the fell. Clouds raced one another with a streaming animosity above the Penrith road. They were ill-dispositioned clouds with the texture of torn and water-soaked wool, lengthening now into thin grasping fingers, now taking the shape of gland-swollen faces, now like hunched discontented shoulders or winged birds of ill-omen. The trees creaked and cracked. Everything was blown away and birds rose and fell like black wisps of paper rising from some conflagration.

Having been severe with the cook, short with Sally, she was summoned to her father's study. Father and daughter faced one another with dislike. His thought was: 'Can it be possible that I was ever responsible for this sallow-faced, ill-conditioned old maid?'

And hers: 'His self-complacency is intolerable. Based also on nothing.'

131

Aloud he said: 'Janet, a week ago I spoke to you about the inadequacy of the bath water. This morning the water was tepid.'

He sat behind his desk, bulky, aggressive, his white hair a little disordered as though the wind without had penetrated the house. There was no smile, no cordial spirit. He and his daughter knew one another too well to waste geniality.

She answered coldly: 'You know that we need a new tank, and higher up the fell. I've spoken about it often enough. Six months ago you promised to write to Lord Tuscover.'

'Well, well,' he answered testily. 'That may be. You know that I've so many things to think of. I will write. Meanwhile surely something may be done.'

'We have,' she answered, her body rigid, her hands folded in front of her (she would die there on his study carpet rather than let him know how severely her temples throbbed, how savagely her throat was aching), 'an extra person in the house. It was difficult enough before, and now--'

'Nonsense,' he answered. 'You're not going to tell me that Rose makes all that difference.' They looked at one another. 'Are you ill?' he asked. 'You seem to be none too well.'

'I'm perfectly well, thank you.'

Something in her voice touched him. Poor old devil! It must be hell to be an old maid, never to have been loved by a man, never to have been kissed with passion. His own pride rose as, looking at his daughter, he thought of all the women to whom, in his long life, he had so successfully made love. He did not think of them individually but only as a rosy cloud, shining colour, movement, hushed whispers, secret laughter. . . .

She was thinking: 'He's really like an animal with his thick neck, his bulging arms. . . . I must get away from here. . . . I've stood it long enough.'

And in her irritation, her voice urged on by her malaise, she said the worst thing in the world. She said:

'By the way, Father, I do wish you'd leave Sally alone.'

'Sally?' His eyes narrowed.

'Yes. You give her the idea that she's a favourite here. The result is that she's impertinent and does her work badly.'

He looked at her, hating her. But he said:

'If she does her work badly, dismiss her.'

'Yes. I think I will.'

She turned to go.

He raised his voice a little.

'Janet!'

'Yes, Father.'

He spoke quietly, tapping the table with the silver-topped paper-knife.

'Run the house as you please, but remember I am master in it.'

'Yes, Father.'

'I have not interfered with you for a long time. Don't exasperate me.'

She made as though she would speak, then decided that she would not. She closed the door softly behind her.

Early in the afternoon she felt so unwell that she could scarcely stand on her feet. At luncheon she had pretended to eat only. A piece of mutton guarded by string beans and a swollen offensive baked potato had seemed to her so maliciously alive that she regarded it with a kind of terror. There are times when the decent romantic screen is lifted and we see with a deep disgust these bodies seated on wooden erections, engaged in shovelling alien substances into a hole surrounded by skin and bone.

Some of these bodies, aesthetically ill-instructed, perform this business without closing the hole at decent intervals. The Colonel, when happy and well at ease with plenty to say, was one of these. At such moments Janet felt a nausea as compelling as any sea-sickness. To-day, with the wind howling about the house, her own aches and pains, her father's happy volubility, this fragment of mutton defied her to leave the table. 'Touch me and see.' She gazed at it slowly congealing, resting between the potato and the beans, immortally satisfied like the navel-stone at Delphi or the Louvre 'Monna Lisa.'

With a ferocious effort of will she cut it in half, raised a piece on her fork, laid it down again. She must indeed be extremely ill, for it seemed to her as if the two pieces had joined together again, and that the beans stirred like weed-tendrils in a pond.

Nevertheless she sat there. She saw the mutton removed, still smirking, and Sally smirking above it. Sally was to lose her job; that at least was one comfort.

She said: 'Oh, do you think so? I like a novel in which everything ends happily. There's so much unpleasantness in life anyway. Why have it in our fiction?'

Rose had observed her, came into the drawing-room as Janet was bending down to stir a reluctant sulky fire and said: 'Oh, Janet! do let me do that! Even though you do hate me I can poke the fire for you.'

Janet straightened herself, then staggered so that Rose must catch her arm.

'Why must you always be facetious, Rose?'

'Come--sit down. You look dreadfully ill. And you ate no lunch at all. I wasn't spying. But I couldn't help seeing.'

Janet sat down. She put her hand to her head.

'Yes, I have a headache, I won't deny.' Then she added: 'I hate mutton.'

Rose, who was on her knees before the fire, looked up.

'It's none of my business, and you run the house beautifully, but I think the cook's lazy.'

'She is,' Janet said. 'I'm giving both the cook and Sally notice before the end of the week.'

'Sally? I am glad!'

The two women looked at one another and exchanged a glance of real comradeship. Both knew why everything might be better without Sally. . . .

Then a wonderful thing happened to Janet. As she looked at Rose, kneeling there on the floor, she was conscious of a sudden exaltation. She felt (not for the first time in her life) maternal. She hated Rose, she wanted her out of the house, she didn't wish to speak to her, yes, she hated her--but she felt maternal. The girl was so young for her age, helpless in spite of Geneva and the League of Nations, helpless at least in this present situation. She looked away out at the trees straining in the wind, and the clouds marching now like an army across the sky-- this sudden protective urgent tenderness would pass. It had in reality nothing to do with Rose whom she hated. Any young thing kneeling like that . . . any young thing who had looked as Rose had looked when John came out of the study . . .

Rose had risen and, after a moment's hesitation, had sat down on the faded green sofa beside Janet and taken her hand.

'Would you mind, Janet, very much if I fetched my thermometer from my room?'

Janet took her hand away.

'Indeed I would. I hate being fussed over.'

'But this isn't fussing. Forget for a moment that I am Rose. I am nothing, simply a disembodied spirit who fetches a thermometer. For you have a temperature. I'm sure that you have.'

'The last thing you look like,' said Janet grimly, 'is a disembodied spirit. And I have myself a thermometer, thank you. As a matter of fact I think I will go and lie down.'

'Why not undress and go to bed?' said Rose. 'One does feel so much better in bed if one has a bad headache. And it isn't a day to stay up for. It's a horrible day.'

Janet was near to tears--tears of aggravation, weakness and pain.

'Would you mind leaving me alone? I don't want to be rude, but when one is unwell the only thing one wants is to be left alone.'

Rose got up from the sofa.

'Yes, I know. It's only that one push from someone outside is some-times useful although always disagreeable. When one ought to go to bed but can't quite make up one's mind--'

Janet got up. The room surged about her. The room, always full of noises, clocks, canaries, and everlasting whisperings, now shouted in her ear.

She staggered and found herself leaning against Rose.

'I can manage perfectly well.'

'No, you can't. You've got to let me help you to your room whether you like it or no.'

'It's only,' murmured Janet, 'a kind of nausea.'

'I know exactly.'

They went upstairs together, Rose's arm round Janet's waist. In Janet's room Janet said:

'If you don't mind--I'd rather be alone.'

'Of course.' Rose left her. 'Only have you some aspirin--and you will take your temperature, won't you?'

'Yes, I have some aspirin, thank you.'

In the drawing-room again Rose waited wondering what she should do. The poor old thing was plainly ill, and for the first time Rose real-ized how lonely Janet was. Except for Rose there was not a soul in the house who would trouble. When Janet had been ill before what had happened? She had lain there in that ugly room, in that dark cold house, and the cook or a discontented, reluctant maid had brought her medicine, seen to her needs. The Colonel would visit her perhaps for a moment but would hasten away, for Rose knew him well enough now to realize that he would hate any kind of illness and fear it. How miserable, how frightened, how deserted she must often have felt! Rose understood, feeling her own health and youth and vigour, how Janet must have detested the weakness that illness would bring her, physical strength being her only asset. Yes, it was a tragic situation met with courage and honesty. She would go up a little later and see how things were.

She had been for the moment absorbed by Janet and stood looking out of the window at the garden. The wind had suddenly fallen and the scene had miraculously changed as it does so often in this country. Blue was breaking through the thin web of grey sky, and little shining white clouds, like ragged snowballs, hinted at an advancing sun. The garden was quite still, and the light, which was not yet there but soon would be gave a silver colour to the new leaves, which had a glitter as though rain had fallen.

She was breathing in delightedly this new peace when she saw a figure open the gate, stand uncertainly and look about him. A moment later she realized that this was Mr. Rackstraw: Mr. Rackstraw, an umbrella in his hand, a soft shapeless hat set crookedly on his head.

Her instant thought was that he must disappear. Her second, where was the Colonel? For the Colonel detested Mr. Rackstraw. Hastily she went into the passage and listened: not a sound save the twittering of the canaries from the drawing-room. She opened the front door and ran out.

As soon as she reached him she realized that he was drunk. He swayed slightly on his feet and as she approached him he raised the umbrella unsteadily and opened it over his head.

Last night she had rested her head on his shoulder, she had kissed his forehead, she had thought him her champion.

'If,' he said, 'it is raining, come under my umbrella.'

She caught him by the elbow, drew him into the road and hurried him out of sight of the house. When they were round the bend he struggled a little.

137

'Miss Clennell'--he bowed, the umbrella bowing with him--'I came to call. I will not be prevented.' His lower lip quivered. With trembling fingers he closed the umbrella. Then looking at her, his eyes full of tears, he whispered:

'I'm sorry. Disgraceful. Beg your pardon.'

She did not know what to say. She was so bitterly disappointed that she could herself have cried. Catching her arm as though he were going to say something very important, he cried:

'But far from dances and the back-blowing torch,

Far off from flowers or any bed of man,

Shall my life be for ever; me the snows

That face the first o' the morning, and cold hills--'

'Mr. Rackstraw,' she interrupted. 'Please, please go home. It will be so bad if you are found here. Please, please.'

(She realized when she looked back on this episode afterwards that he had spoken his poetry with absolute clarity, stumbling over no single word.)

'My dear,' he said, 'I want to help you. I am an old man, a disgraced old man--"far from dances"--yes--"far off from flowers"--but I can offer you a meal--hospit-hospit-hospitality. You shall be saved from your enemies if a wretched worthless old man--'

Then once again her eyes brought comprehension breaking through. 'I'm sorry. I apologize. I hadn't intended, but one glass of whisky is no mortal sin. Who says it's a sin? I defy them! I defy them all!--my only friend. I have no friend. Rightly, you will say--but whether right or wrong that is my punishment. We are all punished in our time. The gods see to it. Forgive me. I need your forgiveness.'

By this time they had reached the turn of the hill and the houses of Threlkeld were in front of them. She stood back from him.

'Please go home, Mr. Rackstraw,' she said quietly. 'You oughtn't to be out like this. It would be unfair if anyone saw you.'

'Yes,' he said gently. 'It would be unfair--but then everything is unfair. Most unfair. Life's only lesson.' He looked up at the sky, which was now an unbroken serene blue, the hills lying against it as though asleep.

'I see that it is not raining,' he said. 'I will go home.'

And very steadily, tapping the road with his umbrella, he walked away. 'And that,' she thought, 'is the end of my champion. There is no one to help me. I must manage this thing myself. Yes, there is Michael. The three of us, it seems, against the world, the flesh and a bottle of whisky.' But, standing in the garden, marvelling at the golden silence and the freshness of it, she sighed for Mr. Rackstraw. 'He'll be so terribly sorry to-morrow,' she thought.

All through the afternoon Janet, having taken as much aspirin as any decent lady ought to take and not consider herself a dope fiend, having extracted a hot-water bottle from Sally, had lain in her bed following the pains that ran like hostile mice from one part of her body to another, keeping misery at bay, for if she is miserable who is there to care?

One thing especially worried her and that was the house. The house had a cold.

Her perceptions were fiery, lit by pain and fever, no imaginary exaggeration was it to perceive how the chimney snuffled, how the ceiling ached, how little chilly tremors ran along the floor, how all the apertures were closing with rheum, how the staircases shivered. Somewhere in the house's middle quite awful pains were stirring; she could in her own feverish state see the house raise, like a hand, the ugly bow-window outside the drawing-room, and heaving a deep sigh of distress through all its Cumberland stone feel the heavy ache of its tiles and plaster while down the channel of the central chimney tears of soot fell softly in sympathy.

The horrible thing was that all the apertures were closing just as her own throat, eyes and nostrils were constricted. Soon there would be no air in the house: fever would heat the rooms and passages, the windows would darken, the very chairs and tables thicken with high temperature.

And she would die in this horrible old room of hers, and at the last, choking, gasping for breath, she would be strangled by her own disease.

She sat up looking wildly about her. She had not switched on the light because she had hoped that she might sleep, and now, in the dusk, it seemed to her that the room was growing smaller. Surely the wardrobe, which appeared now to be double its ordinary size, was nearer the bed than customary!

'I'm crazy,' she thought, 'and nobody will come. If I ring the bell it will only be Sally again. I cannot bear her in the room. I shall die here and nobody will be sorry. There's not a soul in the world but will think it a good riddance.'

There was a gentle knock on the door: it opened and someone was there.

'Why, you're all in the dark!' Then more gently: 'Janet, are you asleep?' Rose turned on the light by the door. 'Only for a moment. Don't let it hurt your eyes. Wait. The lamp by the bed.'

She switched on the lamp and in another moment it was the only light in the room.

'How are you? May I stay for a minute or two?'

'Please,' Janet said.

'How was the temperature?'

'It was a hundred and two.'

'Oh dear! . . . Now may I take it again?'

Janet submitted. She lay there with the thermometer under her tongue and stared in front of her. Rose's fingers were on her wrist. There was silence.

'Yes--it is still a hundred and two. Won't you have a doctor?'

140

'Perhaps it would be best. Doctor Meadows.'

'Do you mind my leaving you a moment while I telephone?'

Again silence.

Rose was in the room again. 'He's coming at once.' She sat beside the bed. 'May I make you more comfortable?'

She smoothed the pillow, lifted Janet so that she lay against her breast.

'Do you mind this eau-de-Cologne? It helps the headache.'

She sat beside the bed, Janet's hot hand in her cool one.

'The house has a cold,' Janet said. It seemed to her that Rose was isolated by a cloud of cool water that surrounded her with a shining nimbus.

'Is there someone standing by the door?'

'No. There's no one there.'

'Only yourself in the room?'

'Yes. Only myself.'

'It was very good of you to come.' Then she said again, breathing with difficulty: 'This house has a cold.'

'It seems to me very warm--too warm.'

'No. I don't mean that. It has the influenza just as I'm sure I have. It's all stuffed up and full of aches and pains.'

'Yes, I know how one feels. But you mustn't talk. Shall I go until the doctor comes?'

'No, don't go. Talk to me a little. Tell me things.'

'Shall I?' Rose stroked her hand. 'I'll tell you one thing I've been thinking this afternoon. That it must have been lonely for you other times when you've been ill here. I don't think this is a good house to be ill in. I was afraid you wouldn't like me coming back to see how you were, but the house is depressing to-day. John's in Keswick with Michael. I don't know where your father is. I'll confess something. I came to see you as much for my sake as yours.'

Janet turned her head on the pillow and looked at her.

'How young you are! Ever since I was so rude to you the other day I've been thinking of that. Not that I'm ashamed. . . . I meant that . . .'

'Hush! you mustn't talk.' Janet shook her head.

'I only want to say one thing.' She took her hand out of Rose's. 'Don't think because I'm ill that I've given in. It was wrong of you to come here--wrong to stay. And to be kind to me. You're only doing it for a purpose, I'm sure. But I'm weak. I'm foolish. I've been lonely so long.'

'Janet, dear. . . . Not now. We'll have it all out one day--but not now.'

Janet gave Rose a feeble little push.

'But you shouldn't stay here. You'll catch the influenza.'

'Well, if I do--then you can nurse me.'

'Yes, I will. Don't imagine I won't do my duty--whatever it may be.' Janet began to speak excitedly. 'I tell you, Rose, I can't help it. I know what's right and wrong.'

'Do you?' said Rose. 'I wish I did.'

'Of course you do. Everyone does. And yet--I see how you love John. I know it now as I didn't the other day.'

'Yes,' said Rose. 'I do. It's changed everything.'

'Well, there it is. We can't alter it and I won't pretend I don't like you to care for me. But perhaps you don't. To be quite honest I don't see how anyone can.'

'I do care for you,' Rose said. 'I didn't expect to but I do. And now please, Janet, don't talk. Lie down. Let me see that the hot-water bottle is all right.'

142

Janet lay down. Rose felt her forehead.

Janet said: 'Let your hand stay there, Rose. It is so cool.'

'No. Wait. This will be cooler.' She had found, when she tele-phoned to the doctor, some ice in the pantry and now she brought from the washbasin an ice-cold towel.

'There! Don't you like that?'

'Yes. Thank you. Don't go till the doctor comes. Will you light that candle, please?'

'A candle?'

'Yes. That one in the silver candlestick. It's one of the few pretty things I have. Mother had a pair. They're really old, I believe. Father has one in his study.'

Rose lit the candle.

'Now will you switch off the lamp?'

There was again silence.

'Isn't it charming? So much nicer than electric light. I've seen my mother doing her needlework under that very candle. She did such beautiful work.'

There was a knock on the door.

'That must be the doctor.'

Rose bent down and kissed Janet on the cheek. Janet threw up her arms and drew Rose's head down for an instant.

Sally said in the doorway: 'It's Doctor Meadows, miss.'

CHAPTER X - FLIGHT FROM DESPOTISM--WITH RUMP

Janet was quite seriously ill with influenza for a week, and during that time Rose devoted herself to the poor lady.

Janet was a good patient, for gratitude worked real havoc in her sentimental heart. When, after so much misery, she sat in her chair, a shawl about her shoulders, sipping chicken broth while Rose read to her a novel by Mr. Albion, she was so weak, so grateful, and so sentimental that tears rolled down her cheeks and salted the broth and nobody heeded. 'We are friends now for life, I suppose,' Rose thought, while she read a moving account of the Squire's difficulties because the ancestral home was mortgaged. This story, she thought, she had read before and it would not please her circle of friends in Geneva, who preferred something more obstetric, but how agreeably English it was and how easy to read aloud was Mr. Albion's prose.

'Oh, how beautiful, dear!' sighed Janet. 'Do read that bit again!'

'Yes, I have her now for life. I am her only friend. I shall never, never be rid of her, and although I shall so very often be irritated I shall more often be glad and say to myself: "Well, anyway there's Janet!"' Looking back she was not surprised at Janet's so sudden surrender, for she has been longing, Rose thought, to love somebody. She's fine, she's brave, of a grand integrity and has a sense of humour most unexpectedly. Also she detests her father the Colonel. She is an ally.

When, later, Janet was sleeping and Rose went down to the drawing-room for an hour's rest she found, to her amazement, Mrs. Parkin.

A frosty eye saluted her. There was no handshake.

'I have come to see Colonel Fawcus.'

'Oh yes. . . .' Rose's eyes sparkled. She did what she had determined to do. 'I have been wanting to apologize, Mrs. Parkin, for losing my temper with your son the other day.'

Mrs. Parkin said nothing, but her little breasts rose and fell under their stout and not very decorative grey covering.

'It was unpardonable when you were a guest here. I do most sincerely apologize. At the same time I do want to say that I do not for a moment regret it.'

'Well, really, Miss Clennell!'

'I quite understand how indignant you must have felt, Mrs. Parkin. I felt indignant too. I think we're all square.'

Mrs. Parkin was so very angry that her hand, holding a little black-beaded bag, trembled and her mouth twitched, but she replied with dignity:

'Miss Clennell, on my side I have nothing to say except that when you arrived here in an invidious position I was friendly and introduced you to my circle. I might have behaved quite otherwise. You have repaid this with violence to my son and rudeness to myself. I am an old friend of Colonel Fawcus, but I'm sure you will agree that, when I visit here, you and I had better meet as polite strangers.'

There was a ring of Charlotte Yonge or Miss Worboise about this speech and Rose was touched. She would behave again as she had behaved before if the same occasion arose: nevertheless she thought Mrs. Parkin rather a pet.

She smiled, then thought her smile must be aggravating and looked serious.

'Yes. I behaved very badly. I often do, I'm afraid. Polite strangers. Yes. I'll do my best,' and she went out of the room.

And John is the other question. What has he been doing?

He thought, when first he heard of his Aunt Janet's sickness, that it was a good thing--and this not from cruelty but simply a judgment from a real boy's acceptance of facts as they are. Aunt Janet in bed meant more freedom for himself, Rump, and the old gardener.

But--it did not turn out like that. Something very strange occurred. His mother paid him no attention at all. It seemed as though the only person in the world for her was Aunt Janet, and this was odd because he had thought that his mother did not like Aunt Janet.

He discovered that he missed his mother's interest in him, and that not at all because he wished that she should be kind to him. Only--she had said that they were to be friends. Was this being friendly?

He had known often before what it was to be lonely, but now it was as though no one had any interest in him at all. Even Mr. Brighouse . . .

During algebra he said: 'When will Aunt Janet be better?'

'She's getting on.' Mr. Brighouse looked at him severely. 'We happen to be doing algebra if you don't mind.' Mr. Brighouse's temper was very uncertain this week. Could it be that he also was missing somebody?

It was then, after considering everything and everybody, that John had an idea. The idea remained; it grew and burgeoned. His grandfather's behaviour made it a fact.

On a very dreary afternoon when, although the sun shone, it seemed that the world was dead, he was summoned into his grandfather's study. He at once took off his coat, preparing for exercises. At the same time he considered how extremely beastly this all was, and in that instant the idea grew a little older and a little stronger.

His grandfather stood up in front of him, looking a mountain of health and strength.

147

'Yes. Now stand with your heels together.'

John did so.

'Your hands at your side.'

John stood as stiff as a steel rod.

'Now listen to me. I have been training you for a considerable time. Why, do you imagine?'

John considered. It seemed that here was occasion for a little propaganda.

'To prepare me for school.'

'Not necessarily. It may be that I shan't send you to school. You are having a better training under me than you'll ever get at school.'

John's nose twitched. He longed to scratch it and that longing revealed to him the true beastliness of his position. Something had happened to him on that day when Roger turned on him. Perhaps some new manliness, perhaps a new disgust. In any case his soul revolted because his nose demanded something that he was not free to give it.

'You're a happy boy, aren't you?'

He was not, but he felt that this was the wrong moment for protest.

'Yes, Grandfather.'

'You certainly ought to be. It is time that you should know what I have in mind for you. I shall in a year or two be seventy. I'm as strong and fit as a man of thirty. When you are seventy you must be as I am.'

'Yes, Grandfather.'

'To be so you must be strongly disciplined. Have you ever heard of Sparta?'

'Yes, Grandfather.'

'Tell me about it.'

'It was a part of Greece where they trained boys to play games and fight and not be frightened.'

'Quite so. Have you heard of the Spartan boy and the fox?'

'Yes, Grandfather.'

'Do you think you would have kept quiet with a fox eating your vitals?'

John considered.

'No,' he said. 'I think I'd have made a noise.'

'Well, that's honest anyway. But the Spartan training was the finest the world has ever seen. Do you know what the Germans are doing?'

'No. I don't think . . . They burnt a lot of books, Mr. Brighouse says--'

'Pish! I don't mean that. Quite right to burn them if they didn't like them. The Germans to-day, under their great leader, Hitler, are doing what the Spartans did. They are training their boys and young men to become the greatest heroes the world has seen since Sparta. They are disciplining them, making them sink all their private wishes and impulses in the service of their country. They are no longer individuals but only members of a great body to whose slightest wish they must be subservient. Instead of the sloppy young men with cigarettes and hair over their eyes, who think of nothing but pleasure and idleness, who won't earn their living even when they have a chance, they are a splendid body of young heroes, ready to live and die for their country at the word of command.'

John, who now was suffering from pins and needles, said:

'Yes, Grandfather.'

The Colonel paused. A kind of transfiguration took place in him. His whole body seemed to swell with a wonderful glory. His eyes were misted, his voice trembled as he said: 'I might be where Goering is to-day had I been born a German.'

John, who had no idea of Goering, simply stared. He also began to be frightened.

'Nevertheless we must do what we can. One English boy at least shall learn what obedience, physical endurance, discipline mean.' He put his hand on John's shoulder, drawing him slightly towards him. 'I love you, John. You are all I have now that I have lost my dear son. I was meant to do great deeds in the world, but fate decided otherwise. You shall do them for me, and when the world acclaims you, remember to whose training you owe your power. So, after all, my life may be of some account.'

John sneezed.

'I'm very sorry, Grandfather. My nose has been tickling. . . .'

'Have you been listening to what I've been saying?'

'Yes, Grandfather.'

The Colonel was feeling his arms, his chest. He pinched his ear.

'You're not very strong yet, are you? No muscle at all--'

'I think if I went to school--'

'Nonsense! We'll see that you're strong before you're much older. We won't do any exercises to-day because I want you to think over what I've been saying to you. From now on you obey me in thought, word and deed. Whatever I tell you to do, you do. Do you understand?'

'Yes, Grandfather.'

'If I wake you up in the middle of the night and order you to run to Keswick, you run, do you understand?'

'Yes, Grandfather.'

'The slightest disobedience and you're punished--because I love you, because I mean to make you a great man, because I'm going to put my spirit into you so that you may do what I should have done after I'm gone.'

'Yes, Grandfather.'

'Come here and kiss me.'

John was enfolded in his grandfather's arms and smelt heathery tweed, tobacco, shaving-soap and hair-oil. His grandfather was now sitting down and John was standing between his legs.

'This is now my life-work. I surrender at last all hopes for myself. You are me, me as I might have been, as I should have been. You are my dear son come back to me again. From to-day we are one. . . . What are we?'

'We are one,' said John.

'Good boy! To-morrow we start. Now you may go.'

John went.

In his own room he stood considering. The Idea was now a Fact. Moreover not a minute was to be wasted. He started at once to pack. The Idea was that he should run away.

He had been approaching this decision ever since the scene with Roger. Not only was life blank and empty without Roger but it was now also extremely unpleasant. There was his mother who said 'Let's be friends,' and then was unfriendly; there was his grandfather who said, 'Now we are one,' when most certainly they were not one and never would be. John was not without humour, although nobody except Rump had ever encouraged humour in him. There was something very comic in his grandfather saying, 'Now we are one.' There was something frightening also. In fact--it was time to depart.

He would, he fancied, have started on his world-adventures ere this had it not been for two things--Roger and the prospect of school. Both were now taken away from him. It was time to go. He had planned his campaign. Almost all the boys in all the books that he had ever read had run away at one time or another, and especially in his favourite book, which was, so old-fashioned was he, David Copperfield. David had walked to Dover. It ought not to be difficult to walk to Carlisle. Once in Carlisle he would be compelled to pawn the gold watch and chain that had belonged to his father in order to travel to London, but, once in London, he did not doubt but that he would find employment. He could be Boots at an hotel, or a messenger boy, or possibly an acrobat, seeing that his grandfather had trained him to stand on his head. Then he could redeem the watch. Moreover, as he was taking Rump with him the two of them might perform for a while in the London streets. No one could call Rump an intelligent dog, but at least he could beg and bark if you said the word 'Policeman.'

He would walk between Skiddaw and Blencathra to Uldale, and thence to Carlisle. He had gone to Skiddaw Forest (which was no forest: there was not a single tree there) with Mr. Brighouse, and, although it was lonely, and, as he had heard, a man had once been killed there in a duel, and there were stones that made singing noises, still he would have Rump with him and he would be afraid of nothing then so deeply as he was afraid of becoming One with his grandfather. Better to starve in the Forest that wasn't a forest than be wakened in the middle of the night by his grandfather and ordered to run to Keswick!

His new-found manliness (he had grown in the last few weeks) made him independent and even cheerful. In fact as he stood in his room and considered his packing he was whistling 'Smoke gets in your Eyes' considerably out of tune.

To-morrow morning would be an excellent day for the adventure because it happened that Mr. Brighouse had been allowed two days' leave to visit some friends in Yorkshire.

He had bequeathed John enough Algebra, History and Geography to last him a month at least. John was very much afraid that, as things were, he would not be learning the Algebra, History and Geography. His grandfather never thought of him till tea-time and his mother would be busy with Aunt Janet. . . .

As to the packing, John had been given two Christmases ago a rucksack by Aunt Janet. This would hold one pair of pyjamas, one pair of stockings, two flannel shirts, a tooth-brush, a piece of soap and a ball of string. He would take with him his three favourite books-- David Copperfield, The Broad Highway and Greenmantle. Also a cricket-ball, which Roger had once given him. Item a collection of cigarette-cards. Item a photograph of his father. He thought that would be about all.

His further plans were somewhat indefinite. As he was not to be allowed to go to school, he might as well begin to be a man at once. There were many possibilities. He might be an explorer and spring from ice-floe to ice-floe as he had seen, in the cinema at Keswick, young men gallantly performing. He might fly an aeroplane from Australia to Croydon or even act in Hollywood as several boys appeared to be doing. The world was full of opportunities and, once a hero, there was a letter to be written to Roger.

It would be something like this:

DEAR ROGER--You have seen, I expect, in the newspapers that I have just flown from Australia [or discovered a new mountain in Iceland, or brought home Pigmies from Africa, as the case might be]. I have enjoyed myself very much and shall shortly be starting another Expedition. If you care to come with me I'll be awfully pleased . . .

Simply that. No reproaches. No glorification. Simply that.

He awoke very early next morning and saw, from his window, that the world was veiled in mist. His gold watch told him that it was seven o'clock, but as Summer Time had been a week in progress, this meant that it was in reality only six.

He dressed very quietly, took his rucksack that had been packed the night before, and stole out to the top of the stairs. Save for the clocks the house was silent. The servants would be about but in the kitchen. He crept downstairs, cautiously opened the door into the garden, and advanced, like an Indian on the trail, to Rump's kennel.

The garden was a sea of mist through which the trees sailed like the masts of leaf-growing ships. Behind the mist there was a faint stirring as though some fire blazed the earth at an infinite distance. Spiders' webs brushed his face, and leaves were wet against his cheek. A bird sang and seemed to follow, with its cry, above his head almost like his own voice. He found Rump's kennel and the dog asleep. He dragged

153

him out. Rump looked at him, wagged his tail feebly, yawned and tried to return to his kennel. John, who had long been accustomed to speak to Rump like a human being, having not too many real humans for intimate conversation, knelt down on the wet grass, put his arm round Rump's neck and explained the adventure.

'Try not to be too much of an idiot. This is the one chance you'll ever get. You'll soon be fat and wheezy as you're going on here, and you know you hate Aunt Janet and Grandfather. You shake whenever they look at you. Coming with me you'll have a chance to do something in the world.'

He thought that he heard a door opening from the house and stopped to listen. He looked back but could see nobody through the mist. He had brought with him some buns, a large piece of cake and some fragments of cold chicken, which he had found in a luckily un-occupied pantry the evening before. He gave Rump half a bun, and Rump, who was always hungry at any time of the day or night, began to look about him a little more hopefully. As with many human beings his fears were always more active than his hopes, but he was not afraid of John--in fact he rather despised him although he also loved him. Like most terrified persons he despised a little those who were kind to him. He never loved so truly as when he was being sycophantic to a tyrant. At the moment, however, John appeared to be the only mortal in this cold, dim and early world, and therefore John should be obeyed. He followed him through the gate and up the fell. John, as he closed very softly the gate behind him, fancied that he heard steps on the gravel path. He listened for a moment before he struck up the fell, but the only sound was the song, steady, joyous, confident, of the garden bird.

For two hours or so they travelled forward together valiantly, but, from the very beginning of this remarkable adventure, it seemed to John that they were accompanied. This was, of course, the effect of the mist, which was not strong enough to confuse his path but actual enough to confuse his mind. He did not feel as though he were starting on an affair that was to change his whole life, but he remembered how, in a book of explorers that he had read, it had been explained that nothing seems extraordinary at the moment of its happening. A true explorer never permitted himself surprise or curiosity, and had not Stanley said: 'Dr. Livingstone, I presume'?

He felt no regret nor 'the lament for loved ones lost.' There were no loved ones in the house now abandoned to the mist. Only, queerly enough, he would have liked one last word with his mother.

It seemed a bit caddish when she had come such a long way to see him and had told him that morning on the fell that she liked him, to go away for ever without a word. Not that he liked her--or if he had begun to like her a little she had dropped him as quickly as she had picked him up. He believed that women and girls were never to be trusted. Roger at least said so.

He did like Mr. Brighouse, who had been awfully decent always, but Mr. Brighouse had other interests. After all, John thought, if I were a man I shouldn't care about boys.

So there was really no one except Rump and the gardener. As to the gardener, he cared for roses and carnations more than for John, whose questions he was tired, as he had said only the other day, of answering.

So there was really no one. . . . He was afraid of his grandfather, he hated his aunt . . . no one at all.

He found the Sanatorium quite easily, struck the path that led along the flank of Skiddaw, and soon was alone, with Rump, in a world of noise and shadow. He had never imagined that there would be so many noises. His own feet in the first place! Whenever he stumbled on a stone he seemed to rouse the echoes of the world. A pebble rolled and the whole ground shook.

Then running water. If he stopped and listened, which he began to do more often than was wise, water seemed to be moving on every side of him. Not friendly water either. One of the things that he had always cared for best in this country, that he loved without as yet knowing it, were the brooks and leaping waters of the hills, the sudden unexpected rivulets through turf, the dark pools under chattering falls, the torrents after rain, the glitter in sunlight of broadening streams.

But these waters were unseen. They occupied the country as though it belonged to them and they resented any invader. In the half-light he felt as though, with an incautious step, he might be involved in water that would hold him and drag him down. That was absurd, for there were no marshes here, but nothing was real in this strange country whose only human inhabitant he was.

Nor was he helped by Rump, who liked the mystery no better than he. Rump followed at John's heels, venturing not a yard away. Rump was not a dog for a crisis.

'I think we'll sit down for a moment,' John said.

He sat down on a boulder and Rump cowered close beside him, pressing against his leg and giving, every once and again, an uncomfortable little shiver.

It was now that John, sitting and listening, heard steps as of men marching. If you strained your ears you heard nothing; if you tried to think of other things, tried to see the true shapes of the climbing fells behind the mist, then the tramp-tramp became insistent, forcing itself up into your actual consciousness. But then, so soon as you applied your actual consciousness to it, off it disappeared again! Then it was easy enough to fancy that you saw figures--figures of listeners, inhabitants of the valley perhaps.

Mr. Brighouse had told him that there was an old tale that, under Skiddaw, the great Cumbrian heroes of the past lived in a vast hall where they drank, sang songs, played games. This was not true, of course, only a story, and yet on a day like this in a place like this anything might be true. And suppose that, in the middle of their festivities, one or two of them stepped up out of their great cave and came to the upper world to look about them--John Peel in his long great-coat, Rogue Herries with the scar on his face, little Hartley Coleridge with his elf-like eyes and wild leaping step--John had heard of these and many more, real people and fairy-tale people, but of all the figures of the place those that dominated his imagination most strongly were the men, the heroes, who had followed Prince Charlie in the '45 and been hunted and killed here and towards Shap by Butcher Cumberland and his cruel men. These were the heroes for John, who had the nature of one to sympathize with the lost, the fallen, the strayed, the martyred.

How vividly he had often seen those men hiding, running, lying in bog and marsh, creeping from boulder to boulder on just such a misty day as this! Down the valley would march Cumberland's soldiers; a shadow would move in the half-light, then the cry, the pursuit, the rolling echo of the shot--one more martyr to the Prince of the splendid Lost Cause!

It did not seem fantastic to him now that hunters and hunted should be moving near him. And what if some of the old ghosts should resent his presence there, or simply out of some maliciousness place their cold hands about his throat and draw him into their company?

He was the kind of boy--he would be later on the kind of man--to whom there would always be two worlds, the unseen more real than the seen. That was why his grandfather had power over him.

Yes, there were footsteps, there were shadowy figures, there was always the running water. . . .

Then, like a true son of his father, he pulled himself together. After all it was very little use, was it, to start on the adventure of his whole life and, after an hour or so, sit on a stone and see ghosts? How about Africa and the Pigmies? How about the Arctic and the floes? So up he got and marched on, surprised to find that his legs were already rather stiff, his rucksack unexpectedly heavy and his stomach remarkably empty!

In these parts light can play odd tricks with natural circumstances, especially during those weeks when Spring is changing into Summer. It is then that the closeness to Nature, a characteristic of these hills, lakes and valleys, seems to slip the barrier between man and his planet. The bursting of a leaf-bud is of more import than the signing of a cheque, and a stream rising mysteriously on a fell-side is more emphatic than a bevy of bridesmaids. A cold in the nose suddenly caught here is an insult to the young bracken, and rheumatoid arthritis a joke to the first piracies of the cuckoo. Mist, which so often veils the hills at this time is not only mist here. It is a covering for the secret life of the mountain-tops and slopes, and from the heart of Skiddaw, Blencathra, Helvellyn and the other immortal possessors of this land a strange radiance may be seen by watchers to proceed, a radiance not only of the sun but of the inner being of the earth, lambent there under soil through winter, issuing now in clouds of light that do not lie on the hills so much as permeate them. Advancing through the mist the

157

watcher is suddenly conscious of a warmth that wraps him like a robe and a glow that comes, as it seems, from his own heart, making him one with the ground at his feet. He is drawn inward and is aware of a life so urgent, permanent and independent of time that, for a brief instant, he fancies that he will snatch the secret of his own immortality. Very swiftly he passes into the colder mists again and, returning to Cumberland ham, matrimony and the Income Tax, wonders at himself for a fool.

The hills, of course, have not been aware of his solemn presence; they have so many real things to occupy them.

It was such a morning now for young John. As he walked forward it was not so much that he could not see as that he saw everything wrong. With Mr. Brighouse he had been able to name peaks; he had turned back and seen Helvellyn through the gap. But now the hills walked with him, trailing clouds of mist like men rising from bed and dragging their blankets with them. It had seemed in clear daylight a short walk from the entrance to the little cottage in the middle of the treeless Forest. But now there was neither beginning nor end.

Everything was on the move, for the vapour, thin now like tissue-paper, shifted in movements without form but filled with purpose. Hills were revealed only to be hidden, and grey streaks of fell stood out with grim stone and lean ragged lines like crocodiles' backs.

Soon he became uncertain of his direction. The unseen running water, the consciousness that others were moving with him, the strange shifting of the hills themselves, all this was illuminated behind the mist as though, he said afterwards, giants were secretly watching him with lanterns.

He stopped to take his bearings and at once the space about him seemed to shake to the tramping of men. He could not find Rump. He felt the fear of loneliness and isolation coming upon him, the same old fear that he had known in dreams, in his grandfather's room. It was of no use to say that he would not be frightened. He was frightened! Giants with lanterns! Giants with lanterns!

He cried out: 'Rump! Rump! Rump!'

The mist flung up its arm, and a jagged rocky peak that appeared jet-black and ringed with sunlight threw out its shoulders at him. A moment after, the sun was gone again as though it had never been. He advanced and stumbled, his rucksack bouncing forward and striking the back of his neck. He was on his knees and it was as though cold hands held him down.

Suppose they were there, standing round him now in a ring? He thought of Roger. He wouldn't allow a little mist and a few stones to stop him, so up he got--but now he didn't know which way to turn. He had stumbled forward, but then, in rising, he had turned. Was he going back? Tramp-tramp! Tramp-tramp! Who are they? Who's here? Who's in this valley?

Who are you?

I'm John Fawcus.

What are you doing here?

I'm going to London.

Oh no! . . . Oh no! . . . He isn't going to London. . . . He isn't going to London. . . .

He began to run, panting. A stone again, and this time he fell flat.

He was breathless. He cried out 'I can't . . . I can't . . . I don't know where--'

And then, miracle of all miracles, a voice cried:

'John! John! Where are you?'

He called back: 'I'm here! I'm here!'

A real figure, no ghost, grew out of the mist. He was on his knees, feeling blood on his cheek, for the stone had cut him. He looked up wildly and saw that despised, useless, interfering woman, his mother. The sense that he had had from the first about her that she was of another nature from other persons was now confirmed in him. Still on his knees, he stared at her.

159

She was wearing the little dark-blue hat and dark-blue costume that were sufficiently familiar, but nevertheless she must be a witch, a bogy, the kind of ghost that he had been fearing. He only expected her to vanish.

However, instead of vanishing she said (and she did not come near to him but stood a little way off): 'I beg your pardon, John. . . . I'm afraid I've been following you. I was just giving Aunt Janet some tea when I heard the stairs creak. I looked out and there you were, crawling downstairs with a bundle on your back. So I followed you.'

He dabbed at his cheek with his now very bloody handkerchief. The mist was clearing. To his right was a thin stream of water, glittering in the sun, running through the rough weedy grass.

'I'll just wash this,' he said. He felt very shy--a most awful fool in fact. What did she mean following him like that? A piece of cheek! But as he knelt in the wet grass, bending down and trickling the water on to his face, he saw the world almost upside down, and, at the same moment as he caught the lower flank of Skiddaw heaving on a sunny air with blue sky slanting fan-shape into vaporous cloud, he knew that he was glad that she had come, that she had taken that trouble, that she wasn't so unfriendly after all.

When he returned (and although he didn't know it he had mud on his nose) she said in a very ordinary voice (he didn't know what he had expected--trumpets? tear-torrents? rages?):

'I brought some food. I'm afraid I stole it from Aunt Janet's room-- some slices of chicken and toast and some oranges.'

'I've got some chicken too,' he said proudly, but when he produced it what a nasty mess it was! Cake, chicken, butter all mashed together. Rump, reassured by the sun, another human being and a pleasant scent of rabbits, enjoyed it.

John and Rose sat on a flat stone together and ate.

'I kept just a little behind you most of the way. In this mist, though, I lost you until I heard you call. Are you angry with me? And would you mind telling me what you were planning to do?'

160

He realized that their relationship was entirely changed. She might almost have been Roger sitting on that stone beside him. Her hand was on his knee and he didn't care. In fact he moved a little closer to her. After all, it was true what she had said, that she was almost his own age. Anyway she looked very young, sitting on that stone with her hat off and her hair blowing about. When he moved a little closer she put an arm round him.

'Don't think I'm making up to you,' she said, 'but I'll be off this stone if I don't hold on to you.'

'I don't mind,' he said, his mouth full of chicken. He hadn't imagined that before eleven in the morning you could be so hungry!

Light was filling the valley. The warmth was radiant now and the sunlit glitter of the thin stream a thread drawn crookedly through green weed-stuff.

'And would you mind telling me, John, where you were going to?'

'I was going to London.'

'London! But how?'

'I was walking to Carlisle and then taking the train.'

'Oh, I see! And what then?'

'I don't know. I'd have earned my living somehow as a messenger boy or an acrobat or something.'

Rose held him a little closer.

'I didn't know you were an acrobat.'

'Grandfather taught me. He makes me stand on my head and all that kind of thing.'

'Stand on your head? But doesn't it hurt?'

'A bit, but he says it's good discipline--like the Spartans.'

'Well--tell me--why did you want to run away?'

161

He looked down at the ground, where Rump, properly gorged, was asleep, his nose on his paws.

'Oh, I don't know. It was slow after Roger went, and Grandfather said that perhaps I wasn't going to school after all--and you were in Aunt Janet's room all the time.'

'Did you mind that?'

'Yes, I did.'

'Then you missed me?'

'Well--you said we were to be friends--and you said--you know what you said that day we had a walk. And then, right after that, you go and don't see me at all.'

'I had to look after Aunt Janet. There wasn't anyone else to do it.'

'She was all right before you came.'

'Then I thought you wouldn't want me fussing.'

'I don't mind. Now Roger's gone there's nobody but you--'

His head was nodding. The sun, the food, the air, the walk, the early start . . .

His head fell forward against her breast. He murmured something. He was fast asleep.

She sat there on the stone, holding him against her, looking at the empty sunlit valley with what her detractors would have described as her 'cock-sparrow' expression.

In any case this was her happiest, most triumphant hour since the day when John's father had told her he loved her.

CHAPTER XI - INSIDE THE COLONEL AS FAR AS ONE DARES

This is now the Colonel's last great opportunity. He is good for--how many?--say ten more fine emphatic years. There is a possibility of twenty, for men with a fine physique have reached ninety ere now and never lost a faculty. Only in his head is there a trifling confusion; the rest of him is superb, heart, lungs, sight, hearing, blood-pressure, appetite . . . only in the brain . . . and there a sort of glorious excitement, everything astir and on the move, so that the clocks tell the time as though with a special private message to him, and the trees wave with a regal obeisance and clouds at his bidding refuse to obey the sun. He stands at his bedroom window, stripped to the splendid buff, and raises his arms. But, stooping later to find his disobedient sock-suspenders, he knows an instant of awful alarm. As he bends, there is a cramp in his left side. He sees the rising sun wearing a cock-eyed grin and there is a woodpecker unexpectedly regardless of him. The danger of our egotisms is that they have a theatre-backcloth for scenery, and scene-shifters, who also carry their own egotisms with them, are easily careless. The only impregnable stage-armour is humility, but the dramatic colour of that virtue is tiresomely grey.

The Colonel did not believe in humility, and rightly so, for were the humble just now inheriting the earth? Most certainly they were not. He stood in front of his window again, wearing now his socks and sock-suspenders. His chest was inflated, his buttocks shone in the morning sun whom, in the manner of the German Neo-Paganism, he greeted as an equal. He was paying a visit to the town of Keswick this morning and the thought of this visit gave him pause.

He realized, with only too actual a consciousness, that Keswick did not seem to need him any more. It is very easy to despise the citizens of a small town neighbouring you--easy but not wise. The Colonel knew this, for he had lived here all his life. The citizens of Keswick are, it may be supposed, of common clay like the rest of us, but for a certain kind of honesty, independence and loyalty they are worth a common man's friendship. The Colonel had never felt that he was a common man: nevertheless he had respected Keswick and been proud to lead it along the right paths of patriotism and civic virtue.

Although he might not actively realize it, he was proud of every inch of it and would regard fondly the windows of Mr. Chaplin's bookshop, the photographs of Mr. Abraham and Mr. Mayson, the silver of Mr. Telford, the groceries of Mr. Bawden, as though, God-like, he had created the whole of them.

Now, brushing his beautiful white hair with his beautiful ivory brushes, he was conscious that he was not a Justice of the Peace nor on any particular Committee, not even on one of the innumerable Lake-Preservation-Town-Planning-Save-Us-from- the-Vandal Societies. It was more than three years since the Keswick Lecture Society had asked him to address them on one of his Antiquarian subjects. . . .

It was in this unsatisfactory state of mind that he visited Keswick on this particular morning. Despots are dangerous, but a despot without authority, although a contradiction in terms, is a menace to all his neighbours. All despots are self-justified and feel that they are working for the people's good, but a despot wishing his people good and unable to benefit them is a man mad with righteous indignation. So with the Colonel on this important morning.

During one short walk from the War Memorial to the Post Office he was like God visiting the children of Israel. Everything exasperated him. In Chaplin's he could not obtain the Spectator and was maddened to observe that the place was littered with Mr. Bauman's Lakeland novels. He detested that red-faced, self-satisfied bounder who had never called on him or shown him any respect whatever. Passing Telford's he encountered a fleet of perambulators all directed by sauntering, gossiping young women who pushed him ruthlessly off the pavement. At that dangerous corner that leads to the town Square he was all but sacrificed to a Juggernaut of a charabanc, in the Post Office itself the fact that he needed stamps immediately seemed altogether unobserved by the lady behind the counter, who deliberately preferred to him a young farmer, a stout woman in spectacles, and an old man with a parcel to register.

Here, I'm sorry to say, he lost his temper and, like everyone who is noisily cross in public, realized, with a wave of indignant self-pity, that there are many other egoists in the world.

With a general maddened impression that he was going to report everyone to somebody he was in the street again and face to face with Mr. Rackstraw.

Now if there was one man on the face of this wearisomely restless globe whom he both despised and repudiated, that one was Mr. Rackstraw. A drunken parson, a reprobate, a scandal, a brazen hypocrite.

The little man stood in his way.

'Good morning, Colonel.'

The Colonel would have passed him without a word. Mr. Rackstraw was ubiquitous.

'Fine day, Colonel,' Mr. Rackstraw said. 'I'm glad I've met you because I'm hoping to pay a call. When am I likely to find you at home?'

The Colonel answered to the point.

'Never, Mr. Rackstraw. I have no wish for our future acquaintance.'

Rackstraw smiled.

'I'm afraid you've got to see me. It's a matter of some importance.'

'There can be nothing of importance for us to discuss. I may surely be allowed to choose my own acquaintance.'

'Certainly, Colonel. Certainly.'

'Well, then--good day.'

Then an astonishing thing occurred, which later, in retrospect, the Colonel altogether failed to understand. Mr. Rackstraw laid his hand on the Colonel's arm, and the Colonel neither moved away nor attempted to restrain him.

Mr. Rackstraw's appearance was displeasing, for he wore a shabby soft black hat, he had cut himself shaving, and between his left knickerbocker and his grey worsted stocking there was an interval showing a streak of white woollen pants. The Colonel on the other hand was, as usual, resplendent.

Yet Mr. Rackstraw there, outside the Post Office in full public view, restrained the Colonel, and anyone passing might, in view of their physical intimacy, consider them friends.

'Excuse me, Colonel,' said Mr. Rackstraw gently. 'It isn't for my own sake that I wish to see you. Rather for yours.'

'For mine? What the devil--!'

'Give me only a quarter of an hour. I'm sure that you don't realize the danger you're in--'

'Danger!'

'Yes.' Mr. Rackstraw pressed his fingers on his arm. 'Oh, not what you mean! Not from any person. But you are contemplating an act that is likely to be deeply resented. Oh, don't misunderstand me! I repeat-- not by any human being. But you can't do things here as you can in other places. Surely you know that! You've lived here all your life. Every larch tree is dangerous, and as for stone walls--'

'Will you be so kind as to take your hand off my coat? That you're crazy is well known--'

'I'm drunk sometimes,' Mr. Rackstraw, who was perhaps a little too fond of mentioning the fact, remarked. 'But crazy--no! I mean every word I say. Don't run the risk, Colonel. Sink your pride and let them go--otherwise look out for rolling boulders, rivers running through your dining-room, and a wild tree or two.'

'Let them go? Let who go? Upon my word, the police--'

'Nonsense! You know what I mean. I'm not being offensive. It isn't offensive to try and save a man from destruction--especially a man you don't like. Give me half an hour and I'll show you the risks you're running.'

'Give you half an hour! Give you a year in gaol more likely!' And this time the Colonel did break away, striding up the street to his car in such a temper that all the Keswickians, calm and controlled and rich in a sense of humour, enjoyed immensely the spectacle.

As he drove himself away he could only with the greatest difficulty control the wheel. The impertinent and insulting thirty-mile limit was a further source of intense aggravation, for the Colonel, like many another, felt the restriction as a personal insult to himself, his ancestors and all his present relations. Then, turning away from the river and up the hill, his mood of self-pity gathered power. He should not have lost his temper in the Post Office. A pity! A pity! Lose your temper, yes, but only when it is a tactical wisdom to do so! It had seemed but yesterday that he had been nothing but smiles and kindliness in Keswick! With how buoyantly paternal a gesture had he patronized the local Easter light opera, sitting in the second row of the stalls next the Reverend Mr. Lewin of St. John's, turning round and greeting Mr. Abraham or Mr. Bawden, charming, charming, charming--yes, feeling his whole heart warm to his fellow-beings who liked him, whom he himself liked. Going then, in the interval, behind the scenes to congratulate them all, crying out in his hearty welcoming way that he had seen The New Moon in London, indeed, indeed he had and, yes, this was good, very good indeed. London must look to its laurels. Thanks, a cup of coffee would be pleasant--wonderful on so small a stage how well they managed (seeing, as though in an all-surrounding mirror, this fine vigorous, robust figure, the snow-white hair, the friendly smile, with voices, voices everywhere murmuring 'How friendly the Colonel is! How generous the Colonel! How delightful to hear what he thinks!').

And now this was gone. They had been rude to him in the Post Office, the perambulators had driven him into the gutter, Rackstraw had insulted him. Very well then! He nodded at himself in the little mirror. If they would not have him as a benevolent friend they should have him as a man of quiet, unrelenting power. He would begin at home-- John, Rose, Janet, Michael Brighouse. He had been indulgent to the world long enough. John was growing, Rose was an intelligent woman, young Brighouse would do as he was told, Mrs. Parkin should be influenced. There were men in Keswick who would soon be eating out of his hand. Once a power here, how quickly it would spread to Penrith, Cockermouth, Carlisle! The voices that had been dimmed returned: 'You don't know Colonel Fawcus? He's really the man. I'll give you a letter to him. He's well over seventy but has more influence than anyone else in the North. Why has the North gone Fascist of late? There's your answer. When they say that it's youth that runs the world to-day I think of that wonderful old man. . . . If you saw him you wouldn't think, except for his white hair, that he's a day more than forty. . . . Oh yes, that's his grandson. Clever young fellow. Owes everything to his grandfather. Ask him what he thinks of the old man. He'll tell you. It's his settled conviction that we would never have had Fascism in England if it hadn't been for his grandfather. If Baldwin hadn't paid that visit to Keswick in the spring of 1937 . . . You remember?'

The voices were so loud that the Colonel all but clashed with a small Bentley, and it was a marvellous vision of an irate vulgar face that leaned from the car and cursed him in that instant of transition.

'He wouldn't have been so violent,' the Colonel, now happily restored to his easy good-nature, thought, 'if he had known . . .'

He passed, like a benevolent Jove, into his house.

Meanwhile, in his own canary-chanting drawing-room, there had occurred in his absence a little scene that contributed, considerably, to later events.

Mrs. Parkin had been paying a morning call. She had called to enquire after the health of poor Janet Fawcus and had been fortunate enough to find Janet downstairs for the first time, very gaunt and pale, wrapped in shawls and sipping beef-tea. Fortunate indeed! The one person in the world with whom Mrs. Parkin wished to have a quiet little talk. Not that she liked Janet; she was also well aware that Janet had always disliked herself. But all minor dislikes were now swallowed up in the one great major dislike that, Mrs. Parkin was assured, they both shared for Rose Clennell.

Since her quarrel with Rose an odd thing had happened to Mrs. Parkin. She had found it exceedingly difficult to keep away from the Hall. Like many other ladies who have not quite enough to do, her relations with her neighbours filled her days with drama. She wished to be despot even as the Colonel, but only for the very best possible reasons. She served on Committees, helped with Sales of Work and Bazaars, because she was sincerely convinced that without her everything would crumble to pieces. She often complained with genuine weariness that the number of things she had to do would certainly kill her; her efforts after Culture in this very barren neighbourhood were making her an old woman before her time. Nevertheless she gladly gave herself; it was the least one could do. She kept a smiling face; no one knew how she dragged herself to bed more dead than alive, what the arranging of just a small musical party meant in sheer physical energy!

It followed, therefore, that anyone who opposed her in even the smallest degree was Public Enemy Number One. There was no private malice in her resentment. She felt for him as Queen Victoria felt for Gladstone, Lenin for Kerensky. They were simply in the way of the world's progress, these bad people. And Rose Clennell now obsessed her. She thought of her in her lying down and her rising up, she absorbed her in her soup, she threw her to the dogs when she flung a bone to her red setter out of the sitting-room window! What was she doing, this wicked, immoral creature? What were the stories to be told, where the scandals to be spread? Janet Fawcus, who so rightly hated the woman, would have them all.

So she set off, with a brief word to Mr. Parkin: 'Poor Miss Fawcus! I must go and cheer her up!'

'Thought you detested the woman,' Mr. Parkin murmured.

'Nonsense! You can't detest a poor old maid like that. You know I'm not one to bear malice.'

Later, sitting in the room opposite Janet, she could not feel the patronizing self-pleasure that she would wish. For she was a kind woman by instinct and if she had lived in the old days, the wife of some rich and important squire, there would have been no limit to her generosities. She would have been satisfied with her position and, a happy woman, could be busy in beneficences. As it was she was frustrated.

Moreover poor Janet was sadly ill, yellow-faced, gaunt-eyed, sticking her chin out of her shawls as though it were her only feature for dignity. Nor did she believe in Emmeline Parkin's protestations of sympathy. The little woman, sitting upright on the edge of her chair, with her red-brown costume that would never belong to her, however hard she wished it, wanted something out of her.

What she wanted was soon apparent.

'But, Janet, how miserable for you! Influenza you say? I wonder how you caught it. And it pulls you down so. I expect you feel as weak as a kitten!'

'I'm getting along nicely, thank you.'

'I'm sure you are. But now's the time to be careful. Pneumonia, you know. That's the danger.'

'I'll not be having pneumonia.'

'No, of course you won't. But all the same you can't be too careful. What a cheerful noise those canaries make! Are you sure they don't worry you?'

'I'm used to them.'

'Yes, of course you are! But I always think that when one's been ill little things are apt to irritate.'

There was a silence. Janet was not helping at all. She sat propped up against her pillows, without moving, staring in front of her.

'How is everything?' Mrs. Parkin began at last.

'Everything?'

'Yes. Everything and everybody.'

'I don't know. I've been in bed.'

'Of course. So dreary for you! How is dear John? Roger goes back in a few days' time. I so regret that little trouble. But John mustn't mind. He must come out to us again just as he used to do.'

'I'm afraid John does mind.'

Emmeline felt irritation stirring within her. Tiresome old thing! But agreeable one had come to be and agreeable one must remain.

'It was most unfortunate. I'm not a hasty woman as you know, but really'--here she dropped her voice and looked at the canaries hopping to the sunlight as though she would strangle them--'I know you'll agree with me--Miss Clennell, considering her very awkward situation, is bold to a degree. How much longer will she remain here, do you think?'

'I'm sure I can't say.'

'Oh, of course not. There! Let me arrange those pillows for you. They look so very uncomfortable.'

'No, thank you. I can manage.'

'Well--what was I saying? Oh yes. Of course everybody is talking. Simply everybody. We are all broad-minded these days and no one wanted to help her more than I did. But as it's turned out--she really is . . . How unpleasant for you it must all be!'

'Unpleasant--in what way?'

'But, Janet! my dear! It's very noble of you, of course. But to have a woman of no morality at all, brazen-faced, you might call it, planted here without your even being asked--'

'Yes. It was all my father's idea--'

'I know. So very odd of the Colonel! Not that it's for me to criticize, and if only she behaved herself!' She leaned forward until her little ramrod body was almost off the chair. 'Tell me. Is she simply too dreadful to you? You keep her in her place of course. I've seen the way you behave, and very right and just too.'

'How do I behave?'

'Oh! I've seen you! I tell everybody when they ask--Janet is exactly right, behaves with absolute dignity. As of course she would. But tell me--is she rude to you? Is she behaving badly with that young tutor?'

'Behaving badly? In what way exactly?'

'Oh, you know what I mean. In these days with everyone talking about birth-control and the awful books that are published, and of course she's one of these modern young women--'

'I don't know about birth-control,' Janet said. 'It's not my business anyway.'

'No, of course it's not your business. What I mean is--aren't you going to make some sort of protest? Is she to stay here for ever? And John hates her. He was so ashamed at the way she behaved to Roger. The poor boy! I was so sorry for him. It was really far worse for him than it was for Roger and me! But what I want to say is that if there's anything I can do to help you . . . Perhaps I could say a word to the Colonel. Someone from outside, a friend of the family, can often assist with a judicious word. And the Colonel values my opinion, I know.'

'As a matter of fact,' said Janet slowly, looking into her cup to see whether any beef-tea remained, for her appetite, thank God, was returning, 'I don't want her to go. I like her very much.'

'You--what?'

'Yes. I like her. She's a fine woman.' How greatly Janet enjoyed this moment! With a sparkling merry eye she stared at the two large brown spots on the right side of Emmeline's little nose.

'But,' Emmeline stammered, 'I don't understand. I do not really. I'm stupid, I'm slow.' (And within she was thinking: 'Stupid old fool. She's only saying this to irritate me. She doesn't mean a word of it.') 'Of course I know your good-nature. You mean to see the best side of her, of course. But I can't believe--I really cannot . . .'

'Can't believe what, Emmeline?'

'Why, that you find her anything but intolerable.' (And here Emmeline's irritated indignation began to get the better of her although she knew that it should not.) 'You've not been well, dear. You've been very unwell indeed and so you see things from a different angle. Influenza especially. I know when I had it last September. You remember. The Colonel was so kind, sending those flowers. I know that I saw people quite oddly--not at all as they were.'

'No,' said Janet with quiet pleasure, 'I'm not a lunatic, Emmeline, in spite of the influenza. Rose Clennell is one of the best women I have ever met. I'm proud to be her friend.'

Mrs. Parkin got up and smoothed down her dress with trembling hand. 'I don't understand this,' she said. 'There's something very odd going on in this house. First the Colonel, now you. . . . All I can say is that people will be amazed. . . .'

'I don't care a damn,' Janet said, 'what people think.'

After that there was nothing more to be said--or only this:

'Well, Janet dear, I'm delighted to find you so much better. Delighted. All the same--do be careful. Influenza can be very dangerous in its effects.'

'I know exactly what you're going to tell everybody, Emmeline. "Poor Janet Fawcus. I went in to see her. You know these old maids. Well, if Janet Fawcus isn't in an asylum two years from now . . ."'

'Janet! How can you! How monstrous! Are you sure those canaries don't worry you? They would me. I must say you're in splendid spirits. I'll be in to see you again if I may. Give my love to the Colonel.'

'Good-bye, Emmeline. No, you'd better not kiss me. I'm still infectious, I expect. So good of you to come. I'll be out and about in a day or two.'

And how much better that visit had made her! She was aware of a new triumphant exultation. She had a friend whom she might defend. If she could not love, then she must hate, but how greatly she preferred to love! She had a friend, she had a friend! She was alone in the world no longer, and this child (for really Rose was no more than a child) needed her championship. Battles! Battles! Janet loved a battle--and here at last was Father . . .

173

'Where have you been, Father?'

'In Keswick. In Keswick. Where else could I have been? The Post Office is scandalous. I must make an official complaint.'

'What did they do to you, Father?'

'Do to me? How do you mean--do to me? Really, Janet, you put things in the oddest way. Simply incompetence. Badly staffed.' He stood there eyeing her. Poor yellow-faced, skinny creature. His daughter! It gave him the queerest turn. 'You don't look too well. You should be in bed.'

'I'm feeling wonderfully better.' She raised herself on her pillows. 'Emmeline Parkin has been here.'

'Oh, has she? And what did she want?'

'Just came to see how I was--and to talk a little scandal.'

'Scandal? About whom?'

'Rose--whether Rose was misbehaving with Michael.'

The Colonel enjoyed that. He laughed, throwing back his head, and all the canaries chirruped in sympathy.

'Rose! That's a good one! What did you tell her?'

'I told her nothing.'

'That's right. She'll think the more.' He reconsidered the Post Office, Mr. Rackstraw and the rude man in the passing car, so he decided on immediate authority.

'Well, well. . . . Mustn't stay down too long the first day, Janet. I'll help you up to your room.'

Janet looked down quietly at her folded hands, then up at her father again.

'Oh no, thank you, Father. I'm very comfortable.'

'Ah, yes, you think so. But I know what's good for you. Now--lean on me. I'll lift you up.'

'No, Father. Thank you. I shall stay where I am.'

'Come, Janet. Don't be foolish. We can't have you bad again.'

He moved towards the chair, then stopped. She had a strange light in her eye. She laughed.

'You're very strong, I know. But a struggling, kicking woman is no joke. I might even bite.'

He frowned.

'You'd better do what I ask.'

Janet smiled.

'Dear Father! I'm a grown woman. You've not bothered me while I was ill--why bother me now?'

'Are you trying to be impertinent, Janet? Because if so--'

'Impertinent? No, of course not. But I'm going to stay downstairs. Rose is looking after me.'

'Never mind Rose. I wish you to go upstairs.'

'And I wish to remain.'

'Then it is impertinence. I think--'

But what he thought was for the moment concealed, for Michael Brighouse came in.

'Fine to see you down, Janet!' He smiled at the Colonel. 'That's better, isn't it, sir?'

The Colonel, without a word, left the room.

'He's in a temper,' Michael said.

'Yes, he wants me to go to my room and I won't.'

'Mr. Barrett, Elizabeth, Mr. Browning,' Michael said, laughing.

'All the same,' Janet remarked, 'I'm old enough to be your mother, Michael--or nearly. I'm also a witch. I make prophecies. I prophesy storm.'

Later on Rose put Janet to bed and then she went to her room. She sat on her bed, swinging her legs, looking at the dark picture of Abraham and Isaac and the pale, pale silver-mauve that now washed the sky above the fell. The fell opened out to her fancy: it split in half like the kernel of a nut and fold upon fold of hill lay behind it. These hills were all gentle in shape, between the folds lay pools of mouse-silver water, and grey stone walls bound them. Over these slopes sheep moved. Hill after hill unfolded and behind each were hills again. There was no end to this pattern of shape behind shape, and the peace that lay upon them was in the form, in the colour, in the promise of refuge. The sheep gathered into multitudes, stars fell into the pools of water, and someone said 'Hush!'

She found that she had fallen asleep, sitting there on the bed. She pulled herself together, yawned, stretched her arms and realized her great happiness. She was happier than she had been at any time since Humphrey's death. Why? She stood up and smiled at Abraham and Isaac.

Because of John. He was hers, at last, and she was his. She remembered Cynthia Bones, in her room at Geneva, flipping ash all over the carpet and saying: 'Children are nothing but a damned nuisance. Take it from me.' Well, she had at the moment taken it from Cynthia. She could see now that room with the copy of some Degas ballet-dancers on the wall, young Freddie Bones looking up from the piano where he was attempting, badly, some fragments of Arnold Bax and saying rather wistfully:

'Of course it isn't the thing now to care about children. All the same in the days of Eric, or Little by Little, they were happier, a lot happier.'

'Oh, happiness!' Cynthia had said scornfully.

So they had talked and here was reality. John lay within her breast, in form threefold. He was the baby she had suckled, he was the man who, on her body, had begotten him, he was the boy now in this house, standing, his figure alert, his eyes fixed gravely upon her, ready to start for any journey that she named.

As the baby he was there with her in the room, for there was no such thing as time. He lay on the sofa propped with cushions, for he was not as yet strong enough to sit upright, but he had the devil of a driving force in him, for he pushed against her with his legs, his fat shapeless knees rising and falling, his toes kicking at her breast, while his ancient, cynical, sarcastic eyes gazed into space and he shoved and shoved, his mouth obstinately set.

While she kept his head above the water, he kicked in the bath, pushing out his feet. While he lay on her lap to be dried his face puckered for a howl, but he changed his intention and suddenly smiled, gurgling with pleasure at some thought, malicious, cynical, derisive. Then, his arms about her neck as she carried him to his cot, he rubbed his cheek against hers and, speculatively, pushed his fingers into her eye, sighing with sleep, submitting to her, trusting to her, recovering his innocence.

She had given him up: incredible, shameful act. And now she had won him back again, her life was full, glorious, rich in every possibility. She had been treated better, so very much better, than she deserved.

She looked out of window and counted five stars. So once with Humphrey at Assisi she had looked out of window to see stars in the sky myriad-thick and hear a bell ringing from the church. And the next thing, she thought, is to get him away, for get him away she must. His flight had shown her how urgent this was if nothing else had shown her.

It was at this point that she stopped dead there on the floor where she was, to realize almost superhuman difficulties. It was surely not a hard thing to walk with John to Keswick and take a train. Well, they might try it, but something told her that they would not achieve it. From to-day on they would be watched, and the Colonel eternally round the corner. John was not hers. He was the Colonel's. Once far enough away, she might defy him. He would, perhaps, as Rackstraw had said, fear a public scandal. But to be caught, in the streets of Keswick! There was only one car belonging to the house and she would

177

not be allowed to use it. She might order a taxi from Keswick to meet her somewhere, but the Colonel would know. . . . How would he know? Why was she so sure of his omnipotence?

It was time to dress for dinner. She slipped off her frock and stood again, considering. The situation had the elements of melodrama and yet she was no heroine nor was the Colonel a villain. The motives in this affair were too subtle for melodrama, which demanded simplicity and colour, black and white. There were no such colours. She slipped on a dressing-gown and moved towards the little bathroom, when melodrama, after all, comically obtruded. There was a tap on her door and there was the dear man, his white hair ruffled, two ivory brushes in his hands, himself in stiff shirt and dress-trousers, standing and smiling.

The door was open behind him, he did not attempt to close it; he only said: 'Look here, Rose! What have you been doing to Janet?'

She smiled back at him, but drew her dressing-gown (it was of black and silver) more carefully about her.

'Done to Janet?'

'Yes.' He came further in and closed the door. He began, as it were absent-mindedly, to brush his hair with one of the brushes. 'Forgive my coming in like this, my dear. It's unconventional, I know. But I was passing . . . the idea struck me.'

'What's the matter with Janet? I've just put her to bed.'

'Oh, you have, have you? She wouldn't go when I told her.'

'No. She said something about that. She said she wasn't a child any longer.'

He laughed at that. 'A child! No, I should think she isn't! All the same I'm still her father. I know what's best for her.'

She said nothing to that but simply stood waiting for him to go.

He looked at her.

'For the matter of that I know what's best for all of you.'

She laughingly defied him.

'Oh, do you? I don't think so. No one knows what's best for me but myself.'

He came nearer to her.

'Do you like this room?'

'Yes, very much.'

'It was Humphrey's, you know.'

'Yes. I recognized it at once. He described it to me.'

He looked about him.

'The furniture's a bit shabby. But that's true of most of the house. I'll have it renovated--as you're going to stay you may as well have a decent room.'

'Who says I'm going to stay?'

'I do.'

He was now almost touching her and in his face was a look of triumphant elation.

'You don't think I'm going to let you go, do you?'

'You can't keep me.'

'Oh, can't I? I told you when we took that little walk the other day.' He went on, his voice deeper: 'I can't help it if you're so pretty. That isn't my fault. You came here of your own free will, you know.'

She turned back towards the dressing-table.

'I've got to dress. It's nearly dinner-time.'

'Is it?' He patted her shoulder with one of the hair-brushes. 'All right. . . . I'll have this room done in any way that you suggest.' And he went out.

She found, as she sat at the little table, brushing her hair, that her whole body was trembling. He thinks he can do this now. He thinks he can come into my room while I'm dressing. Why didn't I lock the door? But I will. . . . She steadied herself. He can't do anything to me. We're not living in the Middle Ages. I refuse to be frightened. I need all my wits for John and myself. I need all my wits. . . .

So she put on her best frock--peach-coloured with silver strands, long and pleated. What's come to him? It's as though he knew something that we none of us know.

She came out of her room very quietly, looking down the passage to see that no one was there. She tiptoed along, moved softly up some stairs and came to John's room. There was no one about. She opened the door and saw that his light was still on. He was lying in bed reading a book.

'Hullo, Mother,' he said.

She closed the door, came over and sat on the bed.

'You ought to be asleep.'

'Why, it's only half-past seven. As a matter of fact,' he said confidentially, 'I think it's about time I stayed up later--until nine anyway.'

'Listen. Speak softly. I don't want anyone to hear.'

She took his hand. He said, staring at her:

'What a ripping dress!'

'Yes, it's my best. In fact it's the only decent one I've got. I'm glad you like it.'

'Yes, I do.' He studied her critically. 'I don't notice generally what women wear. I haven't had much chance, have I? There's only been Aunt Janet.'

'Listen,' she said again and she pressed his hand. 'Do you think, John, if a chance comes you'd run away with me?'

'Run away!' His eyes widened.

'Yes. The two of us. You're not to say a word. Your grandfather will never let us go of his own accord and I think you've been here long enough--I have, too, as a matter of fact.'

'My word! Do you mean in the night or something?'

'I don't know. I've got to think things out. We needn't stay away always, only you tried to go yourself the other day and I hate it here.'

'Do you? I thought you liked Grandfather.'

'Well--he's rather odd. Don't you agree?'

John nodded his head. 'Yes. He is odd. He wants me to be like the Nazis.'

'Exactly.' She bent forward and kissed his forehead. 'You shan't be--not if I have anything to do with it.'

'Should I go to school if we went away together?'

'Yes. I've promised you that already.'

He looked at her and she saw that now at last he trusted her.

'All right. I don't mind.'

She kissed him again and got up from the bed.

'I must go down to dinner. There's the gong. Your grandfather hates to be kept waiting. Not a word to a soul, not even to Mr. Brighouse. Do you swear?'

'I swear,' he said, very solemnly indeed.

She stole to the door, blew him a kiss, opened it with the greatest caution and hurried down to the hall, where the gong was raging like a wounded beast.

They went in together, the three of them, the Colonel gallantly giving her his arm. Seated at table Rose saw that Michael could only stare at her, his mouth a little open. It was her dress, she supposed, and he fancied that he was in love with her, dear boy. The truth was that she was radiant and reckless with happiness because John was hers. Not for ever! Oh no--not for ever! No one was yours for ever, but consider only this moment and how he looked at her as he said so solemnly, Hamlet to his father's ghost, 'I swear!'

But although she was happy she was also apprehensive. This meal was the most dangerous that she had yet had in that house. Of how much was Michael aware? Moving her lips very slightly, smiling across the table at him, she said:

'Close-fitting house of velvet, foxglove bell,

My heart within your walls . . .

And you, like rose, upturned by infinite seas,

To bleach here on the foam-remembering fell.'

'What's that?' the Colonel asked sharply.

'Oh, nothing . . . part of a poem that Michael taught me when I first came here.'

She knew that Michael understood. He shifted in his chair, looked at the door as though he were on guard against it.

'Now poetry,' said the Colonel, looking at the sole on his plate benevolently as though, out of the generosity of his heart, he had created it. 'That's a funny thing. I could have written poetry if I'd had a mind to. But it softens you--it weakens a man. That your own poetry, Michael?'

'Oh no, sir. I can't write poetry.'

'Literature,' the Colonel continued, 'can be very dangerous. Tell the cook, Sally, that this sole is quite eatable. Yes, as to literature--'

('Sally is still here,' Rose thought. 'And the cook. Wicked old man! He says they're to go, but they don't.')

'--as to literature, it can pervert the State--Shelley, you know, and Swinburne. That's why the Germans burnt all those Jewish books. No use to anyone anyway.'

'Don't you believe in the freedom of the Press, then, sir?' Michael asked, picking his words delicately.

'No. Not if it does the State harm. We are the State's servants.'

'By the State, sir, you mean a despot--like Mussolini or Hitler?'

'Well--why not? You can't deny that Italy and Germany are immensely improved. Why, Italy's another country! People aren't ready for freedom, don't know how to use it.'

'I'd hate not to be free,' Michael murmured, looking at Rose.

'But you aren't free,' the Colonel said, smiling. 'We are none of us free--so why pretend? By the way, my boy, how did you enjoy your Yorkshire visit? I've had no time to ask you.'

'Not much,' said Michael. 'I wanted to be back here.'

'Good. Good,' cried the Colonel heartily. He was carving the roast chicken. He did this extremely well, as though he had been dismembering one thing or another his whole life long. 'Glad you missed us. How did John work in your absence?'

'Oh, all right, I think.' Rose's lips moved. Michael looked at Rose. Sally, holding the cauliflower, looked at Michael.

'Yes,' said the Colonel. 'He's a good boy. We three'--he paused, looking at the door--'will make something of him.'

'Do you know,' the Colonel went on, 'I was in the garden this afternoon and I was thinking how curiously isolated this house is. Yes, even in these days.'

'Isolated?' Rose asked.

'Yes, my dear. Of course, as it is, we have plenty of callers--and there are our friends the Parkins and so on. But suppose someone were ill--Janet, for example--and I let it be understood that we did not wish to be disturbed--well, I think no one would bother us.'

183

Michael laughed.

'You wouldn't like that, sir.'

'Wouldn't I? I don't know. Go into the outer world and you're bound to be irritated. I was this morning, for example. Damned impertinent at the Post Office. And there was that drunken scallywag Rackstraw, caught my arm in the middle of the street and went on jabbering. I was pretty short with him. People think more of you if they don't see you--physically, I mean. Of course you can make yourself felt without being seen.'

Rose said: 'I think this house would get on my nerves if I didn't escape from it sometimes.'

The Colonel agreed. 'Oh, it would. It's old, you know, and a bit shabby. It wants doing up. Full of the past. And not such a remote past either. A hundred years ago some people called Meakin had it. He shut his wife up. Never let anyone see her. People said she was mad and they used to hear her screaming as they went along the road at night. There's some of their furniture in the house still. Try the port, Michael. It's not so bad.'

'Thank you, sir, I will,' said Michael.

Then they went into the drawing-room where a fire was brightly burning and silver, brass and gold all gleaming.

They sat comfortably round the fire, the Colonel and Michael, one at each end of the sofa, Rose in a grey and white arm-chair.

'Pretty, that flame-colour against the white,' said the Colonel appreciatively.

'It isn't flame,' said Rose. 'It's peach.'

'My mistake,' said the Colonel.

They had drunk their coffee. Sally was gone, the door closed.

'And now,' said the Colonel, stretching out his stout legs, 'I want to tell you two how glad I am that you are here. I have been thinking in these last days. I have come to certain conclusions. You are young.

John is very young. I am old and in another five years will be very old--or ten.'

'Oh no, sir,' Michael said politely.

'Oh yes, my boy. At eighty? Very few men are much good after eighty. However, I'm not eighty yet. We have in front of us, say, five years of growth and energy. At the end of that time John will be nearly eighteen. You and Michael, Rose, will by then have thoroughly imbibed (a bad word but it will serve) my ideas. I intend you, all three, during those five years to be my pupils. You are all happy here, I think--I on my side am fond, very fond, of you. It should work admirably.'

There was a pause; then Michael said:

'I'm very sorry, sir. Five years? But I've no intention of remaining here. I have my life to make. Also--it's a thing I've been wanting to speak of for some time--John, in my opinion, ought to go to school.'

'As to your going away, my dear boy, of course you are free. You can go to-morrow if you wish. Tutors are easily obtainable, but not, I fear, young men as agreeable as yourself. Only--there's Rose. You are such good friends. You don't want to leave her, do you?'

Rose broke in:

'If Michael wishes,' she said, 'we'll be able to meet in London. Dear Colonel Fawcus--'

'I'm your father-in-law, dear Rose,' he murmured.

But she went on: 'I'm not here for five years either. You've been immensely kind to me, but I too have work to do--'

'Exactly. Of course you have,' he said, taking a cigar out of his case. 'Thank you, my dear--a match. Over there on the little table. You are perfectly free. Go to London whenever you wish. Only--if you go--you can't, I'm afraid, see John again.'

Michael very slightly nodded his head. So that was it. Michael--Rose, John. Michael stays for Rose, Rose stays for John, John stays . .

'No?' Rose handed him the little silver matchbox. 'But--surely--you can't keep John a prisoner?'

'I can't? Why not? I'm a peculiar man, dear Rose. These are peculiar circumstances. That boy is mine--mine by your own act. He is the child of my son. He is going to be moulded into a pattern of myself. It is now the one and only intention and purpose of my life. Listen!' He leaned forward, resting his arm on his broad thigh, his rosy face full of energy and kindly earnestness, his portrait, fresh and virile, beaming down on him from above the mantelpiece. 'I'm not mad--or only in so far as we all are a little. It is simply that I've realized that this is my last great chance. I'll be frank with you both. I regard myself as an extraordinary man--one in a million. That isn't only megalomania-- there's a truth in it. I have a force and a power that, if they'd been applied in the right place and time, would have taken me anywhere. But the time and place have failed me. Some of it has been my own fault. I've missed chances I might have taken. Well, I'm not going to miss this one. John shall be a great man, and if you're wise you'll both stay here and help me to make him one. But if you won't--I can't help it. I'll do it alone.'

It was a trick of light, of the fire, of the lamp whose orange shade was up-tilted, but the shine on his glasses made them blank, so that to Rose he had no eyes, only two gleaming orbs of nothingness.

'But you can't,' Rose said gently. 'You can't. John isn't that sort of boy. You can't turn him into just what you like. He has spirit, independence--'

'No. Can't I? You don't know, dear Rose, what happens in my study. Already. His obedience, his discipline, is most remarkable. Already. In another two years . . .'

Michael half rose. Rose motioned with her lips that he should not move.

Rose got up, turned down the shade of the lamp, then, standing there, said:

'This is completely unreal. You can't behave like a tyrant in a Victorian novel. You must see how silly it is.'

'It isn't silly at all,' he answered her. 'Not at all. You'd have said a year or two ago that it was silly of Hitler to think that he'd ever be able to do what he liked with the German people--'

'John isn't a German,' Rose broke out indignantly.

'No, of course not. But are the English so different? Or would they be if times went badly for them as they've gone in the last ten years in Germany?'

He put out a hand towards her. 'Come on, Rose. Sit down. Let's be friends. I've told you my little plan. There's nothing strange in it. I think I'm being very generous about John. He's mine, altogether mine, but I've invited you here, wanted you to stay and now am asking you to be here altogether. Michael too. Nothing will make me happier than for him also to remain. What do you say?'

Michael--Rose, John. Michael and Rose exchanged one more glance.

'But I can't--' she began.

Then an odd thing happened.

The naked blazing glasses stared at her. She saw nothing.

From a great distance she heard a voice say:

'Stand just where you are, dear Rose. You look so lovely. Your charming dress--'

She could not move. The glasses grew larger and larger, rounder and rounder. She saw nothing but the deep, deep emptiness blazing with light, hot and fiery now, while all about them the space was cold. She was aware that she was removed from all sound. She could not hear the fire humming nor the clocks ticking nor that little under-buzz as of stirring insects that belonged to this room. She could not see. She would like to put her hand to her face. She could not move it.

She was terrified.

Then she heard the Colonel's voice again:

'Peach-colour. I must remember. A lovely dress, my dear. . . .'

187

She saw suddenly his shirt-front with the two little black pearl studs, then his thick neck above the shining collar, then his round rosy face.

A trick of light.

All the room was visible now and the sounds had returned.

'I do hope you'll think it over, both of you,' she heard the Colonel saying. 'It will be such a happy thing for me if you decide to stay.'

CHAPTER XII - JANET COMES TO LIFE AND IS IMPRISONED

'In fine,' thought the Colonel, 'I never felt better. My digestion is really magnificent these days.' He heard the key turn in the door. 'They're both inside there. Well, well. . . . How disgraceful!' He smiled. He stretched his arms and yawned. 'I'll tell them about it later.'

Rose turned from the door and looked at Michael, who was sitting on the edge of the bed.

'Was it wise to do that?' he asked.

'He isn't coming in again as he did the other day. I was only half dressed. All the same I wouldn't like him to know that I'd locked us both in here.' She hesitated, looking at the door. 'But he can't. He isn't back from the Parkins' yet, I'm certain. And then there's Sally prowling round. She tells him everything. You mustn't stay long.'

'Don't you realize,' he said, 'that, loving you as I do, it's a little difficult for me to be locked up in your bedroom with you?'

'What are you going to do with me?' she asked, laughing. 'Throw me on the bed?'

'I should like very much to kiss you.'

'You may, Michael, you may.' She went over to him. 'But you won't want to long. There's no response. I can't help it. It's not my fault.

Then we'll be friends always, lovers never--and later, when you love someone else, a friend like me will be useful.'

Trembling, he put his hand on her shoulder and kissed her. Then he sighed.

'You see,' she said, 'locked doors and bedrooms don't mean anything. With some men--well, frankly, I wouldn't be alone with them in a room full of open doors and windows. Michael, I'm thinking of only one thing and so must you be. Until we're safely away you've really got to be a knight, all that the modern poets disbelieve in. You've got to be selfless, coldly chaste, a knight without fear or reproach.' She stood and put her hands on his shoulders. 'I'm mad with impatience. I've never been like this before--but now I shan't eat or sleep or rest until I've got John and myself out of this. Is he mad, do you think? Is he crazy? Or is the world full of him?'

'I think,' Michael said, putting his hand up, touching hers, then taking his hand away, 'the world is full of elderly gentlemen and ladies who'd like to do just what he's doing. They're in boarding-houses, flats, hotels, slums, offices, shops--wherever there's two or three gathered together. They read their papers, go to the cinema, watch their neighbours, argue with one another at the club or cocktail parties, or in bed with their wives and husbands. What they'd adore to have would be power--heaps and heaps of it. To say to someone: "Stand there! Take your hat off! Kneel down! Kiss my shoes!" They read of Mussolini answering the salute of thousands of little Italian boys and they sigh with desire.

'They haven't the chance, but if they had . . . The Colonel has his chance. He has Janet and you and me and John. John's his chance. He isn't mad but he's frustrated. He may be mad before he's finished, though.'

Rose looked at him.

'I believe you're right. But now, there's very little time. He may go about the house calling for you at any moment. And I must go to Janet. We've got to be practical. We've got to work something out with time-tables, trains. And first we've got to discover how to get away from this house. I believe that everything's changed since he talked to us last night. He's sure that something's up on our side. I'm confident that

Sally, the cook, and probably old Lewcomb have all been given their instructions. I'm certain that if I telephoned to Keswick for a taxi it would be known in a minute. I believe that if I walked out of this house alone I'd be allowed to do it, but I'd never see John again. Being sure of all this, what's the thing to do?'

'We must trick him,' Michael said. 'Night's the time. When he's asleep.'

'Yes,' she said thoughtfully. 'Night. But getting out of the house won't be so easy. And what then? Do we walk to Keswick?'

'There's a train to London early in the morning.'

'No. Not nearly early enough. Not, I think, before seven-forty. That's daylight. I'll risk no scene at the station with old Lewcomb popping out behind a porter and shaking a spade at us, or Sally suddenly emerging from a bookstall and saying: "Master forbids you to go, miss." Once I put myself in the wrong position we're in a hole. It's he who has to be in the wrong. . . .' She thought, walking about the room. 'It's better now than it would have been a fortnight ago. John's ready for anything, Janet's my friend. If it weren't for John I could snap my fingers at him, but John's the whole case.

'Owing to my idiocy he's got him. As we've said dozens of times, if we once get properly away and he has to take it to the Courts to get John back he'll probably funk it. What with Sally and John's discipline in the study and the rest. But to get away--how? When?'

She stopped to listen.

'I'm sure there's someone outside the door. Wait.'

She went to it, turned the key softly, then Michael heard her say:

'Yes, Sally, what is it?'

'Nothing, miss. Only two towels for the bathroom.'

'Thank you. I'll take them.'

She came back.

'There! Do you see?'

191

'Yes, I do. Leave me to think it out.'

It was tea-time and to everyone's surprise Janet appeared, dressed, on her feet, in her right and vigorous mind.

To explain this there is her Journal of the evening before:

'I am alive! I am alive! My bones are still water, but no matter my bones--feeble, ugly and mean-spirited as they are. Sally says, "Here's a nice omelette, miss," and I say to Sally, "Where are you going at the end of the month? Have you got a nice place yet?" and Sally says, "The master wants us to stay on a bit." So I explain to her why she won't. Funny! She's a pinch-faced, ivory-coloured little thing. What does dear Father see in her?

'"I shan't give you a character of any kind," I say. "And you go at the end of the month." So, looking at me very impertinently, she asks me what I have against her and reminds me that the omelette is grow-ing cold. So I tell her what I have against her, quite simply. "You're not a good servant," I say. "You don't do your job." She says nothing, only smiles.

'I'm gay. I'm almost indecent, for I have put on my Chinese jacket that old Uncle Prosper sent me once from Pekin. It has red flowers, purple leaves and gold thread. I look at myself in the glass and laugh, for I seem now to have the strength of ten old maids, ten old maids who have at last a purpose in life, someone to care for, their hatred turned into love.'

But Janet was not wearing her Chinese coat when she came down to tea, but rather her plain brown tailor-made with the severe buttons. Brown was the worst colour in the world for her.

The Colonel, Rose, Michael all looked up in astonished surprise.

'But, Janet!'

'Yes, I know. I'm tottering on my legs. Thank you, Rose. No, I don't want to lie down. This chair will do. Yes, my legs are feeble but my temperature's normal, I've got a fine appetite, I'm ready for any-thing.'

192

The Colonel was in handsome spirits. 'Splendid! Splendid! But don't you overdo it, my dear. Pneumonia is the danger. You're a bit pale.'

'I'm always pale, Father. Pasty if you like. . . . Now tell me the news. What have you all been up to?'

'Up to? Up to? What should we be up to?'

'I don't know, Father. How can I tell?' She enjoyed her tea.

'There's a lot to be done,' she said at last reflectively, 'with Sally and the cook both going at the end of the month. I must try the agency in Carlisle.'

The Colonel laughed.

'Sally's all right, my dear. She's been very good while you've been ill.'

Janet smiled, a prim housekeeping smile. 'I'm glad to hear it. What do you think, Rose?'

Rose took Janet's cup and refilled it. 'Oh, I don't like her. I think she's impertinent and careless. I thought it was understood that she was going.'

The Colonel stood up, swinging himself a little on his legs. Then he carefully cut himself a piece of rich damp gingerbread cake.

'The cook can make gingerbread cake all right. You know that poor devil Armstrong at High Fell. Well, he has diabetes and gingerbread cake's his vice. He simply can't keep off it. He goes to the larder secretly and gorges. Then he's fearfully ill and is only saved by gigantic doses of insulin. What a life! . . . Are you two ladies in conspiracy against me?'

'In conspiracy?' asked Rose. 'Why, of course not. What makes you think that? Oh, I suppose what I said about Sally. But I don't like her. I can't help my feelings.'

'And I can't help mine,' said the Colonel, going up to the canary-cage and pushing a minute piece of gingerbread between the bars.

'How the wind's blowing up! All the trees in the garden are getting frantic.'

'And there's old Lewcomb,' said Rose, 'with a sack over his shoulders.'

'Yes,' said the Colonel. 'He's old but he does what I tell him.'

'I expect he does,' said Rose.

'I like Sally,' the Colonel said, coming back and sitting down again. 'And because I like her she's going to stay.'

'Then you've broken your word,' Janet said. 'You promised me before I was ill--'

'My dear Janet,' said her father, 'everything's changed since you were ill. You've no idea how different things are!'

What Janet would have replied no one will ever know, for the door opened and John came in. It was plain that he had made preparations for tea, because his hair was freshly plastered down, all save the fair strong tuft that stuck up obstinately, and his hands had that shining raw look that belongs to the newly-washed hands of little boys.

'Where have you been?' the Colonel asked him. 'Tea's nearly over.'

'I'm sorry, Grandfather. I've been with Rump. I didn't know it was so late.'

'You should have known.'

Yes, he should, and now, like a spy in the camp of the Indians, he looked around him and took in all the dangers. Good Lord! Aunt Janet was down again. She was yellow in the face, but otherwise, it seemed, restored to her natural condition, wearing her ugly brown clothes. Enemy Number One!

There was something strange about them all, he thought, almost as though they had been having a quarrel before he came in. Then, using an art that he had long cultivated, he looked at the food as though he were not looking at it. There was gingerbread-cake! His heart leapt up. There was also a honeycomb. Would he by ingenious subtleties succeed in obtaining some of both? He sat down, very modestly, on a little straight chair near a table.

'Like some honey, my boy?'

'Thank you, Grandfather.'

Having won half his victory, he was able to consider a little. How the trees were blowing in the garden! Yes, the grown-ups were talking as though they didn't mean a word they said. How well he knew that curious toneless empty conversation in which his elders, when gathered together, indulged. And then, when one or two had departed, what life suddenly sprang into the talk of the remainder! They were eloquent, amused, even as five minutes ago they had been indifferent! He had often wondered about it.

He considered his mother and at once he himself knew a fresh activity. How very beautiful she had looked when she had come into his room and told him that they were going to run away together! But it wasn't her beauty of which he was especially now aware. It was rather that she was, most unexpectedly, beginning to acquire some of the qualities of Roger. She remained a woman, of course, and that was a pity, but he was beginning to have confidence and trust in her as he had had in Roger. He was not old enough as yet to analyse his feelings about people, but he was already, subconsciously, a good judge of his fellow-beings. He didn't think his mother wonderful as he had thought Roger wonderful. Rose indeed wasn't wonderful in any way, but she was honest, courageous and loyal, and now that he had overcome his first distrust of her he began to perceive those qualities and rely on them. Since his attempted flight he had been swung, he found, into a real adventure. He had become a conspirator--the thing above all others that a small boy loves to be.

And, indeed, within a very few minutes he was to become in actual fact a real conspirator.

'That, my dear boy,' his grandfather was saying to Mr. Brighouse, 'is bosh--sentimental bosh. Abolish capital punishment and you take away the one restraining influence over criminals. Hanging's too good for many of them if you ask me, and if I had my way I'd flog them as well. I haven't a scrap of cruelty in my nature, but if there's one thing I hate it's sloppy sentimentality.'

He was lying back in his chair in his favourite attitude with his back turned to the window. The others there were also looking into the fire, and it was mere chance that John, one eye on the gingerbread-cake, had his other eye on the groaning and tossing trees in the garden. The grey clouds were rushing across the sky and, in the centre of all this storm and stress, his old black coat flapping about his legs, quite close to the window--was Mr. Rackstraw!

For a moment John thought that this must be a strange Arabian Nights kind of fantasy--but no. It was certain. Mr. Rackstraw was there and he was making signs. Very quickly John realized that what Mr. Rackstraw wanted was that he, John, should join him in the garden. There was, at the same time, something very absurd and ludicrous in Mr. Rackstraw's movements, for he held on his shabby black hat with one hand while with the other he made wild gestures. In addition to this he watched the other occupants of the room and disappeared out of sight when he thought one of them about to turn towards the window. The grins and gestures meanwhile that he made to John might be considered frantic, and a lasting memory he was likely to be, the eccentric figure with the clouds rushing over his head, the trees swaying, his black coat flapping and his features tortured with anxiety.

John nodded. The figure disappeared. He put his piece of bread and honey down on his plate.

'Will you excuse me one moment, please?' he asked very politely.

Good manners reigned. It is wise to allow little boys to leave the room when they wish.

Very quickly and quietly John had opened the front door and was almost blown into Mr. Rackstraw's arms.

'That's a good boy. Come round this tree out of sight of the windows. Phew! What a wind!'

Sheltered between trees and the garden wall, Mr. Rackstraw breathed again.

'My word! I didn't think you were ever going to look my way. And that old devil, your grandfather, kept going to the window.'

'What can I do for you?' John said, speaking with a polite maturity, as, he felt, fitted the case. 'I mustn't be long. They think I only left the room for a minute.'

'I know,' said Mr. Rackstraw, nodding his head. 'To the doubleyou. That gives you five minutes--I won't keep you so long. It's only this letter.' He fumbled in his pocket. 'Here it is. I want you to give it to your mother, will you?'

'Of course I will,' John said, taking it.

'I didn't know how to get it to her safely. I don't trust the post nor the maids. And you're not to let anyone see you give it to her.'

Mr. Rackstraw put his finger on his lip, then he shook John's hand very emphatically.

'You're a good boy. You'll help your mother all you can, won't you?'

'Of course I will.'

'What does he do?' Mr. Rackstraw said suddenly. 'Beat you?'

'Only once or twice if I haven't done right.'

'Haven't done right,' Mr. Rackstraw repeated scornfully. 'I'll give him "haven't done right." I tell you what, my boy, he ought to take a look at the trees and the way they're all bearing down on him. That'll teach him something. Don't you notice it yourself?'

'They certainly do seem very stormy,' John said.

'Stormy! They'll give him stormy! Now, you let your mother have that letter, and no one's to see you hand it to her. No one. Not your precious aunt nor the servants nor anyone. Do you understand?'

'Certainly, Mr. Rackstraw.'

'That's a good boy. When you've leisure read Gibbon. He'll show you how to deal with your grandfather. Now don't you move till I'm in the road. Safer. No one can see us together.'

In a flash of time, as though in truth he had been caught up by a drift of wind and carried off, with his hat and head one way and his spindly, unsteady legs another, a second after he had repeated, 'Gibbon. Don't you forget. That's the man for your grandfather,' Mr. Rackstraw was in the road making way for home.

John's adventure, however, was not yet concluded. He had started for the house when, most unexpectedly, created out of nowhere, there appeared old Lewcomb the gardener, a sack over his shoulders, a tattered broom under his arm.

'Hi! Master Johnnie! Where you bin?'

'I came to fetch something.'

'Fetch something, Master Johnnie? Why, you's all to tea in the 'ouse. I see you settin' there. Didn't I see you with someone?'

'Not that I know.'

'I did, Master Johnnie, and all. Don't you start lyin' to me.'

'I'm not lying.'

'Aye. That's what you're after. Telling me lies. What did 'e give you?'

'He didn't give me anything. There wasn't anyone.'

'You be 'shamed of yourself, Master Johnnie. You be 'shamed of yourself. Tell me what he give t'yer.' He laid a gnarled, filthy and knotted hand on John's shoulder.

'Look here, Barty,' John said. 'If you don't believe the word of a gentleman--' He finished lamely: 'Well, I haven't got anything and I haven't been with anyone and it's none of your business anyway.'

He had once adored old Barty Lewcomb, but now, although as time went it was a matter of weeks, it seemed, that adoration, of another age. Instead of it there was, at this dramatic moment, something very like hatred.

Regrettable, but he gave old Lewcomb a push. He ran into the house and all the trees waved their arms at the old gardener derisively. Regrettable, for he was a good gardener.

He re-entered the drawing-room to find them all very much as he had left them--only he saw at once that his chance of gingerbread-cake was gone. Sally was removing the tea things. She had also taken away his half-finished piece of bread and honey.

He sat down in his little straight chair.

'I don't think Master John had finished his tea, Sally,' said Aunt Janet.

Well, who'd have thought? Aunt Janet to speak up for him like that! Before her illness she would have reproved him for eating too much!

'That's all right!' said his grandfather. 'Won't hurt him to go without his tea for once. Good discipline. Why have you been so long?'

A question confusing to a small boy's nature, so John murmured something about not knowing he had been long.

'In my young days,' said the Colonel, 'we were trained to be quick about things like that.' Then he said sharply: 'Why, there's a leaf sticking to your chin. Have you been out?'

'I just went to the door for a moment,' John said, brushing off the leaf, 'to see the wind. It's blowing like anything.'

'You can see that from indoors, can't you?' All this was in his charming jocular way, and a more benevolent, healthy, elderly gentleman you couldn't find in all England, thought Michael. Really he isn't a bad old cock in his own way.

'Come here,' said the Colonel, spreading out his legs. John came over. The legs closed in upon him.

'I'm going to ask you a question or two. See whether you've been working. Let's see. What about history? Whose daughter was the wife of William the Third of England?'

'James the Second's.'

'Good for you. What was the battle that finished the Jacobite hopes in England?'

'Culloden,' said John scornfully. As though, living where they did, everyone didn't know that!

'Right! When did Queen Victoria come to the throne?'

'1837.'

'You're a bright boy. . . . Now show them how you stand on your head.'

John, very lightly and easily, turned over and stood on his head.

'Good. Now go to the window and wait until I order you to return.'

John went. He stood, looking into the garden, his heels close together, his hands at his side.

Quite suddenly, and without actual reason, it was more than the other three persons in the room could endure. Something was there? Was it in the Colonel's eyes behind the round, thick glasses? Was it in the twittering of the canaries, in the heat of the fire, in the wild swinging of the trees?

Janet said:

'That's enough, Father. Leave the boy alone.'

No one spoke. John waited at the window. At last (and to Michael the packed excitement of that moment of silence was deafening, like the explosion of a mine) the Colonel said:

'Come here, John.'

John came.

'Go along upstairs and read, play. Anything you like. Only keep quiet.'

John went.

Then, thrusting his hand through his white hair, regarding Janet speculatively, the Colonel said:

200

'You'd be better in bed, my dear.'

Rose got up and moved to the door. Janet stopped her.

'No, Rose, don't go. I've got something to say, Father, and I want Rose and Michael to hear.'

All the Colonel said was:

'Be careful, Janet. Be careful.'

'What have I to be careful of?' Janet asked scornfully.

The Colonel didn't answer. He had risen and was standing quite near to her, over her, looking down at her. She got up and faced him, and Michael thought that he had never seen a plainer, worse-dressed lady. He had also, he reflected, never seen her fuller of energy, determination, and almost a sort of ecstasy. Her pale face was mottled with patches of red, but her eyes, he noticed, were clear, bright and, at this moment, beautiful.

Unfortunately her knees trembled because of her days in bed, so she must sit down and she did--on the straight little chair that John had occupied.

'I'll go in a moment,' she said, 'but first I want to say one thing. There seems to be no one else in this house who can, so I must. I've been thinking while I was in bed.'

'I'm glad of that,' said the Colonel, who was sometimes very child-like in his humour.

'I want to know what you intend to do about John.'

'Is that your business?' the Colonel asked.

'It's the business of all of us in this room. It's mine in so far as I've been in this house ever since he came here as a baby. He's never liked me, but I don't wonder at that, because I can't be very attractive to children. One can't help, however, being fond of him. And then there's Rose. She let her rights in him go, like a fool, her civil rights anyway, but that doesn't mean she hasn't got human ones. She has more rights to him than you have, Father.' She paused; then, with a sharp click of her tongue, as though she were snapping a bag: 'When is the boy going to school?'

The Colonel looked at her very steadily. There was a sort of amused disgust at the corners of his mouth as though he were saying to himself: 'Fancy this nauseating old thing striking out like this! But she'll be sorry in a minute.'

At last he said:

'John is probably not going to school at all. I have already explained to Rose that I think his education will be better carried on here.'

'Oh, you have, have you? Well, I know what Rose thinks. I know what I think. I know what Michael thinks. If John isn't sent to school within the next six months I shall--' She paused for breath.

'Yes?' said the Colonel.

'I shall make a public scandal of it. The whole world shall know.'

The Colonel, looking at her with great surprise, felt his nose, then stroked it reflectively.

'The influenza's turned your brain a bit, Janet. It does sometimes. You're making a scene, a thing you've always had a horror of.'

'I'm not making a scene in the least,' she answered. 'This is quite deliberate. I'm perfectly cool and collected. For years and years now,' she went on, 'I've never interfered in anything you wanted to do. What I've thought about it is another matter. But I've never said a word. However, I can stand this no longer. On three separate occasions I've seen John come from your room crying. What you do to him there I've no idea--make him stand on his head, I suppose, to judge by your pride in that ridiculous exhibition just now. Rose is careful to say nothing because she knows what the difficulties of her position are. But I can and I will.'

'Apparently you have,' the Colonel said. He looked at all three of them, considering. At last he said: 'You're a bit of a fool, Janet. You'll be very sorry, very sorry indeed. I don't forgive a public exhibition like this. I don't know what Rose and Michael must be thinking.'

'I don't care in the least,' Janet answered, 'whether you forgive me or not. There have been too many things between us for too many years for there to be a question of forgiveness. Rose and Michael haven't been here long enough to know, but your conceit and arrogance have grown on you until you don't know who you are or where you are. Well'--she got up--'I've told you what I mean to do. If you don't send John to school and stop all this nonsense you'll be sorry.' At the door she added: 'And Sally and the cook are going whether you like it or no.'

When she had gone there was a very awkward silence. It was extremely embarrassing both for Rose and for Michael, who knew that here was an occasion when silence was quite golden. The Colonel walked about the room a little. He looked out of the window.

'The rain's come at last. Poor Janet! The influenza's left its consequences. There's no doubt about it. Don't you think so, Rose?'

Rose smiled. 'I suppose,' she said, 'she has been worrying about John. She always says what she thinks.'

'Oh yes, she does,' said the Colonel. 'That's quite true. She always has. She gets that from me. And so,' he ended cordially, 'that's that,' and, humming a little tune, he left them.

An hour or so later he knocked on Janet's door, then he entered. Janet was in bed, wearing her spectacles, a very ugly yellow shawl round her shoulders, reading.

'Hullo, my dear,' he said genially, standing by the door.

She put down her book, took off her spectacles.

'Well, Father, what is it?' she asked.

'I only came to say that I have no ill-feeling whatever about your extraordinary behaviour just now.'

'I don't care in the least,' she said, 'whether you have or not.'

'I don't understand it. I don't know what's come over you.'

'Nothing's come over me. I meant every word I said.'

He didn't move except to jingle the money in his pocket.

'I'm afraid what I said is true--that the effects of the influenza are pretty serious.'

'They're not in the least. I'm perfectly well. In another day or so I shall be quite my usual self.'

'I'm glad you think so. I'm afraid I can't agree with you. We'll see how you are in a week or so. Meanwhile I dare not--for the sake of the servants, Rose, John, give you your liberty.'

He took the key out of the door.

She sat up, staring at him.

'For the time being I'm afraid you must keep to your room--'

'Indeed I shall not--' she began.

'I'm afraid you must. Sally will bring you your food and see to your wants. The door will be locked and I shall keep the key. Good night.'

In the passage he turned and locked the door. He dropped the key into his pocket.

END OF PART II

PART III - FIVE DAYS

CHAPTER XIII - MAY 14TH: HOW MR. RACKSTRAW QUOTED LANDOR, MICHAEL TORE HIS TROUSERS, AND JANET COUNTED THE DAISIES

On the morning following these remarkable events Rose woke to an early sunlit silent house and realized at once that she was now living in a strange world indeed.

The first thought that struck her was incongruous but pertinent to the situation--namely that they were now half-way through May, and that Janet had insisted that Sally and the cook should depart at the end of the month, not realizing that the end of the month was already over. No wonder that Sally had been laughing at them!

This led her to Janet and to an instant recovery of the dramatic moment when, just before dinner, the Colonel had said to her:

'Janet won't be coming down to dinner, I fear.'

'Why ever not?' Rose had asked. 'Isn't she as well? I must go--'

And then the Colonel had explained that she mustn't go, that he had been in to see her and she had talked to him in so queer a fashion that there was no doubt but that the influenza had, for the moment, disordered her brain. He had been compelled to lock her door and he was afraid that just at present no one must see her.

So that was it!

Had a doctor been telephoned to, Rose asked. No, the Colonel had gravely replied. He thought it better not for the moment. He did not wish outsiders to know poor Janet's condition. After all, a week or so might see her in her normal state again.

So that was it!

'But surely I--' Rose had begun.

No, the Colonel thought it better not. Sally would see to her needs. Rose might excite her.

Of the many things that Rose wanted to say she breathed not a word. After dinner she quietly played backgammon with the Colonel, who laughed, joked, lost with a good grace and kissed her paternally on the forehead as he wished her a good night.

So that there was handsome reason for her early waking!

After Janet, John.

As he left her to go to bed he had with a dexterity worthy of the cleverest detective stories slipped into her hand a letter.

'Good night, my dear boy,' said the Colonel benevolently. 'And God bless you.'

'Good night, Grandfather,' John replied, and went to bed like a lamb.

She thought now of the letter. She had been too deeply disturbed as she undressed to trouble about it, but now she stretched her hand to the little table and secured it. If it had been composed in sobriety it might contain something of value--and even if it hadn't!

This was the letter. It was written in red ink and in a most beautiful (and certainly sober) hand.

DEAR MISS CLENNELL--I might begin this with a closer intimacy were it not that I fear you will wish, after our last meeting, to
have nothing more to do with me. I cannot blame you if that is so and
yet I beg you at least to read this letter and give me the benefit of your
generous doubt this once.

I would urge you, quite selfishly, to give me this one opportunity of
making a lonely old age of unhappy and useless repentances capable
of one act of usefulness. I am at your service in any and every capacity
and I swear to you most solemnly that not one drop of spirituous liquor
shall pass these lips until I have seen you and your boy safely out of
your present discomforts. I realize, better perhaps than you do yourself, the danger of your present situation. You will discover that every
step you now take is watched and that the Old Man of the Mountain,
having allowed a Notion to grow into a Tyranny, will become with
every day more tenacious of his purpose.

You must escape and quickly. I suggest:

(1) Night-time. Best hours 2-5 a.m.

(2) By car.

(3) Warm clothing against the night air.

(4) Communication with myself in the hollow under the first oak-
tree on the left of the road past your gate towards the village. I will
communicate in the same manner.

(5) No time lost.

May I add some lines from one of my favourite poets, that lion-
hearted old man who would, had he been here, have dealt with your
Man of the Mountain as he deserves, the great Walter Savage Landor:

From heaven descend two gifts alone;

The graceful line's eternal zone

And Beauty, that too soon must die.

207

Exposed and lonely Genius stands,

Like Memnon in the Egyptian sands,

    At whom barbarian javelins fly.

For mutual succour heaven designed

The lovely form and vigorous mind

    To seek each other and unite.

Genius! thy wing shall beat down

Hate, And Beauty tilt her fears at Fate

    Until her rescuer meet her sight.

Beware the barbarian javelins!

I am, dear lady,

Your devoted servant,

HENRY HURLEY RACKSTRAW

She regarded this letter with tenderness. Then she sighed. 'Beware the barbarian javelins!' Yes, indeed.

Two things frighten me, she thought: one is the urgency and the other the unreality. He is right: there is no time to be lost, no time for myself or John or Janet. But what are we to do? How are we to act?' The first oak tree on the left of the road . . .' But that is absurd. It is like something out of Wilkie Collins--almost like something out of Dorothy Sayers. There is also a touch of George Moore about the letter, and it may be that now in the ghostly rooms of Ebury Street the Conversations are still proceeding, those Conversations about the virtues of poor Anne Brontë and the vileness of Thomas Hardy's style that it would do the Colonel so much good to hear.

For he is not wicked, she considered. He is no villain. I can imagine that at tea-time this afternoon, under the chatter of the canaries, while in the garden on this lovely day the shadows from the fell stretch in long fingers over the lawn, myself, Janet, Michael, with John in the background, will accept all the Colonel's intentions. Ah, then how happy he will be! He will blossom like the rose and with kindly smile, eager like a boy, he will show us what we must do. We will be his disciples, his propagandists, and soon he will fancy that his power is spreading, that John is becoming like him. He will marshal us and discipline us, every morning we shall receive our orders. And in the end? He will be a feeble old man at our mercy. We will be tyrants, Janet and I. We will lie to him, and laugh at him, and spend his money, and he will recline, half asleep in his chair, dreaming that he is Goering and Goebbels and Hitler and Pilsudski and Stalin and Mussolini all in one, while we wipe the dribble off his chin and forbid a second helping of potato.

But it can't be. That will take too long and, meanwhile, there is real danger.

It was that that made her jump out of bed and stand in her rose-coloured pyjamas upon the sun-bathed floor. The danger was real! The danger was real!

Was it not entirely fantastic that in this month of May in the year 1935 she and her son should be, to all practical effect, prisoners in a not very remote house in the county of Cumberland? Was there no wireless? Were there not motor-cars and trains and even aeroplanes? And these modern things made this old-fashioned situation only the more fantastic because she was held captive, just as she might have been three hundred years ago, by her son and by a maiden lady. Yes, here was a new factor, for now, even if John were not here, she could not leave Janet. She had two prisoners now to deliver.

She sat down on the bed looking down at her silver mules. Of all the absurd affairs! What would Geneva think of it? And yet the trouble was as actual as a divorce, a breach of promise, an operation for duodenal ulcer, desertion by a lover, or inability to pay the rent.

She tested the reality by the things about her. Through an open window the sun poured in. It shone upon Abraham and Isaac by the other window, emphasizing the cracks in the paint, the whiteness of Abraham's beard, the blackness of the thunder-cloud, the now faded ruby of young Isaac's thigh. It shone upon the few personal things she had brought with her--Humphrey's photograph in its blue-leather frame, a small copy of the Pompeian 'Boy with the Wine-bag,' the red-leather box that had her few pieces of jewellery, the two or three books that never left her, a Shakespeare, the essays of Montaigne, and a volume of seventeenth-century poetry. All these things were real just as the thin tall glass with the orange and red tulips was real, as her hair-brushes and manicure things were real.

As real as all these was the fact that the Colonel, although no villain, might, in an excess of vanity, murder any one of them. Such things were not done? Were they not? They were done every day. There were also certain physical perils to herself not pleasant to contemplate. But by far more important than the rest were the perils to John's soul and spirit. For herself and Michael and Janet the world had wrought this much--it had acquainted them with evil, with the meanness and cruelty and lust that is part of the nobility of man. But John was unsoiled.

At that a sort of despair seized her. She kicked her feet until the silver mules shot across the room. This was like some ballet or play or macabre cinema film in which, from this corner or that, from the roof-tops, from the top cellar-stair, out of some dark and shadowless window, the head and shoulders of the puppet demon are suddenly popping! Stravinsky or Dr. Mabuse or even the old dark musty figure of Hoffmann!

So here. The scene is sunlit, the house fair and square, smoke rising peacefully from its chimneys, the housemaid on her knees washing the front-door steps, bacon frizzling in the kitchen, sheep cropping the herbs of the fell--but we are imprisoned in this house, at every window there is someone watching, behind every door a listener, and, in that room where there is the pale bust of Caesar, a lively old boy warms his heart with the fancied indulgence of a nonexistent power.

'I must be practical,' she thought, and got into bed again.

The first effects of her early-morning thinking were tested that same afternoon. She had decided that, before anything else, she must discover whether, after all, herself and John were not free to go. She was sure that they were not, but she would test it.

She would walk with John straight out of the house that afternoon and see what happened. Then, supposing that by a miracle they reached Keswick undisturbed, she would find a car and drive straight to Carlisle. But what about Janet? She was certain that she would not reach Keswick, but if she did--why, then she feared that the temptation to go on would be too strong for her. She would leave John in London with friends and return here at once to fight Janet's battle. Janet would understand and would know that she had not deserted her.

The morning passed most peacefully. No sound from Janet's room, no uneasy word spoken at luncheon, all morning John did his lessons quietly with Michael. The sun poured down in glorious splendour and a little breeze turned leaf and flower into sparkling, trembling colour.

After luncheon Rose gave John a sign and then, without another glance at him, went straight to her bedroom. Five minutes later John had followed her. The boy was no fool!

The door closed. Rose began hurriedly.

'Listen, John. In another ten minutes we're going for a walk. We shall step straight out of the house and along the road to Keswick. If we get to Keswick we'll take a car to Carlisle and the train to London.'

The boy, his eyes fixed on her face, drew a deep breath.

'I don't suppose for a minute that we shall get as far as Keswick without being stopped. I want to test it. But if we do--you're willing?'

'Yes,' he said.

'I want you to understand. If we do get away your grandfather may come after us. He may come to London. He may start a suit in the Courts to get you back, although I don't think he will. You'll be perfectly free to return to him if you want to. You needn't come with me this afternoon. You're absolutely free.'

211

'That's all right,' he said. 'I told you the night you wore the lovely dress. Don't we take any clothes and what about Rump?'

'We can't take anything. We go out of the house as though we were having a stroll. I'm afraid Rump will have to be left behind. Mind you, I don't think we'll get even as far as the Druids' Circle. But I want to see.'

'What'll they do? Shoot us?' he asked hopefully.

'No, nothing like that. Not yet anyway.'

'Do you mind my giving you a kiss?' she asked carelessly. 'You see, this is a bit of an adventure.'

He went up to her and flung his arms round her neck.

'I'm glad there's no one else coming,' he said.

Ten minutes later they opened the front door, crossed the little path and were out, through the gate on to the road.

Not a soul was stirring. The house except for its thin wavering pennon of chimney-smoke was dead, the windows blank. No one was to be seen in the garden. The hills and fields, purple-shadowed, were like a painted scene. They walked with slow casualness along the road. The Hall grounds ran for a considerable length and were bordered from the road by a high stone wall.

'I think,' John said in an almost breathless whisper, 'that nobody saw us.'

'On the contrary,' Rose said, 'I expect that everybody saw us. Sally was behind one window, the cook behind another, Lewcomb behind a tree, and your grandfather looking over the top of the chimney.'

'Will we ever get our things again,' John asked, 'the things we've left behind? There are my books and two catapults and a cricket bat--'

'Never mind your things,' Rose said hastily. 'If we reach Keswick I'll give you fifty bats--'

She stopped abruptly. They had reached the turn of the wall that marked the end of the Hall property. In the wall was a small wicket gate, and in the gate was standing the Colonel.

'Why, where on earth are you two going?' he asked cheerfully.

'Only taking a little stroll,' said Rose with a smile. 'It's such a glorious day.'

'Yes, isn't it? Shall I come too?'

'Of course, we'll love it. But we mustn't be out long. I promised Michael a game of chess.'

'Chess?' They were now strolling up the hill together. 'I didn't know Michael played.'

'Oh, he doesn't. Not to call it playing. Nor do I. But he's suddenly become keen. He bought a book by Lasker or somebody and that stirred him up again. He used to play as a boy.'

'Yes. Start as a boy. That's the thing.'

'He's going to teach John.'

'Is he? Splendid! And the winter's long here. You'll find it a relaxation, both of you.'

They were climbing the hill.

'Sure you weren't making for anywhere particular?' the Colonel asked.

'Oh no,' Rose answered. 'We thought we'd go up to the Circle perhaps and look at the hills.'

'Good idea. We will.'

Rose said: 'Have you seen Janet? I do hope she's better to-day? Perhaps she'll be able to come downstairs for a little this evening?'

The Colonel looked grave.

'I'm afraid not. It's her head she complains of.'

213

'Has the doctor been?'

'Not yet. It's hardly a case for a doctor. Nerves. That's the trouble.' The Colonel gave Rose a severe condemnatory look. What game was she playing? Why was she talking like this in front of the boy? Didn't she know any better? But Rose smiled serenely. He thought, 'How lovely she is! She is the most beautiful, the freshest creature that has ever come into my life! And now that I've got her I'll keep her! I've never,' he thought, his heart pounding, 'failed with a woman I've cared for yet.'

And then the sensation that he had often noticed lately occurred again--an expanding, as it seemed to him, of his whole person, a lightness as though he floated rather than walked, and the strangest consciousness of power as though, if he now raised a hand, the hills would sink, the trees bend, the streams come running to his feet. . . .

They were soon in the centre of the Druids' Circle, and now it seemed toRose also that the hills surrounding them floated towards them; the air was so light, so sun-lit that the strong line of the Helvellyn range passed into the crystal intangibility of the ether. A great sweep of pale white, orange, blue elements merged into one dazzling quivering brilliance, although there was no heat, only a gentle warmth tempered by the little breeze.

In all this light the Stones stood defiantly concrete, of a monstrous weight, solidity, defined form. It was as though they were so ancient that they had withstood again and again this attack of light. They had been placed there by man, and yet, long before man, they were, and the brilliance of this sky, the determined encircling of these hills had in wave after wave of light assaulted them, and scornfully they had kept their own darkness and the independent spirit of their eternal secret.

Rose would not forget this moment, for even as the Colonel laid his hand on her shoulder (she remembered as an incredible dream that she had once liked his touch) saying 'Very indistinct the hills are this afternoon' she was praying to a deity in whom she didn't believe.

'Oh, God! help me out of this! Get us away. Let John and me escape--and soon!'

Then they turned home.

Tea was finished, the chessboard was set out, she and Michael were opposite one another.

The Colonel, in the big arm-chair, his legs stretched in front of him, seemed to be asleep.

'I say, sir,' Michael called, 'do you feel that open window behind you?'

There was no answer.

Michael's questioning sign to Rose was: 'Do you think he's asleep?' Rose's eyebrows answered: 'I don't know. Look out!'

They talked casually.

'Which hand will you have?'

'The right.' That hand held the white pawn. 'You begin, then.'

Rose moved her king's pawn.

Soon Michael said: 'That's one of the few things I remember. If you don't know much about the game get your knights out. At any rate you won't fall to Fool's Mate.'

The Colonel was snoring.

Rose moved.

Michael said: 'Oh, look here, I shouldn't do that. Is he asleep, do you think? Because if you do, your bishop's caught.'

'Oh, I see--how stupid of me! No, I don't think he is. There! I'll move that pawn instead.'

'You oughtn't to let my knight get so far down the board; get your other bishop out. That leaves you free to castle. Don't say a word--I don't trust him.'

They played for a little.

'Check to your queen.'

215

'To my queen?' said Rose. 'I thought you only checked the king.'

'Yes,' said Michael. 'It's only my good manners. I'm warning you that your queen will be taken if you don't do something about it.'

'Oh, I see,' said Rose. 'Thank you. There! I've put my bishop in front of it.'

Then occurred an unexpected interruption.

Sally put her head through the door.

'What is it, Sally?'

'The master--'

The Colonel shouted from his chair. 'Hullo! What is it?'

'May I speak to you a moment? It's rather important.'

'Yes, I'll come,' he said. He strode out.

'Quick,' Michael said. 'We've got a moment. Look at the board so that if he comes back unexpectedly . . . Listen! I've found a way to communicate with Janet.'

'Yes,' said Rose.

'Below her window a corner of the porch juts out just below a part of the house wall. That gives me climbing opportunity. I can get up half-way to her window and could tap on it with a stick, take things from her and hand things up.'

'Yes,' said Rose quickly. 'But we're watched all the time. John and I hadn't got ten yards down the road this afternoon before the Colonel joined us. Lewcomb is everywhere.'

'I know. I'll try something after seven; there's a good half-hour between the dressing-bell and eight o'clock. He always has his bath then and the servants are in the kitchen and the dining-room. Lewcomb goes home at seven.'

'He's supposed to,' Rose said, 'but last night he had supper in the kitchen. I saw him about nine o'clock.' She went on in the same voice.

216

'Look here. It doesn't matter my asking you because I'm learning, but will something awful happen if I move the rook down on to your back line? That would be check, wouldn't it?'

'I wouldn't,' said Michael gravely, 'because my king can easily get out of it and your king will be entirely undefended. Look out for my queen and bishop. If my bishop takes that pawn--'

The Colonel had come in and was standing over them.

'As a boy,' he said, 'I played exceptionally well. I won the junior tournament at my school, I remember, and then--too many calls on my time--too many calls on my time--I had to give it up.'

They went on playing.

'Check,' said Michael.

'I don't see . . . oh yes! I'll put my knight there.'

'What people especially suffer from in this district,' said the Colonel, 'is rheumatism. Poor old Lewcomb now. He's a martyr to it. Don't know how he does his work as well as he does.'

'Check,' said Michael.

'I've never had a touch of it myself. If I had I should know I was breaking up. Once the poison's in your system you may as well throw up the sponge. When rheumatism gets me I'll confess myself an old man. But there's no reason why it ever should--not leading the life I lead. I flatter myself I'll go to my grave without knowing what a rheumatic twinge is!'

'Checkmate!' said Michael.

'Oh no--is it? Oh, surely I can get out of that!'

'I don't think you can.'

The Colonel got up from his chair and stood over them.

'Finished your game?'

'Yes--I think so.'

'That's good--because I want you, Michael, for a moment in my study.' He looked at them both benevolently. 'By the way, you two,' he said, 'when you want to have a very private conversation together I shouldn't have it in Rose's bedroom with the door locked. Servants talk, you know.'

The gong rang for dressing. Rose turned the top corner of the stairs, and Michael (from where he had come she had no idea) was at her side.

'Here. Take this. I managed it. It's from Janet.' He put something into her hand.

'Oh . . . did you?'

'Yes. I don't think I was seen. Unfortunately I tore the seat of my trousers--on a nail just above the porch. But I tapped at her window; she opened it and without a word or waiting an instant dropped this into my hand--wonderful woman. It's addressed to you.'

'Did anyone see you?'

'I don't think so. You can't tell, of course, but afterwards I saw old Lewcomb looking out of the pantry window. I don't--'

There were steps on the stair. They separated and Rose, as she closed the door, heard the Colonel's cheery voice.

'Like your bath first, Michael? There's time for both of us.' And then in a deeper tone of astonishment: 'My God, what have you been doing to your trousers?'

She did not hear Michael's reply. In her room, her door locked, she read Janet's letter. It was scribbled in pencil over several sheets of notepaper and was sometimes almost illegible and once at least seemed to have no meaning.

'I am sure that, sooner or later, Michael will be able to get to my window or something, so I will have this ready. I expect I shall have to begin it and stop it and hide it and begin it. . . . It won't be very coherent either. I never have been--not my nature. And at present I'm so indignant. That's a mild word. I've got the temper of a devil, you know, Rose, and have smashed up several of the best things in my life with it. My hand is trembling with rage as I write. To have a door locked on me at my age and by Sally! Doesn't she enjoy doing it too! However, let's be practical. I could smash the door down, I suppose. I've got an old hockey-stick in the cupboard. I used to play for the Ladies of Cumberland. Did I ever tell you? Outside right. Anyway, the point is that if I were alone in this I'd undoubtedly do something of the kind, but I'm not alone. You and John are in this too. Also I could, I fancy, climb out of the window although I'm not as agile as I used to be. If Michael can get half-way up I can get down. But that doesn't solve anything either, nor do I relish being caught by old Lewcomb in the garden. Still, at about three in the morning I fancy I could get away. Something serious stops me--something so serious, dear Rose, that for the very first time in my life I'm frightened. He's been in once to-day. Didn't stay long. Looked at me with real kindness. "Come on, Janet," he said. "Stop this nonsense." I asked him what nonsense. Interference. I told him I stuck to what I'd said--that he was to leave John and yourself alone and that he might keep me here for the rest of my life and I wouldn't alter. Then, in a few well-chosen words, he told me that he'd seen it coming for a long time, that other people had also, that he might have to take medical steps.

'Oh, Rose, do you know what that means? Do you know--of course you can't--what it is to be a middle-aged old maid whose thoughts have been so long isolated in her brain that they've been at times a little riotous, a little disorderly? My loneliness--my loneliness--my loneliness.

'And there have been hours in the early morning perhaps when I have said to myself that I'm losing control, when I've seen three, four, five of myself, shadow upon shadow . . . but not that . . . not . . . I have had command, I have command now . . . absolute . . . never stronger than now because you have come and I'm alone no longer. But as he stood there softly suggesting that others too have noticed . . . have they, do you think? Dear Emmeline, with the two moles at the side of her nose. Just before her Quartet attempt (and fail so lamentably) at their little bit of Schumann, can't you hear her saying: "But she did, my dear. In the middle of the night. Yes, out of her window. They found her in Keswick. Terrible for the poor Colonel, isn't it, but she's

219

been queer for a long time. We've all noticed it." Oh no, no. No, Rose. Don't I know how we take a suggestion from others?

"'Tis like a camel indeed,

Now methinks it is like a weasel.

It is backed like a weasel.

Or like a whale?"

Well then . . . here's sanity. Here's good sober sense. I must get out of this. And you also. The three of us and no loss of time. We have our means of communication now and you don't know what that means to me. I count the yellow daisies on the wall. Have you not always hated them? Between the mirror and the window one hundred and thirty-two from floor to ceiling. And what do you think? Only three books in the room, that novel by Mr. Albion you've already read to me. No matter. This is waste of time. Remember I'm ready for anything. Only watch everyone in the house. I can see from Sally's malicious lips that she is having the time of her life. Don't come near my room. After dark is better for Michael. Someone is coming. . . .'

It ended there.

CHAPTER XIV - MAY 15TH: HOW THE COLONEL HAD A BIRTHDAY

The following day, May 15th, was the Colonel's birthday and so for him a very great day indeed. He was sixty-nine years of age and he felt, as do many survivors of sixty, that with every added year he was securing an astonishing personal triumph over some secret and sinister enemy. He knew that after sixty many people quite suddenly broke up, crumbled, had nothing left for them but to prepare for death. He had for so long thought about his splendid physical vigour that he could not conceive any kind of life without it. Many of us as we grow older are prepared for almost any catastrophe at any moment--a cancer, the sudden treachery of friends, and, worst of all, the revelation to ourselves of our own meanness or falsity. Not so the Colonel. Everything good was rightly his that came to him; he had not received his sufficient due. That was all.

So his birthday was Nature curtseying to him, and a very nice curtsey on this occasion she made. For the weather was lovely, his health was superb, and he was playing a game that he was greatly enjoying.

To tell the truth, locking his daughter into her room had whetted his appetite for more. He had felt an entirely new sensation when he dropped that key into his pocket, and to discover a new sensation at sixty-nine is something.

He did not wish to be cruel, in fact he had never liked his daughter so much as now. Soon she would say to him: 'Father, you'd better have your way with John. And we'll all help you.' And Rose would say: 'Very well, Janet's given in. I'll give in too.' Dear Rose! Dear, dear Rose! What a companion for his old age she was going to be!

But locking Janet's door had stirred him to further activities. He had been, he must confess, surprised at the eagerness with which old Lewcomb had agreed to 'keep an eye open.' The Colonel had given no reasons. He had simply said: 'I don't want anyone to leave this place for a day or two without my knowing.' The barest word, of course, was all that Sally had needed. And how Sally hated Rose and Janet! You wouldn't have thought she could hold so much feeling in her little skinny body!

This was all a new game for the Colonel.

On the breakfast-table there were presents, an amber cigarette-holder from Rose, a tobacco-pouch from John, some ties from Michael. Nothing from Janet.

'Nothing from Janet,' he said, smiling across at Rose. 'She hasn't, of course, been able to go out and get anything.'

'Will she be coming down to-day?' asked Rose.

'I'm afraid not, my dear. Rest is what she needs. Rest and seclusion.'

And how happy he was! It did your heart good to see him. He was wearing a carnation in the button-hole of his light grey tweed. He was so clean and healthy and shining that he made Michael feel quite shabby.

'Thank you, my dears. Thank you, thank you a thousand times. Kidneys, Michael? Oh, you should. They smell so good. What about giving John a holiday, Michael? I'll take him out in the car. Like that, John? What are your plans to-day, Rose? Such a peach of a day.'

'I don't know. I thought of taking John into Keswick. He can go for a drive as well.'

'Oh, we'll all go into Keswick. We'll have coffee at Storm's. How I adore presents! I remember as a small boy--' He picked up one of Michael's ties, a purple heather-coloured one. 'Just my colour, my boy. How did you guess?'

'Oh, I don't know. I knew it would suit you.'

'Did you? Well, you guessed right. My God, I'm sixty-nine--just think of it! And touched my toes after my bath as though I were twenty. Michael, you're having no breakfast. What about an egg?'

'No, thanks.' Michael got up. 'Then John's to have no lessons to-day?'

'No. He shall spend the day with me. Like that, John?'

'Yes, Grandfather.'

'That's good. That's good.'

He polished his spectacles with his dark red silk handkerchief, then got up, and went off to the study humming.

Rose followed him.

She stood in the doorway.

'What is it, my dear?'

She closed the door. She was by her own wish shut in with him, alone with him and the pale naked head of the saturnine Caesar.

Then quite suddenly and altogether to her own surprise she lost control--that control that she had lost only once since arrival here, on that occasion when, in the passage, she had smacked Roger's face. It was a witness to the change in her perhaps that never, during all those years at Geneva, had she lost control about anything, not even when the First Secretary of the Ellonian Legation had asked her to stay with him at the Rocklitz Hotel for two nights.

She had intended now to be calm, but he was holding John's to-bacco-pouch in his hand and appraising it.

'You ought to be ashamed to be holding it!' she cried. 'If I'd had my way he wouldn't have given you anything at all!' She really was aston-ished at the sound of her own voice. It was as though a third person were with them in the room. But in fact she caught sight of the third person. There was a small cheap gilt mirror hanging on the left of the door. It was hanging crookedly and swayed ever so slightly on its nail. Its surface was blurred and a trifle distorted; it reflected one corner of the Colonel's desk, his arm and shoulder, sometimes his full face, sometimes his nose and cheek only; the cheek was swollen, bulging as though the Colonel were sucking toffee, and as the mirror so gently swung, so the Colonel swung as though he were a marionette on a string.

Rose could see this mirror and its reflection from where she stood.

'My dear! Why, you're in a temper--and my birthday too!'

'No. I'm not in a temper, but I'm angry. . . . Oh, stop swinging . . . no, never mind. I'm a little incoherent.'

She came close to his desk, her eyes shining, her face flushed (as bald-pated Caesar observed) with her eagerness.

'Listen. What are you doing with Janet? What about John and myself? Don't you see how ridiculous and unreal it all is? You can't lock me up as well as Janet. What do you do if I go out and tell everyone that it isn't Janet who's mad, but you? What will you say if I tell them that you ill-treat John and make love to your housemaids? You've locked Janet up all right, but I'm free--I'm free! You can't stop me!'

'Yes, dear Rose, I can. After all, John's mine, isn't he?'

'Not if I prove that you're crazy, that you--'

'Oh, but I'm not crazy, not in the very least. There's not a soberer, quieter gentleman in the North of England. Say what you like. Who's to believe you? Everyone knows that you have no right in John. Everyone is prepared for you to say anything crazy in order to get him back again. Who's to believe you, my dear? Mrs. Parkin doesn't love you and she's taken care, I'm sure, to spread abroad her opinion of you. I'm sorry to say that Sally and the cook don't love you either. There's only young Michael and everyone knows that he's fallen a slave to your beauty and isn't to be trusted, poor young man. No, no, I should have the best of it there and you'd never see John again.'

Then he did an odd thing. He took off his glasses and laid them carefully on the table.

'Look at me, my dear. There, that's right. I know you don't like my spectacles. See, I've taken them off. Now, look at me. You can't say I'm not a friendly old man who means well. I do. I do indeed. We are two people all of us. Jekyll and Hyde if you like--a very old story. If I am rude or thoughtless or arrogant to somebody he or she sees me unpleasantly. I am charitable, generous, honest--lo, I'm an angel! I'm neither devil nor angel any more than the rest of us. There is a third, the real true creature whom so few people know. Won't you be one of them, my dear? Won't you try and understand this ambition of mine, the last of my life? If I lose John I lose everything at the moment of losing him--my health, my vigour, everything will go. I've looked after him, fed him, clothed him, brought him up. Who else but I? Why shouldn't I fight to keep him and to keep you too?'

'You can't! You can't!' she answered passionately. 'You can't imprison us here. We must have our freedom. Don't you see that? Forgive me if I'm excited.' She suddenly smiled. 'Don't mind that. Don't notice it. Things have been so strange in this house during the last week. What you say is true, I'm sure. Well then. Let John and me go. We'll come back. John shall go to school, but he'll write to you every week and this shall be his home as it shall be mine if you wish it. Don't you see that it's the only way? You can't keep us here. You can't really. John shall be yours just as much--'

'John is mine.' He put on his spectacles again. 'I can't keep you--no. But John I can keep and will. Is the door shut, my dear? There's a draught.'

She went to the door.

'Yes, it's closed.'

'That's right. Think it over. Don't be upset. We'll go to Keswick and have a real birthday party.'

'And Janet?'

225

'Ah, there you are going a bit too far. After all she's my daughter and I know many things about her that you can't know. Poor Janet! I've seen this coming for a long time.'

'But she's perfectly sane!' Rose cried. 'There's nothing the matter with her whatever.'

'That's what you think, dear Rose.'

'It's hopeless then,' Rose said quietly. 'I've done all I can.'

'Are you threatening me?' he asked her, smiling.

But she had left the room. The mirror swung on its cord. He got up to straighten it.

She found Michael.

'Listen,' she said. 'It's all settled. I've had my last talk with him. There's nothing more to be done with him--now or ever.'

She looked about her.

'Where we've got to talk is right in the middle of the lawn where everybody can see us and no one can overhear us.'

They went out and walked slowly up and down the lawn while the sun blazed down on them.

The queer thing was that Rose felt, as she took those few steps into the garden, as though they were the first steps of her life into freedom. The grass in the light of that sun ran like water to the purple-leaden shadow under the big oak, and this sense of movement under her feet made her part of the honey-scented air, the blue hills, and a sky so stainless that it fell into deeper and deeper spaces of light shadowing light. The thing was that she was suddenly sure of her freedom, and so, looking at Michael, loved him like a sister.

'This is final, then,' she said, and saw old Lewcomb, with his sleeves rolled up and his thin-pointed stern towards them, bending down over a flower-bed. 'I've given him his chance. I've put it to him for the last time. Now what we've got to do is to get out of here at the first possible moment.'

'Yes,' said Michael, 'to-morrow night.'

'Perhaps that's too soon,' Rose said. 'There's Mr. Rackstraw to be consulted. I propose that I write him a note now, at once, saying that we're leaving immediately and at night. When can he be ready? You will shortly stroll up the road and leave the note in the tree as he explained.'

'Why shouldn't I go straight to his house? What's to stop me?'

'Nothing's to stop you except that he must have had some reason for advising otherwise. In any case we don't want Lewcomb or Sally running at once to the Colonel with the news that you've been to see Rackstraw. If you're clever you can drop the note into the tree without anyone seeing you.'

'All right. I'll do it,' Michael said.

'Doesn't it give you the very strangest feeling walking up and down this patch of grass? Lewcomb is watching us from under his armpits. Sally and the cook are looking at us from the kitchen window, the Colonel from his study. But here we are on magical ground, in sanctuary. No one can come to us and say we are doing wrong, no one can overhear us, the fells look down protecting us.

"And you, like rose, upturned by infinite seas,

To bleach here on the foam-remembering fell."

Don't you see, Michael? You can be free anywhere inside the prison walls. There's the sun-scattered patch, you can see the fells if you wish it!'

He saw that she was beside herself with happiness.

'What is it?' he asked.

'For the first time in my life I see my way. I shall love the Colonel the rest of my days for showing me. And when you've escaped with us, Michael, and we're all together in London, I'm never going to bother any more at the small things that used to worry me--chagrins, piques, disappointments--for there we'll be, all four of us, Janet, you, John and me, on our square of sunlit grass, and people can lock doors or look out of windows, they can't touch us, they can't touch us. We're ourselves, independent . . . and then we can be of use to others. Don't you see? Only after we can stand by ourselves.' She caught his shoulder, she gave him for a brief moment a hug. 'Now. They've all seen that. They're wondering, they're speculating. They are sure that soon we shall be sleeping together, I the siren, you the poor hapless young.'

'The only thing is,' Michael said, 'that when you go I'm not coming with you.'

'Not coming?' She turned in her steps and stared at him and, for that moment, loved him--his youth, his loyalty, his devotion to herself. He saw in her eyes something that he had never seen there before, and for that instant they stood there, entranced, on that golden sun-scented lawn.

Then he knew that it was illusion.

'No, I'm not coming.'

'But why? Of course you're--'

'No. I must stay behind. To tell him for one thing. That's a pleasure you mustn't deprive me of, Rose, dear. For another, in my case it would be running away.'

'Well, we are running away--the lot of us!'

'With you it's different. He's been violent to Janet and refused freedom to yourself and John. He hasn't refused me anything. As a matter of fact he's been very decent to me always, in every way. I'd much rather stay and have it out with him. To tell you the truth, I'm rather fond of him.'

'So, as a matter of fact,' said Rose slowly, 'am I. That's what makes this whole affair so absurd and unreal. I hate him when he makes love

228

to me and is crazy to John, and it's because he does things like that we've got to go--but the rest of him . . . Don't you think,' she said, 'that when we have got away all will be well? He'll come and see us in London. We'll make him.'

Michael shook his head. 'Never. It's a cruel thing we're doing. We can't help ourselves, but it's cruel all the same. He'll never get over it! The jokes in the neighbourhood, the failure, the loneliness . . .'

Rose turned to the house.

'Oh, isn't it beastly!' she cried. 'Either way. Whether we go or we stay. Whether--'

But he was coming out of the house towards them.

'He couldn't bear it any longer,' Michael said. 'He had to know--'

'Well, my dears,' the Colonel cried. 'What about our trip to Keswick? Where's young John?'

Half an hour later the three of them, the Colonel, Rose and John, were seated in Storm's Café. This is the meeting-place for the Keswick gossipers of a morning, and on a fine day it is one of the most cheerful places in the universe.

From where you sit you can look out on to the town Square, see the motor-cars marshalled into their resting-places by the genial lame man who is like a mother to them, watch the figures pass, hurrying to their business or staying for laughing conversation, see the sheep driven wandering-fashion from point to point, consider the visitor from the outside world who lingers from shop to shop. This is the human world, and the other world above it and around it is also human, for this little huddle of brick and mortar is planted in the very cup of the hills. You cannot ever forget Skiddaw breaking like a flower, Blencathra with its serried edge, the two Lakes spreading on either side, one to the Border country deep in battle, foray and sudden death, the other to the most beautiful small valley in the world, enclosed immortally by imperishable hills. Nothing changes here. Motor-cars may come and go, from the hotel opposite faintly may be heard the strains of the midday radio

music, still the sheep scatter by on silent feet, Southey wrapped in con-
templation of the new box of books from London walks solitary,
Hartley Coleridge takes a skip and a jump, snapping his fingers, and
darkly, more ghostly, behind these, the thick-set German miners, with
their Elizabethan colours, stand, cautious, foreign, while the hump-
backed pedlar strikes the sun with his silver and cheap gold.

Nevertheless what Rose saw was that, holding the centre of the
room and greeting the Colonel with the most cordial of welcomes,
were Mrs. Parkin, Mrs. Lincoln and the Morphew family!

Well, what of it? In another two days they would be as the dust of
yesterday's road! She was aware, however, that their own arrival created in the café almost a frenzy of excitement. For here was the
wicked woman and her bastard child, here the unfortunate father of the
lunatic lady! Never, however, had that unfortunate father been more
gay, more brilliantly alive.

'Now, if that isn't splendid! On my birthday too! Did you know it
was my birthday, Emmeline? I bet you didn't. Yes, coffee. Coffee.
Your very best on this splendid morning! An ice for you, John? Coffee, vanilla, strawberry?'

'Vanilla and strawberry, please,' John said.

Conversation continued and Rose forgot everything else in her
pride in her son. He had gained, she thought, new poise and independence in the last few weeks. That might of course be her imagination,
but she was assured that he felt himself freed from some bondage. He
sat in his chair next to the pale and despondent Miss Morphew, and
Rose heard him say: 'Yes, it is a lovely day, isn't it?'

Mrs. Parkin beamed and words flowed from her. 'No, I had forgotten! How careless of me! But I'm sure you don't remember my
birthday! Not that I want it to be remembered because I'm really the
most terrible age! What we ought to do is to serenade you with some
music. What do you say, Hilda darling?' (This to Mrs. Lincoln.)

'Music! Rather! Not that I'm in very good voice.'

'Nonsense, Hilda! I never heard you sing better than the other evening. That song about Celicia. What was it? Brahms, Wagner . . . ?'

'Strauss, darling, and her name wasn't . . .'

'Never mind. It was lovely.' Then Mrs. Parkin really began. 'But I forgot. A serenade would never do for poor Janet. How is Janet?'

Everyone listened--even Miss Morphew, who had just been saying to John: 'But I don't care for animals. I know everyone thinks I do. As a matter of fact I'm sick--'

'Janet isn't too well,' the Colonel said gravely. 'What we fear is a nervous breakdown. She's been doing altogether too much, and then that influenza . . . No, Janet will have to go carefully--'

'Oh, isn't that terrible!' Mrs. Parkin's eyes sparkled with excitement. 'As a matter of fact when I came over to see her the other day and had a little talk with her I thought she wasn't at all herself. Very excited and--'

'Do you know,' Rose broke in, 'I think she's perfectly well. You'll be seeing her about in a day or two. The rest will have done her a lot of good.'

There was a silence. Rose could hear the undertone: 'Fancy! That woman daring . . . ! The poor Colonel! But he brought it on himself!'

And the Colonel said, beaming on them all: 'I dare say Miss Clennell is right! We shall see! We shall see!' After a while, wiping his spectacles, he got up. 'We must be moving on. Finished your ice, my boy?'

John had not, but being a proper guest he murmured that he had. The Colonel paid and into the sunlit Square they went. John was a step behind them. The Colonel said:

'Dangerous, my dear, dangerous.'

And then, as they approached the car: 'How you women do stick together!'

On the return journey Rose realized that the battle had advanced another stage. He was furious--but he made her the prettiest speeches. His voice was now so refined and delicate that the feelings concealed were like lions and tigers behind bars.

231

'Now this is a day!' he said. 'Dear Rose, aren't you learning to love this country? Will you ever be able to leave it again? I do hope not. Can you write? Novels, I mean? I wish you'd try and put that wretched Bauman out of existence. Although as a matter of fact it's a native who ought to write the epic of this soil--someone born and bred here.' So he chattered on, and the incongruity between words and feelings was so great that she was reminded of various oddities--of John Lacey who told her that he always had a volume of Proust by his side when he worked and yet he wrote like a navvy, or of a white-haired American publisher once pointed out to her at the Savoy, shepherding intellectuals like May Tooney and Consett into luncheon, and he with not a notion of literature in him!

'He would like,' she thought, 'to take my neck between his red hands and snap it. What won't he do if we give him time!'

But to give him time was just what they mustn't. And then, so absurd was this affair that she had an unexpected movement of affection towards him as they moved into the house. She touched his arm.

'Please,' she murmured. 'Think it over again. Just give the other plan a trial. See how it works. Let Janet free. Give John and myself a week in London. I promise we'll return.'

He didn't answer her. He didn't look at her. He turned back.

'John! John, my boy!'

'Yes, Grandfather?'

John came running up.

'Come into my study a moment, will you?'

Then, after John had passed him, he said to Rose:

'John is mine and by your own wish. I love you, dear Rose, but I don't trust you an inch.' He bent forward and very lightly kissed her cheek. 'Funny thing, I've never trusted a woman all my life long.'

So, after luncheon in her own room, Rose wrote her note to Mr. Rackstraw.

DEAR MR. RACKSTRAW--Everything's been done that can be done--in the line of persuasion I mean. The funny thing is that in a way I understand him. This is his last chance to prove to himself that he is still something--that he has the power that he's always wanted so much. But what's the use? We can't all be sacrificed to his desire to prove himself. As a matter of fact I think I'm going a little crazy in this house--Michael and Janet too. The only one of us who is perfectly happy and enjoying it all is John. So we must get away as soon as possible. There's no time to be lost. Janet is locked in her room but Michael can get her out through the window. I feel the absurdity of writing this, as though we were living in a detective novel, but it's real enough, as poor Janet knows. As you say, night is the only time and, I think, two nights from now. That is the night of the 17th to 18th. The morning of the 18th between one and two. I don't know what your advice will be, but I've thought it out and I'm sure that the best thing will be to motor to Seathwaite, leave the car there, walk over Stye Head to Wastdale, get something there to take us to Seascale and then catch a London train. Anything from Keswick is impossible. There isn't a train till 7.40, which will be full daylight. He won't--if we get away--know of it till the morning. Michael, brave boy, will stay behind (by his own insistent wish) and tell him that we've gone although not where we've gone. By that time we should be at Seascale and well in the train before he gets there. Let me know what you think of this. I think if your car is waiting at the tree where I put this note that will be best. It is good of you to help us. I shall never forget it.

Yours,

R. C.

As had been already arranged, she came out of her room and Michael crossed the passage at the same moment. They brushed together; she made some laughing remark; the note was in his pocket.

At the same moment the cook's head appeared at the top of the stairs.

'Excuse me, miss--'

'Yes, what is it?'

'It's only about dinner, Miss Clennell. I was wondering whether you'd fancy a nice little bit of veal.'

Rose burst out laughing. The cook looked at her suspiciously, then her rather long sallow face (a sheep's head with some dark hairs on the upper lip) slowly flushed.

'Yes, miss?'

'Oh, it's nothing. Forgive me, Mrs. Button. I was thinking of something. Yes, veal will be splendid.'

'Very good, miss. I'm not wanting to bother Miss Janet with the meals just now.'

She had disappeared.

Rose returned to her room. From one window she could see the garden, now misty with accumulated sunlight as though it had been stored through the day; from the other the fells, now stripped bare with warmth, a nakedness of heat. But it was the window over the garden from which she watched, standing behind the curtain. She also could see the road for a considerable way before it turned.

First she saw old Lewcomb on his knees before a flower-bed. Then she saw Michael saunter out with Rump at his heels. Through the open window she heard Michael's voice: 'Coming for a run, old boy?' She saw Rump wag his tail ecstatically, then give Michael a suspicious look as to say: 'Is this another plot to lead me into some impossible situation?' He was reassured and ran wildly to the gate. She saw Michael saunter through. A moment later Lewcomb rose to his feet, looked cautiously about him, then, carrying a flower-pot in one hand and a rake in the other, wandered with a kind of lop-sided casualness to the gate. He opened it and moved into the road, but he had taken too long over his plotting. Michael was returning. They met ten paces down the road and Rose heard, through the clear sunny air: 'Hullo,

Lewcomb. What are you doing in the road with a flower-pot? Planting flowers in the hedges? I forgot my pipe.' And he came up the garden path humming. The note had been delivered to the tree.

Only one further incident of this day need be recorded.

One night of the week John had a hot bath. Rose passed the bathroom door and heard from within a voice singing 'Smoke gets in your Eyes' greatly out of tune. She knocked and entered. He was lying flat, wriggling the toes of one foot.

'Do you mind me, John?'

He rubbed the water out of his eyes with his knuckles.

'No, of course not.' He smiled, but this time not cautiously. 'I say,' he whispered hoarsely, 'how's the plot going?'

'It's very hot in here, isn't it?' She sat down on the little cane-bottomed chair beside the bath.

'You bet it is. The hotter the better.' He turned over on his side. 'I've been wanting to see you all the afternoon. When are we going, Mother?'

She leaned towards him. 'Two nights from now, I expect.'

'Golly!' He sat up. 'You know,' he said, 'it's funny, but I'm looking forward to it like anything.'

'Looking forward to what?'

'Going away with you. Only we'll see Grandfather sometimes, won't we?'

'Of course.'

'He's very decent sometimes. Then other times he isn't. It would be better not seeing him always. What school am I going to?'

'I don't know yet. Where would you like to go to?'

'Oh, Rugby, I think. I met a chap at the Parkins' who said they've got an awfully decent Head there now. How are we going to run away?'

'In the middle of the night. Mr. Rackstraw's taking us in his car.'

'I say--won't that be fine! Is Aunt Janet coming?'

'Yes.'

His face fell.

'You don't like her?' Rose asked.

'Not exactly. . . . It's . . . I can tell you everything now, can't I?'

'Of course you can.'

'I don't like women--except you. And I didn't like you at first.'

'You haven't seen many, have you?'

'Oh, I don't know. There's Mrs. Parkin and Aunt Janet and Mrs. Lincoln, the singing one, you know, and Mrs. Morphew and Sally and Mrs. Button--'

'Well, there are others!' Rose said slowly. 'You do like me now, then?'

'Oh yes, awfully.'

'I'm glad.'

He sponged his face. 'I think I'll get out now.'

He stepped out and stood in front of her.

'Do you mind my drying you?'

'No, of course not. Only you'll get awfully wet.'

'No, I won't. I'll put this towel over my dress.'

She had his body in her arms. She wrapped the towel round him, held him tightly, then kissed the back of his neck.

He paid no attention but went on chattering like a little bird.

'It will be frightfully exciting in the middle of the night. We'll have to go downstairs as quietly as anything. Have you noticed? They're awfully creaky? And there's another thing . . .'

He was unaware with what agitation her heart was beating against his steady one.

CHAPTER XV - MAY 16th: THIS DAY BELONGS TO JANET

This is Janet's third day of imprisonment. Her room has become her world.

'And praise the Lord that I didn't prevent him putting in those bath-rooms five years ago. Two of them. My room and Rose's. The funny thing is that he holds to that small Spartan bedroom of his own and trots across the passage every morning to the general bath carrying his big sponge like a banner and tap-tapping with his bedroom slippers. . .

But now on the third morning she is thankful for nothing. A kind of terror has crept in. It is as though the walls were closing.

Yes, it was a lovely summer morning. She had flung both her windows wide open, and now she stood, as she had done already so many times, in her pyjamas and dressing-gown, looking into the outer world. From the main window that looked into a garden alive with bird-song, the abode now of sunlit peace (old Lewcomb was not about as yet), the jump was tremendous for a middle-aged lady. The old house was a high one. There was nothing to break the fall.

From the other (as she now well knew) the descent would not be difficult could she make up her mind to it. Twice now Michael had visited her. She took from the pocket of her dressing-gown the note of the evening before:

Courage, Janet dear. We have settled on Friday night. (By the way, tear this up as soon as you have received it.) I have word from Mr. Rackstraw that he agrees with our plan to leave between one and two on the morning of the 18th (night 17th-18th). He will take us in his car. More to-morrow evening. Love. R.

She had not obeyed her orders. She tore the note up now into little fragments and dropped them into the w.c. in the bathroom.

She considered the descent. First she must climb on to the window-sill. (She would have the window open all night so that it should not creak with the opening.) Then she must slip (and here for a moment she shut her eyes) down the length of pipe until she reached the roof of the porch. Here Michael would be to secure her. Then she must jump. She must jump out and away so that she landed on the lawn and she must trust to luck that she did not break a leg or an arm or sprain an ankle. The distance was not great and for most people an easy jump. Michael would jump first and he had told her that he was strong enough to catch her, but she was no light weight, was clumsy and awkward. Nevertheless she had once played hockey for the Ladies of Cumberland and she could do what she had a mind to!

She turned from the window with a quaver at her heart!

She had lived in this house her life long, and now she must jump from a window to escape from it! Incongruous incident for a sober-living spinster!

She returned to her bed and steeled herself for another day. Last night she had slept scarcely at all. She had heard every hour strike from the crazy old clock on the stairs that went first 'Boom!' as though it meant a terrible business, then hesitated clearing its throat, then faltered into a pitiful whisper of strokes, apologizing for its very existence. With every hour struck, the room, large though it was, had seemed smaller.

At no time had it been beautiful, for Janet did not care for aesthetic beauty. 'Serviceable' was what she wanted things to be. She could appreciate a vague nebulous rotundity of words, like the prose in Mr. Albion's novels; a sunset could stir her were it large enough, and Mrs. Lincoln's singing appealed to her because of the noise that it made. But she would not have her room littered with trifles. Tidiness was what she demanded. Tidy it was, but now that same sparseness was beginning to be terrifying. The large gaunt wardrobe, the squat chest-of-drawers, the dressing-table with its ugly mirror, an old photograph of her father and mother, taken shortly after their marriage, a very large and gloomy coloured engraving of 'The Massacre of Glencoe'; these objects, familiar to her for so long, seemed now on this third morning to be threatening her with some personal malevolence. She had never lived with them so long at a time before. She had gone in and out of that room a thousand thousand times, she had dressed and undressed there, had slept there, but her life--that had seemed to her so active and filled with important detail--had conquered the room and made of it a colourless background.

Now it was her whole life, her world, and it had already in these few days witnessed some scenes, unpleasant enough, wounding enough, humiliating enough to give that furniture a new arrogance, a fresh wicked assurance. The wardrobe had appeared to her simply as a convenient piece of furniture. Now its broad flat surface was, she was sure, studded with pale quirks and rounds, that if you looked at them continuously stirred rather as evil-looking jellies waver in a sea-pond.

She might even fancy that at times this wardrobe surged with a kind of inside life, and it would, she told herself, need only a trifle more of energy for it to move forward with some secret purpose.

But it was, after all, the swinging mirror at her dressing-table that gave the room its increasingly active spirit. It had always been of an evil nature, this thing, swinging forward when you least expected it, sticking with obstinate peevishness at its screws so that no pulling nor tugging could make the nasty thing budge.

But now, for no reason at all, it would swing, and the whole room would take up a horrid activity, the very chairs seeming to be endowed with life, and all of them, even the pictures on the wall, fixing their eyes on her, as they would say: 'We have you now locked in with us and it is we who are now of importance, not you. And this you will be made to understand before you are very much older.'

But it was that riot of the daisies that was the worst. She had never liked them, wide, flat-faced things with small white eyes that sprang at you, as you looked at them, from a hundred places on the wall.

It was her attempt to count them that was causing them now to obsess her. It seemed that they were scornfully delighted with her effort and, once she had made it, they would not let her alone. They would show her what they could do, so now they rioted from pattern to pattern, their little white eyes running together into one pallid indecent eye or separating into hundreds upon hundreds of eyes all daring her to count them.

It was not also imagination merely that persuaded her that the room was smaller than it had been three days ago. The door to the bathroom and both windows were open and yet the closeness of the air was not to be denied. She had a passion for fresh air; it had always been so, and never until now had she thought this room close or confined. She had not realized before how little space there was for walking. Now she would stride, her arms locked behind her, her head forward, from end to end, but always she must avoid a chair or the wooden foot of the bed or the sharp edge of the dressing-table. It was almost as though they came forward to meet her.

Her physical strength was restored--she felt no longer any of the influenza weakness--but it seemed that the furniture also had its own strength, challenging her and saying: 'As the days go on you will grow weaker and we stronger. You will see.'

But the days must not go on, and thank God they would not! Why, to-morrow night she would be free unless, in her escape, some accident befell her. The thought of that possibility increased with every moment of the day. If she fell and damaged some limb not only would she be ignominiously held (and this time for ever) but the others would be held too. Did she let her imagination work there was no end to the horrors that she could picture!

But she must not! Lying in bed she picked up the book beside it, a novel, Kate O'Brien's Ante-Room, that already, although she had read but little, comforted her with its beauty, with its pity for the weak and indulgence for sinners, with its wisdom and reticence. She was no judge of literary merit, but her soul could respond actively to the soul

242

of another, and so here it responded. And how proud she was that this beautiful book had been written by a woman! How wonderful women were to-day, how understanding, fine-minded, courageous in their passion for freedom! Did she escape from this she would show Rose what a woman's loyalty and affection could be! And to think that so short a while ago she had hated her, wished to do her harm! But it was love that she had needed, love for which she had been starved!

So, with a more cheerful spirit, she bathed and dressed. Then she prepared for the horrible irruption of Sally with her breakfast. At every visit this thing became harder to bear. First the unlocking of the door (to Sally only her father lent the key), then the appearance of that hated face, smirking above the tray, the body superciliously triumphant. Janet was silent.

Sally said: 'Hope you're feeling better, miss. I've brought you nice egg and bacon for your breakfast.' Then she would smile as much as to say: 'You thought you'd be rid of me, didn't you? Well, you see what you've brought on yourself, silly old thing.'

Later she would appear again to do the room, and this, although carried out in silence, was eloquent with suggestion. Sometimes their eyes would meet and it would, alas, be Janet who dropped hers before that bold, contemptuous stare. But Janet was not unfair. The girl hated her because from the first Janet had taken no steps to create any contact with her. She could look back now, in this new light that experience was bringing her, and see that all servants in the house had disliked her. In her pride at her own good management she had seen servants as automata in an arrangement whose perfect pattern must be preserved.

She had deserved this, but it did not mean that she loathed Sally any the less. With every day she loathed her more.

Once again the key in the lock. . . . Janet was sitting very thoroughly dressed in her green tweed, which looked so warm on this fine day that it made the determined snows of Glencoe falter.

'Come in,' she said, and straightened her back, for she knew it was Papa. She thought grimly of Wimpole Street, whose Victorian bedroom had appeared to her, two years ago, in a London theatre. 'Ba' too. But then 'Ba' was a genius and Janet was not.

243

She regarded him sternly.

'Well?' she said.

He stood looking at her rather sheepishly. It would not have been unexpected that he should suck his thumb.

'Now, my dear, my dear,' he said reproachfully.

How can he look so firm, so solid, so healthy at his age, she wondered? And yet there is disease in him somewhere. Quite suddenly an ache in the thumb, a twist in the groin, and he will be an old helpless man. Or he may not be. In these days sixty-nine is nothing. . . . How I wish I knew which it is going to be?

'Well, Janet?' He was still reproachful as he moved into the middle of the room and glanced about him. 'He is looking,' she thought, 'to see whether there is a rope-ladder or a man in hiding or possibly a bomb. He walks carefully as one does in Blindman's-buff.'

'Why don't you say something?' he asked irritably, impatience and perhaps a certain moral awkwardness strangling his good-temper.

'There's nothing to say.' She looked at him calmly, taking The Ante-Room from the little table and laying it on her lap. 'Except that the weather's lovely. . . . Oh yes, and thank you for my delightful breakfast.'

He moved nearer to her. 'Now, Janet, let's end this. Say the word and you shall go downstairs as free as--as free as--as ever you were.'

'I never was free,' Janet answered. 'I've only discovered that in the last three days. But--what word do you wish me to say?'

'You know perfectly well. All I want is that you should promise me something. Promise that you will not interfere, either by word or deed, with my plans for John. That's all there is in it. Anyway it's no affair of yours. Can't you see that, my dear? In many ways you're such an intelligent woman. I cannot understand what's put you up to this. I suppose you and Rose have been setting your heads together--'

'Rose has had nothing whatever to do with this,' Janet quickly interrupted. 'You are entirely responsible, Father, for this whole absurdity.

Locking a middle-aged woman into her room! Why, that's Victorian melodrama! Of course,' she went on reflectively, 'I could take it into the law courts. I have been considering that.'

He drew a quick breath. 'Janet, please--When you talk like this it confirms my worst fears--the fears of everyone.'

Her own heart beat at that and her hands tightened on the book.

'You know,' she said, 'that I'm as sane as Rose, as anybody.'

(But did she herself know? Did she know?)

He drew a chair close to hers.

'Please, please, Janet, give in about this. Don't you see that I've had to put my foot down? John is mine. What right have you or Rose or anybody to take him from me? Can't you see that?'

'What right have you,' she answered quickly, 'to deprive that boy of his freedom? Don't you see that you can't keep him this way? Lock him up as you have done me. Starve him. Beat him. He'll leave you just the same. But let him go, give him his freedom, and he'll not leave you. . . . Father, this is madness, really it is. You are wanting to show your power in the wrong way. You can't stop freedom by shouting about it, imprisoning people, making laws. You can have your prison camps, your armies, your tortures, for a time, but it never lasts and soon you're swept away, you're--' She put her hand to her head. 'I'm talking like a newspaper. . . . The chief point about our situation is that it's ridiculous. You can't lock me up for ever. You can't go on--'

'No,' he said quickly (and she noticed that some other strange passion was working in him). 'But there are other places where you can be kept--until you're better, until you see things sanely again.'

He got up.

'This isn't recent, you know. It isn't just because of John's affair. We've been fighting one another for years--in this house. You've resisted me at every step, you've--'

'Well, then,' she said, 'let me go away. Let me lead my own life somewhere independently.'

'Yes. Certainly. If you promise not to interfere about John.'

She did not reply. She looked in front of her at the horrible wardrobe with the pale swaying lozenges. . . .

She saw at once that she could not promise. That would be to desert Rose, tobe false to her new friendship. For Rose, she saw so clearly, must fight to the very last to get possession of John, and she must be at Rose's side.

'No, I can't promise that.'

'All right then!' He was shaking with anger. 'You're a fool, Janet-- an obstinate, mulish fool.'

'It doesn't help calling names,' she answered. But he was gone and once more she heard the key turn in the lock.

'So that's that.' She turned back to her book, but she could not read now, for the room was surely smaller and closer than it had been half an hour before.

As she could not read she wrote in her Journal. It was an ugly saffron-coloured leather volume with a red line at the side of every page as in an account-book. Her spectacles were tilted at the end of her nose, and her pale forehead wrinkled as she wrote.

'Father has been and gone. His visit this time has made one thing quite clear--that escape is the only thing--no other alternative, none other whatever. So I must look at this quite normally being the woman I am, a sane normal woman with no nonsense about her. Blot. Blot. It's this damned pen that drips like a cold in the nose. I must say to myself, "Janet, climbing out of a window in the middle of the night is as normal as brushing your hair. Feel no kind of alarm." (By the way, this book is carefully locked after every writing and dear Father will have to tear it open over my dead body if he find it.) Step on to the window-sill--first movement. Grip the pipe firmly with both hands--second movement. Close your eyes and slide--third movement. You will then find yourself in Michael's arms. Then the jump. Oh! the jump! The jump! What a nightmare! But make it normal. Force it to be. Make it like tying your shoelace. Make it so, Janet. Make it! Michael will jump first. That's one thing. And the distance is very short, the gravel path very narrow. He will be there on the lawn to break my fall. And even if I do break a leg or twist an ankle, I'll stick it. I'll set my teeth and they shall carry me to the car. And if I faint I shall at least have the satisfaction of unconsciousness. Where are they going to? Kendal, Carlisle, Penrith, Cockermouth? Not Carlisle nor Cockermouth, I should imagine. They are too obvious.

'My slow mind moves forward, for it is slow. I am only now beginning to realize what this escape, if it comes off, will mean to me. For I'm middle-aged and haven't a friend in the world save Michael and Rose. It's all very well to say that I intend to devote myself to Rose and John--but will they want that devotion? Rose and Michael are young and all their lives are before them. Rose is sweet, warm-hearted, loyal, but she is impetuous, full of energy. She will make some new grand life for herself and John, and in that what place can an old maid have? I am very plain and shall be very poor. I have a pittance from my mother that father can't touch, but that depends on investments. All the same I can work. That I'm a good organizer I know, and I will try in the future to love people more, to forget myself in their interests. But can I? Don't I want love to be romantic, emotional? Don't I hunger and thirst for the kind of warmth and reciprocation that I've never all my life had from anybody? And how can anyone give it me? I have no charm, no culture, no interesting brain. Yes, but there must be many, many women in the world even as I who long for affection from someone, who are lonely and plain as I am. Yes, but can I give my affection to someone who is plain and uninteresting? Don't I need someone who is pretty and clever like Rose to rouse it in me? But what am I demanding? Who ever said that life was bound to give me the best things? What obligation is there in life? None whatever. It is my part, as it is everyone's, to fit into what one is given, not to make impossible demands. And fit I will. That I swear.

'The house is very silent. I have two more days to pass here in this horrible room. I found myself, in the middle of the night, telling myself over some of the things I love as though I would never see or touch them again. Is this a prophecy? Oh, God forbid! I thought of ridiculous things--turning over spools of silk in a shop, having an ice-cream at Storm's, standing on the top of Stye Head with the wind blowing about my legs, picking roses in the garden for the drawing-room, a trip to London after a long time here when, as the dirty houses close about one, one realizes that in three minutes one will be in the London station, shopping in Keswick, exchanging greetings (I never realized until now that I loved the Keswick people), changing a novel at Smith's and listening to Mr. Birkenshaw's advice, people coming to tea and seeing that everything is nice, the silver shining, the flowers fresh, the tea-cake hot, going to Emmeline's or anywhere else for a little party, wondering for the thousandth time whether on this occasion I shall not be at last bright, beautiful, engaging, reading in the garden with the sun coming off the fell, hot and strong, yes, even going to the cinema in Keswick and seeing some lovely creature like Garbo or Dietrich and imagining that we are close, intimate friends, overhearing Dietrich say: "Yes, but Janet Fawcus is my real friend--without her I don't know what I'd do!"

'Folly! Nonsense! Are other women as foolish?'

But after tea was the time. Every day worse but to-day quite horrible. All the afternoon there had been no sound. The sun had bound the house tightly about. In that mesh of light the garden swam but no one moved there. Only at 4.30 Sally came in, set the tea on the table and went. From 5 until 7.30 the expectancy lasted and with that expectancy every kind of suspense. Suppose Rose were ill--an influenza? Or suppose a discovery, something overheard, some letter read?

And then after seven had struck there was the agony of anticipating Michael. She sat, bolt upright, in her green tweed as though she were about to leave for a journey, her heart hammering, her mouth dry, her eyes dim with a film of intense watchfulness. Her eyes fixed on the window, but she could not see it. It was as though a web of lawn blew to and fro. . . .

To-night no one came.

At eight o'clock Sally brought her dinner--chicken, brussels sprouts, and the potato that she hated machined into fragments. After that, nothing.

No word. No movement. Only the whirring grumble of the clock.

Shivering as though with cold, she started to undress for bed.

248

CHAPTER XVI - MAY 17TH-18TH: FLIGHT OUT OF EGYPT

'There is no doubt but that at this time the blind obstinacy of James prevented him from seeing the true facts; and it may be noticed how again and again the crises of world events are prepared for by just such obstinate personalities--'

'Give some other examples of this,' said Michael.

'Charles the First,' said John.

'Yes. What was the belief that made Charles the First so obstinate?'

'Divine Right--' began John.

His mind was distracted. Rump was scratching at the door.

'May I let him in?'

'Yes. I suppose so. He's no right here.'

'This will be the last day,' John whispered.

He went to the door, opened it, and Rump entered, not joyfully but with caution.

'It's almost as though he knows,' John said.

'Here. Close the door. Rump, lie down.' Michael leaned across the table and looked at John with great seriousness.

'John, I want you to understand. This isn't just a grand lark, you getting away to-night.'

'I don't think it is a lark,' John said, 'but it's awfully exciting.'

'Oh, it's exciting all right, but the point is that it's more than exciting--it's dangerous, and for no one more than yourself. Listen. In the eyes of the law your grandfather has absolute right in you. If you get clear away there are reasons why he won't probably press his claims. But you've all got to get away--'

'You're coming too, aren't you?'

'No, I'm not. I'm going to stay behind and tell your grandfather in the morning.'

'By Jove, won't he be angry!'

'Yes, he may be, but I can look after myself. What I want you to realize is that it's been very important that your mother shouldn't put herself in the wrong. If something fails to-night that's just what she will do. We shall all be here, just as we are now, but your grandfather will be able to say that we've been conspiring to steal you. Things aren't too easy. Your Aunt Janet for instance. I couldn't get to her last night and I dare not this evening. She may not be ready--'

'Isn't it a pity,' John said frankly, 'that Aunt Janet's got to come?'

'Use your imagination a moment. Would you like to be locked up?'

'I'd get out of the window.'

'That's exactly what we hope your aunt's going to do.'

'She'll have to jump, won't she?' said John, greatly excited. 'And I don't expect she's much good at jumping.'

'It isn't far and she's plucky. But of course someone may be awake, looking out of the window, and there's old Lewcomb. You see, John, what I want you to realize is that a lot will depend on you. Whatever happens, keep quiet. Don't cry out or shout or anything.'

'Of course I'll keep quiet,' said John indignantly.

'It may not be so easy. You've got to help every way you can, but without a sound, do you understand?'

But John's mind was already travelling forward.

'Don't you think,' he said, 'that you could put something in Grandfather's coffee at dinner? Not to hurt him or anything--just to make him sleep sound? I know it's often done.'

'Well, it's not going to be done this time. I thought you were fond of your grandfather.'

'So I am. But as we're escaping we may as well do the thing thoroughly. It wouldn't hurt him.'

Michael considered John. How greatly he had changed from the sensitive shy boy of a few months ago! Or had he not changed? Rose had brought something out of him.

At that Michael felt a miserable unhappiness that had, through all this week, been growing on him. To-night would see the end of his romance, his very one-sided sterile romance! Rose would be in the house no longer. His own personal worldly prospect would not be too cheerful, for no one could foretell the kind of vengeance that the Colonel would be likely to take! But for that he cared little. For Rose he would sacrifice his very life and future!

But here, in this house, he would see her no more, nor warm his heart at her smile, nor feel the touch of her hand, nor hear her voice. He pulled himself up.

'All right, John, I see you understand. You're doing this for your mother, you know.'

'I think she's grand, don't you?' said John.

'Yes, I do. You'd better get on with that history. Read pages a hundred and six to a hundred and twenty before I come back. . . .'

For with every minute of this last day there was pressing upon him the necessity of being with Rose for every second of the time! If he could! If he could! If he could only, in these final hours, gather from her some word, some look that would promise to him in the future

251

some change in her feeling! Something that he could store, conjure over, remember! It might be, he thought, that his actions to-night would stir her! She would realize, as she had not before, the stuff of which he was made, that here was someone whom she would not be likely to find, the world over. . . .

Once more he beat down his desires, his hopes, his longings. He was a brave and unselfish young man, quite as brave and chivalrous as any young Elizabethan, to whom, like many of his generation, he was, in spirit, true brother. Left alone with Rump, John had also his own distresses. He could not take Rump with him. He would never see him again. Considered simply as a dog Rump was nothing. There were thousands and thousands of dogs more beautiful, more wonderful, and certainly more intelligent. But beauty and brain have little to do with lasting friendship. That very lack of qualities had created in John's heart a maternal care and a deep affection.

What would Rump do when he was gone? Neither Sally nor the cook cared for dogs. Rump was simply a nuisance to them, and to Lewcomb, his more constant companion, he was less than the dust that he raised with his ragged old broom.

Moreover if you do not care for a dog he does not show you what he has in him. Rump had qualities. He did understand your moods and suffer them all, that principal reason for the attraction that dogs have for humans; he was only too ready to suffer them. But he had also a life of his own; he knew, it might well be, the cursed inhibitions of his own cowardice, and when he rose above these, his joy and sudden vigour were very pleasant to share.

The tragedy of leaving a dog is that he does not know the reasons why you have left him. Cynics, non-dog-lovers, that strange and incomplete kind of man, say that it is only for their bellies that dogs pretend to love you, and if you do not love them that is true. No one who has loved a dog but knows that there is more in it than that. There can be a relationship so human between dog and man that that puzzling entity, the soul, must be called into question. John, as yet, knew very little about the soul, and Rump nothing, but they did know where their relationship lay, and that it was a precious thing.

John felt that he was committing a cowardly and treacherous act--perhaps the most treacherous deed of all his life. For five minutes or so, as he sat there with Rump lying at his feet, he was tempted almost to say that he would not go unless he could take Rump with him. Of course he could not take Rump. One excited bark and all was in ruins. Could he not wrap something round Rump's head? But no--that meant a visit to the other side of the house, where the kennel was, an infinite delay. Perhaps he could send for him later? No. There would be no mercy on his grandfather's side. He might even destroy him.

At that horrible thought John was in a passion of distress. He took the dog on to his lap, a clumsy and ungainly business, for Rump had always, and quite rightly, refused to be any kind of a lap-dog. But of what now was he aware? For instead of his customary wriggle, his refusal to be held by any hand, his scorn for soft places, he huddled himself into John, fitting his legs under his belly, a thing that he hated to do, and then attempted to lick John's face, a thing that, in his turn, John also hated.

So John sat there and considered the scene. It was a day altogether unlike those glorious ones that had preceded it. At breakfast-time a faint sun, dim as a fried egg, had fought a feeble battle with filmy clouds and trailing mists. But it had been beaten, as it had known from the first that it must be. Even the mists had been but half-hearted in their victory, wandering among the trees as though looking for a resting-place, crawling across the lawn as though they were thinking out some splendid plan for strangling the whole world, in a minute abandoning all their purpose and vanishing, only to leave behind them grey-packed clouds that seemed to hold in their heart the wails of disconsolate cows and the bleatings of forlorn lambs looking for their mothers on the fell.

Rain had threatened but it had not fallen, and this imminence of some minor catastrophe hung in the air so that in the stillness the flowers drooped and the trees dejectedly turned their leaves to see whether they might not be more handsome on the other side.

'This is a beastly day,' John thought. 'I wish there would be a noise somewhere.' But more than that how he longed that he might explain to the dog, whose heart he could feel beating against his thigh, all the reasons for his going, show him that it had to be, that he must stand by his mother to whom he had now sworn allegiance, that go to school he must or he would grow up without having had any fun at all, and that he would do his best, his absolute best, to secure him again, and that if he did so manage, Rump would find his new life most wonderfully superior to his old one. But he could say nothing of this. He could only stroke the dog, and pull his ugly ears, and (what Rump preferred to all things other than a fine meal and running after stones) turn him over and tickle his belly.

But even to this last Rump to-day did not respond as was his custom with little sighs of ecstasy, kicking of the legs, and a frenzied wagging of his tail. He lay still and passive, only once and again making that always frustrated attempt to lick John's face.

Such was the urgency of his feelings that at last John spoke aloud.

'I'll do my best to come back, or if I can't do that I'll have you sent to me. You won't like the actual train, but after that, when you see me at the station waiting for you, it will be splendid. We shall probably live in the country somewhere and when I'm away at school Mother will look after you and see that you have everything you want. She likes dogs, which nobody here but me does.'

However, it was of no use. Rump understood nothing. John put him on the floor and there he stood, sniffing around for a stone, which, in his stupidity, he expected to find in any place and at any time. Then, when he abandoned that hope, he lay patiently down at his master's feet again.

During the afternoon the mists lifted and patches of faint blue like the blue of an old faded quilt appeared above the trees. There was no life anywhere and no heat. It was as though the sun had, in a fit of exasperation, decided to bother no further with this silly planet, and, lending still just enough warmth for life, had wandered off to see whether some other star might not prove more rewarding.

For Rose and Michael it was an incredible afternoon and evening. It seemed impossible that when such a plot was about to burst upon the world there should be no stir either in heaven or earth.

The house itself was the voice of ordinary tranquillity. After tea, as on another occasion, the two of them played chess while the Colonel, his eyes now wide open, watched them, hummed to himself a little, and broke once and again into reminiscence to which he required no answer.

'Oh, you're really too good for me, Michael,' Rose said. 'There's my queen gone!'

She played in a dream and it seemed to her that all this had been enacted in her presence before. Somewhere there had been a game of chess over which hung the menace of a great catastrophe. Somewhere, at some time, she had wondered: 'Now if I exchange knights here my bishop can move forward and threaten the rook'--while beneath this surface preoccupation she had thought: 'If that door opens I must run for it. Can I get to that tree in safety?'

'I remember once,' said the Colonel, looking at his pipe to see whether it were still alight, 'that I wrote to Baldwin about the Housing Problem. I never had an answer. I never really expected one. But he must have taken notice, for my suggestions were on all-fours with what they are doing now. Only think of all the years wasted!' He picked up the Daily Record that was on the floor beside him. 'Now what I like about the Record,' he said, 'is that you know exactly where you are with it. No shilly-shallying, none of this modern effeminacy. It says what it thinks without fear or favour.'

'Check!' said Rose. 'Oh, Michael, I've got your queen. I've forked you!'

'I never saw it,' Michael said, pulling himself up, staring at her so that she was suddenly herself aware of him.

'Now I've got a chance of winning,' she said.

'Yes, you have.' Michael looked at the Colonel, who was now in reality deep in his paper.

'I love you,' Michael said softly. 'Whatever happens, don't ever forget that that is true.'

'No,' she answered. 'I'll never forget it.'

When she came down to dinner the same unreality pervaded the scene. There was the Colonel, very fresh indeed after his bath, his shirt-front gleaming, carving the chicken.

There sat Michael opposite her, the silver shone on the sideboard, and the yellow daisies that she disliked so much stared at her from the centre of the table.

The Colonel looked up from above the chicken.

'What will you have, my dear? Wing or leg?'

'I'll be greedy and have the wing,' Rose answered. 'Not very much, thank you. I'm not hungry.'

'Hullo! Not hungry? Not going to be ill, I hope?'

'Oh no. I had too big a tea, I expect.'

'Push those flowers a little to the side, will you? I can't see you properly. Yes, you look a bit pale. If it's fine to-morrow we'll have a run in the car. What about taking a run over to Ullswater and then over Kirkstone home?'

'Not if it's a day like this.' She was, in spite of all her efforts, shivering.

'No, of course not. We wasted those lovely days. Never mind. You wait until you've had June here. June is generally glorious weather, isn't it, Michael?'

'Very often,' said Michael.

What would the old man do if things went wrong for them? Would Rose after all be sitting opposite to him to-morrow night? Would they be perhaps all locked into their rooms? No, that was fantastic. . . .

A little later the Colonel said: 'Ah, ginger pudding! Now if there's one thing I like . . . !'

'Ha! ha!' said the Colonel (and all the clocks had just struck eleven: the grumbling clock on the staircase, the ladylike clocks in the draw-ing-room, the old gentleman clock in the dining-room and the little sandy-faced cuckoo-clock in John's room--'Cuckoo! Cuckoo! Cuckoo!'

most derisively). 'This is what they call poetry,' and he read from his paper these lines. (He was derisive like the cuckoo-clock, and for the same sound reason.)

'Men lower nets, unconscious of the fact that they are desecrating a grave, and row quickly away--the blades of the oars moving together like the feet of water-spiders as if there were no such thing as death.

The wrinkles progress upon themselves in a phalanx--beautiful under networks of foam, and fade breathlessly while the sea rustles in and out of the sea-weed.'

He read every word scornfully, but also carefully as though he were afraid lest a phrase or a sentence might unawares jump up and bite him.

'I think that's beautiful,' Rose said. She heard the clocks striking. She looked at Michael, who was reading. 'What's that you're reading, Michael?' she asked. She knew that the Colonel never now would go to bed before they did--no, let him be ever so sleepy.

'Sylvie and Bruno.'

'It's not so good as Alice, is it?'

'No. Not so good. There are some grand things though.'

'And that's what they call poetry!' said the Colonel, throwing down the paper impatiently. 'Poetry! Now Kipling's a poet!' He looked about him with defiance, for Rose had incomprehensible notions about the arts.

All she said was, raising one arm and yawning:

'Well, I'm for bed. Good night all.'

'Good night,' they said. 'Good night. Good night.'

'Do you call that poetry, Michael?' the Colonel said, stumping about.

257

'I suppose there are all sorts,' Michael said. Then, after a little pause: 'I'm for bed too, sir, if you don't mind.'

'Not at all. Not at all, my boy. Sleep well.'

So the Colonel was left alone. But not alone for long.

The door opened and Sally came in. She stood there quietly, looking at him with her small but lively eyes. Her eyes lived when she saw a man who once had kissed her. The Colonel once had kissed her but not now.

He stood, jingling his money in his pocket. His speculative, unenterprising gaze was that of a man who has kissed in the past but will not again.

'All well, Sally?'

'Oh yes, sir. I think so. Miss Janet very silent to-day. Not said a blooming word.'

'Oh, hasn't she? No one tried to get into her room?'

'Oh no, sir. Nothing doing anywhere as you might say.' She looked at him expectantly. She was afraid of him and not afraid of him.

All he said was: 'Very good, Sally. Thank you. Good night.'

She closed the door quietly behind her.

Servants spying. He really didn't like it. But also he did like it. All the strings in his hand. He owned this house and everyone in it. . . .

So he too went up to bed.

Standing only in his vest, half an hour later, he, greatly to his own surprise, sighed. What would this all come to? Would it be as he wished? He closed and unclosed his hand. He brushed his teeth. He put on his pyjamas. He climbed into bed and stretched out his hand for The Death in the Bathroom, the story that he was then reading.

Why had he sighed? He felt a vague melancholy, a curious loneliness. Soon he turned out the light and five minutes later was asleep.

Sally, taking off her stockings, said to the cook: 'I'm going to give my notice. There's no fun in this house any more.'

The cook, standing in her voluminous nightdress like a vast white lighthouse, said:

'I shouldn't, Sally. There's more fun coming, I give you my word.'

Sally shivered.

'Ough . . . I don't know. Got the willies tonight somehow. That woman in her room not speaking--I 'ates taking her meals in, honest I do. What's his game anyway?'

Then she saw that the cook was on her knees saying her prayers. For some obscure reason she resented this.

'Might give us a room to ourselves anyway,' she thought. 'Big house like this. Beastly old house if you ask me.'

Rose undressed. Michael undressed. John undressed. Those were the orders, for who, at any moment, might come knocking at your door? But Janet had had no orders. This had been a day of terror for her. She had abandoned hope. Something had gone wrong with the plans, some discovery had been made. . . .

For two days now she had had no word from her friends. Nevertheless she undressed and lay in the bed, gripping her hands tightly, staring at the foul wardrobe. What she was doing was summoning her courage.

'Whichever way it goes I can face it. Nothing will happen. There will be silence. Not a word to-morrow from anyone. I can stand that. And then perhaps in a few days' time I shall be ordered to get up and go to some strange place. I'll fight that, fight like the devil. And if it comes to that, Rose will be there to help me. For whatever else happens I know that Rose won't desert me. Whatever happens that will be true. . . .

'But I can't endure this room much longer. It isn't cowardice, it's a kind of nausea. The windows are open but the room is full of smells, of furniture, of food, of cats. Yes, there is really a smell of cat. Shall I get up and look? No, not yet. Once I am up I shall walk about and then the furniture begins to move with me. This afternoon I found myself in the middle of the room afraid to go right or left. I can see through the window that there is a faint moon and a lot of mist--a light that would be moonlight if it were just a little stronger. That is half-past twelve striking. Why didn't Michael come? No one will ever come again. They have given it up. They have abandoned me. Yes, I must look. Soon I shall be sick. I will get out of bed and look. In any case when half-past one strikes I will dress and be ready.'

As the clocks struck two the thin, lunatic, whey-faced moon pushed her swaddling clouds aside and crept warily into the open. Spare spider light mildewed the landing: across it the three figures at intervals of some minutes appeared, vanished. They had made no sound and their passing was so swift that the two mice exploring from the small hole to the left of the grumbling clock lost consciousness of them almost as soon as they had caught it.

Michael had been first. He wore a dark suit and no shoes. The grass would be dry. There had been no rain for days. His only weapon was a long coil of strong thin cord, this for helping Janet. It might not, it almost certainly would not . . . but you never knew.

He paused for only a brief moment before he started down the stairs, caught by an almost irresistible impulse to shout at the top of his voice. It was as though some stranger, hopping from the moonlight, had caught him by the shoulders and said: 'Now yell!'

It was the consequence perhaps of the strain of waiting during those long hours in his room when his brain, on fire, had gone over every possible contingency, every aspect of almost certain disaster.

But this instant of time when he paused at the head of the stairs lasted, it seemed, an eternity.

'Yell, you blackguard! Yell!'

He put his hands to his throat and the stranger was gone back into silence again. For the stranger was himself, carried now tightly in his pocket.

No stair creaked, but the small sitting-room door had to be opened. They had decided on this exit because, although the door was locked (the Colonel locked all doors before going to bed and all windows, save fortunately in the bedrooms), it was, they had found, a key that easily and softly turned.

This was a small, unused room neighbouring the drawing-room, filled with bookcases loaded with old dust-laden volumes of Cornhill and Temple Bar. He had reconnoitred it and knew that there was a table; also four chairs and a writing-desk. The blinds were drawn and it was dark. The handle of the first door moved silently. Inside the room he drew a breath and felt as though he were so crowded about that every step meant danger. He brushed with his hands as though against a thousand spider-webs, then he had found the key, turned it, and lightly jumping the gravel from grass to grass, was on the lawn.

Rose was second. As she opened her bedroom door she heard, but so lightly that it was like the blowing of a leaf against a wall, the touch of Michael's foot as he reached the bottom of the stairs. She paused too, but not from Michael's impulse. It was rather to go to John's door and see that he was awake and ready. They had agreed that she must not do this because to go to his room meant mounting several stairs and a grave increase of every kind of risk.

John had been given, beyond any question of confusion, his orders. He was to wear his cricket shirt, shorts, grey stockings, gym shoes, and over them his thick dark winter coat. When he heard two strike he was to come out, go straight down to the Book Room, as it was called, and thence on to the lawn. Michael would be there and show him where to stand so that he would not be seen while the rescue of Aunt Janet proceeded.

He had listened intelligently and repeated instructions exactly. There could be no mistake. Nevertheless Rose's impulse now was all but irresistible. It might be (it was indeed likely) that with the excitement and suspense of these last days he had fallen asleep. If, when Rose joined Michael on the lawn, John was not there, then Michael must return, climb the stairs again, go to his room, wake him . . . a dreadful increase of danger of discovery.

How easily now she could slip up the stairs, open the door. . . . Sally and the cook were on that same passage. . . . She had given her word.

But the impulse was stronger than any physical expediency. She had a crazy instinct that in this single act of leaving the house she was abandoning her child for the second time. It was as though her own consciousness told her: 'For your own safety, security, you do this . . .' and afterwards, looking back, she was to realize that this was one of the deepest, most significant moments of her growth, arising from depths of her real self, a new self in which the old was embedded. She would give now much more than her life for John. The impulse passed as swiftly as it came. She had given her word. If she did not depend on John now, acting for himself, in his own self-reliance, she would never depend on him.

She was at the bottom of the stairs, through the Book Room, and with Michael on the lawn just as an owl, with its frustrated and lonely melancholy, called from the moon-shadowed darkness.

John had not slept. He had found the lying in bed not at all tiresome, for he had had the idea (no novel one, of course) that he was a Red Indian scouting on a dark and difficult trail.

Balanced on a tree branch, enveloped in the damp darkness of the surrounding forest, alive to the chatter of the monkeys, the occasional scream of a bird, the far-distant roar of the prowling tiger, he had waited without moving, his ears alert, for the first sound of the advancing enemy. His nostrils were filled with the warm humid stench of the forest, and so alert was he, so practised, that the breaking of a twig, the fall of a leaf was as thunder to his consciousness. . . .

At half-past one he left the forest, got out of bed and dressed. Then he waited, sitting on a chair, until it should strike two. When it did so he put on his shoes, slipped into his pocket his jack-knife, a ball of string and a packet of nut chocolate (this last altogether his own idea), opened his door, heard from Cook's room a snore like the beating of a small drum, and set out on his adventure.

He had a notion that he would like to say good-bye to his grandfather, as though he might go into his grandfather's room, jog his arm with: 'Grandfather, I'm off now!'

So ridiculous was this that he almost laughed.

A moment later he was with Michael and his mother on the lawn.

In Janet's room all was half-darkness. She had turned on no light lest it should show under the door into the passage, but no blind was drawn, so the first unreal curdled shadow of the veiled and unveiled moon was pallid like milk across the floor, against the wall, on the bed.

In the centre of this pallor, upright in a straight chair, was the motionless figure of Janet. She did not move, because her ears were straining for every sound. She was wearing her brown costume and on her head was a small shell-shaped brown hat pulled sharply on to her forehead: it suited her very ill. In one hand she held tightly, as though afraid that it might escape her, a brown reticule. In this reticule were a handkerchief, a brown faded daguerreotype of her mother as a young girl, her Journal, a little red address-book, a bottle of smelling-salts and a recipe for heartburn cut from the newspaper. This, with another extract from a newspaper telling of a hockey match between the Ladies of Cumberland and the Ladies of Lancashire, was inside the address-book. She had been dressed by half-past one and she would sit there until half-past three. If no one came by that time she would know that the adventure had failed and she would return to bed and await the morning.

She was, by now, quite certain that the adventure had failed. She was not surprised. Her father was very clever where his own interests were concerned.

But the thought of her own future was so terrifying that she dared not look at it. So she simply sat there, thinking of nothing, staring at the window.

263

She heard two strike. As happens when one is waiting at an appointment and is going to be disappointed, the time moved with astonishing rapidity.

It seemed to be only a moment after the striking of the hour that the ferrule of a stick tapped very gently on her window-pane.

With that sound she was instantly changed from the despairing apprehensive virgin of the last two days to the practical determined Janet Fawcus of her ordinary life. That her heart was beating with almost tumultuous joy did not stop her for a single moment. She went straight to the window and very, very quietly raised the lower pane.

'Can you hear me?' came the whisper from below.

'Yes.'

'There's not a moment to lose. Look here. Do just as I say.'

'Yes.'

'First, sit on the window-sill.'

'Yes.' She was on the window-sill, grasping the wood with one hand; in the other she held her bag. She was no good at heights--even the ridge of Blencathra made her sick. The moon had gone behind its attendant clouds again and she could see only the things nearest to her--otherwise the world was a slightly swaying, grey-coloured soup made of trees and soil. The night breeze blew up her legs and under her skirt.

'Can you see the pipe?'

'Yes.'

'Good. Now listen. There's plenty of room for you to get your arms round it. Lean slightly forward and clasp it. Then hug it. Let yourself go and slide gently down it. I'm here to catch you.'

She was once again the frightened virgin. Something inside her said: 'Don't be such a fool! Get back into the room. You'll miss the pipe and fall headlong.'

Indeed the effort to lean forward and touch the pipe was more, surely far more than she could ever do. She was balancing on the sill,

264

her head went round like a twirling globe, she was balanced over that soupy, swaying darkness. She could not do it. She preferred to die. But she had done it. She had touched it. She had clasped it. She clutched it now with an almost maniacal ferocity. It seemed to pull her from the window-ledge, and, her hands clasped round the pipe (hands and bag together), she found that she was slipping. Then she could have screamed. She was (oh, traitress to Rose and friendship) about to shriek when she found herself in Michael's arms.

She was almost on her knees, but the stone beneath her was solid, giving her reassurance, although the ledge was not very broad. He whispered in her ear: 'That's splendid! splendid! Now what you've got to do is to jump. It's nothing. It's no distance. Only jump forward so that you land on the grass.'

'But I can't see. I can't see anything.'

'It's better for us not to have the moon all the same. You don't want to see. You've only got to jump out and forward. There's nothing in the way--nothing to hurt you. What's that you have in your hand?'

'My bag.'

'Give it to me. I'll throw it down first. You might hurt yourself with it.'

But here a mule-like obstinacy seized Janet. She would not give up her bag.

'I can't. It has everything I value.'

'Nonsense. Please. There's no time.'

'You shan't have it! You shan't have it!'

'Oh, blast!' She felt his hand on her shoulder trying to shake her. 'Keep it then! Now listen! I'm going to jump first! Wait for a moment after I've gone and then jump.' And he jumped. Or she supposed that he did. She heard no sound. She saw nothing. She only knew that she was quite alone on a ledge of the world in the middle of the night. He had told her to jump. Well, she could not jump. That was all there was to it. If God Himself had commanded her to jump she must have re-fused Him. She could not jump. She would not jump.

265

But also she could not go back. She was unable to climb that pipe. Hot burning tears filled her eyes. How monstrous of them to force her into this hideous position! They were mocking her. How beautiful and lovely seemed the room that she had just left! How unutterable a fool herself to join in this mad insane attempt!

Her knees trembled under her. Wildly she looked about her. She could see nothing but in a faint haze a pipe, a wall and somewhere a threatening, clutching tree. Overhead the changing clouds that hovered and soon would swoop. . . .

She would not jump: and she jumped.

She fell on her knees, spreading out her hands--her bag vanished into space. Michael's arm was about her waist. She leaned back against him looking up at the moon, now both sheep-faced and sly, that slipped from under a cloud and threw a glitter as of fish-scales on the turning world. 'Sheep, fish-scales, how ridiculous!' she thought, 'and the jump was nothing!' Then she heard Michael's mutter: 'Oh, my God!'

After that things happened quickly. For the moon, pleased with her appropriate gesture, showed them Lewcomb in a shirt and riding-breeches with, of all things, on his head, an old nightcap like a stocking-end, Lewcomb thus, straight on their heels. (Michael for curiosity asked at a later date about the nightcap. It was, it seemed, a family heirloom and worn against rheumatics.)

He was at them so silently that all that Janet, still on her knees, perceived was his opening mouth. He was about to shout, to cry, to bay the listening moon.

But he did not--and this next was, in fact, so swift that time had no place in it.

Michael too had seen the gaping mouth, and with the vision of it came the action of stopping it, for he had the old man on the ground and his hand over the tooth or two left to him before the cry was born.

All he whispered was, 'Quick, the cord!' and to John's everlasting pride it was John only who knew what that intended. The coil was lying on the grass in friendly company, as it happened, with Janet's bag.

John in no time at all had the cord and his jack-knife at Michael's service.

No one, by the way, has ever understood why Rump was silent during this turmoil. But he had never been a very good watchdog.

After that John held hard at Lewcomb's ankles. The old man struggled and wriggled like an aquarium, but there was Michael's man-size handkerchief over his mouth, the cord about his belly and legs. John surveyed him with seriousness. He had read frequently in his books of 'trussing' your enemy. Now he saw it done.

'The summer-house. That's the best place,' Michael commanded. So they dragged him across the lawn, Rose, Michael and John.

This summer-house was a rather handsome affair built by the Colonel in the preceding year.

'Sorry,' Michael said. 'I've got to tie you to the table-leg.'

Having done so, he whipped off the handkerchief and was out of the door in a twinkling. There was a key, which, after locking, he slipped in his pocket.

Faintly half across the lawn they heard cries as of a swooning vegetarian. They would not break into the Colonel's dreams of power.

The moon was veiled again.

'My bag!' said Janet. She groped on hands and knees.

'Oh, come along! Come along!' said Michael.

'It has my address-book.' She had found it. The clasp was intact in spite of the fall. 'I'm glad,' she thought, 'I bought the more expensive one. I so nearly got the other.'

In the road was the car and Mr. Rackstraw. They climbed in. Rose turned to speak to Michael. He was gone.

CHAPTER XVII - THE TREMBLING SKY

Janet sat beside the driver, Rose and John in the back seat.

The car started off at a tremendous pace, then, at the bottom of the hill, the wheel began to wobble.

'That will be serious if it gets worse,' Mr. Rackstraw said, turning round to them confidentially, 'but we ought to manage Seathwaite all right.' The car was nearly in the hedge.

'Please,' Janet said, 'look where you're going. I don't want to be tiresome, but an accident just now would be so very inconvenient.'

She knew herself and her irritable nature well enough to realize that instead of being, as she ought, elated, triumphant, enchanted at seeing dear Rose again, she was exasperated, not far from tears, extremely conscious of a bruised left leg, aware that one sleeve of her costume was torn, and above all, anxious to reassert her dignity. She realized how ridiculous this last at this time must be. But she could not prevent herself. She had come hurtling through the air, landed on her knees, in front of Michael, Rose and John. The boy especially must have thought it very comic. It was all in the dark--and she was sure that her leg was bleeding inside her stocking.

'Please tell me,' said Mr. Rackstraw, but his gaze was now on the road, 'did you get away without any trouble?'

'There was a little confusion,' Rose said, 'because Lewcomb the gardener came rushing out on us. We had to tie him up and put him in the summer-house.'

'Do you think anyone heard anything?'

'No. I don't think so. We were all very quiet. Of course you can't tell.'

She was thinking of Michael. How deeply she regretted that she had not said anything at the last! But, by his own intention, he had gone! And now he must face the horrible morning without a word from her! She heard again his voice over the chessboard telling her that he loved her. He was young, so very, very young. He would soon feel tranquilly enough about her. Time--even a week or two of absence--wrought such wonders, but the very knowledge that that young love of his would so swiftly be gone saddened her with a sense of loss, of waste. She did not love him--that was not for her ordering--but he was the best friend she had ever had. He should be still her best friend.

The moon was now out to her lugubrious full--not a beautiful presence of silver light but a sick discontented creature, turning all things to malicious unreality.

They were entering Keswick, and in a moment found themselves opposite Chaplin's bookshop, impeded by a group of persons setting out on some expedition.

One or two of these were quite clearly drunk, and the peace of Keswick, which should at this hour be immaculate was broken with song and dance. Two young men with Scotch caps on their heads and plaids about their shoulders were dancing a reel solemnly in the middle of the street. A large car stood near by and out of this two ladies leaned, imploring the dancers to stop their nonsense and take their places.

They, however, refused to move for all Mr. Rackstraw's hootings. Rackstraw stopped. One young man leaned confidentially in to them.

'Are you climbing Great Gable?' he asked in the most friendly fashion. 'Because that's what were going to do. We'll all go together.'

His accent had no trace of the Scottish, as is the case with many wearers of the cap, the plaid and the kilt.

'If you don't get out of the way,' said Rackstraw, 'I'll kill you.'

The young man examined them all with a merry eye.

'Yes, we'll all go together,' he said, 'to see the sunrise.' But before he could speak further he was arrested by a massive woman in Russian boots who, leaping from the other car, advanced on him, dragged him away and flung him rather than persuaded him into the equipage.

Rackstraw drove on.

'That's a nuisance,' he said. 'If anyone's following us they may tell-- and we shall have company on the Pass.'

They got then as far as the Lodore Hotel, only Rose, to whom at this moment life had no bread-and-butter truth about it, was reflecting as the car bumped and jostled that she had read somewhere that there were at least ten different whites--snow white, oyster white, ivory white, seven more--but that this colour of the reluctant moon was shabby like a soiled tennis-shoe. She caught John's hand, for this last jolt is surely too violent for safety, and she heard Rackstraw say: 'It's this damned wheel. It shakes like a jelly.' The car stopped and at the same moment the austere night-front of the Lodore Hotel, curtained, blind and soaked in sleep, was broken by the opening of a door and a porter's voice saying:

'You're all right, sir?'

'Oh, quite all right--all right--all right! I should think we are all right, ha ha!' and a stout gentleman emerged followed by a lanky boy. The gentleman was in bulging knickerbockers, shirt open at the neck and a face all red and bursting with friendliness and good cheer. So strongly marked was this that it could be seen even under the thin pale eye of the moon.

'Now, Edgar, come! We must step up if we are to catch the sun!'

But such was his nature that he must speak to any and every one of his kind be they within speaking distance. He was clearly in the category of men who love to shout down a megaphone at a garden party non-existent through wet weather.

'Hallo, sir! Had some trouble?'

'No, thanks!' said Rackstraw.

'Sorry. No offence meant! Just thought that I might be of some use. Edgar knows about cars, don't you, Edgar?'

The lanky boy said with a sort of ferocious melancholy: 'Should think I do--damned sight too much.'

'Now, now!' said his elder cheerfully. 'Manners, my boy, manners before ladies!' He touched his cap of grey and brown squares politely to Janet and Rose. 'Fine night for a climb, isn't it? Just going up Great Gable, my boy and I. Good for the adipose tissue, what! I live in Manchester and again and again I've said to the wife, "Must see those Lakes." She doesn't care for lakes herself--neither lakes nor mountains. Bridge is her line. Bridge and a bit of shopping, so Manchester suits her, but what I say is that one should like one's own natural beauties-- one's country's, I mean--all very well the Riviera and Switzerland, but when you've got close at hand--'

He had been leaning confidentially on the side of the car and Rackstraw had been examining the engine; the little man with a shake of his head was, on a sudden, back in his seat, the car sprang forward, and the stout gentleman, moonlit astonishment on his countenance, twirled like a knickerbockered top.

Rackstraw did not find words until they were passing Grange bridge.

'Would you believe it? The whole world's--climbing Gable--tonight. You're more private--in the daytime along--this blessed road. What do they want--to choose this night of all--nights? You'd think they'd--all come out to see--us pass as though we were--royalty.'

His words came jerkily indeed, for now the car, tossing its head and twitching its ears, had taken possession of them.

'This damned wheel--I beg your pardon--but if I go slowly--it's worse--and if I go fast--'

There's nothing, except earthquake, like a trembling car-wheel to give you a conviction of life's insecurity, and now they danced and the world danced with them. For along that valley road where once witches had been dragged, Chinese murderers had persuaded their reluctant brides, and the taunting cuckoo had derided the sincere and obstinate natives, this little merry car triumphed in its freedom.

Rose's arm was around John and she stared defiantly at fate. We are free! We are free! And if this is our final moment of consciousness at least we are at liberty. No walls confine us, we need not whisper, for overhearing Sally and the cook are snoring in their beds and the canaries are held in slumber.

'It's all right, John. It's all right. It's only the wheel's a bit loose. We're nearly there.'

'Oh, I don't mind,' he answered. 'It's fun, don't you think? Did you see?--that boy had a wig--'

'Nonsense, dear. I'm sure he hadn't--a wig--'

'But he did, Mother. You could see--the back of his neck--there were bits ofthe hair--sticking up right away--from his head--'

The country jumped at them. As they spun through Rosthwaite village the blind houses danced at them and the garden wall of the Scawfell Hotel skipped like a ram. . . .

At the turning to Stonethwaite where the little gate is, the car pulled up. 'Oh! I have enjoyed that!' it hummed. 'Never had such fun in my life!'

Nor would it again. It was destined shortly for the degradation of the rusted and ignominious scrap-heap. Its short sunlit day was done.

For now on the rocky and uncertain path to Seathwaite, Rackstraw drove them at a snail's pace. They tumbled into the wettest place in Great Britain, bruised, battered, but triumphant. They climbed out and stood, a little group, the only sound in all the world the swift chuckling running of the streams.

Now for the first time they felt their real liberty. The cool air touched with gentleness their cheeks, in their nostrils was the smell of peat, fell-grasses, the faintly acrid odour of the farm. A web of cloud, mysteriously milk-white as though reflecting a world of moonlight, caught the hill-bastions into its folds.

After the rattling confusion of the already forgotten car the sound of Taylor Ghyll, running, a steady triumphant voice of the night, was all friendliness and comfort.

They started forward.

'It's ten minutes to three. The sun rises just after four. We have plenty of time.'

They walked on over the stones and pebbles of the little path in single file, exchanging no word, until they reached the Bridge.

Here they paused, waiting, listening for they knew not what. It was a wonderful moment for them all, and the moon, as though recognizing them, stole out once more, now maidenly, gentle; her light was silver now, scattering the running water with shining coin, transmuting the tree that hung over the stream into dark patterns of shadowed jade.

Janet looked almost timidly at Rose.

'I haven't said--now that we're together again. Those last days were awful. What I mean--'

And to the astonishment and dismay of them all, she began to cry, first with a sniff and a snuffle, then taking her handkerchief from a bag, weeping unconstrainedly.

Rose put her arm around her.

'Don't, Janet. It's all right. We're safe now. We're together again. Forget those last days. You'll be laughing to-morrow--'

'Oh yes, it isn't that.' Janet with a great sob threw back her head, breathed in the air. 'It isn't that. I know I'm so silly. You wouldn't believe how seldom I cry. It's only that I've not been myself. If you knew how dreadful that room's been, and with every hour it was worse, and then the last two evenings Michael not coming. But it's all right now, indeed it is. Only how ridiculous you must have thought me jumping out of the window like that, but there really wasn't any other way, was there? However'--she blew her nose and smiled upon them all--'I'm sure you quite understand and if I was a little ridiculous it's allowable once in a way, and I don't suppose it will ever happen again--'

They started up the path. Janet was limping.

'Is your leg bad?' Rose asked.

'I hurt it when I fell. It's only scraped and bruised.'

'Shall we stop and see what's the matter?'

'Oh no!' cried Janet. 'Oh no! With every step it's better!'

And so she felt it was, for now a kind of grand insane exultation seized her.

Stye Head has been trodden by many hundreds of thousands of persons, but it has some very queer magical properties. There are many passes in Cumberland and Westmorland lonelier, more desolate, and yet it can have a quality of loneliness richer than any of them. It is a path leading to the very heart of this small district's character. If, when you have climbed the Pass and reached Sprinkling Tarn, when you have walked up over the gradual slope to Esk Hause, looked over to the Langdales, down into Eskdale, greeted Scawfell, if then you say that this is poor beside the Scottish hills and nothing at all compared with Mont Blanc, then hurry down, catch your train at Keswick or Windermere and never return.

Only a few miles distant, only a minute in time as the aeroplane flies, are towns, factory chimneys, all the business of man; Stye Head miraculously assures you that you can escape.

It was this sense of successful flight achieved that elated them now. With every climbing step they were escaping far more than the Colonel. It really seemed that they were moving into another world, for against the mouse-grey of the night sky a whirlwind of small clouds, ivory in colour, blew like feathers hither and thither while the moon shone and darkened, and shone again. To this eyeflash of light and dark the country responded. They had climbed as far as the little gate and, looking down, could see the Borrowdale valley, closed in by Castle Crag, and beyond it Skiddaw and Blencathra. These hills, and the

Borrowdale Glaramara, stood like funeral pyres of ebony until the light struck them, when it was as though water flooded down their flanks, pouring into the valley, which was suddenly transmuted into a silence of silver, holding its breath lest a sound should disturb it.

For the brief moment before the cloud, itself silver-edged, came over, so expectant was the silence that you waited for a cry, the song of a bird, everyone to 'burst out singing.' After that the immediate darkness that succeeded was not threatening nor sinister, for behind the darkness the light was present.

When at last they reached the flat run of fell, by common consent they stayed, sat on boulders and rested. The moon was gone. They would not see her again. The very air changed. There was a faint movement above them like the stirring of birds; the whirlwind of little airy clouds was gone and the sky from end to end was dove-coloured, of great purity, without a mark or stain upon it. The arm and shoulder of Gable lumbered up into it, for Gable is a lazy hill, of infinite good-nature and human understanding. Only on the side of it where Piers Ghyll cuts to the valley there is danger. 'But why,' says Gable, 'break your little necks on me? Step on to my shoulder and you shall mount with ease and safety to one of the jolliest Tops in the world--or if you want some adventure I offer you the Napes. Go and pay Gavel Neese a visit. But, best of all, I like you here, clambering about my neck, seeing the world with my eyes, touching me with warm hands and feet. I am nearer man and his childlike, trusting, timorous soul than any other hill in the world. Meanwhile I'm sleepy--talk if you like. I enjoy human voices. But don't lose your tempers--and I detest bad manners.'

Rackstraw sat, looking down into the valley across whose floor bales of mist were now rolling.

'Soon I must go back,' he said, 'and wobble that old car home again.'

'Oh no--not yet,' Rose said. 'We will separate at the Tarn if separate we must. Why don't you come on with us to London?'

He smiled and shook his head. They now resembled the gnomes in the half-darkness that held their world.

'You'll think me very rude, I'm afraid, when I tell you that I shall be glad to be rid of you. You've been on my mind for weeks. I've had to make vows that I've hated to keep. It's been like a perpetual Sunday. Not that I haven't enjoyed it, but I've been like a man on diet. One's health's better but one's spirit is deplorably weak. I've loved you all, but--dear me--I shall be very glad to see the last of you.'

'Why, if we've spoiled your life--' Rose said.

'Oh no, you haven't spoiled it. I'm much too strong-minded for that. And anyway it's spoilt already. It's spoilt, the sort of life that people call worthy. But there's another kind--a lost, abandoned, ruined kind that still can be very jolly. It's a mess, of course, with a lot of disgraceful things in it, but it's an exciting mess with many dramatic moments. The fact is that like everyone else one's pulled different ways--one likes people, wants to help, loves company--and then how one detests them, how one aches to get away from the very sound of their voices! Christ was the same, I think. At one moment He said "Love your brother," but after He had said it the one thing He wanted was to get away, on to some hill somewhere, a hill like this, where nobody could reach Him. And He enjoyed flogging the money-changers. There's no doubt He enjoyed it.'

'You've been very good to us,' Rose said. 'Hasn't he, Janet?'

'Oh, he has!' Janet said fervently. 'I must admit to you, Mr. Rackstraw, that until these last weeks I didn't like you at all. It shows how wrong one can be about people.'

'Oh no, it doesn't,' Rackstraw said. 'You wouldn't like me at all, Miss Fawcus, if you knew me. I've lent you my car, not changed my character.'

'Perhaps I've changed mine,' Janet said, rubbing her wounded leg.

'I don't suppose so. You're free now. That makes so much difference.' Dimly they saw him rise.

'Well, I'll go with you as far as the Tarn and then I'll be rid of you.'

They started across the flat, still boggy in many places in spite of the warm dry days. They moved now in a world where they were solitary save for the living presence of the stream that ran below the cleft.

'Comic properties!' Rackstraw suddenly exclaimed. 'Comic properties! That's what they are!'

No one spoke.

'Drunken fool with a Scotch cap, woman in Russian boots, oaf in knickerbockers. They're not here! They're not here!' He called out softly: odd and musical his voice sounded. 'Rose! Rose! They couldn't be here! They wouldn't exist! And I go back to them! I'm going back to them!'

'Yes, yes,' she said reassuringly, for she felt that he needed comforting. 'But you can come here any time.'

'Yes,' she heard him say to himself, 'I can come here any time.'

She was walking a trifle behind the others with John. They were not touching, but he was close beside her and she felt, by an intuition that proved their constantly growing intimacy, that he was dejected.

'John,' she said, 'are you feeling unhappy? You're not tired, are you?'

He waited a moment before answering her.

'Tired? Of course not. Only, I say, Mother--do you think I'll be able to get Rump back again?'

'Oh, Rump!' That was the last thing of which she'd been thinking. 'Why, I don't know--'

She heard him sigh.

'I was afraid I wouldn't. You don't think Grandfather will poison him, do you?'

'Oh no. . . .' She put out her hand, took his arm, drew him close to her. 'Why should he?'

'He'll be in an awful temper, won't he? And there'll just be Rump and Mr. Brighouse for him to let out over.'

Yes. Michael. . . .

'He isn't unkind like that. He wouldn't hurt a dog.'

'Anyway it will be rotten for Rump. He isn't a dog you'd like at first sight. But he's got feelings like anything . . .'

She held his arm tightly.

'We'll do our best to get him for you. I think we can.'

John sighed again, but this time with satisfaction. He was beginning to trust his mother completely.

'John--when we start our new life together we'll confide in one another. I don't mean that I'll want you to tell me everything. That's nonsense. No one ever tells anyone everything. But I don't want you to think I'll be shocked or angry. I'm really only beginning to live myself. My life with your father was a kind of a fairy-story. And after that it was nothing. So we're really starting together. When you go to school don't forget I'm there. Boys do, you know.'

'Yes, but then those are mothers. I mean, boys have had mothers all their lives and they think of them as mothers. But I've never had a mother and so you aren't one exactly. I'll tell you things just as though you were Roger. Although you aren't Roger, of course. What I'd like best would be for Roger to see one day I'd made a lot of runs at cricket or played in the Public Schools Rugger and scored five tries. Of course, you can't. No one ever scores five tries. All the same it might happen. . . . The best thing is,' he added, 'that we like being with one another, don't we?'

'Yes, we do,' she said.

She looked about her and saw that through the opaque forms were emerging. She could see Rackstraw and Janet, ahead of them, quite clearly now. She looked up and it seemed to her the sky was trembling. Although there was as yet no colour it was as though every colour threatened, and she had fantastic notions that behind that thin white skin-like texture anything might be. Because she was weary and

279

exalted and happy her imagination was extravagant. Yes, behind this trembling sky, dragons with green tails, red parchment with letters in tarnished gold, fields of flowers--lupin, larkspur, gentian, high rocks of crystal, and, raising its head in solitary splendour, 'the greenish orchid fond of snow. . . .'

But this was elaborate, this was false. The reality was more lovely than any imaginings. Veils were stripped from the earth. A clear light began to glow. The sky, trembling in every breath, shed its coverings, which broke into myriads of small clouds rosy-tipped. The colour was so faint that it was like the ashen rose of sea-shells washed pale by the sea. And again, as the sea murmurs its path through the mist into a shadow of blue upon white, so now the sky foretold the blue that it held with a blue so pale that it had no substance, no reality, only prom- ise. They were at the Tarn, black and without life, but here, too, even as they approached it, the new day's breeze touched it and it trembled.

They stood together, Rackstraw, Rose, Janet, John. They looked back across the flat land between the hills and saw the light increase.

They saw too, striding towards them, the Colonel.

The little group stood with the Tarn behind them, instinctively close together, as though on their guard against the enemy. The Colo- nel strode with his customary activity, throwing his whole body into the good work. He wore no head-covering, and his white hair was in the increasing light an aureole.

When he was within speaking distance he stopped. No one spoke.

He cleared his throat as though he were going to make a speech; then he said sternly:

'You didn't expect me.'

Rose, who knew that this meeting was a climax to matters of such seriousness that the only proper behaviour was to laugh, said:

'No. We didn't. Have you got guns about your person?'

'If you think this a joke--!' he answered furiously.

280

Rose, who was watching him closely, saw that he was trembling violently--from anger, excitement, hurried climbing and walking, and also from advancing years.

This made her suddenly tender, anxious, as though he were in her care. She wanted him to sit down and rest. She went towards him.

'Must we stand at such distances? Come and sit down with us. We can't fight with our fists. There's nothing to be done but to talk about it.'

But as she advanced towards him he retreated.

'Certainly I'm not going to sit down with you. I've come to demand my rights. John, you are to come home with me immediately.'

'Oh no,' John said. 'I can't--not after all the trouble we've taken.'

'You can't!' the Colonel began. 'You dare to say can't to me?' And then he stopped abruptly because he saw, clearly enough, that in this place with Gable and Scawfell in attendance the words were simply foolish. You could talk like that in the study at the Hall--but most certainly not here.

They all felt that. There was a general awkwardness, for the hills quite certainly were laughing at them all.

Rose sat down. Janet, aware of her leg, did the same.

'Well, what do we do now?' Janet said. 'We're on our way to Wastdale, Father.'

'Oh, you are, are you--' He broke off, aware again that fury was here a mockery. He looked at his daughter with angry curiosity.

'Do you mean to say that you jumped from that window?'

'I slid down the pipe first,' Janet said, 'and then I jumped. I hurt myleg in doing so--'

'I'm glad you did.' He put his hand to his forehead. He was at a complete loss. There were those people who had defied him. Here was he. But what next? It was the surroundings that stupefied him. Had he a gun, had Rackstraw a gun, they might shoot one another. But no one

281

had a gun. He and Rackstraw could not fight one another with their fists. He could not step forward, catch John by the arm and drag him away. John would elude him and there was a whole world of space in which the eluding could be done.

'Tell us first,' Rose said, 'before we go any further. How ever did you track us down?'

He could not help it. Rose was so beautiful, Rose was so tender, would make so lovely a wife for his old age did not the law and Rose herself forbid. He found himself replying quite mildly.

'I sleep with my window open, of course. I woke up to hear a noise like a house falling in the garden. I put on some clothes, went out and found it was Lewcomb trying to kick the door of the summer-house down. I released him. He had heard the car, so I drove into Keswick. There I saw a drunken young man sitting on the kerb--a Scotsman it seemed. He told me that you'd gone, his party and yours, to see the sun rise on Gable. A talkative man in knickerbockers on the Borrowdale road confirmed it. In Seathwaite I saw the car.' He was rather proud of this detective work. The pride was in his voice. He realized that he was quite frightfully tired. He had climbed Stye Head at a pace and he was in his seventieth year. He longed to sit down. Death rather.

But his voice was steadier and more reasonable as he went on.

'Never mind that. It doesn't matter how I got here. The point is that I have the law behind me. John's mine and must return with me. The rest of you can go to the devil.'

Rose answered, after a pause:

'That's all very well. Perhaps we are breaking the law, but if we are you've driven us to it, you know. Later you must do what you think right about that, but I warn you that if it's a case in the Courts we won't stop from any kind of evidence we can get showing that you aren't the right man to have John.' She waited, but he said nothing, so she went on. 'I don't believe you'll want that. Don't you see?--I warned you. I did everything I could to make you change your mind. So long as you had us there, in the house, you had the power, but the moment we'd climbed Stye Head--you can see for yourself everything's different.

'All the same--there's John. It's now and always for him to decide. If he wants to go back to you I won't dream of preventing him. It's up to John.' She looked round for him. He was standing close behind her. 'John--will you go back to the Hall or come on with me?'

He said at once without a moment's delay:

'I like you very much, Grandfather, but I'd rather go with Mother if you don't mind.'

The Colonel waited; it seemed to them all a period of silence infinitely long.

At last he said:

'I can't stop you here. I see that. I don't know what I had in mind when I started out.' He raised his voice, he began to shout. 'But don't think you're going to get away with this. It's monstrous, monstrous, that's what it is.'

'I told you you couldn't,' Rackstraw said. 'I told you power wouldn't work that way.'

The Colonel turned upon the ugly shabby little man as though he were seeing him for the first time.

'You--you drunken sot--you disgrace--you swine--'

But he could not. No angry voice here but was lost in the attending hills, but must surrender to the new light flooding down on them from the morning sky.

'The police shall deal with you,' he said quite mildly. 'And with all of you. You'll hear from me. You'll see where you get to!'

It was over. He stared at them all like an enraged and puzzled bull. Then he was a bull no longer. He took out his dark red silk handkerchief and rubbed his face.

They must go; nothing more to be done. He would not, of course, shake hands. A pity.

Rose said gently: 'Later on, when you feel differently, we'll meet again. And please--don't be angry with Michael.'

She heard, as though in the air around her, Michael's poem:

Close-fitting house of velvet, foxglove bell,

My heart within your walls . . .

And you, like rose, upturned by infinite seas,

To bleach here on the foam-remembering fell.

Her farewell, sentimental no doubt, true certainly, to Michael.

The Colonel had not heard. Without another word to any of them, he had turned his back and was walking away.

They said good-bye to Rackstraw and started towards Wastdale.

Rackstraw stood there alone, then swiftly followed the solitary figure.

As he neared him the Colonel turned round.

'By God, if you speak to me I'll kill you!'

He walked on. Rackstraw followed. The Colonel stopped. What was it he felt? Had he not had some suspicion of it as he climbed the Pass, a suspicion that he had fiercely denied? What was this pain, a burning, first as of a bee's sting, now as of a fire, in the right thigh?

And now the calf was stiffening--cramp caught the leg and twisted it. He stumbled.

Rackstraw was up with him.

'What is it?'

The Colonel looked at him with the eyes of a frightened baby.

'In my right thigh. Burning like hell . . . cramp. . . . Oh, God!'

He sat down on a stone. Rackstraw sat down beside him.

'That's rheumatism. Sciatica. Here, let me rub it. Wait. We'll go on in a moment. You can take my arm. I'll help you down.'

The Colonel got up. He was not to be beaten. He walked a few steps by himself. He was beaten. He took Rackstraw's arm. They went forward together.

THE END

Also from Benediction Books ...
Wandering Between Two Worlds: Essays on Faith and Art
Anita Mathias
Benediction Books, 2007
152 pages
ISBN: 0955373700

Available from www.amazon.com, www.amazon.co.uk

In these wide-ranging lyrical essays, Anita Mathias writes, in lush, lovely prose, of her naughty Catholic childhood in Jamshedpur, India; her large, eccentric family in Mangalore, a sea-coast town converted by the Portuguese in the sixteenth century; her rebellion and atheism as a teenager in her Himalayan boarding school, run by German missionary nuns, St. Mary's Convent, Nainital; and her abrupt religious conversion after which she entered Mother Teresa's convent in Calcutta as a novice. Later rich, elegant essays explore the dualities of her life as a writer, mother, and Christian in the United States-- Domesticity and Art, Writing and Prayer, and the experience of being "an alien and stranger" as an immigrant in America, sensing the need for roots.

About the Author

Anita Mathias was born in India, has a B.A. and M.A. in English from Somerville College, Oxford University and an M.A. in Creative Writing from the Ohio State University. Her essays have been published in The Washington Post, The London Magazine, The Virginia Quarterly Review, Commonweal, Notre Dame Magazine, America, The Christian Century, Religion Online, The Southwest Review, Contemporary Literary Criticism, New Letters, The Journal, and two of HarperSanFrancisco's The Best Spiritual Writing anthologies. Her non-fiction has won fellowships from The National Endowment for the Arts; The Minnesota State Arts Board; The Jerome Foundation, The Vermont Studio Center; The Virginia Centre for the Creative Arts, and the First Prize for the Best General Interest Article from the Catholic Press Association of the United States and Canada. Anita has taught Creative Writing at the College of William and Mary, and now lives and writes in Oxford, England.

www.anitamathias.com,
christiancogitations.blogspot.com
wanderingbetweentwoworlds.blogspot.com

Anthony Adverse by Hervey Allen (see page 62 of this book for a reference to one of the characters reading *Anthony Adverse* again and again.)
Benediction Books, 2010
1168 pages
ISBN: 9781849026949